Rick Gekoski came from his native America to do a D.Phil at Oxford, and went on to teach English at the University of Warwick. In 1985 he became a full-time rare book dealer, specialising in important twentieth-century first editions and manuscripts. He lives in Salisbury and spends time each year in New Zealand.

Praise for *Darke Matter*

'Clever, witty and perceptive . . . Gekoski writes movingly about love, loss and grief, while handling the difficult issue of assisted dying with considerable balance and finesse. Beautifully written, engrossing and heartbreakingly funny' — *Mail on Sunday*

'Harrowing, funny, tender and nearly always beautifully written' — *Sunday Times*

'An original and bleakly funny portrait of grief' — *Economist*

'Surprising . . . with a warmth that is genuinely and unexpectedly moving' — *Guardian*

'A wondrous book with two fathers, Kingsley Amis and Dante' — Sebastian Barry

'Makes for dark, thrilling reading . . . In James Darke, Gekoski has created a powerful, raging voice' — *Spectator*

'I was beguiled and charmed by the vivid personality being revealed. By that, and by the fact that I couldn't stop reading. Gekoski puts words together with a sure touch and deep craftsmanship' — Philip Pullman

'Rick Gekoski's impressive debut novel . . . Darke is both a tender and hard-hitting examination of grief and the slow, singular healing process . . . A brilliantly vivid creation . . . life-affirming and life-shattering' — *The Herald*

'Staggeringly accomplished. Heartbreakingly true. A shockingly monumental first novel' — John Niven

'Stuffed with more wisdom, bile, wit and tenderness than many writers create in a lifetime. In James Darke we have a hero as troubled and eternal as King Lear . . . And in Rick Gekoski we have a late-flowering genius of a novelist who proves it's never too late to start a glittering career in fiction' — *The Times*

'An immensely enjoyable elegy . . . done with precision and patience' — *The Scotsman*

'Debut delight . . . Just how this gleefully conjured misanthrope came to wall himself off from the world is the mystery at the heart of a singular first novel that evolves into a moving meditation on loss and redemption' — *Mail on Sunday*

DARKE MATTER

A Novel

RICK GEKOSKI

CONSTABLE

CONSTABLE

First published in Great Britain in 2020 by Constable

This paperback edition published in 2021 by Constable

1 3 5 7 9 10 8 6 4 2

Constable
An imprint of
Little, Brown Book Group
Carmelite House
50 Victoria Embankment
London EC4Y 0DZ

An Hachette UK Company
www.hachette.co.uk

www.littlebrown.co.uk

For Andreas

Darkling I listen; and, for many a time
I have been half in love with easeful Death,
Call'd him soft names in many a mused rhyme,
To take into the air my quiet breath;
Now more than ever seems it rich to die,
To cease upon the midnight with no pain,
While thou art pouring forth thy soul abroad
In such an ecstasy!
Still wouldst thou sing, and I have ears in vain—
To thy high requiem become a sod.

John Keats

★

Lucky sod.

James Darke

PART ONE

Darke, Still

Chapter 1

In the year 0, by a remarkable coincidence, our Lord Jesus Christ was born. If that's not sufficient to shuffle your coils, his mother proclaimed herself a virgin.

People still acknowledge the anniversary of these miracles, though in recent times this has gone from a modest tipping of the cap to the commercial jamboree: Christmas. This year, as ever, the festivities will be at my – previously *our* – house, and daughter Lucy and her family will come, and then stay. I undertake this stoically, as an obligation of the season: I'm better at charity than either faith or hope, because, weirdly, charity is recommended over these other virtues.

1) Faith! Believe in God, he's a safe pair of hands: *very good!*
2) Hope! Even if you are Job or Abraham, and God is chortling and tormenting you, don't despair: *excellent!*
3) Charity! There's a lot of needy people out there, despite (1) and (2) above: sow your shekels: *the best!*

They were great psychologists, those old Jews; they reaped plenty in this world and presumably the next. Give a little, get a lot. I have thus resolved to make regular offerings to the good souls on every street corner, box-rattling for Macmillan Nurses or Cancer Research.

In my own home, though, I am blessedly safe from the canvassers, beggars and importuners spreading bubonically from house to house at Yuletide. It is nigh impossible to get my attention, while I am swathed in my domestic gloom. After Suzy's searing, peaceful death, I returned from her funeral, and retired from the world as thoroughly as an urban hermit may manage: cut off my email, cancelled my phone, closed my curtains, revised my door so as to admit neither post nor invasive knocking. And so I stayed for some time, ordering deliveries of oysters and claret, estranged from self and family. How long? I hardly recall. Time disappears in a black hole. Months, many months. And when I eventually crept out, seeking reconnection with Lucy, I had cause to regret it, and did. And didn't.

My doorbell is a single, muffled chime. When I am upstairs, I hardly hear it; and when I do, I don't answer unless I am expecting someone, allow the bell to sound a couple of times, and then the ringer moves on. Nobody home.

But whoever it was kept pressing the bell, which rang and rang again, quietly but irritatingly. And when that ceased, there was a knocking, loud then louder, sustained, insistent. I stomped down the stairs in a strop and opened the door to two middle-aged men in shiny navy suits, with short hair and the erect bearing of zealots. Not sleek and smug enough to be Mormons, nor sufficiently desperate for Christian Scientists or Jehovah's Witnesses. Soiled and baggy of eye, certainly, yet they carried themselves with an authority that didn't seem to emanate from the divine.

The one slightly to the front, as if to assert seniority, had what is often (mis)described as a bullet head, more like a head for butting, was stocky and red-faced, veinous traces round his cheeks and the bridge of his nose. The other was younger and less shop-soiled, with hooded eyes and a sharp pointy nose, forbidding as a falcon with a migraine.

'Do forgive me if this is unclear,' I said firmly. 'The reason I don't answer my door is because I don't wish to be bothered ...'

'Rather an unusual door, sir?' Their front man interrupted me, inappropriately and rudely, looking at the door itself.

'Surely you haven't come to do a survey of the local doors?' I was irritated and bemused, yet flattered that he should admire my modest contribution to the improvement of my neighbourhood.

'I've never seen one without a knocker or a letterbox.'

'Indeed. Neither have I.'

'And the finish of the black is remarkably deep and resonant. It seems more like a fortification than an entrance.' The accent was Edinburgh, educated and precise. He was still scanning the finish of my door, as if seeking imperfections, and returned to meet my eyes, apparently with the same goal in mind.

'Now, see here . . .' I began, but he held up his hand in a gesture that was not designed to placate, neither did it have a Bible in it. It had some sort of ID card, which he thrust forward.

'I am sorry to interrupt you, sir, but we would value a few words.'

'Go away!' I said, without looking at the proffered identification. 'I don't care who you are, I'm not joining, or buying.'

If anything, they moved slightly forward, and I sensed a foot placing itself in the path of my door.

'Just a few questions, sir. You are Dr James Darke, are you not?'

'I am. I don't know where you got my name, but I am not interested in anything you have to offer. Good day.'

As I had anticipated, the foot was there, and the door would not close.

'If you don't go away immediately,' I said, 'I will call the police!'

The fatigued plasticised identity card was again thrust into my face. DS something or other Scottish? I didn't catch the first name. Angus no doubt. The second card was produced. DC something ending in -ic. First name? Slobodan, that would be likely. A Yugoslav – what are they now? I can't keep track of Balkan comings and goings. I have no idea what these initials signify. DC? Dangerous Croat?

These agreeable linguistic speculations were soon cut short.

'We *are* the police, sir. May we come in?'

'I'm sorry, but you cannot. Please go away. I don't want to contribute to your Benevolent Fund, or to help with a neighbourhood watch. Now if you would excuse me ...'

McBullethead looked into a small black notebook that he had taken from his jacket pocket.

'You are the husband, sir, of the late Suzanne Moulton, and the father—'

'Yes, yes, I am. What's it got to do with you?'

He was relentlessly, threateningly, polite.

'If you'd be kind enough to invite us in, sir, and give us a few minutes, I can explain.'

'Explain what?'

A tiny flicker of his nostrils indicated that his patience was wearing thin.

'Just a few inquiries, it shouldn't take long. But if you prefer, sir, we could make an appointment to talk at the local station, which is on Buckingham Palace Road.'

I had no idea what to make of this. Could it have something to do with Bronya, who came from one of Suzy's cleaning agencies? Perhaps she was an illegal alien? Most Bulgarians are. Or might it be to do with the reams of paperwork that accompany a death? I hadn't done any of that, left it to Lucy, who is notoriously slack about such matters. Probate, certificates, tax returns, whatever. Hardly police matters, surely, shouldn't they be out water-boarding terrorists?

'Tell me when I might visit your humble abode.'

'Well, sir, it's Christmas in a few days, things will be slowing down over the holidays. But you should hear from us within a few weeks.'

'That will be fine,' I said, beginning to close the door, now free of foot.

'Thank you, sir, and do have a happy Christmas.'

I have no intention of going to their station, but the mere closing of the door, though it kept them out of sight, hardly banished them from my mind, obsessed as it has been and ever shall be with guilt, world without end, amen.

It gave me an uneasy couple of days, but by the time Lucy and the family arrived I'd almost managed to forget it, or, more properly, almost managed to convince myself to forget it. It lingered in my mind like an incipient migraine. But once the loved ones piled into the house, it was almost impossible to think of anything other than logistics: who slept where and when, what to eat, what to drink. Above all, what to do.

Lucy and Sam have apparently encouraged one or two of their friends to drop by during this period, which will wassail my soul. I do not object to their mouldy, fungal metropolitan acquaintances, I can make myself scarce. But I am already in a state about the wooing and hooing visitor whose presence will define the entire holiday period, which will be dominated by poor dear Suzy, here in spirit as the Ghost of Christmas Past.

Dickens: twice guilty. First, for this particular iniquitous spirit. And second, for all the rest of the Christmas spirits, this overblown charade that passes for religious celebration. Christmas was a muted affair until his Christmas books were published to universal acclaim. Joy be'd unconfine'd, hearts and purses opened, geese and trees were fattened and slaughtered in their millions, halls and persons were bedecked, all sang and celebrated and prayed and rejoiced. Overdid it, it's what Victorians did best. Gorged, disgorged, laughed, wept. Pretended to be happy, and then returned to their miserable, crimped lives.

I don't need the pretence, I'm used to misery and crimp, they suit me just fine.

* * *

7

Since my grandson Rudy's birth, seven or eight years previous, we have celebrated Christmas in London. Lucy is no cook, and her Sam no host, while Suzy revelled in it all, never missed a trimming. Two years ago, she'd left it to the last minute and begged me to accompany her shopping in the West End, promising a good lunch at the end of the ordeal. In the kiddie section of John Lewis there was a foul-smelling clamorous scrum of mums and children, you had to barge your way to the counter, like entering the Tube at rush hour. Not that I do.

I'd made the mistake of dressing in an elegant graphite-grey finely ribbed corduroy suit, with a white cotton shirt and muted Armani tie in light violet. Within the first few minutes a weeping chocolatey toddler had wiped its hand on my trousers. I looked down and gave it a petite whack, quickly turning the other way innocently to peruse the ceiling while humming the 'Ode to Joy'. Its poor, harassed mother was pulling the child, who might have been three, or five, whatever, by the arm, while it – who might have been a boy or a girl, who cares? – howled and remonstrated inconsolably.'

I left before I started to cry too, and promised to meet Suzy at the Wolseley. By the time she arrived, exhausted and be-packaged, I'd made a manly start on a bottle of Meursault. She looked shaken by the experience, good thing I'd saved a bit for her.

I have ordered this year's provisions on time and online, being both unwilling and unable to withstand the noisome crush of my fellows in food halls and stalls. I first suggested a goose, but got a 'Yuck', so have researched turkeys. If we have to consume one of the noxious feathered beasts, please God it shall not taste like blotting paper soaked with gravy. Sam buys his frozen, from Tesco's, and pronounces them top class. Lucy will eat a bit. I have no idea what Rudy eats other than pizza and ice-cream.

I soon located an organic, free-range small turkey producer. It is semantically unclear if the turkeys are small or the producer is, but I suspect they mean the farm itself, though 'farm' is the wrong word – their turkey-raising facility sounds more like a boutique hotel. Prospective buyers are put on a waiting list for a bird, and if you are offered one, you get full disclosure. After a few days I was offered Chanticleer IV, who will weigh in at around 11 pounds. His parents were Miranda and Chanticleer III. I was sent pictures of them all, with their dates of birth, and a price tag that makes my chequebook's eyes water.

I agree to buy Chanticleer IV, though I inform his owners that I am already so attached to him that I am considering putting him up in the guest bedroom, and inviting him to Christmas dinner. They reply suggesting that I eat him. They will do the necessary disembowelling, and when he arrives he will be fit for the oven, and I for the poorhouse.

What to drink? I once allowed Sam to bring the wine, as I had nothing bad enough to offer. He proudly produced two bottles of New Zealand Sauvignon Blanc stinking of grapefruit, so acidic that I could feel the enamel being stripped from my teeth as I drank. At the table he lifted his glass to his nose, sniffed deeply, as if at a toddler's nappy, gargled a bit as he took a first sip, a look of intense concentration upon his features.

'Smooth,' he intoned sagaciously. 'Very smooth.' It is his sole term of approbation when drinking wine: Pinot Gris is smooth, so is claret, so is port. Port? He knows just enough to propose a toast, but not when or how. Last year he sprang up, glass in hand, before I could stifle him. 'Good health,' he said, raising his glass. Suzy was having her chemotherapy and was neither allowed nor able to drink. She didn't eat much either, though she'd cooked all of it.

I wish they'd come for Easter instead. I prefer pop-up Jesus to his new-born incarnation, with all that mewling and puking in the cradle, itinerant sheep herders, and beardy wise men. We could celebrate it with my excellent *lapin au vin*.

The only respite from the unremitting, claustrophobic nightmare lies in Rudy's horse-riding lessons, my Christmas gift to him since he was four. We take a proper black taxi to the stables in Bathurst Mews, near Hyde Park, a cobbled but excavated and newly base-mented terrace of some sixty bijoux residences, purpose-built for horses, now inhabited by small businessmen (large ones wouldn't fit), lawyers, bankers and trust-fund beneficiaries. The stables take up three of these petite homes, which I make out to be a value of £250,000 per stabled horse. As befits residents of such swanky premises, the horses are well behaved, impeccably docile, and suffer the pawings and pokings of small children philosophically. The only miscreant is a grey who is wont to nibble the blooms growing in pots outside a number of the houses, to the consternation of the owners. A sign hangs over the stable office, in full admonitory view:

DO NOT LET ENIGMA EAT THE FLOWERS!

I have adopted this sentiment as my philosophy of life. Enigma is a perfect name for a horse, a being at once so dignified and so subservient. Rudy loves him, and the clapped-out nag has a presence that moves me. No fawning, as a dog might.

From the first ride it has been Enigma or nothing, not because Rudy is aware of the vast philosophical implications of the name but because he thinks it 'so cool' that a horse eats flowers. I point out that since they eat hay, carrots and oats there is no reason not to munch the odd daff. He sees the point of this, but still thinks it's 'silly', which is his favourite critical term. Enigma is silly. So am I.

For the week(s) before Christmases past, Lucy and Suzy would be on the phone daily, making 'arrangements' so extensive that they might have been travel agents constructing itineraries for Ulaanbaatar. They would spend hour after hour yakking away, covering the entire range of viands and victuals, as if scripted by that rancid sweetmeat Dickens himself. This year, in dear Suzy's absence, it has fallen on poor me to field these enquiries.

An unexpected and thoroughly disagreeable conundrum occurred only last week. When you're only four at table, you're hardly in need of *placement*, are you? Of course, I almost forgot. *Five*, not five actually sitting at the table, still five. Baby Amelie is coming for her first Christmas. Start them young like Baby Jesus. She's only a couple of months old. Sam could tell you how many days too. Amelie *Parkin*. The name hardly trips off the tongue, unless you add *-lot* at the end.

I was admonished to keep away at the time of the birth, but grudgingly allowed to visit three weeks later, when I took refuge in the junior suite in my Oxford hotel, though Lucy said there was 'plenty of room' for me in their Abingdon semi. She was relieved when I declined, still sore and exhausted by the birth of the new arrival, and by the demands of breastfeeding. I had no desire to watch my daughter lug her dugs out to pacify the greedy newcomer. Lucy will not remove herself to a private space for these intimacies. *It's natural!* So are murder and incest.

I spent two days failing to find any attractions in the new arrival, made no attempt to hold, to cuddle, to make goo-goo: 'to bond', as Sam calls it. Peered into the crib, bent over stiffly, looked the sprog in the eye, ready to lift up quickly to avoid imminent projectiles. Mostly it slept, guzzled, and slept again. Now and again it made a noise, or a smell, often together. Lucy had some doubts whether Amelie was ready for her first trip to Gampy's, worried about pollution in 'the Smoke', as I cannot get her to stop calling it, as if she were from bloody Sheffield.

I've made a space for the baby's crib in Suzy's old bedroom, where her parents will be sleeping – not that they get much of that – and Rudy can hunker down on the divan in my study. Everything is in order. I have a list. I cross things off. Simple, right?

Wrong. I should have foreseen it. I had given Suzy's clothes, shoes and paraphernalia to charity shops, changed two of the pictures on the walls, put a muted Kashmiri carpet on the floorboards. But Suzy lurked, the room was inhabited by her, the emanations of her long presence penetrated the air, which seemed to breathe her breath, and to shorten mine. I sat with her for the long months of her final illness, listened to her cries for release, mopped and cleaned, and vomited with her. And then both of us had had enough, and one night I gave her a soothing drink to carry her away.

Since the debacle when the pregnant Lucy came to look despondently through her mother's closets, she hadn't entered the room, and was anxious at the prospect. I offered to vacate my own bedroom, but she wouldn't hear of it.

'I have to come to terms with this some day, Dad,' she said, a little less than firmly, 'your room is yours. Mum is gone, so I should be happy to be in her room, and feel a little bit closer to her. But my mind fills with images, and I get frightened.' I listened sympathetically, but couldn't suppress the thought *fills with images!* She didn't know the half of it, was hardly there during that slow descent into helplessness and death, for Suzy kept her at a distance to the very end. *Lest her mind fill with images.* As mine did, and will continue to do, ineradicably.

Her mother's *deathbed*. The transformation of the room itself was complete, but the prospect of sleeping in it was, Lucy confided tearfully, as daunting as spending a night in a cemetery. Without consulting her, I toddled off to the local furniture shop and purchased a new double bed with a brass bedstead, made for a few rupees by impoverished Indians, who will no doubt be grateful for my patronage. At least Suzy hadn't died in this one. Nobody had, as far as I know, though Indians die so quickly and copiously that they hardly know where to do it. One of them might have snuck into this very bed, to have a quick perish. Or a shag. They do a lot of both.

And then Rudy rang to announce that he wants an extra chair at the Christmas dinner table for Granny, with a plate and cutlery and glasses and *everything*!

'Can we, Gampy, *please*?' he pleaded, sensing some lack of enthusiasm on my part. 'Then she'll be with us!'

'No, darling, we can't do that. She is *not* with us any more, except in our hearts, she always will be there. But if we have an empty seat at table it will only make us even sadder.'

'But Gampy, she wants to come too! She could sit next to me!'

'I'm sorry, darling, but the answer is no.' My voice – I could hear it – had sharpened. I was about to continue and to apologise, to explain further, when Lucy took the phone.

'Honestly, Dad . . .' she began.

'Yes,' I said, more sharply than before. 'Yes. Honestly. Very.'

There was a silence, which I interpreted liberally as leave to hang up.

There remained the contentious issue of the Christmas tree. As ever, we must have one. I have grudgingly agreed to this exception to my general rule: nature must be kept in its place, and me in mine. I abhor potted plants, which should go back where they came from. And trees, I have observed, have been created to stay outside, that's why they have roots.

Once a year I gave way and allowed one into the house at Yuletide. It was, at my insistence, *tasteful*. The predominant decorating colour was white, with sparkling tiny bulbs (I reluctantly allowed yellow or gold), shimmering metallic *objets* and mock snowflakes. Suzy spent hours during the week before Christmas, putting them up, then rearranging and reordering them to her satisfaction. Little Lucy loved helping with the task, and was biddable enough with regard to the predominant aesthetic.

Rudy is not. He has been exposed to too many heavily be-tinselled dying conifers, covered with alternating twinkling lights in green and red and yellow and orange, overburdened until the branches droop with hideous hanging Father Christmases, reindeer, baby Jesuses, angels, wise men and magi, shiny bulbs and candy canes – all the effluvia that a modern Christmas generates, and to his mind requires. In his Abingdon home there will be a tree that he is allowed to decorate on his own, and his predominant desire is that no green shows through, as if the decorations were the tree itself.

He and I have discussed this. My view is simple: you in your way, and me in mine. That is eminently reasonable – it's my bloody house, isn't it? – but does not appeal to him. Why shouldn't Gampy have the benefits of his expertise? For the last few years Suzy acceded to Rudy's aesthetic interventions with good grace. I remained largely silent, merely scowling and muttering under my breath; I once described his efforts to him as 'rather vulgar', which pleased him – he thought it meant colourful – and now he is campaigning to be allowed, once again this year, to vulgarise the tree. He has numerous plastic Tesco bags full of ornaments, and enough strings of lights to illuminate the Blackwall Tunnel. He will bring them, he says cheerfully, and he and I can have fun together.

He is not a well-brought-up child. Though he is bright, engaged and inquisitive, and knows a startling amount about a variety of subjects that his iPad has taught him, he has been indulged by his relentlessly modern parents. He lacks the one quality necessary to a well-regulated childhood: the ability to take NO for an answer. He states his case, he argues, he sulks, he argues some more, he gets his way. Though he has moments, many moments, in which you might mistake him for a sentient being, informed, articulate and thoughtful, he regresses too easily, and it would not surprise me, at such times, if he started to suck his thumb. Lucy pacifies him, and claims it makes for an easier life. Not for me, it doesn't.

Aside from his constant use of the term 'silly', which I find especially irritating when applied to myself, his other recurrent working category concerns fairness. 'It's not fair' means that he not only should get his way, but that it is in accord with the dictates of past experience, reasonableness and natural justice. And it is absolutely and comprehensively 'not fair' that our Christmas tree is not going to be decked with his usual flotsam and jetsam.

'Granny loved it. Granny wants it to be like this every year!'

'But darling,' I near as damnit snarled, 'Granny is gone now, and I like it the way I like it. You know, before you were born, Granny and I . . .'

'I don't care. It's not fair!'

When I reluctantly came to consider the matter, it was sadly apparent that Rudy was right. It wasn't fair. I gave in. On Christmas Eve Lucy and Rudy could commandeer the tree, set up shop in the drawing room with their Tesco bags, and get to work.

I went upstairs to my study to smoke, to drink, and to consult my Penguin copy of *A Christmas Carol*. I do not regret the sale of my first edition of it, or any of my other Dickens rarities, trans-formed by Sotheby's into a trust fund for Rudy. I will be gone by the time he comes into the proceeds, thank God, for I would disapprove of almost any way in which he might spend the windfall. Travelling to Australia? Buying a sports car? Getting entangled with a grasping girl? Supporting dubious political causes?

What to spend it on? Bricks and mortar. A small, elegant flat in a good part of London. That and nothing else. Perhaps I ought to buy one such now, give it to an agent to rent out, and leave it to Rudy when he comes of age? Why should he make his own decisions when I can make them for him?

I half fill a whisky glass with Glenmorangie – no water, no ice – and open my book. I cannot bear to reread the whole soppy thing, I am in search only of the Ghost of Christmas Past. Foolish me. I'm sufficiently haunted by my own. By day and most poignantly by night, my dear Suzy occurs and recurs in incarnations both young and old, in health and in sickness, till death did us part. My attachment to my wife, and hers to me, is unrelenting, a constant reminder that it is no attachment at all, save that provided by the persistence of memory. And of love.

Yes, as Sam observed to me only last week, I have re-entered the world, gained weight, and seem to be scratching myself less. He puts this down to the passage of time, and to 'recovery' from the trauma of (he does not say so, but *excessive*) grief. I must allow time to pass. Get out more.

Sam and I have never, quite, fit, or perhaps he would say 'bonded'. When Lucy first brought him home, in her final year at university (Sheffield, alas), he was deeply uneasy, and had stuffed his stocky frame into an ill-fitting suit, with his unnecessary tie at half-mast. Suzy carried the ball – the metaphor appeals, her beau was a rugby player – during the uneasy getting-to-know-you rituals, and though I am usually adept, not exactly at putting people at their ease, but at the social niceties of meeting strangers – a necessary skill for a schoolmaster – I couldn't find any common ground with this social worker in the making. Both of us tried, for a short time, and then left it to the ladies to get on with things.

When they left, blessedly and at long last, Suzy and I had a long drink and a short chat. I knew better than to express disappointment at Lucy's choice – she had form in choosing the wrong sort of chap – and let Suzy do it for me.

'Well,' she said, 'best leave them to it. She'll outgrow him.'

'I hope so. I couldn't find any common ground with him at all.'

Suzy snorted. 'Too much, not too little!'

'I have no idea what you're talking about.'

She offered that superior Dorset county laugh that she'd inherited from her parents.

'It comes down to class. Most things do, and ...'

'I know, I know, not much in common there.'

'Dear James, you are funny. Look at it closely – you're both

Northern boys from modest backgrounds, only you've gone all posh, and he's so close to his roots that they stick out above ground.'

This was rather hurtful. I had made a sustained effort, once away at school and in Oxford, to knock my rough edges into shape, whereas Sam seemed only to have sharpened his.

'I have no idea what you're talking about . . .' I began.

'I know,' she said, 'shall we go out for lunch?'

Everyone has an opinion on what will be good for me. A recent suggestion from Dorothea Thornton, a long-time literary acquaintance of Suzy's, formerly a regularly reviewed novelist, now in the process of being justly forgotten, is that I join her monthly poetry group. Of course I declined. Such meetings are for ladies with not enough to do, who read in the most desultory manner the fashionable works of the day, and then fail to discuss them while drinking and gossiping. Suzy was frequently asked to join such gatherings – until now I never have been – but always sent her regrets, sometimes acerbically. After she gave up writing fiction – though the phrase suggests something chosen, it would be more accurate to say fiction gave up writing her – she read novels omnivorously, and rarely discussed them with anyone. Certainly not with me, I had enough such discussions with my students, I was heartily sick of them. The discussions, I mean. Or do I mean the students? Or the books we discussed?

All of the above. It is impossible to be a schoolmaster over a long period of years without being pulverised by the experience, and spending one's declining years, like a veteran home from the Somme. The prospect of doing some mandatory reading, to prepare for a seminar-like discussion over drinks with a huddle of strangers, is more than unattractive. I hate groups, and I have come to dislike poetry, which bores me.

This response, which I made firmly, did not deter Dorothea. She wrote again, reiterating the invitation, saying that both human company (what other sort is there?) and literature would do me 'the world of good'. The curious thing, the utterly humiliating and unexpected thing about this unwonted and impertinent intrusion, is that I am actually considering joining her and her biblio-fellows, if only for an exploratory session.

Each of the members hosts the group in turn, provides drinks and nibbles, and chooses a poem, which they distribute via email a couple of days before. The others are asked to read the poem in advance, but enjoined not to 'research them', for in their first sessions one of the members showed up with notes so comprehensive as to throttle conversation. He almost ended up throttled himself.

At least reading a short poem only takes a short time. I would find it intolerable to read a novel at someone else's suggestion. Anyway, I don't read them any more. They do go on and on. Yack yack bloody yack. But I can make my way through a poem, as long as it is short (the rule is that it has to fit on a single page: A4 is allowed, six-point type is forbidden). There may be some obverse pleasure in this; I'm tired of my usual detestations, exhausted not by hating things, which I find animating, but by the fact and strain of being. Of being, without. Of being without my Suzy, whose words still echo in the canals of my ears and the arteries of my heart, with whose presence I am filled, and by whose absence I am haunted. Especially now, especially at Christmas, the family gathered like a herd lacking its leader, aimless, disjunct, organically lost . . .

Might the old Christmas slobberer have anything useful to say about being haunted and eviscerated by love? To be visited, nightly, by a ghost?

> *It wore a tunic of the purest white, and round its waist was bound a lustrous belt, the sheen of which was beautiful. It held a branch of fresh green holly in its hand; and, in singular contradiction of that wintry*

emblem, had its dress trimmed with summer flowers. But the strangest thing about it was, that from the crown of its head there sprung a bright clear jet of light, by which all this was visible . . .

I suppressed a BAH, and squashed a HUMBUG. Such a visitation is not unusual, I have similar experiences most nights, visited by a spirit both spectral and spectacularly, but unreliably, corporeal. By my Suzy, calling and recalling. I never get used to it, dread each instance as fervently as I fear there will never be another.

For as its belt sparkled and glittered now in one part and now in another, and what was light one instant, at another time was dark, so the figure itself fluctuated in its distinctness: being now a thing with one arm, now with one leg, now with twenty legs, now a pair of legs without a head, now a head without a body: of which dissolving parts, no outline would be visible in the dense gloom wherein they melted away. And in the very wonder of this, it would be itself again; distinct and clear as ever.

Distinct. And clear as ever.

Chapter 2

On Christmas Eve we met round the fire in the drawing room to settle the presents under the 'tree', while Rudy rummaged round the various parcels, shaking them to assess their contents. Lucy, Sam and I had a nightcap, finished it quickly and were released to go to bed. Rudy would be up early.

'We'll let you lie in, Dad,' Lucy said. 'There's no need . . .'

'Of course there is,' I said. 'Just wake me when you're up, and I'll come down and make coffee and toast.' She and Sam cannot get used to my flat white; it's too 'posh' for them. They brought a jar of their favourite instant brand. She has tutored me in how to make it. Apparently you need a teaspoon.

Though keen to get upstairs and on my own, I was more anxious once I found myself in my bedroom. I turned on the bedside light, tuned in the wireless, and was greeted with a noisome bit of seasonal cheer: Rudolf the brown-nosed reindeer. I turned him off. I'd refilled my glass and brought my drink upstairs, and settled down in the armchair, still shaken by rereading the Ghost of Christmas Past.

It's the most awful twaddle. What's that word they use? *Schmaltzy*. Pure chicken fat. Or *turkey* fat? Woo-woo goes the ghost, takes Scrooge by the hand and they fly through the air back to times of former happiness. I can just about manage that, conjure multitudes of pleasures with Suzy, moments in sun and rain, young and old, dressed and undressed. I can do that. No, what so distressed me was that harrowing image – he can be good, Dickens – of the ghost shimmering, assembling and reassembling its body:

Now a thing with one arm, now with one leg, now with twenty legs, now a pair of legs without a head, now a head without a body . . .

That's what I experience in my night-times, my dear dead wife's body complete and incomplete, her arms, her nose-eyes-ears-cheeks, her once-beautiful breasts as numerous as if in a painting by Dalí, memories of making love, coitus interrupted by images of her final decayed incarnation. Alive and dead, person and ghost, the boundaries and body parts shifting until I sit up in bed, dazed and shaking.

The dying images are the abiding ones: to reanimate our youthfulness I need to strain and can produce only bits; old photographs are inadequate prompts, they're as dead as she is and I soon shall be. The images of Suzy in her final months have an insistence and tenacity that inhabit and define my life. Yes, even after all these months. Grief is not an illness. I'm not recovering. I won't. Nor do I wish to, I think I don't. How can you live with a ghost, when you are rightly frightened of them? How do you recover your former innocence about the human condition? The condition of being a human? How to return to your inno-cent regard for the human body, when it became a source of dismay, and disgust?

I get up to look out of the window, as if to trace the flight of the Ghost and his poor captive Scrooge. But the night sky is as blank and loveless as ever, just enough twinkling to remind you that there is no light. Below and to my right I can just make out next door's garden, formerly the home of my nemesis Spikedog. Ah! The memory of happiness past. I would stand at the window and lob bits of meat spiked with chilli-bombs, which, once the recipe was perfected, caused him distress sufficient to regard me, on our occasional future meetings, with cowed respect. I so enjoyed that.

Spikedog and his equally repellent owner have moved out and on, and the new owners have some sort of blonde spaniel, I think it is, with droopy ears. I don't like it either. Not as much as I like Enigma when Rudy, Natasha and I go for our slow-motion ambles in Hyde Park. I admire horses in principle, and from a distance. Get too attached and the next thing you know you'll be dressing and talking like a damn fool, and harrying foxes.

Dean Swift understood this: horses were merely a means to transport him (if I may be allowed the metaphor) to his favoured topics, the corruption of human society and of the human body. My sixth-formers were bored by Gulliver's numerous satirical references to social and political themes of Swift's day; the major thing that caught their attention – naturally enough, or perhaps I mean unnaturally – was what some critic described as Swift's 'excremental vision'. They liked that, and connected it to Yeats's 'Crazy Jane and the Bishop': 'for love has pitched his mansion in the place of excrement'.

Not for Swift it hadn't. He was in love with a woman he called Stella, 'the most beautiful, graceful and agreeable young woman in London'. But when she appears in one of his poems, lightly disguised as Celia, there is no gainsaying the fact that his loved one was that most disablingly dreadful thing, a person. With human needs and functions. Thus Swift's peeping Tom intrudes into Celia's dressing room, only to recoil at the ultimate undermining truth:

Thus finishing his grand survey,
Disgusted Strephon stole away
Repeating in his amorous fits,
Oh! Celia, Celia, Celia shits!
But Vengeance, goddess never sleeping
Soon punished Strephon for his peeping;
His foul imagination links
Each Dame he sees with all her stinks . . .

Once a poet fully realises this – they're highly sensitive, poets, and have enhanced sensual powers – it overwhelms him, and there is no escaping what T. S. Eliot once called the *stench*. Like Swift he assigned it only to women.

Poor nosy Dean Swift and fastidious Mr Eliot to be so *sniffy*. Mr D. H. Lawrence, a fearless explorer of the human underworld, replied vigorously in Celia's defence. He preferred such organic matters just as they are, and where they are. Thus the scene in *Lady Chatterley's Lover*, in which the (*Earthy! Natural!*) gamekeeper Mellors is rummaging about in the naked Lady C's nethers, and discovers a lot to write home about: *Here tha shits and here tha pisses: an' I lay my hand on 'em both, an' I like thee for it.*

All this yucky human stuff is why angels were invented. There are no lavatories in heaven, no human plumbing, no need to find a place of relief. Angels have as little body as is necessary to make them credible and imaginable, they're hardly distinguishable from humanoid swans. Nothing gross about your angels, nothing *human*: neither piss nor shit, no sputum, saliva, vomit, sperm, vaginal oils and essences and discharges, bloody encrustation, pimples and weeping sores, scabs, pus, mucus, foreskin gunge, semen dribbles, snot ropes, anal remnants. They're angels: sanitised, nature-free zones. Heavenly!

Such thoughts murder sleep. I tiptoed quietly to my study to check my (very occasional) emails. There was yet another inviting me to the monthly poetry group, urging it upon me as if a tonic. It was signed *Dorothea xx*. I do not know what this signifies. I would never stoop to such marks. Kisses, is that it? She sends kisses? Would I be right to detect a hint of wooing in this ardent invitation, this care for my welfare, this double *xx* intrusion?

The very thought of holding her elderly body in my arms, all that kissing and undressing and smelling and revealing what needs hiding and masking, those flabby breasts and saggy buttocks, my withdrawn, attenuated bits and varicosities, the images flash and make me reel.

Just because I feel better doesn't mean I am better. I am worse. I am losing my objective correlative. If the first stage of grief eviscerates, during the latter stages – it never ends – the pain of immediate loss is replaced by the droning ache of being. Rage recedes, I no longer scream at God, just admonish him wearily as one would a child who has failed his crucial tests.

I cannot bear the passage of the hours, I am a tempus fugitive. I retreat to my bedroom, slink under the sheets, turn out the light, and fail to sleep. It is past midnight.

And so, as that neurasthenic dwarf Tiny Tim said, 'A Happy Christmas to us all; God bless us, every one!'

At six my alarm rang, and I woke ungroggy, not having had enough sleep from which to recover. Combed my hair, did my ablutions, pulled on my silk dressing gown and my leather slippers. There was a sound of crying down the hallway. Rudy, over-tired, over-excited, protesting at having to brush his teeth. *It's Christmas, it's not fair.* Lucy will give in. I hope she and Sam have the decency to brush theirs, all I need is their morning breath souring the air. It's sour enough already. I hurry out of my room, down the stairs to the kitchen. Put the kettle on, the seeded brown sourdough slices in the toaster, lay the table, put out the unsalted butter from

Normandy, gooseberry jam and Seville orange marmalade, and a jug of gold-top milk.

Sam and Lucy appear a few minutes later, rubbing their eyes, hair all over the place, dressed in terry-towelling robes that have never seen better days. They are barefooted, unwashed, exhausted. I would feel sorry for them, but it's their own bloody fault, all this gratuitous baby-producing. Suzy and I knew when to desist.

Rudy has gone straight to the drawing room, to check whether Father Christmas has drunk his glass of sherry and eaten his short-breads. He has. That's why he's fat as a house, Rudy says. He likes keeping to the old scripts.

Soon he is rummaging amidst the presents, calling out.

'Mummy! Dad! Gampy! Come quick! It's Christmas!'

Soon he is tearing through the parcels at a furious pace, never pausing to express interest, much less gratitude. Though my present to him – his Enigma rides – has been both thoughtful and expensive, Lucy nevertheless insisted that there be something under the tree from me as well. I suggested some well-wrapped horse manure. Apparently that wasn't funny.

I acceded, it makes for an easier life, and Rudy loved his new Sheffield United kit, the ugliest assemblage of unnatural fabric and atrocious design to be found anywhere south of Sheffield. He throws off his jammies, puts on the shorts and shirt, and runs upstairs to admire himself in the mirror.

When he gets back he informs us that Amelie is crying, and Lucy rises wearily to go upstairs, returning a few moments later with a red-faced, screaming, wet and smelly bundle in her arms, which she hands over to Sam.

'Will you change her, darling? Then I'll feed her, poor thing, she's starving.'

He looks reluctant, but rises obediently, and takes the baby back upstairs. I cannot assume that the feeding will take place there, or whether Lucy might choose the comfort of the drawing room, *en famille*. I repair to the kitchen post-haste, to get the turkey stuffed and ready, make myself another coffee, and kill time until I confirm that wherever the feeding is going to take place, I won't be there.

Hours later, we are five at the table, having made space for Amelie's crib, because she is fretful and Lucy wants to be able to sit down without having to go upstairs every five minutes. This seems an entirely disagreeable compromise, but of course I shut up.

We were each assigned jobs. I uncorked the wine, a few hours ahead of the meal, and left it to breathe to make sure it was smooth. Lucy put her fish out, and cooked the vegetables; Sam laid the table, though he hardly knows how to deploy the cutlery in its proper places, and Rudy insisted that he be allowed to bring the food from the kitchen to the table. He did this with the studied care of a butler, and no less solemnity, walking at measured pace, holding each dish in front of him with both hands, like a trainee waiter at Simpson's in the Strand. Lucy has overfilled the bowl with cranberry sauce, but Rudy insists he won't spill a drop, and doesn't. He does equally well with the gravy, sprouts and potatoes, and protests mightily when he is not allowed to carry the turkey, surrounded by sausage, on its large platter.

It is agreed that I have cooked the bird perfectly, though only Sam is keen on eating it. Rudy has a slice of white meat, still yearning for pizza, and I fill my plate with the unappealing organic pap, just to show willing. Lucy is happy with her poached salmon. We help ourselves to vegetables, don humiliating paper hats, fill our glasses, and before Sam can even think of it, I rise to make the toast.

'To our absent loved one. To Suzy.'

Sam and Lucy raise their glasses and clink them, Rudy solemnly lifts his glass of juice to his lips. We eat as quickly as possible, and manage to keep our mouths sufficiently full not to have to talk too much. There is too much to say, and it is unsayable. Though Rudy's notion that we should set a place for Suzy has been thwarted, she is there nonetheless: the Ghost of Christmas Present. Lucy's eyes are watered, Rudy unusually solemn, and whatever gets into my mouth finds difficulty making its way to my stomach.

I am father and grandfather and host, it's my responsibility to keep things going before we descend into silence and tears. To demonstrate my seasonal benevolence, I manage what little table talk there is. Rudy witters on about Sheffield United, who apparently have four fixtures over the holiday period. He tells us about each. Lucy slumps wearily, having been up twice in the night with Amelie, about which she does not wish to talk. I turn to Sam.

'Tell me what you're up to?' I ask, to his considerable surprise. What might I mean? As in, are you up to bleeding a radiator, or changing a tyre? His forehead crinkles.

'You know, work, what are you working on?'

Now he looks more than puzzled, he looks bemused. I've never asked him that before. I can see on his features the imminent announcement that he needs a wee.

'Well, you know . . .'

'I don't,' I said, 'that's why I'm asking.'

'Well, James, since you ask, it's been a very exciting period. As you know, I do some clinical work, running groups and seeing occasional clients.'

Very occasional, I'd bet. What's a 'running group' – some kind of exercise class?

I nodded and twitched an eyebrow.

'You know, since we lost Suzy . . .'

There, he has said it, almost. The truth is on the table. Rudy looks uncomfortable, but I find myself grateful, though irritated.

Died. That's what she did, no seat at the table for Suzy, we are getting on with life as best we can. In her absence. They are, anyway.

'... I have got more and more interested in the grieving process? In the last few months I've put together a group of the newly bereaved, who've lost a parent or a partner. I try to avoid couples who have lost a child, that's a different gestalt entirely ...'

'Of course,' I nodded. 'Quite a different gestalt.'

Even Sam, relentlessly self-engrossed as he was, could hear a hint of mockery in my voice, but he soldiered on.

'The group comes alive once they have *processed* the initial feelings ...'

I raised an interrogative finger.

'Processed? You mean, like cheeses in the supermarket?'

Sam looked not so much insulted – that would have been agreeable, and appropriate – as bemused.

'I don't understand,' he said, casting a sidelong glance at Lucy, who wasn't bemused at all, she's used to me. 'What's Jesus got to do with it?' His brow corrugated as he pondered. *And what's He doing at Tesco's?*

Lucy glared at me. She hates it when I try to be funny at the expense of others, especially of Sam. I look suitably chastened. I don't say *but that's what others are for.* Anyway, if he had any gumption he'd tell me to go to hell. That's what gump is for.

Never mind 'gestalt', whatever that signifies, I particularly detest the term *lost* meaning *dead*. Something that is lost can be found, a sock or set of car keys. The dead are not lost, they are no more. Nor have they *passed*, or *passed on*. We know what's implied: not gone, they've just moved house, to *there*, not *here* but on the other side, with God. Now they're angels, basking in the celestial nothing.

That wouldn't suit Suzy for a minute, much less for ever. She'd find it more congenial in that other place, more action there, more interesting people. After all, what would an angel find to talk about? She'd be as listless and irritable up there as I am down here, bereft and alone. The thought offers the odd consolation that we are nevertheless together. Suzy and Darke, still.

Suzy is dead. Suzy was my angel once, now her body lies in the ground. I sometimes imagine her, entombed and decaying, then struggle to banish the images. Sometimes I can't. Rudy puts flowers on her grave. When I visit it I go behind the yew tree and cry. I think that's what it's there for, good thing nobody cut it down for vulgarising.

I'm sure Sam thinks he could help me, him and his group: Sammy and the Grievers. They could put on blackface, and sing uplifting spirituals like a gospel choir, and wave their hands in the air. *Oh, Lawdy Lawdy, praise da Lawd!* They'd feel better after that gestalt.

Encouraged, Sam carried on. Apparently – he lapses into jargon at the drop of a cliché – he works 'phenomenologically'. He quickly explains that this means soliciting what his Grievers actually feel and *working* from there. Yahoo! What else would he do, work from what they don't actually feel? He adds the further, and apparently crucial, fact that he regards himself as a *member* of his group, as well as its leader!

Lucy tried to elucidate.

'That's actually uncommon, Dad, and pretty revolutionary. Sam doesn't just sit back and listen and interpret and ask questions – the group responds to him just like they do to each other.'

Sam nodded modestly and popped a sprout.

'The key is to understand the demographics …'

I must have looked more puzzled, and produced one of those looks that Lucy calls 'lemony'.

'You know, the make-up of the group. I quantify it, and put it on a spreadsheet: age, marital status, nature of loss, gender, social class, ethnicity, religious orientation, you know, all of that? It helps remind me how different they all are, in spite of sharing grief.'

I restrained a strong impulse to twirl my hands in the air, singing 'Nobody Know da Troubles I Seen'.

Best ask a question, more amusing that way.

'I see,' I said sagaciously. If I had a beard, I would have tugged it. 'Tell me how you quantify religious orientation, that seems a bit problematic. Or do you just mean Catholic, C of E, Jew, Hindu, or None of the Above?'

He smirked at my ignorance.

'Nothing as simple as that. What I am interested in is the strength and nature of their spiritual beliefs: whether they believe in God and the afterlife, rewards and punishments, you know? We've got all sorts. And I include myself in the Excel chart too, because I am also a member of the group. It's very enabling, it allows us to work things through on an equal basis.'

'I see. And you can . . . *quantify* this? However would that work?'

'On a scale of one to ten,' said Sam.

We fill our bowls with trifle on an equal basis, process and work it through, push our chairs back, groan and do stomach pats. Sam and Lucy are going for a walk in the park, to give Rudy some exercise, Amelie some fresh air, and themselves some respite from me. I closed the door as they left, waving goodbye like a dignified queen, and went upstairs to bed, to recover, to recover myself and my dear wife. I bury my head in the pillow and inhale her.

The enticing smell of her scent, with which I regularly season my pillows, brings her closer, for an illusory moment transports her to my side. Since discovering the dousing ritual, I spend more and happier times in bed, inhaling my lost one. I smell my fingers, the penetrating sweetness made acrid by the day's residue, inhale with the satisfaction of an undergraduate after a hot date. As I was, as we were, during those early years in Oxford, Suzy teaching bedtime etiquette, me learning, not exactly fast, but steadily. The mornings after, alone in my college bed, I rolled my finger under my nostrils, coated my upper lip, snuffling like a sated piglet.

Lying down in the now quiet house, I close my eyes, drift into the haze, reach out to hold her hand, which is dry and emaciated in mine, until slowly it fills out, warms and rounds, and clasps mine back. She has accepted my role in her death, is grateful. My eyes fill as we turn, into each other's arms. Soothed, I am soon asleep, but not for long. It's not that easy to escape.

I soon stumbled downstairs to join the noisy returning throng, plumped myself into my chair, and closed my eyes. At five o'clock precisely – I checked my watch – the doorbell rang.

'Why don't you answer it, Dad?' said Lucy with an uninterpretable look on her face. She glanced over at Sam, who was similarly unwilling to get up. Yet it must be some friends or other of theirs – I don't have anyone to expect. Unless, of course, it is those policemen. But they said I could come to them next time, we will exchange visits, as new acquaintances do.

I rose slowly, the effect of too much rich food, two glasses of claret, my nap, and Her Majesty droning on the telly, shook myself and made my way to the door, opening it slowly and anxiously.

On the doorstep was Bronya. My former cleaner! And ... somebody else. A man.

Before I could move away, she had clasped me in a hug.

'Happy Christmas!' she said. I had little choice but to agree, and to return the wish, if not the hug. She looked at me intently.

'Is good. You gain weight!'

This required no response, and got none save a faint nod.

'And this,' she said, as they stepped into the hallway, 'is Thomas.' She pronounced it in the Eastern European way: Toe-mass. He had his arm round her waist, as if to indicate from the onset of our embarrassing meeting – what *can* Lucy have been thinking? – that Bronya was his, now. Not that she was ever mine, of course not, though there was an embarrassing scene in the kitchen, last time I saw her, when we were close to being closer. Thank God we weren't. I assumed I would never see her again, which I then regretted, a little.

I shook Toe-mass's hand, and wished him a happy Christmas.

'Won't you come in? Do let me take your coats.' He didn't have one, though it was cold. He was wearing a white T-shirt under a flimsy, crumpled black linen suit, with outlandish dark red suede shoes. Nor had he bothered to shave, nor even to comb his hair.

By now Lucy had joined us, a happy smirk on her face, gave both of her visitors the double kiss, and showed them into the drawing room, where Sam rose to greet them warmly and Rudy looked up for a moment from his Xbox, to say, 'Hi, Bronya,' though he did not seem to recognise Toe-Mass. Bronya went over to him and tousled his hair, but his eyes and fingers never left the screen.

'Well,' I said, 'who'd like a drink? Can I offer a glass of champagne, or perhaps you'd prefer tea?'

'But first,' said Bronya firmly, 'is presents.' She took several wrapped parcels from her bag, looked at them carefully, and read the hanging tags. 'Rudy! Is for you.'

He stopped his playing reluctantly, and wandered over, hand outstretched. It was a thin offering, too small to be a book. He unwrapped it greedily.

'Oh, cool. It's the best!' He rushed to give Bronya a hug, and she redirected him to Toe-mass, who got one too.

'Is from both of us. Toe-mass knows games.'

Lucy and Sam were given a single gift, which they unwrapped, to find a new cookery book.

'Is recipes. Stuffed cabbage, you like that.'

Lucy looked doubtful.

'Isn't it very hard to make?'

'No worries, I help you.'

Bronya looked my way, but I was shirking in the corner, mortified not to be able to respond in kind, until Lucy gave a little cough, and a wink, as she rummaged under the tree.

I was given a book too, the latest biography of Charles Dickens. Of course Bronya didn't know that he and I had fallen out. She'd be pleased to hear it, never having warmed to the old hypocrite.

'How perfect, I will start it immediately. It had marvellous reviews. In *The Times*, I think . . .'

'Yes,' said Toe-mass, 'and the *Telegraph*. The Dickens demographic.'

I took another look at him, puzzled. The tone was near-as-damnit urbane, not exactly clubland, more like a TASS foreign correspondent who'd taken Philby's English seminar.

Lucy and Sam stood shoulder to shoulder to dispense our guests' presents, that were, she announced, from all of us. For Bronya she'd found first editions of Suzy's two novels, and for Toe-mass a modern edition of Henry Mayhew's *London Labour and the London Poor*. Both recipients announced themselves delighted.

Bronya was now looking round the room methodically, at each wall, across the ceiling, at the carpets and furniture, inventorising – had anything changed? – but also, I surmised, checking out the quality of the cleaning. Who'd taken her place? Was she looking after me properly? She walked to the wall, between the windows that overlook the street, and perused my Palmer etching. Examined the frame. Was it dusty?

There was something irritating, touching and mildly delusional about this. Bronya was a rotten cleaner: not only did she leave cobwebs round the corners of the architraves, she merely dabbed at the picture frames, and left them askew to provide evidence that she'd been there. Her replacement, bless her – I do not know her name – is much more efficient in both time and quality of work, and has as little desire to talk to me as I to her, a most satisfactory relationship. By the end of my brief period with Bronya, I was looking after her as much as she was me, and I resented this near equality.

I had three takers for champagne, none for tea, and Bronya for coffee. I suspect she was nostalgic for the Gaggia and our times round the kitchen table, and sure enough she followed me in, unbidden. Toe-mass had settled next to Rudy, and was watching him play his little game, making occasional observations acute enough to catch Rudy's attention. He hit the pause button and looked up wonderingly.

'It's so cool, I got it for my birthday. It's called Sonic Forces . . .'

'I know,' said Toe-mass, 'I love it, but I'm not as good as you. Show me your avatar.'

In the kitchen, Bronya looked around, pulled out a chair and sat herself down familiarly.

'Is looking good . . .' she began, and then, after a pause and a shy smile, corrected herself. 'It is looking good.' She said this haltingly, with less assurance than her normal broken English, less flow. It made her seem a stranger, to me and to herself.

She blushed at my renewed attention.

'Toe-mass is helping improve my English. He speaks . . .' She paused. 'Very well. He has been here longer than me.'

This halting delivery had something pedantic and studied about it, no doubt she was trying to impress upon me how far she had come. She was smartly dressed in an elegant black shift, with a wide red scarf tied round her waist and some sort of black-and-red fat Chinese beady necklace. But then again, I had only ever seen her in her cleaning clothes, and after all it was Christmas. Her haircut was more London, less Sofia. She looked slimmer, happier, and had something of the glow that goes, as I recall it, with being in love.

'It's good to see you, but rather a surprise. I didn't know you and Lucy were friends?'

She nodded. 'Yes. Never mind. You tell me about you . . . about yourself. Lucy says you are doing better . . . Is right?'

No. Was wrong.

'Much better. Would you like hot milk with your coffee?'

She smiled.

'Flat white, yes. I see you are better, but am worried about Lucy ...'

I heated the milk and began to hand-froth it, as the Gaggia warmed up.

'She's all right, just a bit overwrought. You know, tired ...'

She nodded, uncertainly.

'Tell me about Toe-mass.'

She stood up and walked to the window, lest I see the expression on her face, and I presume the accompanying blushes. She looked out over the garden, up at the sky, composed herself.

'Is old friend from school. We meet again in London, at party at our embassy. He working there now.'

When they first came into the house, I reflexively formed an idea of him as some sort of itinerant tradesman. He had the healthy indoor glow of a plumber or electrician; the waterworks and lights would go out all over London without our Eastern European imported labour. Much as we blather about the benefits of work, we English don't actually do much of it. Though I weary of waitresses whose English is inadequate to direct you to the right cutlet or lavatory, the country would grind to a halt without them. As for the NHS? Ban the brown nurses and doctors and all the patients would expire.

'He is sometimes interpreter,' said Bronya, 'translates many documents into best English, but profession is journalist. He very well known at home, and he write "Letter from London" for the newspaper in Sofia.'

The Bulgarian Alistair Cooke! God knows what he must make of us.

'And how long have you been ... seeing him?' I was chagrined to find that this mattered to me, that it would have been insulting, or inappropriate, for her to have embarked upon her little liaison while still in my employ. And presumably under my thrall?

I began totting up the months, getting the calendar right, as if she were pregnant and I had to discover whether the baby might be mine. It was now December, she'd left in, was it May? Well, not left. I'd fired her. I'd felt myself getting close – no, a bit closer – to her, and I nipped her in the bud. After which there was only the brief meeting when she entered the house with her copied key, scared me half to death, and tried to talk some sense into me about Lucy, with whom she had formed an alliance. As we had tea in the kitchen while I calmed down, I experienced more in the way of feeling than made me comfortable. Nothing happened, of course, I'm not that daft, though she may well have been. It hardly bears thinking about, but now and again I do. And, it seems, Lucy and she have bonded over my sad and parlous state.

'I don't know,' she said, 'maybe start of summer? It was surprise to see him again.'

I should have been happy for her; she had struggled, never complained, made something for and of herself. I'd had a role in this, through my admittedly callous treatment of her, as if she were a pigeon I had freed from the coop and released into the air. But they're supposed to head back home, aren't they? They're pigeons, not bloody cuckoos. I don't know which I resented more, that she had chosen Lucy, or Toe-mass, over me.

I left the kitchen, carrying a tray with our coffees and champagne for the others, to find Sam and Toe-mass sighing, laughing and comparing notes on how bad their national football teams were. England had crashed out of the World Cup. Bulgaria weren't even in it. They looked guilty as we entered, desisted, sat still and upright, like bad boys. Rudy was slumped in his chair, thumbs busy and eyes fixed. Lucy had gone off for somatic interaction with Amelie.

Wrong time, wrong place and people, wrong demographic. Bad gestalt. Conversation started, spluttered and died. We drank our drinks, refilled them, praised the contents, drank them.

'This is a very beautiful house . . .' began Toe-mass.

'Thank you.'

'I wonder – maybe 1720?'

'Perhaps a touch later, the terrace went up in bits and bobs, as they so often did when the money ran out, or the builders did . . .'

He nodded, looking round the room.

'I started a piece a few years ago about Georgian terraces in England, but it was superficial, too much information. London, Bath, Cheltenham . . . I threw it away.'

'Maybe you should have narrowed your topic? There's some fine terraces in Docklands, from developments contemporary with this one. Deptford, Rotherhithe, places along there, where nobody goes unless they live there. They'd make for an interesting article.'

He didn't seem very interested.

'I'm sick of the beautiful and the picturesque. The problem with England is that it's too comfortable, the political issues are trivial, and there are no social ones worth taking to the streets for . . .'

'Thank God for that,' I said. 'You probably don't know about the miner's strike, but . . .'

'I've read about it,' said Toe-mass. 'I admired Arthur Scargill very much.'

'How marvellous,' I said.

Bronya was looking from one of us to the other, first worried, then puzzled, and finally that little bit relieved. We were getting on, in our unyielding fashion.

'Is good,' she said. 'And thank you for drinks, but now we must be going . . .' She looked around. 'Where is Lucy?'

Lucy was hurrying down the stairs, anxious about how it was all going.

'Oh, must you? We've just got started . . .'

'I'm so sorry,' said Toe-mass. 'We're going to a carol service and we've only just got time. Thanks so much for asking us.'

'Me too,' said Bronya.

As she left, she gave me another hug.

'You have good day,' she said fondly.

'I have other plans,' I said, releasing her and closing my beloved door.

Chapter 3

Dear Dorothea,

Thank you for your reiterated invitation to join your little group.

Alas, I am neither in the right frame of mind, nor am I the right sort of person to enhance such a gathering. I read very little poetry these days – how clever of you to keep your eyes on short objects, like Gulliver in Lilliput – and God knows I once read rather a lot of it, back when. I remember enjoying some, which was mildly uplifting, and disliking most of it, which I enjoyed more. Better than gushing like an Eton Mess. If I ever meet another reader who adores Yeats's 'The Lake Isle of Innisfree' I will disembowel them in a bee-loud glade.

Anyway, as Groucho Marx said, why would I wish to join a club that wants to have me in it?

Very best wishes, and apologies,

James

A short, sharp shock. Surely no one could withstand such a comprehensive rejection.

Her answer was immediate.

Darling James,

Of course you feel like that, all of us did, in one way or the other, before signing on. And most of us – though we've had a couple of drop-outs, why wouldn't we? — have come to regard the group as an occasion that graces our calendars, and sometimes — is this a wee bit tendentious? I hope so! — our very lives.

If you had not initially resisted my invitation, it would have disappointed me. To have qualms, but nevertheless give it a try — come, just for a session or two! — that would be reasonable. It is what I did, and I was coming out of a situation, as you may recall, not dissimilar to your own.

It's a lovely group: there are usually six to eight of us, not all 'literary', though we do have a senior editor at Little, Brown, a literary agent, and a translator of Dante. There's also Philip Massingham, the human-rights lawyer, and Patricia Bond, who is a consultant at the Chelsea and Westminster. Good people, very good readers. I'll fill you in on their vitae — and more! — before you come.

We've given up on the idea of cooking for each other, which got a tad competitive, so we meet after supper, at 8.00 in each of our homes in turn, and the host reads their choice of poem, and leads the discussion. This keeps things orderly, and gives focus. The host will supply drink and something to nibble, which can be amusing when done imaginatively.

Come! What's to lose?

Dorothea xxx

She intended to sound arch, but it's pure childishness. Like Rudy, she will not take NO for an answer: precocious, entitled, likely to insist and to sulk, indomitable. And, I suppose, amusing enough if you fall for it, charm is such a racket.

Oh dear. All right, I will go, if only to confirm that I will dislike it, and them, just as much as they will dislike me. It's easier than getting into an interminable email chain with Dorothea in which the entreaties and *xx*-kisses multiply. *Relentless*, Suzy called her, a tireless promoter of causes, the major one of which was herself and her increasingly unpopular novels. She herded literary editors to lunches, wrote reams of billets-doux to reviewers, handed out so many books with charming inscriptions that the second-hand bookseller catalogues describe unadorned copies as 'not inscribed by the author, and rare in this state', and charge more for them. Suzy had a shelf-ful, before she tried to donate them to Oxfam and was turned away. On the way home she chucked them in a skip.

Darling James!

Well, aren't you a sweetie! I'm sure you'll be a great hit. The next meeting is on January 23rd, at 8.00. I will confirm the details, it's at Miles's house in Ladbroke Grove. Very chic!

As you are a new member, it would be unkind to throw you in at the deep end, so why don't you circulate a poem of your choice for one of our next couple of meetings, once you get the lay of the land?

Bestest love,

Dorothea xxxx

On receipt of this, I closed my computer lid with undue force, filled with remorse and anxiety. I didn't want to go, I don't want to go. I suspected what 'the lay of the land' heralded: it was one of Dorothea's nicknames at Oxford. I could beg off on the grounds of my forthcoming trip to Ulaanbaatar, from which I could no doubt return with yak's-milk poisoning. But such lies have a way of catching up with you, and I am no dissembler, having had since childhood a disarming and unmanning propensity to tell the truth. Lies get you in trouble, as my father once said as he unloosed his belt.

I will go to Notting Hill, much as I dislike people who reside in pastel houses, like Hindus lacking spirit. And before my time comes I will begin choosing a poem. I'll make up a longlist, then a shortlist, then a winner: like one of those recurrent, boring literary prizes that Dorothea-*xx* has failed ever to win, despite having laid a landfill of judges.

Criteria for entry on my longlist? Something that none of them might have chosen. Does it have to be something I admire? Or better yet, might it be something I detest? I presume the chooser is also the reader: poems exist in the ear as well as on the page. When I taught modern poetry at school, I tried to find a recording of the poet reading their own work. The poet: not some damned thespian! There is a recording of some actress declaiming *The Waste Land* in such a histrionic fashion that it curdles your blood and makes you shriek with dismay. When you hear Eliot reading it himself, grating his way across his wasted land, crusty dry, definitive, you understand the poem as it was meant to be understood.

But I can hardly bring it to the group: it's too long, and most literary people are sick of it, on the grounds that they know much of it by heart, and understand it tolerably enough. They don't. Anyway, it cannot fit on a page, like all Americans he's a windbag.

If I am to read a poem aloud, it has to be by a man. Men read men, women, women. As nature intended. Anyhow, there're so few women poets worth reading. Emily Dickinson? Of course, marvellous. But that awful Plath woman, all that overheated emoting like a devil with period pains, though when she overheated her hubby's manuscripts in a bonfire in their garden, it did a service to the world of poetry.

Poets are ghastly. Novelists may be abstracted, self-important, wordy, boring. But poets? Convinced they are the inheritors of the bardic torch – givers of light and warmth, suns, gods – they dress up, tousle their hair, proclaim themselves the unacknowledged legislators of the world, never having noticed that all legislators are pompous halfwits. Imagine living with a poet, being subservient to and taken advantage of by so noble a being. What a life, to be such a wife: the abandoned Caitlin Thomas, Maud Gonne pursued by limp Willie, Miss Plath with her head in the oven, the bleeding Vivienne Eliot deposited in the bin like a used tampon, Dorothy

Wordsworth, the old bore's real missus, writing his poems for him, the cringing cheeks of the harassed Lady Byron. The downtrodden *muses* incinerated by the torch. *The Wives of the Poets: A Monograph*. Having conceived this stonking idea, I shared it with Suzy. Mistake. She thought for a moment.

'*Wife*,' she said, 'rhymes with *Life*.'

'How discerning of you!' I responded, noting that it also rhymes with *Strife*.

'Husband,' she replied, 'doesn't rhyme with anything.'

I go through my small collection of LPs of poets reading their own work. Eliot, of course, Dylan Thomas welshing, Philip Larkin the lugubrious pussy-hound, Robert Frost, cod-wise. There're too many poets, and they do go on and on. Death by droning. Does anyone actually care any more, save a small band of fanatics similar to trainspotters or birdwatchers?

I hate this reading group already. Can you quit something you haven't yet joined? I compose a regretful email in my head, but I'd regret Dorothea's reply even more, with the attendant multiplying kisses. She'd love it if I continued to resist, might even appear at the door, clutching her bosom (she'd need both hands) and her poetic texts, imploring.

Make a choice of poem. No hurry. Then circulate it. Drink and nibble. Read. Regret. Resign.

During our visits I am tasked with reading Rudy's bedtime story. I am grateful for and pleased by this, for I am determined to extend the range of his literary exposure. His father has forbidden works about talking animals, citing some ludicrous published research by an imaginatively bereft Canadian academic. I suppose that if you live amongst the bears and wolves you wouldn't want to cosy up to them. Look what happened to Little Red Riding Hood. But we who are fortunate in our owls and badgers and piglets are happy to commune with our garrulous little friends.

As a result of Sam's injunction, which decimates English books for children, I have offered Rudy a suitably shortened version of *Gulliver's Travels*. He was excited hearing about 'a whole country run by horses! That's so cool!'

It was an ambitious project, though Sam initially disapproved of the idea.

'You're going to read *Gulliver's Travels* to Rudy? In the original?'

'I am,' I said firmly, without explanation or excuse. And not entirely accurately. Of course I will cut out those long disquisitions about contemporary affairs, politics and religion, with which Gulliver bores his interlocutors large and small, and his readers, large and small as well. But what is left after these excisions I would preserve in the 'original' language.

Rudy will more than cope, he will engage. His reading may be limited, but he is highly intelligent, a touch precocious perhaps, and keen to learn. He has memorised all of Roald Dahl's children's books – I was unfamiliar with them, but they're rather good in their scratchy, antic fashion. But he will respond to something more demanding. Children do not need to understand every word of what they read. Adults don't.

If Rudy struggled somewhat reading the *original* text, he would still feel proud having read it.

'For pity's sake, James,' said Sam. 'He's only eight years old.'

It has never been clear to me what pity is, that it should have a sake.

'Surely you could find something else to read him, that's more age-appropriate?'

When Sam is thinking his eyes tend to cross, as if he were studying his nose. He went quiet. It was clearly my turn to say something, but I wouldn't. I could see him analysing how far 'on the spectrum' he would place me.

He waited me out. I capitulated.

'Children need to be respected, and challenged. Rudy wants me to read it to him, and to learn to read it himself.'

Sam raised his finger high into the air and wiggled its tip about, as if goosing an angel.

'But have you told him the language is very old-fashioned?'

'For goodness' sake,' I expostulated wearily, sufficiently cross that I could almost see my own nose, 'in the nineteenth century, when children were properly educated, they read at an adult level well before they were ten. John Stuart Mill could read Latin and Greek by Rudy's age!'

Sam opened his mouth a little, and puckered his lips like a gold-fish sucking its flakes.

It was cruel of me. I should have helped him out.

'He was a nineteenth-century philosopher . . .'

'I know who he was,' said Sam firmly. 'But he's hardly a good example, is he?'

'What do you mean?'

'He may have been a hothouse genius, but by the time he was twenty he was profoundly depressed.'

'Ah yes . . . indeed. Do you know that he was worried, according to the laws of probability, that all melodies would inevitably be used up, and that new music would be impossible?'

Sam scowled, and corrected me sharply. 'I suspect he was really talking about internal harmonies, and that what was being used up was *him*.'

I was lagging behind, slow to take this in. Sam knew who Mill was? He had opinions about him? And *diagnoses*?

I retreated further up my own spectrum, and waited to hear what would happen next.

'I did an essay on him when I was at uni,' Sam said. 'I love *On Liberty*, it's been right useful to me in my professional life.'

He paused for a moment, as if remembering something.

'But you're right, James. Mill thought it is a "moral crime" not to educate children properly. And Rudy's primary school always stoops to the lowest common denominator . . .'

Aha! Surely I had him, at last. We'd spent many uncomfortable moments discussing Rudy's education, and I had offered again and again to pay for him to go to a decent prep school. I was about to reopen this discussion and to renew my offer, but he saw me reaching, as it were, for my wallet.

'It is politically essential that children be educated in state schools, the more and the less able together. It teaches them lessons essential in a democracy. So if his little school in Abingdon doesn't stretch him sufficiently, it is our role ...' he looked me in the eye, I was included, 'to do it ourselves. So by all means, James, read him your original *Gulliver's Travels*, you're right. Anyway, it'll be his bedtime story: if he doesn't follow it, he'll fall asleep.'

It was fair comment. I do too, sometimes.

Rummaging about my bookshelves, I located my Penguin edition of *Gulliver*, edited so thoroughly by an estimable Italian professor that the resultant burgeoning text has had to be squeezed by its publisher into tiny type. I read it with a magnifying glass in one hand, and a pen for crossing out and amending passages in the other. The book was splayed out on my desk – I had to crack the spine to do this, which served it right – with paperweights to hold down the pages on both sides. I shall cut the text down to size, but leave in the episodes about pissing on the fire and the buckets of poo, children love that. Rudy's favourite book is about a farting giant.

Our first reading was a mitigated success, not that he understood it all, but because he wanted more. When he stays with me, or more occasionally when I visit him in Abingdon, he begs for a further chapter at bedtime. He is rightly impatient – 'When do we get to the horses, Gampy?' – hence I'd constructed a précis of Books I and II, and excised the intolerable 'Voyage to Laputa'. Rudy listened to the first chapters with good grace, more than tolerated but enjoyed the tiny people and the gigantic ones, knowing the four-legged were still to come.

When I eventually read him my edited version of the 'Voyage to the Land of Houyhnhnms', he was attentive beyond anything I could have imagined, lay with his head on the pillow, eyes closed, rapt. Having been starved of articulate animals, he was delighted by the talking horses, and he laughed at the images of the Yahoos, hardly thinking himself or his Gampy a member of that accursed race.

Soon enough we reached the end of *Gulliver's Travels*, with our poor, broken hero mired back home in Redriff, withdrawn and miserable, stabled with his horses. When I closed the covers, Rudy began to snuffle.

'What is it, darling? Is it too sad for you . . .?'

'No, Gampy. I mean, it is sad, but what is going to happen to him? What happens next?'

'Nothing, darling. I'm sorry, that's where Mr Swift ends the book. It's finished, see . . .' I showed him the final page of the text.

'It's silly! It's not fair! I want more!'

I put the book on the bedside table, leant over to comfort him and turned off the lamp.

'Never you mind, just go to sleep now. If you want more, perhaps we can read it again.'

He yawned and turned away.

'Soon, Gampy?'

'Very soon. You go to sleep now.'

I tucked him in, and sat in the darkness, listening to his breathing as he fell into sleep. Of course, he was right. It isn't fair. *Gulliver's Travels* lacks a proper resolution. The homecoming raises more problems than it resolves. When I taught the book to my sixth-formers we all felt similarly. *What happens next?* I did some research, but apparently no one had undertaken an extension of the text. It would seem extraneous, and impertinent. How many children had Lady Macbeth? Nothing is said of it. What happens next to Captain

Gulliver? Nothing is said of that either. Books end. Get over it. Reread.

Sitting in the darkness next to my grandson, I wondered if I might reanimate, and try to resolve, my decades-old frustration at the lack of a suitable conclusion to Swift's text. I need a project, having given up writing my monograph about sloppy-puss Dickens. Might I, instead, turn to Dean Swift, with his disgust and misanthropic rage? I'm happier in his company. And if he was too reticent to reveal what lay ahead for his hero, perhaps I might give it a whirl?

Even having the temerity to consider such a project makes me anxious. Of course I could improvise some childish extension to the story that would pacify Rudy, but it wouldn't satisfy me. I need to do it as best I can. It will take time, and during that time it would please Rudy to reread Gulliver together, which would help me to recall the rhythms of the language.

If Swift wouldn't do it, I'll try. I will write the bloody ending myself.

Yet I have no confidence, none whatsoever, that my pastiche of Swift's language will be anything other than a B-minus. Over the years I have reread *Gulliver's Travels* with varying degrees of pleasure, finding it sometimes witty and provocative, at others tiresomely embedded in long-dead controversies. Nevertheless I cannot replicate the subtle intricacies of its prose, which while simple, has a characteristic voice, and timbre, that make it instantly recognisable: Swiftian.

I am no linguist. I stumbled through my schoolboy Greek and Latin, before abandoning both on entering Oxford. I picked up enough French to make myself understood on my occasional visits to that extravagantly peculiar land, though to be fair a shrug of the shoulders and the single word '*d'accord*' gets you a long way in Paris society. If you light a Gitanes while saying this, and flip your hands about in the air, you are instantly recognised not merely as literate, but eloquent.

Not wanting to make an entire fool of myself on my extension of Gulliver, I may send my paltry efforts to my old chum George, who though mired in the nineteenth century is not rooted in it, and has a knowledge of Augustan literature far in excess of mine, as well as a much better ear.

We were at Oxford together, though he was two years my senior, and had little idea who I was. But he was instantly recognisable: neither a dandy nor a show-off, but that much rarer entity, an eccentric. He sported a silk paisley cravat, velvet jacket, and moleskin trousers from Hall Brothers, and highly polished brogues from Duckers. It was said that he spent much of his time walking in the Oxfordshire countryside, reciting Matthew Arnold's *Thyrsis* and *The Scholar Gypsy*, both of which he knew by heart.

He had a prodigious memory, and an almost equally enormous grasp. He'd founded the University Tennyson Society, which claimed three members, though he was accused of having made up the other two. George was also at ease with Chaucer, spoke Middle English like a reeve, had gobbled Shakespeare whole, and was batty about Swift and Pope. Of course, he got a congratulatory First, disregarded his tutor's instructions to embark on postgraduate research, and obtained a position as English master at our esteemed public school, at the age of twenty-two. He'd spent his life there, and counted himself the most fortunate man alive.

When I later joined the common room, we established the kind of friendship that doesn't necessitate actually being friends. But when I need help of one sort or another – not very often – I can rely on him. After Suzy's death, when I immured myself from the world, wounded and desperate, blocked my door, cut off my emails and phone, huddled away for months, it was George who, at my instigation, fielded enquiries, received my redirected mail and shielded me from the light.

His only failure in this regard, which I greatly resented, was in insisting on coming to the house to deliver a stack of letters that Lucy had written to me, and which he had parcelled together with a black ribbon, a Victorian affectation that he thought might move me as much as it did him. I gave him tea, took the letters, and hustled him out with the assurance that I would read them.

I did, slumped in the kitchen; the series began with sympathetic letters, worried about my mental health. And spiritual. Hah. Of course I hadn't answered, as I hadn't received them. The following letters were progressively more distraught, and the final one was, well, final. Either I responded, or there was no sense responding. She didn't mean it, but she meant it. I was scalded and boiled. I suppose George's impertinent intervention was efficacious, because not very long thereafter I went to Oxfordshire to attempt a reconciliation with my daughter.

If I were to write a pastiche of Swift's prose, George would be my man. The resulting critical humiliation might do me a bit of good, and improve my text considerably.

Daunting? Yes.

So what?

Yet another heavily be-*xxx*-ed email has arrived from Dorothea, confirming the fateful day and place of the next meeting, and attaching a poem for consideration. It has been submitted through her, as the group's protocol insists, because in the past individual members had accompanied their suggested texts with commentary and assorted effusions: *Why I chose this poem. How much I love it. A little background reading . . .*

This month's poem, chosen by Miles the literary agent, is by Rupert Brooke: 'The Dead'.

These hearts were woven of human joys and cares,
Washed marvellously with sorrow, swift to mirth.
The years had given them kindness. Dawn was theirs,
And sunset, and the colours of the earth.
These had seen movement, and heard music; known
Slumber and waking; loved; gone proudly friended;
Felt the quick stir of wonder; sat alone;
Touched flowers and furs and cheeks. All this is ended.

There are waters blown by changing winds to laughter
And lit by the rich skies, all day. And after,
Frost, with a gesture, stays the waves that dance
And wandering loveliness. He leaves a white
Unbroken glory, a gathered radiance,
A width, a shining peace, under the night.

This smells of rat. Not your crawl-about-in-the-trenches-corpse-muncher, much to be expected in such environs, no. Much worse. A literary rat. A plot, I suspect a plot. A burial plot.

I write by return to Dorothea, thanking her, and asking if she could send me the previous few months of members' choices. Mistaking my enquiry for enthusiasm, she sends the list, which is (as I had feared) composed entirely of poems about loss, mortality, decay, death, grief. Some grindingly earnest Wordsworth, over-upholstered Shakespeare, witty and unconsoling Marvell, a pint-sized draught of Dylan Thomas, a smelly snatch of T. S. Eliot, some bardy Yeats ...

So that's why she wants me. I can sniff her gestalt: the poetical enthusiasts – median age seventy-four – are actually some sort of therapy or encounter group, 'coming to terms' with mortality, their dead partners, their shrinking selves. I will benefit from their accumulating wisdom, and they will have a new mourner hot from the pot.

Another Group of Grievers. Choosing poems that don't merely express grief but encourage others to do so themselves. *Cathartic*, that's what they call it, so good for you. The problem, of course, is that hardly anyone knows what catharsis is. The notion is attributed to that classical know-it-all Aristotle, and was misunderstood not merely by him, but virtually everyone since.

Catharsis is apparently what happens after you watch a tragedy. First you sit through the unbearable experiences of watching Oedipus kill his father, bed his mother, then gouge his own eyes out, and at the end you supposedly feel better, having had the emotions of fear and pity tuned up and balanced, like a car engine on its annual service. Rubbish! At the conclusion of *Oedipus*, if you have so-called emotional intelligence, you are distraught and exhausted. And if, God help you, you have attended a performance of *King Lear*, with the demented old man carrying the dead body of his lovely Cordelia, the notion that the experience is cathartic is risible, deeply stupid – and widely held.

Suzy. I'm writing about Suzy, what else is there to write about? Every day, most every hour, is filled with her absence, and that absence is the abiding presence of my life. I see her in whole and in part, I talk to her, she responds, we commune, in bits. I do not want her catharted or purged. I don't want my feelings about Suzy to go away, I don't want her to go away, I am inhabited by her, filled with her, tormented mind and body. She is my wife, still; I am James Darke, still.

I neither want to rid myself of this, nor to express it. The only thing more painful than this daily agony would be its absence. No more pain means no more Suzy.

I am tasked – how did I allow this? – with finding some bloody poem to share with the Catharsis Club, members of the Purgation Party. All this is enough – I don't need a lot – to make me detest poetry, and poets, and their readers. *The best possible words in the best possible order?* Nonsense. The best possible words, when you are mourning your dead, are no words at all. Silence is the respect we give, the testimony to our loss, the only adequate and respectful 'expression' of how bereft and adrift we are. I am.

I reread the Rupert Brooke, which I remember clearly from school. I must have been – what, fourteen? – when I first encountered it, and was commensurately moved by its sentiments. All those poor young men, lost! The lives they had, and could have had! I remember blinking back a tear, deeply moved by my own sensitivity. Reading it again after all these years – I would never have set it for my own pupils – I regret that I cannot post an immediate response to circulate amongst the members: *What utter twaddle.*

It will be better, I sense, to hold and to refine this criticism – hearts are *woven*? Like mittens, I presume – and bring its fuller incarnation to the group. It will be a perfect test of the discrimination of the members: anyone who could admire this risible effusion is hardly worth sharing a drink with, much less a poem, and an evening.

Dorothea has decided that, after 'this marvellous and so aptly chosen' poem, it will soon be my turn to be host, and to submit my own choice. Before that auspicious initiation, she suggests that it would be useful for the two us to meet, perhaps for a light lunch at hers, so that she can get me 'up to speed' on my fellow members. The prospect is appalling: there is nothing 'light' about Dorothea's person, and I am sure her lunches would be similarly fatty and unappealing. Brackish pâté out of a tin, over-crisp crostini, aged, wrinkled cornichons, bleeding beetroot and feta salad, a bottle of insipid Riesling . . . And as for getting 'up to speed', a loathsome metaphor – why would one use it to describe a bunch of superannuated, sofa-bound litterateurs, contemplating their impending doom? The yet further *xxx*-es seem to suggest that after lunch might it not be agreeable . . . ? I must never allow myself to be alone with this woman, or soon enough the sticky treacle will be mine own.

I decline the invitation with elegant grace, and Dorothea

promises, instead, a description of the various members – she is known to have enjoyed quite a lot of members – though she assumes that I know most of them. I don't. Her missive arrived the next day, she apparently having spent the whole night composing her little character sketches – there is (at least) a full page about each member, with links to their Wikipedia entries. If no one will now publish her boring novels, she has this, at least, to occupy her compositional time, and to demonstrate to me the acuity of her observation.

The translator, a well-known beardy seducer, is described as a 'man of capacious appetite, worldly, warm-hearted and generous, *with a big brain*'. No doubt she observed this between her legs, but sadly, Dorothea had to admit, 'he hardly ever comes'.

Her descriptive language was suffused with a sexuality that might have been camp had it been witting. When she called a woman 'impenetrable' she presumably intended it to mean Scottish and rectitudinous. And when her advances had been turned down, the relevant gentleman was infallibly described as limp and joyless.

I scanned, then deleted, the descriptions. Why participate in a group if you have such disdain for the members, the process, the themes and topics, and most of the poems themselves?

What? It would be more amusing slouched at home, drowsily missing the *News at Ten*. Or, worse, actually watching it, perhaps seeing the ubiquitous Golde, my former pupil, now our Minister for Education, talking rubbish about schools and schooling. His schoolboy face comes back to me when I watch him, indeed, it is still there, it abides in his 'adult' incarnation, the sixteen-year-old sexually obsessed, creepily ingratiating toady.

Miles's residence is in Elgin Crescent, three stacked storeys as pink as a wedding cake from Tesco's, and a glossy grey door and windows that had recently been repainted. Like its owner, the house glistened with wealth and self-importance. The head of his eponymous agency, Miles represented authors distinguished more for their sales than their literary quality. 'Any pompous arsehole can represent Teddy St Aubyn,' he said. 'It takes genius to represent Jordan. Tits sell a lot better than racks of literary novels!' They'd sold well enough to buy this house, and a bolthole outside Lucca, where he spent much of the summer.

Dorothea described him as an assiduous and intermittently successful Lothario, though he preferred the term 'shagger', which he would mouth lasciviously in a mock East End accent, a linguistic affectation common in the literary world of his generation. 'Oi, guvnor,' I once heard the head of one major publishing house say to another, like Michael Caine trying to sound like a cockney. "Ow's bizness?'

By Dorothy's account, with a few drinks in him Miles was sparkly and infectiously attractive, with a few more a bore, and at parties, between the poles of his spectrum, he would spend his time trying to pick up women. The fact that his advances and routines now hardly ever hit pay dirt did not daunt him in the least. In his middle seventies he was still a flirt, a blue pill ready in his jacket pocket in case he got any encouragement, though to be fair even that little helper rarely enabled him – he would confess with a giggle – to stand up for the occasion.

'Never mind,' he'd say, 'I can always lie down.'

'The problem is,' he'd told Dorothea, who immediately told everyone else, 'when young women see me they see a dirty old man. But I'm not. I'm a dirty young man, always was and always will be, only now I'm disguised in an old man's body. This can be helpful – it means any young woman will talk to me, because I'm presumed to be as safe as an old queen.'

As I entered the house Miles clasped my shoulder fraternally, accompanying the gesture with what might pass, in other circumstances, as a leer, complete with raised eyebrows à la Groucho Marx.

'Lovely to see you again,' he said.

'You must forgive me,' I said, 'ravages of age, my memory is shot. Remind me when we met? Some time ago was it?'

He did another funny look, somewhere between a moue and a smirk.

'Yes, many years, at one of Suzy's parties. When she couldn't place her next novel I acted as her agent for a time ...' He laughed. 'But alas, I didn't have much luck. The spirit of the age was against her, I fear, which was a shame, she was very talented ...'

He still had his arm on my shoulder, but I soon moved away and was shortly approached by Dorothea, who was lingering and listening, and given a glass of an utterly disgusting resinated white wine, and a piece of sticky, stale baklava.

Miles soon raised a toast: 'In honour of poor dear Rupert, who died just off the coast of Skyros. It was difficult sourcing one of the local wines ... but I trust it will give the right flavour to our evening.' He nodded smugly. If he expected applause he didn't get any. The wine, like dear Rupert himself, didn't travel very well: it tasted as though it too had fatal septicaemia.

There were a couple of absentees, as usual with 'such a distinguished' group, as Dorothea would have it. Philip was in The Hague, fighting for the rights of some human, and Patricia was in hospital doing whatever an oncologist does, for a private patient, no doubt. Tim the translator was eating out somewhere, or someone.

The room was easy and welcoming, ostentatiously undemanding. There were Persian carpets on top of Persian carpets, a painted coffee table, Indian, with a glass top revealing a narrow vitrine with a few ethnic trinkets displayed: carved toy animals – elephants, monkeys, snakes, tigers, no cows. There were a couple of shimmery David Jones watercolours, one on top of the other, on the far wall. Bookshelves on either side of the mantle, stuffed precariously. Not a *collector* of books, Miles would smirk, merely 'an accumulator'. A considerable number of them, he said modestly, had charming *dédicaces* to him. I had a look, just before we began. Most said 'For

Miles, with best wishes', which is a common authorial way of saying bugger off.

He'd had a good number of wives, who had buggered off as well, though he claimed not to recall quite how many. 'They do come and go,' he said with the wry smile that ladies apparently found so attractive. 'I prefer divorce to marriage, *such* a sense of freedom.' He could afford it, and had maintained good relations with his former partners, having as many exes as an email from Dorothea (whose email description of him had labelled him as frisky and spunky).

He stood in the middle of the room, as we made our way to places of rest. Dorothea subsided into a sofa more upholstered even than she, and shoved over to make a place for poor me. Her hip greeted me warmly, as Miles stood to offer his poem. He knew it by heart and recited it gracefully enough. His eyes filled as he did so, and we responded with the requisite silence.

Ethel McVeigh gave a small cough. She must be in her early eighties, a rectitudinous Scottish spinster who had spent her erotic life under the covers of a book. Known as Ethel the Wellread, she had given her heart only to words. Though she still does some freelance editorial work, she resigned her position at Cape some years ago, to the considerable relief of her authors and colleagues. She had been feared and respected for the forthrightness of her views. Being edited by her was apparently like having a root canal.

'Darling Miles,' she said, 'this will be so painful for you, it's very brave …'

Dorothea leant over to whisper in my ear, 'His grandson was wounded in Afghanistan, he was in Stoke Mandeville for a year afterwards, so very tragic …'

I nodded with appropriate solemnity, listening to Suzy's voice, remonstrating in my head, *Don't you dare, James. Do shut up!* She had an infallible sense of when I was about to say something objectionable, something she called *horrid*. I am sometimes, and the provocation was immense. I didn't know this Miles person, and could still feel his horny hand's imprint on my shoulder, nor did I care about his presumably paraplegic grandson. I resent being suborned into sympathy. It is certainly a sad story. I say *sad* rather than *tragic*. Tragedy is something that happens on the stage, not in real lives, unless they are scripted by Sophocles. There is nothing tragic about being blown up by a mine. If you're a soldier, you expect such things, they will certainly happen, and if you're lucky it will be your comrade and not yourself who is maimed.

I cannot understand what has happened. Demographically, as Sam would have it. I know the young are gratuitously prone to broadcasting how they feel, tooting and tweetle-ing and promiscuously sharing pictures of themselves. But our assembled group are elderly, sophisticated and ironic, representatives of an English generation who knew how and when to button their mouths, dry their eyes and stiffen their lips.

And here we have Miles, gaudily bedecked in his Paul Smith suit and technicolour tie – most inappropriate, one might think – blubbing, and offering to share his consoling Rupert Brooke effusion with us. Rupert Brooke! If he hadn't been so pretty and died so young, nobody would look at his poems twice, having developed sufficient contempt for them on a first reading. This lyric is not poetry at all: it stinks of forced feeling, ill-assimilated and badly expressed, and if you reformatted it as prose, it would contain sentiments apt only for greetings cards. The sort that say **CONDOLENCES** on the front cover.

I have come to the group armed. Gone through the poem line by line, locating and eviscerating one cliché or empty gesture after another. If it were a prisoner in the dock, charged with disorderly linguistic conduct, it would be convicted immediately, and sentenced to transportation to Australia. They know what to do with limp Poms over there.

The group admire the poem, I suspect, because they are moved by Miles's bravery in offering it, and circle round its sentiments reverently. I close my eyes, and tilt my head back. Suzy would love hating all of this, I can hear her snorts. We commune together silently. I sink back into the sofa, graciously allow my glass to be refilled, twice, and say no words save *goodnight*, as soon as I possibly can.

As I get home, an email is waiting from Dorothea *xxx* enquiring why I was so silent, asking if the experience was 'too much for me'?

I didn't answer. In the morning there were two more emails, increasingly urgent, which would be followed by a phone call if she had my number, which I have refused to give on the (spurious) grounds that my mobile is in hospital.

My Poetry Evenings, like my days, are numbered. The only question is how small that number will be.

Chapter 4

I may not read Rudy every word of my addition to *Gulliver's Travels*, but it's irresistible trying to get it all down, to reincarnate in the privacy of my thoughts as Lemuel Gulliver, redux.

I have not run this effort through George, whose critical eye would reduce, even ruin, what I hope is a childlike amateurishness in my composition, which is written for one and only one reader, who will not understand much of it. I have apologised to George for leading him on, knowing he will have been waiting impatiently, blue pencil in hand in readiness to correct my many errors of language, fact and judgement. I'd rather leave them in. Not that I can tell which one is which.

He responded to my dismissal with a curt missive, in his impeccable italic script, wishing me luck with my 'unexpected little memoir'.

One night I read my beginning section to Rudy, more than a little anxious to gauge his reaction, for if it bored him, the further and larger project would hardly be worth pursuing.

INTRODUCTION

G*ulliver's Travels is frequently mistaken for a children's book, but its full text would bore any but the most precocious child. In* *bookshops you will always find a shortened and bowdlerised version in the children's section, with the giant Gulliver pictured on the cover, tied down and surrounded by tiny Lilliputians. What a wonderful fancy!*

In the next chapter, it is he who is tiny, and the inhabitants of the land of Brobdingnag who are big! In each case, the same lesson is learned: when the little ones look at big Gulliver, they see a creature with disgusting physical deformities. His small friend 'discovers great Holes in my Skin, that the Stumps of my Beard were ten times stronger than the Bristles of a Boar, and my Complexion made up of several Colours altogether disagreeable'. In the next voyage Swift turns it the other way round, and when Gulliver looks up at the gigantic Brobdingnagians, he is horrified by their bodies, their skins pitted by pustules and cancers, festooned by cavorting lice.

By the time our hero goes on his fourth Voyage, he is ready for the ultimate lesson, when he encounters the Yahoos in the land of the Houyhnhnms. These creatures, as he cannot fail to recognise, are like humans, though they have longer claws and nails, more hair and an animal gait. They are morally and physically corrupt, malodorous, malicious, libidinous and deceitful.

I read this slowly, trying in my modest way to build expectation. Rudy, wearing his Junior Blade jimjams, was sitting up in his bed, his night-time Ribena in a glass on the table at his side, where a lava lamp displayed blobby colour changes. At this point, I stopped to offer explanations of the meaning of 'malodorous' and 'libidinous'.

He waved his hands crossly, feeling patronised.

'Just read, Gampy.'

It was wise of him – after all, we had read most of the book, so my précis covered familiar ground. We could discuss what he made of it if he wished. His eyes were hooded, and I could sense that he was falling off.

*W*hen the Yahoos approach him, Gulliver takes refuge under a tree, which they climb so as to shit on his head. Though repelled and revolted, he cannot escape the biological recognition: they are kin. He's one of them.

Fleeing from the Yahoo pack, he encounters a horse, then a substantial settlement of horses. He is astonished to discover signs of intelligence in them, but not as astonished as they, to discover such signs in him. Who could believe it? A thinking horse! A thinking Yahoo! The implications and consequences of this wondrous meeting make up the final section of Gulliver's Travels, and are the most compelling and memorable section of the book.

Gulliver lives for some years amongst the Houyhnhnms, learns their ways and language at the feet of his Master, until he is at last able to give a sustained account of himself, and of human civilisation: its foolishness, vanity and perfidy. His Master and his fellows can hardly comprehend this, for they have no concept of selfish, wicked or unreasonable behaviour, cannot see the point of it, and accuse Gulliver of saying 'the thing that is not'.

These Noble Houyhnhnms 'are endowed by Nature with a general Disposition to all Virtues, and have no Conceptions or Ideas of what is Evil ... so their grand Maxim is, to cultivate Reason, and to be wholly governed by it'. Before long Gulliver is referring to them as persons, and the inversion is complete: the civilised and rational beings are horses, the human creatures (Yahoos) are beasts.

After years of getting to know our traveller, however, the Houyhnhnms continue to regard him, merely, as a Yahoo with some glimmerings of reason and an occasional smattering of virtue. Though Gulliver can talk the talk and walk the walk of a horse, the Council of the land decree that he be banished, never to return. It is a cruel punishment. Yet Gulliver, believing that Houyhnhnms are creatures of perfect reason and immaculate justice, accepts his exile without demur. They help him build a boat, create sails from the skins of Yahoos, and he sets off to find a fertile but uninhabited island on which to spend the remainder of his miserable days.

To his dismay, he is rescued by a benevolent Yahoo, a Portuguese ship's captain, who insists on returning the poor madman to London. During the long voyage, Gulliver cringes in a tiny cabin, revolted by the smell and ugliness of the Yahoos who man the ship. He reluctantly wears fresh new clothes, eats as little as possible, and finally disembarks in his home country in a state of utter desolation, marooned amongst the English savages.

Yet Swift misses the final trick, and it truncates the reader's pleasure. Gulliver has returned to England and rejoined his family, who disgust him, and with whom he is unable to live in comfort. And there the book ends, just where it should be carrying on, for we know the cause of his distressed mental state, but hardly witness the effects and any possible resolution.

Swift's contemporary Alexander Pope was best able to catch the implications of poor Gulliver's madness. Pope sees Gulliver's return from his wife's point of view. What a tragedy! He will not embrace her or their children, and flees to take residence in the stables with the much more congenial horses.

Her husband is clearly mad, but to talk to the mad you have to share their delusion, or there is no way or manner in which you can converse. So she must accept that there is such a land as the one he mentions. His is rather a wonderful story, and he tells it convincingly, while his extraordinary equine demeanour seems testimony to the truth of his experience.

Gulliver's travels are not over; the most interesting has only just begun. How does his remarkable final journey progress? How will it end? What happens on his final Voyage, to Redriff?

* * *

Rudy was still awake, just, as I finished reading. He turned on his side, ready for sleep. I switched off the light and sat beside his bed in the darkness.

It's going well so far, our little project. There are stories to be told: Gulliver's, Rudy's. Mine.

PART TWO

Darkeness, Visible

Chapter 5

I have led an unimaginative, unadventurous, reprehensively placid life. It suits me. My only previous experience with the police came when I was twenty-four and was given a speeding ticket for doing eighty on Park Lane, driving home late from a party at the Dorchester. 'A fair cop!' I said to the blonde policeman, who wasn't amused, and threatened to haul me in.

I'm still unclear what the visitation by my two policemen was all about. They couriered a letter offering an appointment late in January, at their local station, and of course I did not go. Some weeks have since passed, and no word from them. I hope it was some bit of administrative nonsense that has been forgotten or abandoned. I have to presume this, because if it is not, it is ominous. Yet I cannot work out how, or why, the police should be making inquiries of me. Unless ... Might it concern the circumstances of Suzy's death? How could they know about that? Surely not via Dr Larry, her sometime doubles partner, lover and later physician, who issued the death certificate ... ? He'd worried that she had died a tad prematurely, gave me a searching look over her deathbed, but was easily enough warned off by Lucy.

The police will be back. There will be trouble unthinkable, inconceivable.

* * *

My only other exposure to the machinery of the law occurred last year, when I was suborned into jury service at the Old Bailey. Having spent the time since Suzy's death cringing in the darkness of my house, I had not gone outside for months, as if I were an extreme agoraphobic. I wasn't. I was people-phobic. They disgusted me. Nothing, not fire not illness not loneliness, nothing, could draw me out of my darkness. Nothing was what I had chosen, and preferred. I'd planned impeccably, foreseen everything. I was not going out of doors, not at all. Until one day I received an email from George headed URGENT, into which he copied a letter requiring me to report for jury service at the Central Criminal Court of London.

It appeared, according to this missive, that I had previously postponed my obligation to serve, and that not even Jesus could do so for a second time. I had no memory of this. Perhaps I was busy examining, or off on holiday? Maybe Suzy dealt with it? The very thought of jury service distresses me, as do most of my citizenly obligations.

A phone call to old Jeremy Fenchurch, whose sharp lawyerly capacities are decades behind him, found him half asleep in his rooms after a bibulous lunch. Even he recognised that I had a problem.

'No way out of it, old boy. Bite the bullet. You might even enjoy it if you get a good case. Nice juicy murder sort of thing ...'

'You're not listening to me. I do not wish to serve.'

He was listening to me. I had no choice.

'Jolly interesting place, the Old Bailey. You'd make a good chairman of a jury. Why not take a positive attitude?'

A positive attitude. Me? I remembered why I disliked Fenchurch. I had long ago resolved never to use him again, without having found a replacement, largely through want of looking for one.

Perhaps I could get some sort of medical exemption?

'Unless you have a pre-existing medical condition, you have

to go,' he advised, suggesting I that might visit my doctor so he could poke me about for any disabling forms of mental or physical instability. He sounded hopeful that the doctor might find several.

It was a restless weekend, punctuated by snatches of sleep, a time of increased anxiety and commensurate increase of tranquillisers. By the time I departed for the court on the Monday morning, I felt semi-comatose yet acutely apprehensive, and could barely stagger my way to the kerbside into the waiting car service.

'Old Bailey, sir?'

'Yes.'

He regarded me quizzically. Perhaps I was heading off to stand trial?

I sat down heavily, my briefcase at my side, and opened *The Times* as a way of staving off enquiry. The driver looked at me in his rear-view mirror fidgeting and sweating, adjusting my tie, studying my hands for promising patches of dry skin, which I picked at assiduously, until they began to bleed more copiously than usual. I carry a silk handkerchief for such emergencies, in a pleasing maroon hue, designed to staunch blood without revealing it. I held it to my palm, in the hope that the bleeding would stop before we arrived.

I didn't look up during the ensuing forty-seven minutes, for fear of catching the driver's eye, or those of the people thronging the streets. My breathing was shallow and my pulse racing. Finger on wrist I counted it at somewhere in the mid-170s, my heart a gerbil trapped in a handbag. Remembering our natural child-birth classes in Oxford before Lucy was born, I began the requisite breathing exercise. *We're going to have a baby!* Deep breath, deeper protracted release. Again, repeat. Eyes closed. *A baby! A baby!*

Delivered, bloody and breathless, in the street outside the courts, I entered the building cautiously. and was directed into a small passageway on the right, instructed to allow my bag to be scanned, then to walk through an upright scanner myself.

I refused.

'There is very good evidence,' I said firmly, 'that these X-ray machines cause cancer.' The woman queueing behind me gasped, though whether at the newly revealed risk or at my insubordination was unclear.

'They're entirely safe, sir,' said the attendant, in the irritated, patient voice you use with a balky infant. 'Same as airports. You've gone through those, haven't you?'

He'd no doubt encountered the problem before and wasn't about to argue.

'Come round the side, sir, I can search you manually.'

He was rather rough with my thigh as he frisked me, and rummaging through my briefcase entirely disarranged the contents of my Parma-ham-on-sourdough sandwich, bits of rocket and caperberries escaping into the leather pocket.

'You're free to go, sir. Up in the lift to the jurors' room.'

Once I'd signed in, and had my papers inspected, I was free to do ... nothing. A hundred or so of us had been encased in a featureless room filled with abandoned furniture, torn, worn, forlorn. The people were cognate with their surroundings: lumpy proletarians, dressed in charity-shop rejects that made most of them, slouched wearily into the dilapidated chairs, look like an installation by that modern British (con) artist Rimington (S.), an old boy of our esteemed school, and like many, a charlatan and a chancer.

I had dressed with care, aware of the gravitas of the juror's role, in a navy pinstripe with a white cotton shirt, and black-and-maroon-striped tie. I was not merely the only person wearing a suit, I was one of only four with a tie and jacket. Many – perhaps half – were in jeans and trainers. Whoever's peers these jurists were going to be, they palpably weren't mine. They seemed fit only to try one another. And it was these riff and raff who were going to sit in judgement on many men (and women) better educated, smarter, more successful, wilier than they, though perhaps a little rotten at the core. Or not. It's often hard to tell, and this lot didn't have the discrimination to tell a bad apple from a good one, being themselves largely the former.

As on an aeroplane, I sat rigidly upright and refused to meet the eyes of the people seated near me, fearful that they might be familiar. But it was clear – as I glanced over the edge of my *Times* – that they had no desire to engage with me either. They'd taken an instant dislike to my stiffness and withdrawal, the miasma of disdain I emitted, the refusal to meet the eye or share a smile, and turned their shoulders, anxious to avoid contact. I was grateful for that. They read their newspapers, thumbed through paperbacks, played with mobile phones, napped and groaned and passed the time of day, and wind.

The overheated foul air was filled with dust motes, which would have shone in the morning light if the windows hadn't been begrimed. It smelled of unwashed clothing and people, tannic-thick tea from the café next door, the stench of cheap bacon. I would have poured a coffee from my Thermos, but it would have sent my heart rate into the 200s.

The first few jurors who'd been called had already departed. Best go for a walk, nothing further was going to happen for hours. Outside the room, anonymous minor officials conferred languidly in the corridors, abstracted and exhausted lawyers shuffled from one court to another, clumps of jurors ascending from cavernous depths emerged from the lifts, pasty and anxious in their sluggish pursuit of justice. Whatever that is, it would be conducted by elderly and irascible judges in absurd wigs, anxious to find somebody, anybody, in contempt, and juries made up of inarticulate know-nothings. It was ridiculous, implacable, meaningless, and vaguely threatening.

Kafkaesque? I don't much like the term, which is largely used by people who have never read Kafka. I prefer *absurd* (as did he). I had a heightened sense of exposure, could sense the eyes upon me not because I was different, offensively other, but because in this court of law I felt (and must have looked) indelibly guilty, not a juror but one of the judged. I had a strong desire to flee, to make my way down the stairs – carefully, the walls were swaying, and I felt uncertain on my feet – to stumble out the door, hail a taxi. Get the hell out of that damned and damning corridor. There is a Bulgarian saying, 'A guilty person runs when he isn't chased', which seemed apposite.

I had an impulse to make a public declaration, a speech in my defence (like Kafka's Josef K. in *The Trial*): ignorance of the law, extenuating circumstances, good intentions, previously excellent record. But one look at the grey and listless practitioners of the law confirmed that I would not get any sort of hearing, much less any sort of justice. In their eyes I was guilty. I am, aren't I? Am I? The walls swayed and dampened as I was regarded with merciless incuriosity, yet another sad guilty petitioner.

My armpits sticky and forehead dripping, faint, hardly able to breathe, aware of nothing save the throbbing of my heart, I put my still-bleeding hands against the wall to keep from falling and stumbled back to the jurors' waiting area. I sat down for a moment, cradling my head until I felt sufficiently fit to approach the lardy, inert functionary, who regarded me with distaste from behind her table.

'I'm afraid I am ill. Could you please call a doctor?'

I'd tried to keep my voice down – indeed, I'm not sure I could have kept it up – but the hostile woman raised hers perceptibly. People looked up from their slouching, pleased to be offered some form of entertainment.

'But sir, you are a doctor.'

'Not that sort.'

Her voice rose, and her wry satisfaction at my state was transmitted to our growing audience.

'What sort are you then?'

'Never mind about that. I need to see a physician. Is there some way in which you could summon one?'

She considered. The watchers gawped. We waited as she made up her mind. I was obviously in some sort of state, though probably not having a heart attack or acute appendicitis. But – I could see the thoughts flowing sluggishly across her brow – if I was seriously ill, and she didn't call a doctor, she'd be found negligent, and I, dead.

'Can I help?'

A youngish woman, dressed in proper clothes, had risen from one of the chairs and briskly approached the desk.

'I'm a doctor, here is my card. Perhaps I might . . . If I may.'

She took my arm and steered me out of the room and into a quiet corner of the café, where she sat me down and took my pulse.

'Your heart rate is up.' She felt my forehead. 'You're sweaty and may have a fever. Are you prone to anxiety attacks, perhaps?'

'Particularly in the last year or so . . .'

'I see. And are you on any medication?'

'Digoxin Diazepam, when I have an attack.'

'Have you taken any this morning?'

'Ten milligrams before I came.'

'I see.'

'Do you think,' I said, 'I might be sent home? I can't . . .'

'No,' she said. 'You can't carry on. Let's go back and talk to the Registrar. I can write you a note.'

The functionary and equally inert jurors-in-waiting looked up with some pleasure as we re-entered the room, anxious to see how the next episode in our mini-drama might play out.

'This gentleman is unwell, and needs to be released from duty.'

'In that case, sir, you are excused due to your physical and mental state.' The stress was on the *mental*. The functionary, roused out of her torpor, had raised her voice. Our audience looked at me with contempt unalloyed by the least trace of pity. I could imagine what they were thinking.

'Ha, that stuck-up git is a nutter. Could've told you!'

And the truth? At that one and very moment, I was.

I slunk home, having learned a lot. Just because my lawyer said I must go was no good reason to obey either him or the summons of the law. I will not make the same mistake again. I thought the experience would be a bore. But I'd hardly behaved as if bored. Didn't slouch in a seat, fiddle with my phone, slurp paper cups of teeth-staining tea, like the other, somnolent prospective jurors. No, I fidgeted, walked about anxiously, sweated and palpitated and ventilated. A panic attack is what the young doctor called it. A passing judge, interrogating my symptoms, would have had no doubts that I was one of the accused, and guilty.

Which, of course, I was, though such accusations were kept in the family. After Suzy's funeral Lucy had tearfully accused me of murdering her mother, and Sam maintained that my concocting of some final relief – I thought of it as her last right – for my hideously suffering wife was 'a grave matter'. I was horrified by their moral clarity, though I shared their dismay. Suzy died because I gave her a fatal draught. It made me feel dreadful, but I was proud that I'd been able to do it. What's so hard to understand about that?

Lucy forgave me, in time, even admitted she would have done as I did, had she had the means and the courage. As for Sam? I never know what he thinks, nor do I much care. We haven't forgotten about the subject, never will, but there's nothing left to discuss. Why disinter it? It won't come back to life. Best we keep it underground, like Suzy, only less dead.

There are *gradations* of deadness? It sounds wrong, unless applied to Christ, J., who popped in and out of death, though even he could only do it for a few days. When I was a boy I wondered, partly on the shining example of Jesus, whether, since someone could cheat death, it couldn't be done again, and for longer? I was thinking of myself, of course. Later I was assured by our school chaplain that we could all do that and enter life eternal, if only we believed and behaved in the right way, which meant not touching each other's willies, or even our own save for the ablutional necessities.

Life, and death. What else is there? Things come, and they go: the only universal truth worth noticing. Poets have observed this occasionally, though most of them prefer poncing about with words. I am busy planning the Grief Lives meeting at my house, making ice-cream. It's taking some time finding the right recipes, as most of what is now publicly offered as ice-cream is disgustingly filled with emulsifiers and various agents to make it creamy, which it is not.

The process is easily learned, it's the ingredients that challenge. None of Rudy's Cherry Garcia, nor the usual chocolates or vanillas, nor additional fruits, I need something snatched, as Keats would have it 'from the penetralium of mystery'. No, a penetralium is not a brand of ice-cream maker. A Magimix is, from which name I got this brilliant idea for what I will call Wisdom Ices. Frankincense. And Myrrh. They were gifts to Jesus – worth more than their weight in gold – and babies love sweet stuff. These Middle Eastern saps – the resins not the Magi – are allegedly so beneficial in both physical and spiritual matters that they may be regarded as a universal panacea: the ingredients allegedly ease arthritis, cure piles and fungal infections, and have magical astringent and diuretic properties. I hardly know how our ageing and infirm poetry grievers managed to live without these remedies, which will simultaneously raise their spirits and shrink their haemorrhoids. So much better than the other way around.

The biblical recipes for my proposed ices are not very promising, even Monsieur Roux would struggle to locate the ingredients and to follow the recipe.

And the LORD said unto Moses, Take unto thee sweet spices, stacte, and onycha, and galbanum; these sweet spices with pure frankincense: of each shall there be a like weight:

And thou shalt make it a perfume, a confection after the art of the apothecary, tempered together, pure and holy:

And thou shalt beat some of it very small, and put of it before the testimony in the tabernacle of the congregation, where I will meet with thee: it shall be unto you most holy.

Of course it would have been difficult to freeze the resulting mixture, and put it in cones, so the ancients did the best they could, made a sort of pudding, spooned it in to the divine infant mouth. *OOOH!* crooned baby Jesus. *Yum yum!*

I spend a day with tubs of various mixes of ingredients: change the proportions of frankincense to myrrh, add ginger to some of the pots and Sicilian lemon to others, a touch of vanilla pod adds depth, and some high-quality coconut sugar helps too. Jersey cream, of course, and the best organic eggs. And then straight into the Magimix.

The resulting gloop tasted somewhere south of disgusting, though it smelled enticing, and might be used as a lotion for a swollen anus. But after many trials, and many errors, I produced a tub of something ... well, unexpected, fragrant, and (once you'd given it half a chance) not at all unpleasant. I will put a yellow parasol and perhaps a sprinkling of pomegranate seeds on top. To complete my biblical offering, an Israeli wine would be fun. I placed on order for a Muscat from the Golan Heights, with a delicate nose of orange blossoms, honey, apricots and gunpowder.

Suzy would say this is all so typical of me, far-fetched and self-displaying. It is. It's a stonking idea, a unique concoction and combination, which will be spoken of for weeks to come, and make its way onto menus in local restaurants.

There is, of course, a further problem. I have, as usual, concentrated my attention on what to eat rather than what to read. I have my lovely ices, but I do not have a poem to go with them, to extend and to deepen the joke. Nothing much comes to mind. I reread Eliot's 'Triumph of the Magi', but it lacks any mention of puddings or sweets, to my mind a damning omission.

I googled the words 'poem about ice-cream and death' and only one popped up – even that was a surprise – by an American insurance salesman named Wallace Stevens. I read it with my usual scepticism, read it again, and then again, aloud. It was not merely fit for purpose, it was perfect.

I have heard nothing further from my two importuning policemen. I should be relieved by this, but their silence is beginning to feel ominous, as if they are lurking behind the hedges, waiting to roust me out. There was an inexorability in their eyes and demeanour, which said *We will have our way. We will have you.* For what, why? And why were they interested in my door? There's nothing suspicious about it, is there?

I have written to Dorothea to say that I am 'not ready just yet' to offer a poem. She wrote back reassuringly, if a little too warmly for my taste, to say that Philip would be happy to go next, though he had just flown in from The Hague, 'and he is increasingly weak, darling, as you know.'

Dorothea suggested that I could host the next month. She probably thinks I have funked it. I haven't. I still need to perfect my Magi ice-cream recipe, and the Golan Heights wine has not yet arrived, presumably because it is travelling on El Al and had to endure prolonged interrogation.

I'd looked forward to meeting Philip Massingham, but also – not a feeling I'd had very often, and of which I am ashamed – I was a tad intimidated by him. He is that rare thing, a public figure who is a good man, on the humane side of most causes. He wrote op-ed pieces and columns for the broadsheets, appeared on *Newsnight*, and could be counted on to give crisp opinions on almost any matter, not because he was facile or attention-seeking, but because he was well-informed, curious, and generous with his time and (if I may be forgiven the term) spirit. Enough, in all, to retard even my panoptic cynicism.

Philip resisted Dorothea's bossy blandishments, insisted that the show must go on, and that it would be good for him. It was unlikely to be good for me, but 50/50, as has been remarked somewhere, is a reasonable percentage. He lives on the sixth floor of a brick mansion block on a quiet road in Holland Park, accessed through a lift so cramped that by the time I exited I was covered in sweat.

He greeted me warmly at the door, which opened into a large, square entrance hall lined on all sides by bookshelves, and placed his hand on my shoulder as if I were an old friend.

'James,' he said, 'I'm so pleased to meet you.' His face was that shade of pale which is frequently but inaccurately described as 'deathly', the bones of his face were beginning to assert them-selves, and his voice had to make up in warmth for what it lacked in vigour. He'd previously been frank with the group about the progress of his various cancers, indeed had written some articles about his coming demise. He was a friend of Patricia Bond, whom he'd met (as a patient, perhaps, they didn't say) at the Chelsea and Westminster, and who had invited him to join her for one of the Poetry Evenings. He later told me that he derived scant consolation from the group, but relished talking about the poems: 'Such a relief from all that legal and political bumf.'

In the drawing room there was a table with finger sandwiches and plates of biscotti, which various members of our group looked at longingly. Behind it a woman dressed starchily in white – some sort of nurse or housekeeper, perhaps? – kept a strict eye on things, as still as a statue in a city square. She was introduced to each member of the group, Katya something or other. I suppose she looked after Philip, whose wife had died some years before.

He stood at the head of the table, and raised his hand gently, and he was accorded the silence and respect due to quality.

'Greetings,' he said warmly. 'I'm delighted everyone could come tonight, and I trust you have enjoyed rereading "Ode to a Nightingale". It is not just a part of our heritage, but a part of ourselves. And I have thought long and hard about what we are to drink, because the poem has a plethora of references to drink and to drugs. Very English, our Mr Keats, a typical medical student. There are hemlock, opiates, draughts of vintage, beakers full of the warm south, beaded bubbles, purple-stained mouths . . . as if the young poet were in some sort of competition for how many such images he could stuff into a few lines. And mouths. When you think of Keats and the south, it is Italy to which you turn, as he did in 1820. And yes, we need a red wine, but what about those bloody beaded bubbles? I am a lawyer, plodding and literal-minded. If the brief is bubbles, then bubbles it must be.

'A red fizz? I have located just the right thing.' He was chuckling to himself as he lifted the bottle, so that we could see the label. I peered over: Lambrusco, one expected that. But I had never seen this one: La Battagliola 'Dosage 15'. Perfect, a drug of choice indeed. I could hardly wait for its bubbles to wink, I need drink to get me through these meetings, and soon enough the Woman in White had filled our glasses, and we raised them in a toast.

'This is a young wine, and it would have benefited from many more years to mature, very like our poet. To John Keats.'

We lifted our glasses and drank. It wasn't as good a wine as it was a joke, but it went down adequately.

We seated ourselves in the drawing room, helped ourselves, at last, to foie-gras sandwiches and biscotti, and waited while Philip opened his book. As previously, the group was silent before the reading of the monthly poem, as if members of a religious congregation. At Miles's soirée, this had irritated me, the unseemly seemliness of it, the ersatz piety. But now it drew me into the quiet. If a dying man reading Keats doesn't elicit feeling, what should?

He read it well. When he put down the book, Philip mused for a few moments.

'The fact is,' he said, 'I've never much liked this poem. So much of it is immature versification, full of grating poeticisms . . .'

'Come now,' said Dorothea grandly. 'It is a most marvellous and perfect poem. A reminder that poets, too, can sing, and that their words are immortal!'

There was a murmur of assent. Philip nodded his head respect-fully enough, though he had hardly listened, having expected such a comment.

'Well,' he said judiciously, 'that is a matter of taste.' What he clearly meant was that actually it is a matter of *judgement*, and that Dorothea didn't have any. 'But,' he continued, 'though I have offered this poem in whole, I am only interested in one part. In the sixth stanza, to be exact.'

We looked at our printout. Ah, yes: 'Darkling I listen', it began. He read it again, as if it could stand alone, and it did, rather well.

He sat down.

'As you all know, I am dying. I do not make a fuss about this, either to myself or to you. We are all dying, though I know why I am, and more than likely when. Perhaps in a year, if I am fortunate.

By the time I die, it will be fortunate, for I will certainly no longer wish to live. What is particularly compelling to me in this stanza is the notion of an "easeful death", which is all that I can now hope for.'

It was clear that he had prepared these words as carefully as his fabled briefs and statements, and we were more than usually respectful, open- and purple-mouthed, winking and nibbling away, enjoying this elegantly expressed feeling.

'What strikes me, returning to this poem after so many years,' he continued, 'is the remarkable, indeed shocking, opening reference to the drinking of hemlock, with its obvious reference to the self-inflicted death of Socrates. We begin with an image of suicide, an act the young tubercular Keats must certainly have considered, for he had the knowledge and the means to do so. He knew that the death that was pressing in upon him was likely to be prolonged and agonising. Why should he not intervene to ease his passage? I have no training in literary criticism, and no idea if this has been noted, but surely what we have here is a paean to what poor dear Hamlet called "self-slaughter" . . . Can this be right?'

It was Patricia Bond who responded, quickly and firmly.

'That's as may be, darling Philip, but Keats died in 1821. The only painkillers then were indeed opiates, and they were very irregularly administered, if at all. Nowadays we are proficient at ameliorating pain, and most deaths now are, as Keats put it, easeful.'

She'd been lurking in the corner, but of a sudden I felt Suzy's presence. No, she hadn't had too much pain at the end, Dr Larry had ameliorated that. But pain is only pain, if I might put it thus bluntly. Suzy avoided copious painkillers for as long as she could, for their effect was to ameliorate not merely pain, but her, herself. What was intolerable about her death was the final terrible struggle to draw breath, the gasping and hacking, the suffocation from within. The images rose inexorably.

Perhaps seeing my distress, the woman in white hastened to refill my glass, and I drank it down in a single swallow, a most ungentlemanly and ugly act.

'I'm sorry,' I said, 'but I can barely tolerate this …'

The requisite murmurs of comfort and understanding ensued, and made me feel worse.

'Do forgive me,' I said, rising, 'but I really must go.'

I am becoming a panic attacker, a bolter, apt retribution for my long addiction to locks and keys.

Philip came to take my arm, and accompanied me to the door, pushed the button for the lift.

'Thank you for …' I began.

'You get home. Have another drink. I quite understand. I so often feel like that myself.'

I returned home in a taxi, leaving my car outside Philip's mansion block, with two firm resolutions. The first was accomplished in a few minutes:

Dear Dorothea,

I was very moved – too moved – by Philip's presentation, the depth of feeling and intelligence, and by his capacity to speak so clearly, so well and yet so discreetly about such intimate matters. I admire him, but I have no desire either to emulate him, nor to reconfigure his words to my own circumstance.

When you kindly invited me to join you all, I had misgivings about which I was frank, and fears too. Both are amply to the fore now. I have given it a try, as you urged. And it is not for me. There are things of which I do not speak, the words are absent in me, or when they are not, they are private. Sometimes I write them down, but I am unused to sharing them, and have no doubt that doing so exacerbates my hollowness and desolation, rather than relieving it.

Thank you for your kindness, and your efforts on my behalf. I will nevertheless soldier on, that's a nice metaphor, and do my stint next

*month. I'm even looking forward to that, in my feeble way. But after
that? Basta.*

   Best wishes,
   James

To my great surprise, and pleasure, I did not receive a return
email full of pleading and festooned with typographic kisses. When
the reply did arrive, a few days later, it was to accept my decision,
to wish me well, and to hope that at our final meeting we might
all say goodbye in a more appropriate manner. And since I was
choosing the poem, she added, it was up to me to curate – I liked
her choice of word – the feeling for the evening. Might that be
possible?

The salutation had only one *x*. I had not supposed her so
sensitive. Not to mention right. I owed them a session, owed it to
myself as well, and I had been preparing the reading and the recipes
for some time. Why not go out with both a bang and a whimper?
Nice title for my autobiography, that.

My other resolution will take longer, but as far as I can tell, I
need not hurry. But who knows when one's time will come? I
must start building my final stash, if only I knew how, and of what.
There are books on the subject, and sources of the right – what
shall I say? – material, to hasten, to cause one's demise, like Mr
Keats's hemlock and opiates? After all, in America tens of thousands
of people a year are apparently dying of opioid overdoses, most of
them unintended. If you can do that by accident, surely you can
do it on purpose.

When I concocted Suzy's final cocktail, it was a spur-of-the-
moment response to the unexpected and unbearable enormity
of her suffering. And, admittedly, of my own. I hadn't planned
ahead, researched the right amounts of the right stuff. I was
guessing. I knew that sufficient Digoxin mixed with a liberal
dose of Diazepam would send her to sleep and presumably into

a coma. And thence, to death. It was a terrible risk, and I was mightily afraid that she might vomit it all up, and wake in even greater distress – if that were possible – than that from which I was trying to relieve her.

But she drifted right off, with what would have been a smile on her face if it were still her face and she could still smile, but a look of quietude and contentment crossed her features, didn't it? I was sure it did. And as she slept, more and more deeply, I held her hand, and some hours later she died.

Sitting beside her I gazed at her departed features for a time. I have no idea how long, time had suspended itself, I sat and she lay there. I was there and she was still there, only she was not, she was in that fleeting transitional moment when she was still Suzy, and not Suzy's body. Corpse. Cadaver. Still she, not *it*.

As I sat, I envisaged for a moment my own coming death, and her poor late face morphed into mine, shrunken and alabaster, withdrawing steadily into the darkness. James Darke, still, on his deathbed. I was startled by the image, and wondered: *Who will be sitting in the chair beside my withdrawing body?* Lucy? I hope not, for her sake. But if it were, could she be counted on to release me, as I had her mother? She'd said, in our fraught conversation in her garden after Suzy's death, that she would have liked to have done what I did – however much she disapproved of it – only she had not the strength.

I said I wished she would do that for me, but I don't, not any more. It is too much to ask, and would create too profound a burden of doubt, and regret. Guilt. No, if someone is going to help me easefully to depart this world, it has to be me.

Drugs, we are insistently and hysterically informed, are every-where and in everybody. And not just your prescription sort, like my Digoxin and Diazepam. No, contraband and illegal substances like heroin are apparently widely available, though nobody says where, exactly. But surely in London there will be curious hotspots, dens of iniquity and opiates, which one could find. I wonder who I can ask?

Or perhaps – London being a tolerably law-abiding sort of place – I might have to search further afield, much as I dislike travel. But for such a noble purpose, why not? It will stiffen my resolve. New York, perhaps. Los Angeles? Detroit? Miami? All heaving with contraband, addicts reeling and smiling and puking and sleeping and dying on every street corner, which their local dealers will have colonised.

I don't like the idea of carrying much cash – so easy to get mugged. I wonder if they take travellers' cheques?

Chapter 6

I hate the bloody telephone, resent pretending to relate to the disembodied. Though she knows how I feel, once at the weekend, Sunday afternoon usually, Lucy will ring just to 'catch up'. Not a lot to catch up on, is there? She feeds her baby and feels exhausted. I sit around, reading bits of books about which I can remember neither text nor title, scribbling away on these pages, watching desultory bits of BBC news. I go out for lunch most days, to my regular spots, none of which is much good, but they know me and my ways. There's no phrase more soothing than 'The usual, sir?' I walk in the park, but it is filled with importuning dogs, who want to sniff me, an invasion for which their owners do not feel compelled to apologise. It is considered impolite to kick them. The dogs. And the owners.

Lucy could talk to her mother for an hour at a time. Suzy would pour herself a large glass of Pinot Gris, sit back in the stuffed chair under the window, prop a cushion under her head, put her feet up, and talk and talk. I would lurk and listen to their phone conversations, but the inflections were foreign to me, the transitions impenetrable, the flow of feeling incomprehensible.

Sometimes I would answer when Lucy called, only to pass the phone over to Suzy as soon as possible. Both of them understood. We almost reached the point where I could just hand it over to

Suzy without saying a word. When Suzy got a mobile phone, at last – she resisted for a long time – the problem was solved.

When I got one too, some time even later, it was solely to write the occasional text. Suzy taught me, it wasn't hard once I got the hang of it. No more awkward silences, long pauses, stilted moments. I sent Lucy funny little texts, indignations really, whenever I had something to 'vent about', as Lucy called it. Once Rudy learned that I could text – he was very impressed – I got a series of them from him too. He tried to teach me WhatsUp, which could do pictures and voices too, but I never warmed to it. Nothing, that's what's up.

When the phone rang that Wednesday evening, showing Lucy's number – it must have been sometime in mid-March – I immediately assumed something was wrong.

'Are you around for the next few days?' she asked.

'I'm always around.'

'Of course ...' She paused, as if digesting unexpected information.

'Is something wrong? You sound a bit peculiar ...'

'No, no, not at all. I was just wondering if I could come down for the weekend, maybe bring the kids?'

'Darling, of course you can. Any time. But do you mean Sam isn't coming? Just you and the children?'

'Yes. Just me and Amelie and Rudy.'

I knew not to say anything.

'Sam's tied up with a lot of things, and has appointments on Saturday, so we'll just come on our own ...'

'How lovely. When will you arrive?'

'We'll leave after Rudy gets out of school on Friday, so we'll be there for supper. Shall I bring anything?'

'Just your good selves. What a treat.'

She knew that I knew that something was up, but it could wait. She and Sam had both been exhausted since the arrival of the baby, who was a bad sleeper, and seemed to suffer from colic and teeth in an unusually fractious way. I can't remember much about Lucy's infancy, or her behaviour at such an early age, I'd left most of that to Suzy. Tried my hand at a few nappies, gagged and surrendered, let them get on with it. There are apparently joys to be had from infants, but aside from the odd captivating smile and gurgle, and their infrequent and not to be relied upon moments of unconsciousness, they are a bore, and a trial in which one is constantly found guilty.

In my desk was my list for their last visit at Christmas. If one reduced the quantities and length of stay, it was still serviceable. I had clean sheets, could order a delivery from Waitrose, with enough Cherry Garcia to keep Rudy happy and his mother disapproving, Rudy and I would wink at each other when we filled his dish, conspirators of the male variety. It was good Sam wasn't coming, he isn't one of us.

Suzy had counselled me, then harangued, then ordered: *keep your opinions to yourself.* They have their own ways, their own theories, their own rights with regard to how they live. Grandparents have to *shut up.* I obeyed. Of course she didn't. She hated how Lucy dressed and did her hair, could not abide the way in which she decorated (!) their house, detested the very house itself. The fact that she rarely said so explicitly apparently excused her obvious disapproval. Lucy was wounded by it, constantly and deeply.

Sam didn't care. I was glad he was unable to come, can hardly bear his gestaltifying presence. The notion that he had appointments and obligations over the weekend didn't convince. He usually took Rudy to the swimming baths or a football pitch on the Saturday, and then they watched sporting contests together on the telly.

When their awful buggish VW wheezed up outside the door and they got out, I put a parking voucher in the window as they struggled out of the cramped confines, looking grey and bedraggled. It was a chilly evening, but the windows of the car were all open, and a quick whiff indicated why. Lucy was wearing her purple feather-tent coat and a pair of jeans, her hair in need of both a brush and a bottle of shampoo. I didn't get too close, fearing she might smell much like the infant (did baby Jesus smell so foul?) who was soon placed into a carrycot, screaming. Rudy was retracted and hardly said a word, wearing his Blades scarf and hat, his eyes on his little screen, as if he might ward off the smells, cold and whatever trouble ailed them all.

He looked up for a moment, only to say, 'Gampy, Amelie is malodorous, will you take her away?'

Lucy gave him a quizzical look. Her eyes were gooey with sleepiness and could it have been tears, as she locked the car, picked up the carrycot, and said, 'For Christ's sake get me a drink, OK? It's been a fucking nightmare!' It had taken three hours from Oxford, some sort of tie-up on the M40, and the baby had screamed for every minute. Lucy had turned on the car radio, which crackled as much as it talked or sang, and Rudy put his headphones on and got his thumbs working.

As soon as the baby was blessedly placed upstairs, and left to scream herself to sleep, I gave Lucy a very large Johnnie Walker Black on the rocks, and Rudy a large bowl of ice-cream. His mother looked askance – they hadn't even had dinner yet – but let it go.

'He can eat backwards,' I said. 'Pudding first, fish fingers and chips after.'

Rudy's mouth was already full.

'Cool,' he said.

By nine they were all in bed, asleep. Nothing had been said about their unusual visit, there was time for that. The baby often slept in the day, and Rudy was easily distracted by his Xbox and the computer. Plenty of time to be alone, to talk. I was rather dreading it. I have little capacity to comfort; I stifle myself and my opinions till I feel I might pop. Nobody comes to me any more for advice, because I too often gave it.

Presumably they'd had a row, and she'd buggered off to clear the air. They have a lot of air that needs it. God knows how people stay married.

I was disappointed not to be able to read to Rudy before he went to sleep, but he was exhausted, and I knew better than to ask. He'd feel guilty, and say, 'Yes, please, Gampy,' and be asleep before the first paragraph was finished. Best save it for tomorrow. We could go to bed right after dinner, and I could read him my first chapter. The composition of Book V has been my only purpose these long weeks; I feel uneasy at my decision not to utilise George's offer of editorial help, but I don't need anyone to tell me it's amateurish. But if a thing is worth doing, it's worth doing badly.

I went to my study, booted my computer, and began to read through my text. I hadn't known they were coming, and it would be wise to knock it into some sort of shape. Eight-year-old shape? Not at all, that would be patronising. He's smarter than an eight-year-old, and anxious to be challenged. Anyway, it's my shape too.

I'm excited, rereading it. I've come to love my Lemuel Gulliver, redux.

In the early morning I was awoken by a murmuring from the garden. I sleep with the window open, cannot bear the claustrophobia of a closed room, and the sound had a curious hushed and insinuating quality, like someone whispering loudly. I pulled off the bedclothes, crept over to the window, and peeped out from behind the side of the curtains. If it was an intruder I would need to call the police. I had my phone in hand, ready to dial 999, remembering with a shiver my terror when Bronya entered the house and snuck into my bedroom.

Lucy was pacing about the grass, phone at her ear, listening intently with a look of ferocious exasperation on her features, spitting out an occasional response. Though it was only just past eight, she'd obviously been up for a while – feeding the baby, I suppose – had washed her hair, and looked fresher to the eye. As ever, her sense of colour startled and repelled me. I am old-fashioned enough to believe that there is such a thing as a clash: some colours do not go together, whatever your Hindu might think. Lucy wore a bright orange cardigan with a lime-green shirt, jeans, and some big fat furry boots that clumped, even on the turf. Her posture was hunched and coiled, and whoever she was talking to was clearly getting a mouthful. As if subliminally aware of my presence, she gazed up towards my window, but I ducked out of sight, and she retreated to the bottom of the garden and sat on the bench under the tree. I could just about make out her final words.

'Don't call me again! And don't you dare come here!'

She pushed the off button and stomped back into the kitchen, drying her eyes with her sleeve.

I showered and dressed slowly, to give her some time to collect herself. Presumably she was talking to Sam – who else might it be? – but the anger and contempt in her voice were startling. Feisty, adversarial and self-protective by nature, she has more opinions than you could compute on an abacus. But even when we had our confrontation in her garden after Suzy's death, when she accused me of murdering her mother, not even then had I heard her speak in such tones. She was angry then, yes, furious, but also bereft, yearning, grieving, lost, begging for reassurance and readmittance into the chambers of love. She wasn't contemptuous towards me, and if I had more than let her down, she was prepared to listen, to engage, and finally to admit that, yes, she wished she could have done the same for her poor mother. Released her, and us, from that suffering, into this.

By the time I got to the kitchen to make my coffee, Lucy was gone. Rudy wasn't up yet, or perhaps he was doing something with his thumbs. She'd left her turquoise leather bag hanging over one of the kitchen chairs, and as ever I picked it up to hang it on the hook on the back of the kitchen door.

I certainly was not rummaging, but I noticed that her phone was on top of the pile of effluvia with which women's bags are stuffed. I put the bag back over the chair, hanging just as it had, listened for sounds of impending arrival, heard nothing, and had a wee peek. Tucked to the side was a phial of prescription pills, labelled 'Sertraline'. I made a note of this, put it back, and removed the phone. I put in her password – 0000 – checked for Calls Received or Calls Missed: there were three, from (I presume) Sam's number, starting just after they arrived last night. Then one at 12.30, then first thing this morning. There was a light blinking for messages, suggesting I call 121. Instead, I pushed the green Messages button, and there were a stream from Sam, unanswered. It seems he'd been up all night.

We need to sort this out, and soon please. I know it's difficult, but we need to talk. Try to calm down, and let's chat in the morning. I love you! X

Please, Lu, please answer when you get up. Your phone is off, don't cut me out like this. We need to be together, now. As always. Your Sam. XX

And first thing this morning:

Am trying to ring! Will you please please ring me back? If I don't hear from you I will come down on the next train, and then we can have it out, all three of us. It's probably best that way!

Ten minutes after receiving this text, she had rung him from the garden.

This involved them, and apparently it involved me: three of us.

I hadn't seen Sam since our protracted uncongenial Christmas together, nor had I spoken to him on the phone. Was something festering, like leftover sprouts stinking and growing mould?

When they left, the day after Boxing Day, things had been cordial, as they often are when people are relieved to be parting. Hugs of self-congratulation. But after they got home, Lucy sent a terse email, thanking me brusquely, but regretting that I had been so critical of Sam over Christmas dinner. 'Goaded' was the term she used.

Gestalt. Phenomenological. A member of the group, not its leader. Processed feelings. 'Goaded' is hardly strong enough for the contempt I feel for this nonsense. Sammy and the Grievers!

Of course, she stood up for him, defended his methods. Said she was proud of him. What could have happened in the ensuing few months? Perhaps my teasing – OK, goading – got under his skin; he'd nursed the injury, attacked me, and Lucy had found herself defending me? Then: a row. Then: a few days' cooling-off period, kids under her arm, an asylum seeker.

A few words of fatherly comfort and advice might help. Marriages go through this sort of thing. Suzy and I once spent a week not talking to each other, boiling, I can't even remember why. Then we got drunk, and went to bed, and the bruises healed, if slowly. Was the row about raising Lucy? She's always been a source of trouble.

Rudy soon tumbled into the kitchen, full of morning beans, demanding his sugary cereal, with milk and a banana. We got out his special bowl.

'Gampy, can we go to that park today? Please? We can feed the ducks, and see the pelicans. I love them!'

'Darling, let's see what Mummy has in mind, she might have other plans . . .'

'She can come. And Amelie, she'd like the pelicans too.'

He gobbled his cereal, getting a nice proportion in his mouth, some on the table, bits of wet flakes on the floor, and bounded towards the bread bin, opened its lid and pulled out the large sourdough loaf I'd had delivered yesterday.

'We can bring this! They'll love it! Have you got a bag?'

I went upstairs to find one – I cannot abide plastic bags in public spaces, for picnics, carrying bread for ducks, school lunches, whatever – and have an elegant maroon canvas carrier upstairs. This gave me a few minutes to search for Sertraline on the Internet. Some sort of antidepressant, an SSRI whatever that is, sometimes prescribed for post-partum depression, as well as for anxiety. Apparently it's alright for breastfeeding – alas – but not good mixed with drink.

It's no wonder Lucy has not recovered the sheen of being that she inherited from her mother: her hair is lank and colourless, her natural lope replaced by trudge, she is either retracted or angry. She says she is still full of grief, and the baby sucks and sucks, leaving her empty. She presents herself dutifully to the chore of motherhood, but has none of the maternal glow that her mother had, nursing her new baby.

On entering the kitchen, Lucy agreed immediately to the proposed outing, a look of relief on her features. She has 'a special place in her heart' for St James's Park, or perhaps she meant it was the special place. When she was Rudy's age, young mum Suzy would take her to feed the ducks and moorhens, the pelicans too if they deigned to eat some bread. When Lucy was in one of her strops, overtired and over-sugared, and made one of her scrunchy faces, Suzy would stare her down and chuckle, 'Ah, my pelican daughter.'

'I'm not a pelican!' Pelicans were ugly and unfriendly. It was an insult. Stupid birds.

'Well, you're my little pelican.'

Of course, Lucy didn't know the reference from King Lear, which is multi-layered; you can spend some time in explication of it. I have. But Suzy merely meant it to tease, I think she would have said *fondly*, but it wasn't entirely.

'I'm not a fucking pelican!' Lucy stomped one day, outraging two grannies, an American tourist, an ice-cream vendor and three moorhens.

St James's Park was laden with multi-generational memory, and Lucy was keen to set off.

'Sure,' she said. 'Great idea, I'll make a picnic.'

'But Mum, they have pasties and sausage rolls. In the café. We can eat there. Please, can we?'

Lucy might well have given in, but I do draw the occasional line, and cafés in parks are one of them. Actually, parks are too. I hate them: the prettified landscape, the prowling sniffer dogs, the screaming children chasing balls and each other, their families leaving litter after they eat, the forced smiles of familiarity – *isn't this lovely!* – the desperate peering up for a friendly ray of sunshine, the vigilant fathers standing at the foot of swings and slides on which their children balance precariously, the mothers gossiping and keeping their eyes out. Killing time, that's what you do with little children, you find a way, even one as crimped as this, just to cross off another day, until they grow old enough to send them off to school and you get your life back.

Our last visit to St James's Park was in Suzy's final year, and we had taken Rudy. He held her hand, they walked to the water's edge. He wanted to feed the endlessly opportuning obese ducks and moorhens, but Suzy would keep hold of his hand, and say, 'Darling, look!'

Always anxious to please, and having looked before with his granny, he would peer over the water intently.

'I can see the pelicans.'

'Good, darling. Show me where.'

He pointed across the water.

'How many?'

He looked about, swung his head slightly left and right.

'Five.'

'Tell me about them,' said Suzy, looking carefully at each. 'Tell me about the one on the left, by the rushes.'

They stood together discussing: which one looked oldest, fattest, happiest, most handsome, least content? And particularly: how could you tell them apart? And if you could, could you recognise them again, even give them names?

The one with the biggest breast was called PellyBelly, and her husband – they were always together – was Fatboy Sam.

A scrawny one missing some feathers, looking anxious, was named Sue-Sue.

Another kept flapping its feathers, as if about to fly, though it stayed in the water. He was called Orville.

The fifth was different from the others because it didn't have their distinguishing features, so you could pick it out in the crowd. It was called Boring.

Rudy thought of it as a game, and liked trying to win. Suzy was introducing him gently to ways of seeing, naming, codifying and enjoying. Particularising, she called it, differentiating the one thing from the other. Rudy soon learned most of Edward Lear's 'Pelican Chorus', which he would sing to a tune of his own:

King and Queen of the Pelicans we;
No other birds so grand we see!
None but we have feet like fins!
With lovely leathery throats and chins!

I don't believe in all this particularising and memorising and getting things straight, it's a waste of time, and I could be acerbic about this to Suzy, who soon enough would not allow me to read drafts of her work. I was an unfit reader, unwilling to *look*. Why should I? Things are as they are, no need to anatomise them, each is very much like itself but not much different from the others. What's the matter? What matters? All is matter. A mango, a pelican, a cricket bat, a politician, a first edition of *Bleak House* . . .

The world is made from words, not things. The difference between one word and another, the infinite possibilities of words, is more important and engrossing than the distinction between pelicans, mangoes and cricket bats. Which are, of course, not things but words, at least until you try to eat one. Things? They dissolve themselves into a dew. Adieu. *A dieu*. God knows. When you understand that all things are the same thing, you are on the road to wisdom, and nothing is more fruitless and sour than that.

Fruitless, sour, finished. Some days, sitting and thinking and trying to write, nothing happens, as if my verbal drains were clogged. My fingers yearn to make sentences, but my head cannot frame them. Curious and unsettling for a dedicated journal-ist. I am running out, out of words. My consciousness, like my urine, once flowed in a steady stream; now it trickles, stops and starts, runs dry until I give it a shake and produce some more dribble, drivel.

As Suzy and Rudy peered and named and distinguished, I walked away feeling excluded, and strolled amongst the heaving, humping, barking dogs, overexcited sticky children and laconic parents, lost in my own ruminations, which consisted largely of fantasising ways of escape. There was no sense sneaking off, or making a run for it – they'd drag me back. I might as well have been on a leash.

I knew this, so had brought *The Times*, found a vacant bench – I don't share – opened our Thermos and poured myself a coffee, a bit Thermos-y, but better than that hot brown water in plastic cups at the café. Suzy could have hers later.

She was there, then, and she's here now, isn't she? Is she? Same bench, same coffee, very slightly different Rudy. Lucy, not Suzy. The universal truth: things come, and they go. Suzy is gone, but not completely; I'm here, but only partially, we're together, still, in our way. I budge over on the bench to make room for her.

There are a lot of indistinguishable pelicans today, looking more like walruses than sparrows. Ugly mangoes with feathers. At lakeside Lucy feigns interest as Rudy scoots about shouting.

'Look. Look! It's Orville. He's called that because he tries to fly but he's no good at it.'

Lucy turned her head from one pelican to the next.

'Oh, yes,' she said. 'Isn't he funny?'

'He's my best,' said Rudy.

I've come to loathe these pelicans, dysfunctional, ungainly, over-beaked, they should beware, they're not constructed to make a quick getaway. They prefer mooching from tourists, or just wading into the lake for a quick nosh. They can fly, though neither well nor high. Made indolent and apparently safe in their lakeside paradise, they would find it impossible to escape a predator, to evade a surreptitious leg trap or a net in the night. Perhaps a crossbow would be fun. I don't know if they make loud noises or cries of distress. Must look that up.

I don't intend doing this mercy-culling myself. As for all troublesome and dirty chores, I will hire someone. I am informed you can arrange a tidy human murder for £500, so the mere snatching and dispatching of a pelican should be simple, and gratifying. Pubs in the East End must be full of prospective, relatively inexpensive pelican snatchers and dispatchers.

I must look up some pelican recipes.

The park, the picnic, the inevitable trip to the Science Museum, Rudy overexcited and needy, Amelie blissfully asleep most of the day, gurgling the rest. Lucy moved from one moment and event to the next, inexorable as one of those contemptible power walkers who stride on listening on earphones, impervious to the world. She talked, yes, she answered, also yes, but she wasn't there. And because she wasn't, I wasn't either. I was grateful for that, having as little desire to 'have a chat' as she apparently did. Before we departed she'd put her phone on the charger in the kitchen, and left it. She didn't want to talk to him either. She wanted to kill the day.

Friday evening? Tick.

Saturday? Tick.

Almost there.

Chapter 7

Rudy is easy these days, disappears for hours on end – it would be days if he were allowed to take provisions to his room – and often he has to be fetched, cajoled, wheedled, tempted, threatened to come down to eat, to watch his allotted time on TV, or just to rejoin the family fray. If he were a teenager you'd know what he was doing, and leave him to it, twice.

Since the arrival of their ubiquitous noisy intruder he has made himself particularly scarce. During Amelie's few agreeable periods, Rudy can be quite taken with his new sister, carries her about like a bundle of groceries, jiggles her in the air as Lucy looks on apprehensively, puts his mouth on her neck and goes BUHHHHH in a vibrating farty sound, which makes her squeal with delight and fill her nappy, after which he gives her back with a disapproving look, and goes to wash his hands.

When he went upstairs after our long day at the park, neither of us minded. Life was hard enough with a new child, and an absent one was a relief. I remarked that it was thoughtful of him, but Lucy smirked.

'You're kidding, right? He's only thinking of himself, and being left in peace to do his things . . .'

Well, I *was* kidding, as she so inelegantly put it. I'm a public schoolmaster (ex-, former, retired, late) and I know boys for what they are: small and imperfectly formed adults. Selfish. Rudy has his own world, and indulges it to the maximum. Plays his Xbox games, surfs the Net (Lucy has put a guard on it so he can't see rude things), creates his designs on the screen, and prints them out. He has a plastic filing box that he puts his pictures in, and sometimes shows them to me. They can be remarkably good.

But when I went upstairs that evening he wasn't in the bedroom. 'Rudy?' I called.

'Here, Gampy.' The sound came from my study. I opened the door, and found him at my desk in front of my computer. I was immediately alarmed. Computers are treacherous and unnavigable devices, prone to shutting themselves down or off, issuing frequent alarming commands, losing words and places as frequently as a granny with Alzheimer's.

I consequently treat mine with the respect due to all capricious dictators. I am deferential, do not ask too much of it, always let it sleep when I am not using it. Not that I employ it very often, for I still prefer to write longhand, which doesn't merely settle one's soul, it expresses it.

I have, though, been using the computer to compose my addition to *Gulliver's Travels*, since I will be reading it to Rudy at bedtimes, and a printout is so much easier to negotiate than my crabbed script. I've had some fun with the presentation of my little *jeu d'esprit*, and designed a title page to show to Rudy, as if it were a real book.

GULLIVER'S TRAVELS
BOOK V: A VOYAGE TO REDRIFF
BY JAMES DARKE, MA (Oxon), PhD (Cantab)

Rudy looked at the computer screen intently, as his face registered a mixture of delight and bemusement.

'What's a Cantab, Gampy? And an Oxon?'

'Oh, those are just me showing off, telling the reader – though you, darling, are the only reader so I was just being silly – what universities I attended. Oxon is Oxford, and Cantab is Cambridge.'

'Can I look?'

He reached towards the keyboard.

I should have been concerned, but allowed him entry to my documents. Anyway, I needed to use the loo. By the time I returned, Rudy's fingers were plonking across my keyboard, no doubt breaking everything they touched.

'I changed the typeface, Gampy! He looked at it proudly. 'It's called Algerian, I tried a lot of others, but this looks coolest.'

GULLIVER'S TRAVELS
BY GAMPY

'Darling Rudy, where is Gampy's page?' My voice was strangulated, a response to my desire to strangle. Myself, not him. Oh, him too. Just him.

He hardly looked up, changing the typefaces rapidly.

'I opened a new window,' he said.

He pushed a button and my original title page reappeared.

'Mine is much better, Gampy.' he said proudly. 'Can we use that instead?'

'We'll see, perhaps.'

'I put them in a file, Gampy, so we have both. It's on your desktop.'

There were now two items, entitled *Gampys Page* and *Rudys Better Page*. He looked at it proudly and then made it go away. God knows how I will ever find it again.

'Can we put it to sleep now? I think it's bedtime for both of you.'

'When can we read it. Gampy? I can't wait.'

'Neither can I, my darling. Soon, I promise.'

He was asleep minutes later, exhausted by his many excitations.

Lucy and I had set this as our goal, to focus entirely on his pleasures, to ensure that we had no time to talk in the evening. Though how she and Sam were to get over their tiff if she wouldn't talk to him was unclear, but of course rows create the very atmosphere in which they cannot be resolved. Wars are like that.

Repairing to my computer, I opened my email program to check my emails, to find one, then another, from Sam. The first was sent on Friday evening, hoping that Lu had arrived safely, adding that he would call on the morrow. By that time, of course, we were out of the house for the day, leaving our phones behind. The second was sent while we were at the park:

Dear James,

Lucy will not respond to my calls or emails or texts, and as you have not answered mine of yesterday, I'm coming down on Sunday morning. Lu will have told you what's going on. I think we can handle it, though it is a tricky situation, and we need to get our ducks in a row, and perhaps solicit some good advice. But we must face the issue, and face it together. The more divided we are, the worse it is going to be.

Best wishes,

Sam

I cringed as I read this inarticulate message. The stronger the provocation, the more important it is to speak concisely and precisely. Sloppy thinking expressed in sloppy words leads to sloppy behaviour. The reason that Churchill – in many ways a most disagreeable man – was a wonderful wartime leader is that, under the most terrible duress, he knew how to say what needed to be heard. England was saved by words.

Sam and his ilk, ironically, are Churchill's legacy, the illiterate progeny of his eloquence. Sam's slangy familiarity is worse, even, than his professional jargon. I still remember with a shudder being urged to 'triangulate' with him and Lucy about Suzy's death ... a most distasteful locution suggesting some sort of orgy. I was so taken aback I almost pinched him.

There is clearly some sort of crisis going on, in his marriage and in his head, and perhaps in his – and our – lives. Who can tell from this garbled gobbledygook gibberish? But to be enjoined to get my ducks in a row is going too far.

As I came downstairs and peered round the door of the kitchen, Lucy was scrolling through her mobile, but quickly put it into her pocket. On the table in front of her was a bottle of Premier Cru Chablis, straight from the fridge. We'd drunk half last night, then vacuum-stoppered it till there wasn't enough air in it to sustain the life of a gnat. She'd emptied it, presumably put it in the recycling, and opened another. She lifted her glass and drank with her right hand, keeping the left resting on the table. Wrapped round the tip of her index finger was a piece of toilet paper, stained red. She bites her fingernails when she is stressed, at other times sucks them just for the recreational pleasure. Suzy once bought her a potion to make nails and cuticles hard to chew, but Lucy gnawed through it like a famished beaver. Then Suzy sourced some disgusting tongue-retarding gunk, but Lucy soon developed a taste for it.

She'd showered after dinner, and was in that old terry-towelling robe that made Suzy recoil with dismay, and offer as gifts a variety of silken Oriental kimonos, which Lucy derided insistently.

'Oh, a Mandarin's robe. How lovely and how useful, that'll look terrific with baby sick all over it!'

I didn't take any notice – I am weary of noticing things, they only upset me – and poured myself a glass of the Chablis.

'I've put Rudy down – he was asleep as soon as he hit the pillow. It's been a long day.'

She shook her head, though her shoulders didn't move, which made her look like a figure in a Punch and Judy show.

'Thanks. Amelie is asleep too. It's good to have a rest and a few minutes to …'

'Darling one,' I said, trying not to sound alarming or invasive, 'do we need to talk about something?'

'Something? What something?'

'I don't know. That's why I'm asking.'

'I did not come to talk. I came to get away.'

I stood up gently and walked over, hearing Suzy's admonition, *When she's like this she needs a cuddle.*

I'm not a natural, but I gave it a go. And in only a few moments Lucy was weeping into my shoulder, shaking and bereft.

'Shhhh, shhhhh, my darling. What is it? It can't be so bad, can it?' Lucy is prone to hysterical overreaction, cries as easily as she takes offence, once spent an afternoon wailing when the neighbour's cat – a most disagreeable scragball – was run over by a milk float. And during those times of the month she – like her mother – can be as zealously confrontational and offended as a nun at a stag party.

Her head shook left to right.

'It's worse!'

'Worse than what, my darling?'

'Worse than bad! The worst!'

She detached herself, wiped her eyes on the terry towelling, which presumably had wonderful absorbent qualities before it stiffened with age, as we all do. Looked me in the eye, though I must have seemed a bit, well, blurry.

'It's the police,' she said. 'They've come ...'

'I would be ever so grateful if you would tell me what's going on. Is there something to be alarmed about?'

She shook her head, impossible to say if yes or no.

At this point, curiously and in retrospect almost incomprehensibly, I made no connection to the two policemen who had knocked on my door, and then invited me to visit their offices. Having been insufficiently alarmed in the first place, I'd more or less forgotten about it.

'But ... does Sam have anything to do with this? You know, I've had an email from him . . .' I started hesitantly enough. She sat still, and worried the tissue round her finger. 'He says he is coming here tomorrow?'

She nodded, yes.

'Well, love, surely that's a good thing. There's no way to resolve whatever this is unless we talk about it, is there?'

Lucy started to cry again, wiped her eyes, and her soggy red finger-wrapping fell onto the table, like an itinerant objective correlative. I picked it up in a piece of kitchen paper and deposited it in the rubbish. She was soon sucking her finger, as if the point of maiming it had been to get it into her mouth for a bit of regressive comfort.

I renewed my cuddle and rubbed her shoulders. I think she was getting ready, at last, to say what was the matter, when there was a crying sound from upstairs. Amelie, hungry and urgent.

Lucy pulled away abruptly.

'I'm so sorry,' she said. 'And feeding her will be all I have left . . .' She grimaced. 'Literally. Drained, nothing left to give. I'll go to sleep after she's finished with me.'

'Quite right. Sleep is best for you.'

'I wish it was,' she said wearily. 'Never mind, it's probably better if we talk tomorrow, after Sam comes. He can explain. After all, this is his fault.'

It didn't matter what that meant. I'd find out soon enough. When Lucy made her weary way upstairs, I stopped at the liquor cabinet to get something stronger than Chablis. I'd hardly taken a sip – rather good Bas-Armagnac, I usually love it – before I'd lain down on my bed and fallen asleep, but not before registering how much I was dreading the coming day.

Sam texted to announce an ETA – he thinks he's a bloody jumbo jet – of 12.47 at Paddington, in the vain and deluded hope that one of us will meet him. Since Abingdon, being an outpost of progress to nowhere, has no train station, he will first catch the bus into Oxford. He wouldn't take a taxi if his mother was dying; in fact, when she was, he didn't, though he unfortunately got to the deathbed in time, otherwise he might have learned a lesson.

Rudy is restless and needy, has fully understood in his inchoate childish way that something is badly wrong, and has followed me into my study, demanding to be read to. This is not the time for it; I'm still finishing the first bit of my *Gulliver*, so I've installed him at my desk – NOT at my computer – with his iPad, and the licence to use it how and as long as he pleases. I don't care if he googles *teenage orgies*, as long as they last for an hour or two.

Soon the house is as peaceful as the twin towers on the evening of 10 September. And 747 JumboSam is on his way. This is fanciful, I like that. Of course, there's nothing dangerous about his imminent arrival; he's too inconsequential to cause more trouble than can be wreaked upon the psyches of his poor grievers.

I know how Suzy would have told it. Or shown it, using that witless dichotomy to which bad readers and critics are addicted: *show, don't tell*. I get bored being shown things, but Suzy was addicted to providing those 'thousands of details' that otherwise sensible novelists recommend and over-employ, as if a novel were some sort of travel documentary with a hand-held camera.

On Sam's sheepish arrival, we gathered round the kitchen table: thin, pale grey ceramic coffee cups, with watery brackish rings left on the blue-and-white tablecloth bought years ago at Saint-Jean-de-Luz (near its twin city, St Rien de Luz), translucent flakes from baguettes with Normandy butter and mature brie, then wine glasses and an empty bottle of Riesling. Smooth. And a seriously depleted box of tissues.

As Lucy repeatedly insisted, 'all this' is Sam's doing. *Fault*, she says, though I am not sure that I think like that. I am thinking as I write. Let your fingers do the thinking. I would give my kingdom and Enigma the horse just to walk out of here, right now.

I don't know how to say this. Suzy thinks, would think, would have thought – curious how tenses and locutions make persons reappear disappear retreat come forward – Suzy is ... there, I've said it, she *is* for me ... I'm not abandoning her *is*-ness so lightly – Suzy is desolate to have caused this problem. *It's all my fault.* Her fault, neither mine nor the hapless Sam's.

If I could have thought properly, I'm so sorry I couldn't, I would have taken the fucking pills myself, left you out of it except as a sort of waiter, serving them up in a cocktail, like you did, for which I am so so grateful. I should have thought ahead. I was never very good at planning, didn't believe in it, took one thing at a time, everything as it comes, came, left the planning to you, and now this. This. I'm so so sorry, my dear one, so sorry to have left you, left you like this, like this.

Sam is not the leader of his group, but a member of it. That's his gestalt. And one afternoon, as they sipped their warm tannic tea out of their chipped unmatched mugs, they were discussing to what extent you can 'help' a person to die. Withhold medication? Water? Food? Who gets to decide? The doctors or nurses or hospice? The dying loved one? The dying loved one's loved one?

And being, all of them, grievers, they all had stories to tell, and apparently told them and told them and told them. And then Sam told one too. Of course, he was discreet about it. Didn't name names, of course he didn't, just outlined a scene in which a dying loved one was helped into the next world by the intervention of her own loved one. Someone he knew, he said. Just that, no harm in that, is there ... was there?

Except when he inadvertently mentioned Lucy, and the

extremities of her confusion and her grief, and the group swooped on him like pelicans, lifted him up into their bills, and swallowed him alive. How gratifying, how nourishing, how delightful that he, a member of the group, would share like this. His wife. They knew her mother had died recently.

And then, of course, naturally, professionally, he couldn't back down, or deny, or prevaricate. He described what had happened, and his own feelings about it. Why not? What's said in the group stays in the group. Doesn't it? Those are not the rules, we don't believe in rules, those are the conventions, without which no one could speak openly, share, cathart and purge, succour and support.

He defended himself: this was how he *worked*, the group shared his methods and believed in them. We all knew that, and Lucy had supported it. There is such a thing as confidentiality, and it had been breached reprehensibly. But not by him!

One of the grievers, a spiky middle-aged matron of the Roman persuasion, had recently lost her father after a protracted and distressing illness. She accepted this as God's will, part of some divine plan that it was her role neither to understand nor, God forbid, to question. He works in mysterious ways, very.

When Sam shared his family story with the group, the RC did not contribute, and stayed silent for the rest of the session, which was a relief to the other members. But as the story emerged and the details were reluctantly filled in by their not-leader-but-member, she was taking it all in, and she was horrified, morally and spiritually disgusted, implacably judgemental.

Her husband, to whom she relayed the story that very evening, was equally but differently judgemental. He was a policeman.

Over the wine, Sam cried, and begged to be forgiven.

Over the wine, Lucy would not forgive him.

Over the wine, I didn't know what to think.

Wine is like that, it affects different people in different ways.

Both Sam and Lucy had recently been visited by my two policemen (the descriptions matched) asking questions about the death of Suzanne Moulton.

Both declined to answer.

Sam cited professional confidentiality. The policeman wrote this down.

Lucy told him to fuck off. He wrote that down too.

The two officers hadn't returned, but they promised to do so when their inquiries were more advanced.

Ah, well. I told Lucy and Sam about my short doorstep interview, the later invitation to the police station, and my disinclination to accept it.

And here we all are, dangling and ripe, ready to fall.

'What I'm terrified of,' said Lucy, still wiping her eyes, 'is that you're going to be arrested, and charged with . . .' She couldn't bring herself to say the word.

'Murder?' I enquired mildly.

She nodded and snuffled. Sam did too. It should have been bringing them together like grievers, but it wasn't. Lucy hadn't met his eye, not once, looked out, and up, and down, at her mug, her glass, her father.

'Well, James,' said Sam, 'at least this is out in the open, and we can . . .'

If he'd said *get our ducks in a row* I would have Riesling-bottled him smoothly, but he settled, for once, for something both simple and appropriate.

'At least we can all tell the same story, because it will be – if it comes to that, and I'm sure it won't – essential to your defence . . .'

I stopped to think about this, which surprised him mightily.

'I don't need to get some damn lawyer to argue me as if I were a case. What I did was humane, morally and emotionally correct. I have no desire, and no need, to defend myself.'

They competed to get their *Buts* in first. Lucy won.

'We've been through this argument before, but the situation has changed and you need to ...'

She looked exhausted and alarmed, her features retracted and reconfigured until she looked – as she so often does when under duress – like someone auditioning as a witch.

'Darling Lucy,' I said, 'I know you sometimes need to be protected from my opinions—'

I was interrupted sharply by what might be characterised as a cackle, sharp and harsh, dismissive.

'You don't understand, do you? You really don't get it, at all!'

'What? What?'

'The person who needs to be protected from your opinions is you!'

Chapter 8

I understand, I think. I think I understand. I don't feel as if I need to defend myself, or, worse, have someone else do so. Nor do I wish to feel defensive, though I do. So: what is the opposite of defending? Hiding under a bush? That's what I have been doing since Suzy died. In many ways it is how I've spent my life. But, thanks to my son-in-law, that is no longer an option. What I really feel like doing is not defending, but attacking.

Attacking? Whom? How? When? Where? Why? All that the word signifies, in this, its first iteration, is that I will not be bullied, and that I'm bloody, and bloody-mindedly, angry. I have behaved well, and my actions could provide the basis for a universal imperative. But I have no idea what to do, and am unpractised at soliciting help. Like most masters from the great public schools I have a Filofax full of successful former pupils, some of whom might welcome a summons. But since I have never welcomed their attempts – soon abandoned – to keep in touch with me, it would be asking too much.

No, the only name that comes to mind is that of Philip Massingham. And before I talk myself out of it – I have only met him once, and behaved badly – I pick up the phone. Even composing an email would be torturous, and give me too many temptations to scarper. Better to stumble and bumble in person.

He answers at the second ring.

'Philip Massingham.'

The formality of the salutation almost makes me put down the phone. I hesitate.

'Hello?' he says. 'Are you there?' His voice is firmer than it had been at the meeting of the poetry group; now he sounds crisp, thoroughly confident and assured.

'Yes, yes, sorry. It's me, James. James Darke.'

I wince as I stumble, humiliated. It was him I expected to be feeble, but now it is me.

'James, how lovely to hear from you. I trust you're feeling better?'

'I am, Philip. And I can hear that you are too.'

'Yes, yes,' he says. 'Much better, thanks. On a good day.'

'Let me tell you why I am calling. It's a bit presumptuous, I hope you don't mind, but I really need some advice . . .'

He lets me go on.

'I am in a situation that I don't entirely understand, and I need some legal advice, or counsel really . . .'

'Ah, James, I wish I could help. But I'm not a proper lawyer, haven't been for zonks. If you can give me some idea of what the problem is, I can put you on to someone first class . . .'

'No, no,' I say, aware I am going to be misunderstood. 'Let me clarify. The situation concerns Suzy's death − my late wife, you know − and I need some advice about how to handle an emerging problem.'

'What sort of problem? If it is a matter of the estate, I know just the right chap.'

'No, no. I'm sorry to be so inarticulate, but this is all just starting, and I'm a bit overwhelmed . . .'

'Overwhelmed?'

'Yes. You see, it involves the police . . .'

'Ah, yes, how might that be?'

He was being patient, but both of us had limited reserves of energy, and it became clear that an approach over the phone had been a mistake. A judicious email would have been better, if I'd felt able to compose one, and myself.

'The fact is, I cannot understand what is likely to happen to me, and why, and how. And the advice I need is not lawyerly in a mounting-a-defence sort of way. I need to know something about human rights ...'

'Go on.' For the first time his voice engages, and he sounds interested.

'Well, it touches on the subject that so distressed me at your reading, and about which you are obviously exercised as well.'

'I'm not sure what you mean.' He is a precise and exacting man, formidable. I am suddenly awash with shame.

'Philip, I am so sorry to bother you like this. I shouldn't ...'

'Quite right,' he says. 'Wrong to talk over the phone. Can I give you lunch one day? If you can do Wednesday, that would work for me. Is the Athenaeum all right? The food is tolerable, and it won't be crowded, so we can get a quiet table overlooking the garden. Say at one o'clock?'

On the day, I arrived early enough to have a walk in St James's Park to settle myself and to check out how Fatboy Sam was getting on. He was perched on a bank, sunning himself indolently, looking more delicious than ever, ripe for the pot. I looked round furtively, afraid that my birdicidal thoughts might be visible on my features, computing lines of approach, and escape.

I trudged up the grand flight of steps into Waterloo Place, where the Athenaeum loomed over the car park. I've never much enjoyed dining there, feeling that little bit uncomfortable amongst the great and the good, but I was greeted civilly by the porter. Mr Massingham was expecting me. It was lunchtime, the bar filled with hearty drinkers celebrating themselves and the triumph of their class.

You find them here in clubland, you find them there: in hats at Ascot and red cord trousers at Henley, with picnics at Glyndebourne, blooming at the Chelsea Flower Show, in wellies at country weekends in Gloucestershire. They prefer their own company, and companies. Or do I mean, however uneasily, not they, but *we*? Am I one of them, by now?

We are the products of prep schools: untimely ripped from our mothers' arms, deposited like orphans onto the doorsteps of strangers. The grief of that exile is unassuageable and unassimilable, which is what we call 'character forming'. During the first few weeks we used as many tissues for tears as we would later do for semen.

When my parents first delivered me, shrunken and disconsolate, into the enveloping embrace of a jolly school matron, my mother looked away after a brief hug, and my father patted me on the shoulder. As he left, he shook my hand.

'Buck up, boy!' he said firmly, and almost fondly. 'You'll be fine.'

I kept my lips both closed and stiff, the dual qualities that lead to that strangulated utterance so characteristic of an English upper-class accent.

'All right,' I murmured, 'see you soon.'

'That's a brave chap. Don't forget to write to Mummy.'

For the first term I did, frequently, and she answered, twice.

Later I became a public-school teacher: the return of the repressed. I reassured myself with the knowledge that the homes from which our little charges were banished were often so emotionally retarded that they were well worth leaving.

And here we are, enlarged, grizzled schoolboys, unconsoled, in the bar of this great club, our thin veneer of cultivated urbanity circled by fear and cellared by rage. I entered the braying throng to find Philip engaged in conversation with Michael Golde, my former pupil and now our Minister of Education, who looked up, and produced a Whitehall smile.

'Sir! How lovely to see you.'

I allowed some time to pass, and manufactured a look of bewilderment to replace the rictus of distaste that was competing for my facial time.

'I'm so sorry,' I said. 'Effects of old age, no doubt, shocking memory. Do remind me who you are?'

And there I was thinking life had all too few moments of amusement. He was mortified.

'Golde, sir. Michael Golde.'

I was relentless. Kept the bewilderment front and centre, didn't give an inch by way of recognition. No widening of the eyes, no wry smile of remembrance.

'From school, sir. Your Friday group . . .'

'Oh, yes. The Friday group, I do remember that. I trust you are doing well . . .'

Sir didn't know who he was, or how important. It was glorious. He'd gained weight, and affected a gravitas that hardly disguised the fact that he was still the sneaky lascivious schoolboy that I remembered so well. If reptilian, now more python than lizard.

'Indeed, indeed I am. And I hope you are too, since your sad news?' He'd written me a formal letter of condolence after Suzy died, which I had had neither the need nor the inclination to answer.

'Yes, thank you.'

Sensing that I was anxious to be timely ripped from Golde's company, Philip took me by the arm, said his farewells and we made our way to the dining room, leaving the forlorn and soundly humiliated Golde propping up the bar.

'I didn't know you knew Golde,' he said, twinkling.

'Old boy of ours.'

'Quite a piece of work, that one. A living example of the workings of the Peter Principle, though I daresay he has higher ambitions . . . the Saint Peter principle, I call it.'

We were seated by an elderly deferential waiter at a table for two, with no one dining at the tables near us. He pulled out Philip's chair slowly and almost tenderly, whispering 'sir', deferring to Philip's increasing weakness.

'I ought to have offered you a drink,' my host said, 'but that awful fellow would have stuck to us like resin. It's better to open a bottle of wine at table, if that suits. Or perhaps you'd like an aperitif of some sort?'

'Wine will be fine.'

'The fish is good here, perhaps a bottle of our rather good Pouilly Fuissé . . .'

The wine arrived, was sampled and poured, and we both ordered the sea trout, with new potatoes, French beans, sprinkled with a few unnecessary slivers of almonds.

'So,' he said, in a voice mellower and less intimidating than on the phone, 'tell me what's going on.'

I did, in detail, from the onset of Suzy's illness to the administering of the fatal draught and the subsequent police visits.

He listened attentively, cocking his head to the side. A smile crossed his features; he finished a first glass and the waiter refilled it, and then mine.

'Can you remember – this may be important later on – exactly what it was you said when you told Lucy and her husband? About what you did?'

I'd been wondering about this myself. I can recall, of course, the gist of it, the confession, the explanation, the rationale. But what had I said *exactly*? Who the hell knows? Memory is tricky and unreliable, and what we recall is not so much inexact as fictive: we make up and refine our stories to have a satisfying narrative arc, not to tell some literal 'truth'.

Philip allowed me time to think, and ate a small slice of his fish. By then I'd almost finished mine, forced myself to slow down – it's rude to empty one's plate before one's host – and as a result was soon on my third glass of wine. I was reminded of Suzy in her last months, picking at a tiny morsel of cod, eating a carrot stick or boiled potato, making an effort to appear engaged with food when increasingly it revolted her, the smells and textures, the indigestibility. Philip was more ill than he let on.

'Let me think. It's so hard to recall. Lucy accused me of murdering her mother. And I remember thinking that she and Sam were entirely incapable, by training or inclination, of understanding or sympathising with a situation where the usual, simple categories don't pertain ...'

He nodded, forked a French bean, shook off the almond flakes, and nibbled at it.

'I see.' I didn't need to explain further.

'I reminded them that Suzy wanted to die, was begging to be released. I think I said that I *helped* her. That I'd put aside some tablets and put them in her tea, with honey. And after she drank it she went, I suppose it was into a coma, and I sat with her until she died some hours later ...'

Philip finished his wine, drank some water.

'Begging to be released? Does that mean she asked you to finish it ...?

'No. I took that as implied ...'

He nodded, and was silent for a moment.

'How did you decide which tablets to give her? And how many?'

'I was guessing. I didn't look up a recipe ...'

'It matters. If, for instance, you were googling, or reading about, how to concoct a fatal cocktail of drugs, that is evidence of premeditation ...'

'It was premeditated. I knew what I was doing, more or less. She was so weak that I assumed that a mixture of Digoxin and Diazepam would ...' I paused, not entirely clear what I had been thinking. I remember saying something tendentious to Sam about thinking with my heart, as if he would recognise the Pascalian reference. Or understand it, and if he did, sympathise.

'Now,' said Philip firmly, 'we are at a critical point, which will be of the utmost importance. When you gave her this potion, was it your intention – if I may put it bluntly – to kill her?'

He'd nibbled enough to allow me to finish my meal. The sea trout was fresh, well-cooked and getting cold.

'You're right,' I said. 'The fish is lovely.'

'Go on.'

'I'm afraid, Philip, the answer is that I don't know. I didn't know then, and I don't know now. Both of us were at the end of our tether, it was over, we were over. Finished. I was trying to end the pain, to release her from it.'

'Which is different in your understanding to ending her life?'

'I don't know. No. Yes. In that moment I just wanted her suffering – our suffering – to be over ... I remember saying to Lucy that when our cats and dogs are dying we treat them more lovingly than our dying friends and relations. Take them to the vet, put them down gently. No pain. Easeful death.'

'I've always thought vets are kinder than doctors. Kinder than God, really.'

I finished the last of my wine, suddenly conscious of Suzy's immanence, a diffuse presence that made the air darken and sway. Unexpectedly, Philip reached across the table and put his hand over mine. It wasn't comforting, but it was generous. He was dying too.

He smiled, laughed.

'I understand, I do. But I don't know that many police officers will, nor many judges either, if it comes to that ...'

'So I'm in trouble. I understand that.'

'I suppose,' he said, 'it depends how you play your cards. First, you and Lucy and Sam need to rehearse this story together, so that it is unambiguous. And then, the CPS will have to take a view. They don't generally prosecute unless they have a fair chance of success ...'

'I see. Do tell me, though: prosecute for what?'

There was a long pause, as in a film: the musical score would get louder just now. Stringed instruments, portentous.

'Murder. Or manslaughter. Has to be one or the other.'

'What's your guess?'

'I hate guessing. It will depend on what you say in your police interview. Let's see what develops ... Would you like pudding? Coffee?'

'No, thank you.'

He gestured to the waiter.

He rose slowly, holding the back of the chair for support. I started to put my arm in his, hesitated and withdrew. He noticed, nodded.

'Thank you so much for coming,' he said warmly. 'I'm interested in your problem. Do keep in touch.'

'Thank you. I will need help, or advice, or support. Not sure which. I suppose it depends on what happens next. But I am resolved that, if things develop towards some sort of charge, I will fight back.'

He paused, straightened, turned to face me directly.

'Fight back?'

'Absolutely. The way we treat suffering and dying is both disgraceful and immoral, and I am looking forward to saying so, publicly. And making myself, and Suzy, into a sort of test case, if that's not an inappropriate metaphor?'

There was a pause, as he considered this.

'What would this actually entail?'

'I'm not sure yet. I may write something for the newspapers. Perhaps publish a little booklet, like a pamphleteer in the eighteenth century, and distribute it through bookshops.'

'I suppose you could put it online too.' He paused, considered. 'Are you saying you want to, well, initiate some sort of … campaign?'

He looked at me closely, as if scanning for the requisite qualities of political savvy, toughness and obduracy. One by one he ticked them off: no, no, not at all.

I must have grimaced, and he gave me an interrogatory look, as if about to offer Rennies or paracetamol.

'No. I loathe leaders, and movements. To be frank, I have never even voted, so deep is my loathing of politicians.'

He looked mildly displeased to hear this.

'Choices,' he said. 'We are obliged to make the choices. And if you want to influence public thought, how do you see your role?'

'I don't. Haven't got that far yet. But I need to do something, and to start something … Because otherwise I shall die, not of my unreliable heart, but of rage and regret.'

'Good luck,' said Philip. 'Let's hope you light your fire.'

He knew the world better than I, and obviously doubted that I would make any impact. Probably end up huddled in jail like poor deluded Oscar Wilde, having killed the thing I loved.

We parted warmly, two tired old men.

First the thank-you note, which I posted that afternoon, before taking to my bed, not the effect of the wine at lunch, but because the encounter with Philip, his precision, scepticism and intensity of focus, had dampened whatever passes for my spirits. He is too correct to have said, 'For goodness sake, James, don't be a damn fool,' but the message was evident in the slight pinking of his cheek, the lines appearing on his brow, the tapping of the fingertip on the table, until he noticed he was doing it, and stopped hastily, a guilty look on his face.

Of course, the guilty one is me. Or perhaps will be me, when the time comes, because the time is coming: to insist that Suzy was not a victim, nor will I be a victim of the forensic and judicial process of accounting for her death, investigating it, categorising it, pursuing it. The force of the forces is released and on the prowl, sniffing and snorting at my door. DC and DS. I have no choice but to accommodate them.

My head burdened with such prospects, I closed the curtains upstairs and down, dimmed the lights, retreated to my former incarcerated incarnation as a be-gloomed ruminant of the entropics, took to my bed, pulled the covers over my head, tried to sleep, failed. Yearned to connect to the still presence of Suzy, reached for her hand but it wouldn't appear, or perhaps she was gone?

Of late I see her only in lifeless photographs, in the matched leather albums that she put together: Family, Oxford, Travels, Teaching and School, London, Lucy ... which only remind me how cold she is, and dumb. Let the lamp affix its beam, and I see only images of a non-person who increasingly has nothing to do with me. And her voice? I heard it night and day for months after she left me, but now it is limited to the occasional snort or expostulation. If I go onto YouTube, there she is being interviewed, full of self and opinion, laughing, snide, a confident presence. But it's not Suzy, not my poor diminishing Suzy, just a videographic impostor doing an impression good enough to fool them, but in no manner convincing to me. These aides-memoir, visual and acoustic, merely confirm her absence. Suzy is gone.

And I, I wish I were, too. But every morning when I check in the mirror, I'm still here, shrunken and diminished in health and heart, hardly fit for purpose. Yet here I am, embarking, readying myself to embark, thinking about perhaps embarking, on a fraught project guaranteed to test the resolve and strength of a man half my age and twice my powers. Perhaps the only consolation I may have, and a relief from these anxieties, is that it is not me who is choosing this project, indeed, it is choosing me. I shall have to confront my DS and DC, visit them in their lair, be scrutinised, and if Philip is right, charged. And then what am I to do? Lie down under a bush with my legs in the air, whimpering, or rise up, nip and threaten?

I had a reply from Philip the next day by email.

Yes, it was good to see you too. I have been thinking about your proposed pamphlet. Much amusement in it, and provocation too – I suspect you will respond to both.

Might 'Do You Love Your Dog More Than Your Mother?' work as a title? Something along those lines? Though of course half the people I know actually do prefer their pets to their mothers, and in many cases – I know the dogs and mothers – one quite understands why.

In the meantime, remember what I said: it is not unlikely that the police will interview, and may well arrest you. And most likely search your home. Best be prepared.

I remain agnostic about the feasibility, much less the desirability, of your project. I suppose that, like God, it is up to you to reveal yourself? Or not, as in His case.

All best,

Philip

Chapter 9

Two days later I was in Oxford, staying as previously at the Old Parsonage Hotel – *Ah, Dr Darke, so good to see you again* – and they'd put me in my usual junior suite. It was Rudy's eight-and-a-half-year birthday, designed by Lucy at his insistence because I missed his eighth when I was locked away in London. So I owe him.

As a special treat we were meeting just up the road for lunch at Browns Brasserie, which is pretty, has tolerable if basic food and is Rudy's *best*. I'd bought him a present with which I was distinctly pleased. Though his parents wouldn't understand it, he would. He'd been intrigued by my Dickens collection before I sold it, loved the red cloth covers with the gilt stamping, the feel and texture of the paper, and above all the illustrations. He was disappointed when the books were removed, for he didn't know that he would eventually be the recipient of the proceeds.

I'd purchased a first edition of the Arthur Rackham-illustrated *Gulliver's Travels*. It's a tad blowsy, with lashings of gilt on the blue front covers, and illustrations that, while vulgar to my eye, nevertheless demand attention. Rudy would like it. I'd had it gift-wrapped at the swanky Fulham Booksellers, and was excited at the prospect of him opening it. The unwrapping and unravelling took place at speed, and Rudy was – if I say so myself – beyond thrilled, while his father was beyond comprehension that 'such an expensive book' should be given to an eight (and-a-half-) year-old, or indeed to anyone at all. To Sam books are objects of utility, and he never buys any but the cheapest available copies. His home has more bedraggled Penguins and Puffins than Regent's Park Zoo. He regarded my collection of Dickens first editions with the kind of ferocious disapproval he reserves for plutocratic capitalists and shire Tories.

The book was put back into its packaging, Rudy scoffed his burger and chips and drank his Coke – everything was allowed on his half-birthday – and ordered a hot fudge sundae for afters. His parents ate something or other, I had a simple grilled plaice and salad, and drank what was not entirely misdescribed as a glass of Chablis.

When we got back to Abingdon, Rudy did not have the predicted stomach ache, and soon repaired to his bedroom with his new book, excited by my promise that, at bedtime, I would read him our first chapter of *A Voyage to Redriff*. When called to tea at half-six, he announced that he wasn't hungry and was ready to go to bed. Lucy pressed a couple of Marmite sandwiches and a glass of orange juice – a disgusting combination – upon him, which were dispatched in record time.

'Can we go to bed now, Gampy? Please can we?'

I stood up, as anxious as he to start our reading. I had some unease that my text might be a little beyond his powers, at least in part, but then so was a lot of the original and we had coped with that admirably, skipping the boring disquisitions and returning as soon as possible to the action.

I'd printed out the pages of my first section, and as the front cover I had attached, somewhat unwillingly, his suggested typology of the title page. I suppose, if you reconnected to your 'inner child', as it is now called, you might have found it charming. But I don't have an inner child, didn't even have one when I *was* a child. Nor have I an inner adult. I'm not sure I have any inners.

Rudy went to the loo, brushed his teeth and changed into his jimjams, and tucked himself in bed. His birthday gift was on his bedside table. I wondered briefly what poor Dean Swift would have made of it all, but who cares? He's dead.

Rudy beamed as he saw the papers in my hand.

GULLIVER'S TRAVELS
BY GAMPY

'That's so cool!' he said with a mighty smile.

'Shall I begin?'

He plumped his pillows, sat up so he could see the pages, or the backs of the pages, and I began.

GULLIVER'S TRAVELS
BOOK V: A VOYAGE TO REDRIFF
In which Lemuel Gulliver returns to his native land

As soon as I entered the house, my wife took me in her arms, and kissed me, at which having not been used to the touch of that odious animal for so many years, I fell in a swoon for almost an hour. During the first year I could not endure my wife or children in my presence, the very smell of them was intolerable; much less could I suffer them to eat in the same room . . .

As for my lodgings, I could not, of course, enter our former bedchamber, for the noxious smells and degrading memories of our marital accommodation were overwhelming to me. From the very first night I made my lodging in the stables, and soon purchased two young Stone Horses, whom I named Paradox and Enigma, in acknowledgement of the riddle and obscure question of our relations, for it was I who was now Master, little as I desired or deserved such a role, and they who were my subjects. When I introduced myself, the horses were astonished to hear me speaking their language with such fluency. For the first months I would not countenance these noble beings yoked to a carriage for my convenience, but they protested that they would like nothing better than to serve me so, for it would also give them exercise and fresh air.

If there was a true homecoming to relate, this was it, for my wife and my children belonged to a past, a foreign and a noxious former life, and I only felt understood, welcomed, and respected in the company of these horses. To their astonishment, I treated them with a deference and admiration that they had seldom experienced in their servitude to rough Yahoo masters. How, they enquired, had I come to acquire such facility in their tongue?

I was determined, in our first meetings, to give them an account of my voyage to the land of their fellows that was sufficiently detailed, and accurate in every way, so as to assure them that I was not saying the thing that is not. They listened to my story carefully, and were kind enough to suppress exclamations of incredulity. They considered before they spoke, allowing time for rumination, and the ensuing silences were invariably followed by responses both generous and well-expressed.

Room was made for me in one of the empty stalls, and a rough but serviceable mattress made of straw and wrapped in blankets was sufficient for my comfort. I had the groom instal a lock in the stable door, so that no one without the key could intrude upon my solitude, for I wanted no other company than that of my agreeable stable-mates. Twice a day the manservant arrived from the house, bringing me adequate food and renewing our water.

I continued to eat as I had learned during my final voyage, simple oatcakes, sometimes sweetened by honey, and drank only the clearest water. Since my arrival home, though I use this word with the utmost reluctance, I have added fresh berries to this diet. My wife instructed the servants to dig a small bed in which raspberries and currants might grow, and when the fruits later arrived I was most grateful to her.

But immured as I was behind these locked doors, in the half-light, there was hardly occupation enough to pass my time productively. In the land of the Houyhnhnms I was constantly busy, cooking, sewing, making the many things of which I had need – all of which activities were now accomplished by my wife and servants. When I had the company of my Master and his family, as well as the occasional visits of his many friends, I lived richly and fully, replete in mind and spirit. Now I am in Redriff, though I have the company of my amiable stable-mates, they are young and inexperienced, unused to sustained conversation, and their company soon pales.

My wife has accepted these arrangements without complaint, knowing the strength of my aversions and my need for seclusion and privacy. She hopes and prays, she says, that after a sufficient passage of time, I may return to my family, who love and cherish me. But my oldest daughter Lucile, to whom I was greatly attached before my voyages began, cannot accept this new state of things, thinking me not mad but wilful and misguided. She visits frequently, knocking loudly on the stable door, but I do not answer. Often she brings her son Reuben, a comely boy of some eight years, who shouts through the doors that he wants to see me and please to come out, for I am being silly, and it is not fair treatment of his poor mother, who loves me, and of himself, my grandson. One day he brought me a bunch of wild flowers in a glass vase to put on my desk, but Enigma ate them immediately, thinking they were for him.

As I read, Rudy first grinned at the mention of Enigma, and positively beamed when Reuben entered the narrative. I could hear him whispering, as if to himself: 'Cool, that's so cool!'

*R*euben's mother no doubt arranges and encourages his visits, and though I disregard his entreaties, they touch my heart, and I sometimes peek out to see what he now looks like, having seen him only as an infant. Latterly she has taken to writing me letters, which she pushes under the door. I have instructed the groom to remove and to burn them, unopened. Her son, spying this gap under the stable door, has taken to whittling small animals – I think they are meant to be horses – with his sharpest Blade. I keep them on my table, and look on them with simple pleasure.

In order to spend my days profitably, and to deflect my mind from my many tribulations, I began composing an account in which I related, as simply and as truthfully as possible, what had happened to me on each Voyage, and of what the habits and dispositions of the natives of each country consisted.

To this end, and approving entirely of a project which she thought might enhance the return of my sanity, my wife procured for me pens, ink, and writing books bound in fine leather, into which I might enter my new experiences during this, my final, most dangerous and distressing adventure. A simple table and wooden chair were placed against the side wall, and a lamp which – though I was enjoined to tend with the utmost care lest I burn the stables down – would provide sufficient light for me to compose both my thoughts, and myself.

The quiet and reflection of this writing exercise slowly began to soothe me, and my accounts of my previous Voyages slowly grew. I resolved to write plainly, so that neither flight of fancy nor ornament of language might conceal the veracity of my accounts. I did not wish to compose yet another volume of tedious voyages, nor produce something as fanciful as the recently published The Life and Adventures of Robinson Crusoe, a fictive tale of little merit.

I was writing for the benefit of the Yahoos, that those of them capable of at least some minimal understanding and imagination, might learn how small their place in the world is, how much they *lack in moral and intellectual power, and how their unreason might be remedied through study of the most instructive society of the Houyhnhnms.*

When I had the initial drafts of my account in reasonable form, I decided, after much thought and though besieged by doubt, to shew the contents to my ancient and intimate friend Mr Sympson. He was delighted to be summoned, for he had been apprised of my parlous state by dear Mary, and was most anxious to visit me. He is a man of great discrimination and wide reading, and his encouragement, should it be forthcoming, would provide comfort and further incentive to me.

I met him in our drawing room, and he sensitively and wisely kept his distance, though I could see he wished to embrace me.

'Sir,' he said most warmly, 'it is a delight and a privilege to see you once again.'

I replied, though it was not entirely true, that I felt similarly.

'I gather you are writing an account of your Voyages, and seek an opinion of it? I am by no means . . .'

I waved my hand, and he stopped.

'Before you begin reading them, Sir, allow me to tell you the nature of the contents, for mine is the most unusual tale ever related by man.'

He nodded his head appreciatively. 'Sir, I am entirely at your disposal.'

When we rose, perhaps an hour later, his face was lit with wonder and delight.

'I have never heard the like, Captain Gulliver, and I believe you entirely in every word and sentiment. It is a wondrous tale, and I have no doubt that, when you have finished it, the public will rejoice in its every sentence.'

I looked at him steadily, and he dropped his eyes.

'I hope not, Sir, for this is not a fancy designed merely to amuse, like the childish work by Mr Defoe. Mine is a cautionary tale, and has within it some truths so painful that I fear, should the account

ever find its readers, many of them will be grievously offended by it.'

On due reflection, he acceded to the truth of this, adding that nevertheless there would certainly be some readers, who, like himself, would find much to ponder in my account, and many ways in which they might profit from it.

He took his leave warmly, maintaining a safe distance from me.

I had not foreseen what was to happen next, for it did not occur to me that my tale, in its bare outline, would prematurely make its way into the world. Prompted by his overweening enthusiasm for my endeavours, Mr Sympson soon began to tell my stories far and wide, with consequences little short of disastrous.

I finished, and paused. Rudy lay still, hardly expecting the narrative to end at this moment, when it was getting so exciting. When I put the pages down on the bedside table, atop his birthday copy of the Rackham edition, he gave a protracted whimper.

'No, Gampy. I want more. Just a little bit?'

'I'm so pleased you like it, darling, but we've already read such a lot. Are you following it well enough?'

'I love it. I love Reuben! He's me, isn't he? He even has Enigma the horse . . .'

'And his trusty blades.'

He lay back into the pillow, turned his head away.

'I promise we'll have more.'

'Soon, Gampy?'

'Very soon.'

He sat up, pushed my papers aside, and picked up his illustrated edition.

'I'll read more of this, then,' he said. 'But it's not nearly as good.'

Dinner was ready when I came downstairs. Lucy had made her usual effort, and produced the usual disappointment. To herself, really, I am a product of indifferent food, badly cooked and presented, first at school and now on an occasional family basis. She'd googled a Nigel Slater recipe for roast chicken, but it's all very well stuffing a lemon and some garlic up it, roasting at the right temperature for the right time, and basting on schedule. But if you buy a cheap chicken at Tesco's, it will taste like a cheap chicken from Tesco's, which is to say it will not taste at all.

'Delicious,' I said, eating my drumstick slowly. There were also frozen peas and roast baking potatoes to get through. And some smooth wine, which I'd brought with me as some consolation for my many trials.

Philip had urged me to talk to Sam and Lucy about how we would respond when the police renewed their inquiries. Sam could not hide behind client confidentiality for long, as the relevant conversation was not privileged in any way. Nor could Lucy continue to tell them to fuck off, nor would I wish her to. I resolved to make that visit to the police station for a formal interview.

Though he abjured the ducks metaphor, Philip agreed with Sam that the family needed to tell the one story, and though he could not counsel a lie, he could tolerate an ambiguity. That's what lawyers eat for breakfast. Perhaps Sam had misunderstood what I said during our talk in the garden: I was not confessing guilt, and the draught I gave the dying Suzy was intended merely to help her to sleep. This version of events appealed to Lucy, and eventually to Sam, but I was having none of it. I am not a liar. I did nothing that I regard as reprehensible, quite the opposite.

I had agreed to stay in Oxford for two nights, to prolong the half-birthday festivities by taking Rudy to the parks on Sunday, and then for tea at Browns, just the two of us. He had no interest in scones with jam and clotted cream – one of the simple delights of English

137

cuisine when all three are done to perfection (which they never are) – and instead had yet another hot fudge sundae, which to my surprise – he insisted I had a spoonful – was rather good.

'You know, Gampy, I can't stop thinking about what's going to happen next . . .'

'Next, darling?'

'In the story, silly. The one about Captain Gulliver and Reuben and Enigma. Can we go riding again soon, when we come to London?'

'Of course we can, as soon as you come.'

'I can't wait to tell Enigma he's in a book!'

'Thanks. I was pleased with that bit.'

He looked proud but humble, and gave a little nod before spooning in some creamy chocolate. I tried to finish my crumbly and tasteless scone, which was improved by a touch of clotted cream, though the strawberry jam was too sweet and a bit thick for purpose.

It was clear where the conversation was going, and when we got home we agreed that he could have another section of *Gulliver* in the afternoon, as long as he didn't ask for more at bedtime, because it wasn't written yet. This wasn't entirely true, but it was useful. I'd finished it quickly, though I was still tinkering with it, as writers do.

After the passage of the first year, I resolved to attend occasional brief meetings and meals in my former house. I began last week to permit my wife to sit at dinner with me, at the farthest end of a long table, and to answer (but with the utmost brevity) the few questions I asked her. The smell of a Yahoo continuing very offensive, I always keep my nose well stopped with Rue, Lavender, or Tobacco, and my cheeks doused with scent . . .

Rudy sat up, and interrupted.

'But Gampy, I don't understand.'

'Understand what, my darling?'

'Well, Captain Gulliver is a Yahoo too, isn't he? So he must be smelly too. Isn't he?'

'Yes, but—'

'So why didn't the horses think he was smelly?'

Of course he was right. Gulliver's very person, his ablutions and excretions, must have been offensive to his Master, family and friends.

'You're right, clever you. Perhaps horses don't have an acute sense of smell?'

'They do!' said Rudy. 'Not as good as dogs but better than people. I looked it up. It's because they have a long nose cavity.'

'Thank you for telling me.'

'I think it's why they sent him away! They didn't say so because it would have hurt his feelings, but I bet they couldn't get used to having him around! Too . . . malodorous!'

'OK, I will think about this.'

'Read some more!' he said imperiously, before catching himself. 'Please!'

I wished to satisfy myself about the many events which may have occurred in my prolonged absence, though even this curiosity about the cursed Yahoos of the land of my birth was in itself painful to me. I enquired about the affairs of the Court, what wars may have been embarked upon, who was in and who out in Church and State, enjoining my wife most urgently to keep her answers brief and to the point. This was no problem for the poor woman, for she had scant interest in worldly matters, having concerned herself with the raising of her family, and the management of her servants and household, all of which she had done most conscientiously.

In response, she begged to ask a few questions of her own, to which I acceded, resolving to keep my answers equally brief. Upon my arrival

I had given her an abbreviated account of my residence in the land of the Houyhnhnms, and extolled upon the many and various virtues of that Noble race. She had greeted this information with incredulity, unable to understand either how the common horse could be regarded as a creature of supreme wisdom, or how a human being, created in God's own image, could descend to the depravity of the accursed Yahoos.

'But, Sir,' she began, 'when you relate the many excellences of the Houyhnhnms . . .' She struggled to pronounce the word, but had practised sufficiently in private, and with her children, that all of them could now manage a sound that did not entirely offend my ears, and make me swoon with distaste to hear my Master and his kind insulted in such gross pronunciation.

She continued, 'You have said little of their arts and literature. If they are beings, or persons as it pleases you to call them, of height-ened and exalted qualities of reason and of understanding, they must surely produce the most wonderful works for their amusement and instruction. Pray enlighten me about these.'

It was a most judicious question, and brought forth from me the following observations, which, though, were accompanied by such poignant remembrances that for a moment I fell silent, and thence to weeping. My wife stood as if to venture to comfort me, but I waved her away, lest she come too near, and the smell become intol-erable. The very thought of the Houyhnhnms' poetry, and of my Noble Master declaiming it so modestly yet with such clarity and simplicity of feeling, brought with it a wealth of images so painful that I would have terminated the discussion. After a few moments, during which I wiped my tears, and had a sip of water, I was able to answer.

'In poetry, Madam, they must be allowed to excel all other mortals; wherein the justness of their similes, and the minuteness, as well as exactness of their descriptions, are indeed inimitable . . .

Rudy was fidgeting now, the nature of Houyhnhnm poetry of little interest to him; had this passage been entirely for his benefit I would have shortened it, but it amused me, and there was spicier stuff to come. An adventure story cannot be all adventures; the reader needs an occasional rest, a different rhythm. Rudy's seemed to include sleeping occasionally, nodding off only to open his eyes when the story got more exciting.

My wife listened to this gravely, and asked if I might recite some of these exalted verses. I was obliged to decline, for the virtues of the Houyhnhnm language consist of its great clarity and exactness, which hardly bear translation into our barbarous tongue.

'I am chagrined, Sir,' she said after some thought, 'that though you mention friendship and benevolence, you make no mention of love, which is surely the strongest and most exalted of emotions, and most worthy of poetic expression?'

I immediately embarked on an enthusiastic description of the Houyhnhnms' beliefs and practices with regard to marriage, the rearing of children, and the coming of death, these being the major topics upon which any disquisition upon the nature of love must touch.

'Love is neither a concept nor an emotion that Houyhnhnms understand, or experience, nor does their language have a word for it . . . Love, as you are pleased to recommend it, is the illusion that one being is innately preferable to another, which while often true is no reason to make a special attachment to them.'

During the course of this disquisition, which I thought admirably succinct and well-expressed, and could not but convince any impartial listener, my wife began to wring her hands, and tears filled her eyes.

She waved her hand, to beg me to stop.

'But, Sir,' she said in a voice surprising in its firmness, 'surely even these horses . . .' Seeing the look on my face she quickly corrected

herself. '. . . these Houyhnhnms, must regret the passing of their immediate families, and grieve for the loss of those with whom they have shared so much? Surely any reasonable being – as it pleases you to call them – would grieve for the loss of a loved one?'

It was by now clear that poor Mrs Gulliver was incapable of understanding what I had put before her.

'My Master and his race do not base their attachments on love, and regard death as natural and inevitable. They experience no grief at the departure of their attachments, nor does the dying person discover the least regret that he is leaving.'

Mary rose to her feet.

'I do not, Sir, wish to hear anything more of this. That your "noble" race can adhere to such sentiments is sufficient indication that they are a cold and bloodless species, incapable of any exalted feeling or special tenderness towards those whom nature has placed closest together . . .'

I started to interject, but she waved me away.

'I can understand this well enough: you treat me as if I were a beast both contemptible and stupid, a response, I dare say, caused by the delusions that have overtaken you, and from which I hope God may one day grant some respite . . .'

I began to reply, but she was already leaving the room.

'I beg your leave, Sir, for there is nothing to be gained by continuing here. I wish you a good night, and shall see you in the morrow, when I hope we can begin again the process of coming to some fruitful, and mutual, understanding and regard.'

I rose, wanting nothing more than to return to my humble lodgings, and the gentle company of my stable-mates.

I was increasingly worried that as the situation darkened, Rudy would be disturbed by it. Gulliver does not 'love' his family. That means his grandson too; Rudy would hardly fail to note that.

He'd lain more quietly this time, and though I heard a murmur of distress when Mary chastises her husband, he soon settled back, fully engrossed. Reuben had not figured in this section – in retrospect a mistake; perhaps I could add something when I got home – and Rudy may simply have been waiting for him to reappear, which of course he will.

'You know, last night? When we were reading? He should have put up a sign, Gampy.'

'Who should? What sign?'

'Captain Gulliver, silly. *Do not let Enigma eat the flowers!*'

So, it was about him after all, even in his absence! And it is, of course. But not only about him.

'You're entirely right. How clever of you! I'll add that later.'

'Can we have more now? Please?'

'I'm sorry, darling, that's it for today. Gampy is tired now, and so are you. There's still plenty to come.'

I wasn't certain – he was hard to read sometimes – but I suspect he was relieved, really.

Chapter 10

My appointment for interview is in the humble police station in Buckingham Palace Road. 2.00 p.m I have been instructed to present myself at reception, where they will be expecting me. I don't know which 'they' to expect. Will DrearyScot and DopeyCroat pass me on to other inexplicably initialled members of the force? Or do they get to carry on with me, assisting them in their inquiries?

Lucky them. Unlike other suspected villains, I will not prevaricate, do not need to be encouraged, threatened or suborned, will tell the simple truth, if there is such a thing as truth, and if it could ever be simple. They are the police, and they will not understand. Instead, they will write it all down, and pass it on to someone else – higher up the D-Chain – who will not understand it either, or if they think they do, will have no sympathy either for the line of thought, or the predicament that caused it. They are binary folk, reducers. This? Or that? Simplify. Make it clear. Get your category right. Process. Procedure. Progress. Bit like Sam, really, only consequential, though on reflection his behaviour has produced consequences of which none of us could have dreamed.

Philip warned me that I need clearly to understand what will happen in my interview with the Met. Did I realise, he enquired archly, that I was 'not unlikely' – a careful double negative designed both to frighten and to mollify – that I was not unlikely to be arrested, and charged? It was essential to be legally represented during my interview. He recommended a defence lawyer so eminent that even I have heard of him. He is as expensive in his legal field as Chanticleer IV in his organic one.

That was good advice, and I have no intention of following it. Though I'm finished with Dickens, I am of his persuasion with regard to the wearying absurdity and mendacity of the courts of justice, and of lawyers. Kafka's too. *Jarndyce v. Jarndyce* drags into the far horizon, poor Josef K is found guilty without knowing with what he is charged. I will not participate in such absurd rituals, will opt out by opting in. I will simply go to my appointment, alone, and simply tell the simple truth as I see it, which is, if not complicated, at least in need of careful explication.

I tried to explain this at the time, to an incredulous Lucy and that blabbermouth Sam, neither of whom could take in what I was saying: that I was an agent in Suzy's death, and had acted to relieve her distress. Had done both bad and good, was guilty and innocent, together. This seemed simple enough to me at the time. I can tolerate ambiguity and moral complexity; I seek it out, I revel in it. I was educated to do so, unlike the police, who are presumably trained not to.

I explained this to Philip over the phone, insisting that I would represent myself at the interview, and say what I had to say in my own words. He was silent at the other end for longer than strictly necessary, or seemly.

'In that case, James, please, at the very least, write out a statement of the facts as you understand them, in advance, and read it to the police. In that way you will have a record of what you have said, and are less likely to go off piste in your statement, which could be disastrous.'

I agree to this minimum requirement and make a note on my small writing pad: 'Piste, off: NOT.'

'The police will then want to question you about what you have said. You will have no obligation to answer . . .'

'But, Philip, I want to answer. I have nothing to hide.'

'Very admirable,' he said drily. 'Speaking both honestly and without representation is a capital form of integrity, very likely to end with you in jail.'

'I understand that.' I didn't, of course, not really; it still felt hypothetical, literary. I thanked him, and promised to send him a copy of my proposed statement before going to see my DS and DC.

To this point the notion of jail hadn't seriously occurred to me, though it certainly had to Lucy, who was constantly on the phone begging me to get a lawyer, and to shut up, and *not* to help the police in their inquiries.

'Look, Dad, Sam got it wrong, didn't he? What you said in the garden that day was that you *wished* you had given Mum a final dose to end her misery, but that you couldn't go through with it, just helped her get off to sleep. Sam misremembered, and blabbed to his group, but what he said wasn't accurate, and they heard the wrong story, and got the wrong end of the stick. I have talked to him about this . . .' There was a long pause. 'And he now accepts that he got it wrong, and will say so to the police. I will too.'

Ducks. It might even have worked, especially if – or I must mean when – Dr Larry confirms that the death certificate was accurate, and that he had no reason to have doubts about the cause of death. But might the police exhume Suzy's poor body? Determine what was in it other than the requisite maggots? Assuming traces of her final cocktail survived. I know nothing of such things, and don't wish to think of them.

Of course, Lucy wants me to lie, or at least to distort the truth; she cannot face the coming trials both legal and psychological. And the prospect of me going to jail, with my stress-registering heart and fading health, is simply intolerable for her. That's understandable, and I love her and wish to protect her from distress, if I could.

I spent the next few days drafting a form of words to read to the police and emailed it to Philip. I got a response two days later:

Dear James,

This is clear, honest and accurate. It puts you – I almost said therefore – in great peril, and I advise you most strenuously not to make such a statement. But if you insist, I will find you the right representation. I know you fancy representing yourself, Rumpoling about at the Old Bailey, but that would be madness. If you are determined to take the stand in your own defence, you cannot do so if you are representing yourself. You know nothing of the law, and seem determined not to learn. So at least agree to this minimum requirement? Limit yourself to reading the statement, and do not answer subsequent questions. You are under no legal obligation to do so.

It was impossible not to agree, and so I did, regretfully, knowing that when the questions came, I would answer them. I'm a schoolmaster, however retired and retiring. Answering questions is what we do.

The quality of the greeting and processing of we murder suspects at the police station is beyond reproach: polite, efficient, and so mutedly agreeable that I almost expected the young policewoman behind the counter to say she was sorry to hear of my troubles. Instead she suggested I have a seat in one of the nearby waiting areas, until I was called.

It took over an hour. Even my dentist is quicker than that. By the time DroopyScrotum came to collect me, I was in a strop. I hate being kept waiting; it makes me feel undervalued and diminished. Presumably it suits the police to interview suspects whose equilibrium is malfunctioning.

'Ah, Dr Darke,' he said. 'Would you like to follow me?'

As we walked from one corridor to another, ascended in a lift, and traversed several further passages, DS walked a step behind me and to my left, in readiness at any moment to catch hold of my shoulder if I were to bolt. I had no desire to do so, was ambling along in what I can only describe as a state of extreme dissociation of sensibility. Thinking, not feeling. Or, contrariwise, feeling not thinking. At one moment analysing the unrolling process, at the next my hearty gerbil scrabbling about in my chest bag, paradoxically animated by the tranquillisers I'd ingested an hour before.

Bloody T. S. Eliot thought this a regrettable bifurcation, this separation of thinking from feeling, postulating that it first afflicted we poor English some time in the seventeenth century. Before that we had all those histrionic dopes in Shakespeare, making a fuss, simultaneously explaining themselves and tearing their eyes out.

I believe in separating thinking from feeling; it makes one safer, and more rational. Dissociation of sensibility is one of the triumphs of civilisation. To shepherd one's thought into line with every passing emotion, with the thump of the heart or the stirring of the groin, the angry raising of the voice, the hand, the gun? These need to be retarded by reflection. Hold on. Don't let your feelings run away with you. Think!

According to Mr Eliot this is undesirable. Which it may be if you are a button-up puckermouth from Kansas City, keen to distinguish a whore from a Madonna. But for us normal people such a split is to be welcomed.

I didn't feel safe – who could? – but outwardly I tried to appear calm, and had my prepared statement typed on three pages of paper, tucked into an envelope in my jacket pocket. I'd been unsure how to dress for such an occasion. I expected my detective might be in intimidating uniform, but he wore the same old suit, this time without a tie, as if I were not worth the bother of dressing up for. I'd settled on a navy blazer, grey moleskin trousers, white shirt and muted tie in greens with a touch of dark red.

DS stepped ahead of me smartly to open a door, stepped back to allow me to enter. DC was seated at a table, and rose to greet me.

'Dr Darke.' It was said with a very slight upward inflection, as if asking me to confirm my identity. Who the hell else was I? Was this a residual Croatian habit of speech perhaps, a sign of not fully mastered English? His eyes were hooded, as if he were looking forward to an afternoon of ethnic cleansing. Weren't they the bastards who killed the poor Bosnians? I can't get the Balkans straight; they keep shifting about, no matter how much Olivia Manning one reads. I still have no idea where Yugoslavia went. Give me my DrearyScot anytime, at least he was British. An interrogation by my Caledonian peer.

I sat down in the indicated chair, in a room from which all distinguishing characteristics had been stripped: institutional, dusty and windowless. DS read me my rights, and informed me that I would be helping them with their inquiries under caution. I'd internetted the standard form of words, and couldn't see anything to object to, so didn't bother to listen.

When he finished, there was a pause.

'Do you understand this?' he asked.

'Yes.'

'Thank you for helping with this inquiry. Please understand that this interview is being recorded. May I have your mobile phone, please?'

'I don't have it with me.'

'In that case would you please stand up?'

He frisked me efficiently; presumably he rarely met a human unaccompanied by a telephone.

'Let me begin by asking—'

I interrupted quickly, as I'd been advised.

'I would like to make a statement. I will leave it with you when this interview is over. After I have read my statement, I am prepared to answer questions.'

A feral, malicious delight registered on the face of DC Slobodan. I was *prepared* to answer questions? As if I were in charge, and he being interrogated. DS Angus, on the other hand, merely raised an eyebrow, gave the smug grimace that passes for a smile in Edinburgh, and nodded his head gently in tacit admission that I, for just this fleeting moment, might presume myself in charge.

I took the envelope from my jacket packet, opened it, and withdrew the three pages. Put them in order on the table before me, looked up, and began to read.

'You what? You said what? Are you fucking crazy?'

We were sitting in the parlour – as Sam calls it, it tickles me to do the same – in Lucy's house, Sam bustling about in the kitchen pouring water onto granules, Rudy away for the late afternoon, playing at some friend's. He had agreed to this reluctantly, but I had reassured him on the phone the night before that I had finished our Voyage V and was anxious to come to read some more to him.

Thank God he wasn't there. I wish I'd had a friend to go and play with too.

I didn't tell Lucy about my interview at the police station until a few days afterwards, when I could come up to Oxfordshire and break the news to her – to them – in person. I was tempted to do this by email, or even by phone. Emotional life is best conducted at a safe distance; I never understand why it is regarded as more honest, and a higher form of integrity, to say things face to face. I once had a brief flirtation with the mother of one of my pupils, which she ended with a short, courteous note, addressed to me at the school. She knew how to behave, after having misbehaved.

In their parlour, I tried, in my ham-fisted way, to let the narrative unfold slowly. Told them that I had been invited – so much nicer a term than summoned – to help the police with their inquiries, and to make a statement. That I had done so, a few days ago …

Lucy had been crying since she opened the door to me, some fifteen minutes earlier. Hugged me fiercely as I entered, as if trying to squeeze me to death. It hurt.

'What did you say? I don't want a bloody précis – you can't be trusted to get things right. Let me see it.'

I'd brought a printout of my statement. She took it brusquely from my hand, sat down, reading slowly, muttering as she did. She was no longer bothering to wipe her eyes or (even more offensively) her nose. She sat snuffling, dripping and weeping.

'You promised! We agreed we would tell the same story. That Sam –' who was hiding in the kitchen (it wouldn't have surprised me if he had been banished there, and now slept in the oven) – 'had got it wrong: that what I really said was—'

'I'm sorry, darling. That was your idea. I never agreed to it, not for a second.'

She stood up abruptly, be-mucused and glowering.

'You want to, do you? You actually want to go to jail? Are you totally insane? Do you know what this will do?'

It is possible to say the same thing in the same way, or indeed in different ways, too many times. Read Oscar Wilde and you will know what I mean. Was I being accused of killing the things that I loved? There was nothing heroic about the process; it was pure and untrammelled, unadulterated, fine, unrefined egotism. I was doing what I wanted, for my own reasons, whatever the consequences to my family – they'd fall in line, and eventually get over it – and to myself. Following no advice: neither Philip's insistence that I bring counsel to my interrogation, or otherwise remain silent; nor Lucy and Sam's insistence that I adhere to a premeditated lie.

Sam returned with cups of hot brown liquid and a plate of chocolate Hobnobs, and put them down gently on the table, like an ageing butler who fears for his livelihood, obsequious and silent, yet with the temerity to seat himself next to his queen and mistress. Who did not deign to thank or to acknowledge him.

Lucy handed him the three pages, and he lowered his head.

'And then? Then what? You answered questions?'

'Of course.'

'But Philip told you not to. We discussed that – best either to have a lawyer there, or to shut up. You have such a big mouth you can fit both feet in it!'

'But darling, it was just a matter of routine. Same old, same old. Perfectly predictable, and I had anticipated the questions in my statement, and answered them. The key is whether my action was premeditated, and whether my intention was to—'

She was on her feet in a moment, almost knocking over her cup as she banged against the coffee table; she approached me directly, bent over a good deal closer than is agreeable, and put her wet, bedraggled face inches from mine.

'Don't you dare! How dare you? Shut up! Shut the fuck up!'

Even Sam could see that this was threatening to get out of hand, and he summoned a soothing gesture and a placating expression as he rose to put an arm round her shoulders. Lucy didn't so much throw it off as shudder it away, as if an airborne snail had landed on her.

And at that very moment – evidence that there is a Providence that shapes our ends – her phone began to ring. She fished in her pockets, didn't find it, looked about. Sam lifted it from the coffee table just in front of her, handed it over.

'Yes? Lucy here.'

She listened for a moment, her expression by turns weary and furious.

'It's good of you to call, Diana, but I'm sure he's all right. It's just that he knows . . . Yes, yes, put him on.'

I could hear a muted tinny tone.

'Yes, darling, I'm sure it's just a little tummy ache. Maybe Diana could give you something fizzy to settle your stomach?'

She listened for a few more seconds, exasperated but with what may have been a tinge of relief on her features.

'OK then, Daddy will come and pick you up. I'm sure you'll feel better as soon as you get home . . . Yes, yes, I know it hurts, never mind.'

She clicked the off button and put the phone in her pocket, her face filled with such conflicting emotions that her facial features had been replaced by an amorphous mass of tears and snot, anger, anxiety, relief.

I hesitated. There was nothing I could say that wouldn't make things worse. Sam drew the same conclusion, and headed for the door.

'A tummy ache. That's his default position when he wants something he can't have. He'll come in clutching his stomach, and ten minutes later he'll be bright as a button, asking for ice-cream. But what he really wants is you.'

'Maybe,' I said hesitantly, 'maybe that's for the best.'

'It is what it is,' said Lucy. 'When he gets home, you can take him upstairs and read to him. I'm going to have a lie-down – I've had enough of all three of you.'

'I'm sorry we were interrupted . . .'

She snorted.

'But if you have anything else to say?'

'To say? What's left to say? It's a disaster, and you're not merely welcoming it, you're causing it!'

'I look at it,' I said, *evenly* I would call it, 'as an opportunity.'

When Rudy the in-valid returned, he rushed into the parlour, and into my arms. I lifted him up as best I could, and kissed him on the top of his head.

'Is your tummy very bad?' I asked, puckishly.

He was sufficiently cunning to pause for a moment, as if interrogating his symptoms.

'I think it is starting to feel a little better,' he said, slowly. 'Maybe I was hungry.'

Sam went to the kitchen to make fish fingers and chips, which appeared in ten minutes, and disappeared in three. Rudy wiped his lips with his piece of kitchen towelling, rose, and took me by the hand.

'Now, Gampy, can you read to me now?'

'Of course I can.' I was so grateful to be released from the frightful scene with Lucy that I would have read to the Devil himself, and thanked him for indulging me.

By the time I made my way upstairs to Rudy's room, he had pulled up a chair for me at the side of the bed, turned on his lamp, fluffed his pillows, and settled down.

'You remember where we were last time?' I asked. 'You know Gulliver was having—'

'I remember,' he said. 'Carry on!'

After a time, events were to occur that transformed my life, to rob it of ease and regularity, for in the months following my meeting with Mr Sympson, and prompted by his having broadcast my tale with such enthusiasm, I became a figure of interest, and derision. My wife has told me that my story has created a considerable sensation, and that the newspapers make constant reference, though the responses my tale drew from the critics – the most pernicious scallywags of the entire Yahoo congregation – were of scant interest to me.

But they were greatly interesting to others. Learning the location of my marital home, curious crowds began to assemble, and their number grew steadily. Though I tried to limit my appearances in public places to the hours of darkness, and my wife and servants had been enjoined to the utmost discretion with regard to the details of my life, when it was learned that I was, as it was deemed, a madman, who walked and talked like a horse, and lived on oats in a stable, the throng of insatiably curious rabble increased dramatically.

HorseMan! I was called, and mobs of drunken and violent men, women and even children screamed it in front of my humble abode, day and night. My story was broadcast widely over cups of coffee and tobacco, and glasses of ale, on the street corners and in the domestic quarters of many a home. Soon enough the newspapers dubbed me the First HorseMan, presuming whimsically that three more of me might cause the Apocalypse, and herald the extinction of the human race.

I could only wish that were true. During my happy time resident in their land, the Council of the Houyhnhnms contemplated the mass eradication of the Yahoos as a way of cleansing their domain, but were much impressed by my counter-suggestion that it would be more efficient, and less likely to cause an insurrection, simply to castrate all male Yahoos, and let nature take its course. Were the same to happen to the men of humankind it would be a great blessing, and were I still of fathering disposition, I would most certainly submit myself to the surgeon's knife.

Strong stuff. No harm in that. Rudy showed no signs of distress, however, and I was sensible not to interrogate him about how much he understood.

*F*urther demonstrations, parodies and satires followed. I was denounced from pulpits across the land, and several lawyers and churchmen were apparently keen to try me on charges of heresy. Man was made in the image of God! To describe him as a noxious beast, with grace neither in this life nor certainly in the next, was surely actionable!

Soon there was in circulation a rumour of a woundingly offensive poem by Mr Pope, entitled 'Mary Gulliver to Captain Lemuel Gulliver'. This diminutive wit had made it his endeavour to look down upon things, as a corrective to the fact that he spent his entire life-time looking up on whatever passed before him, Yahoo and Horse alike. It is no wonder he aimed the multiple barbs of his malice upon me, as Lilliputians did their arrows, and like those arrows some were irritating, and the cumulative effect wounding, not merely to me (who expected no less) but to my dear wife Mary, most vilely included in this noxious satire.

Many of the braying populace had been apprised of my contempt for their race, their nature, behaviour and ineradicable malice. As if to prove me right they came in increasing numbers, drunken from the taverns, shouting abuse, hurling eggs and vegetables at my stable door, sneaking up in the night to urinate and to defecate on its portals. What had the King of Brobdingnag so rightly called them? 'The most pernicious race of little odious vermin that nature ever suffered to crawl upon the surface of the earth!'

I resolved to rouse myself from my torpor and fearfulness, and to confront the massed crowd in the market square close by my house. To this end I composed a flyer, which I had posted in many local hostelries, churches and places of work and education, inviting the populace to hear a lecture, in which Captain Lemuel Gulliver would recount his many adventures. My wife deemed this enterprise fool-hardy in the extreme, and without apprising me had organised a gang of rough men, who would stand at the front, looking as if they were members of my audience, but who might protect me in case of trouble.

The news passed round quickly, and when the time came some days later, there were some hundreds of people massed, a hum of anticipation, and some hostility too, if I gauged the mood correctly.

Nevertheless, I boarded the constructed platform, and waved my arms for silence. The noise died somewhat, for whatever their animus, there was more amusement to be had in listening to me than in shouting me down. I attempted to moderate my enunciation, for by now I had begun to find comfort in my native tongue, and to sound more man than horse.

When I began with a brief account of my Voyages to Lilliput and Brobdingnag, there were gasps and increasing hoots of derision. I was confident, however, that I had sufficient attention from many of the incredulous mass that they would quieten their fellows and allow me to carry on. Occasional cries of Poppycock! rang out, but I kept their attention until I began to talk about my dear Houyhnhnms, and the dreadful Yahoos, who, I had to admit, were not unlike ourselves. This was too much even for the most patient and open-minded of my audience, and within a few moments of hearing of the supreme virtues of my Master and his kind, there were increasing profanities in the air, and not a few vegetables as well. When one of these, a large and over-ripe tomato, hit me square in the nose, I left the platform, and the derision increased.

'HorseMan!' screamed the crowd. 'Let's ride him!' A number had whips, which they began to flick menacingly through the air. Hiding behind my hired protectors, I made my way back to the house, just managing to close the door.

'Well!' said my wife, both angry and relieved. 'What did I tell you, Sir? This was a most foolhardy attempt. You cannot reason with such rabble, not when the story you wish to tell, and the lessons you wish to convey, are anathema to your audience!'

I was sufficiently shaken by the experience to partake of a glass of port, my first since returning from my travels, which went straight to my head, and I thence to sleep in the nearest chair. I awoke some hours later, chastened, and urgently calling my dear wife, I hastened to apologise most sincerely for putting myself, and all of us, in danger. As I expressed these sentiments, and without thinking better of

*myself, I took her hand, and was about to embrace her when I hesi-
tated, and backed away.*

Rudy leant across the bed, and grasped my hand.

I'd been – what was that nice phrase? – economical with the truth.
Told Lucy what she expected to hear about the questions I'd been
asked after reading my statement, and what my answers had been.
Nothing false about that, just falsifying. Because I hadn't expected
the nature of the questions asked by the police, which had filled
me with anxiety, and admiration, and to a degree, suspense. What
possible line of thought could they have been pursuing?

DS had in front of him, placed squarely on the desk in a
symmetrical manner of which I could only approve, a fat file of
material, encased in a grey folder with some sort of identifying
marks on the front. It was a good two inches thick. He paused for
a look through, pulled out a sheet, perused it, put it back, made a
Scottish face, looked at another. What could the fat file possibly
contain? Certainly not the results of their so far limited and fruitless research. Perhaps they had padded it to intimidate me with the
sheer weight of the evidence, filled it with the football schedules
and results and clippings of Patrick Thistle and other Caledonian
Rangers football teams?

He looked up with the kind of curious thoughtfulness, and
muted scepticism, that I associate with David Hume, one of the
few Scots who wasn't a waste of DNA. Unlike the gabby bibulous
Irish – who have as many pressing issues as a choirboy trapped in a
confessional – the Scots are unfamiliar with literary genius. Imagine
a nation who revere that flatulent haggis Walter Scott!

What an agreeable formulation. My interlocutors could never
have guessed the cause of my quiet smile of self-congratulation.
Flatulent haggis. Marvellous! I roll the new coinage round my
mouth and mind, I taste it, it nourishes my spirits.

In the beginning is the word; a single one can transform good to evil, dead to alive, ugly to beautiful, serious to frivolous. Even God isn't that deft. Is the Almighty benign or malevolent? The answer in a word, sir, is either, it's up to you. And be warned: the wrong choice can send you straight to jail, or to the gallows. And, right here, right now, there's my own linguistic case: consider the word 'merciful'. If you add that to killing – as I did – the transformation is so complete that you generate a new noun: mercy-killing. And that's it, really. That's my words, my case, my defence.

DS waited patiently, put his piece of paper back into the folder, closed and placed in back into its allotted space, looked up, and said with unexpected gentleness, like a pastor in the local kirk, 'Tell me, Dr Darke, did you love your wife?'

Next to him, DopeyCroat could not contain a snort, then some ferocious, bushy eyelid-lowering disapproval. He was the hard cop, and had been glaring at me as if at a hovel full of Bosnians he was about to relocate.

Philip warned me that they might try to catch me off my guard, to be prepared not merely for the obvious questions, but the unexpected ones as well.

'They may try to unsettle you, make you drop your guard. Don't. Think before you answer, if you answer at all. Best to say nothing to all questions and inquiries, expected or otherwise.'

For the next moments, I followed his advice.

DeviousScotsman waited patiently, his eyes seeking but not finding mine, which I had lowered. In thought, and with a sharp – and no doubt prompted – rush of emotion.

He nodded as if delighted to acknowledge the response in my silence, pleased to the chill cynical depths of his Caledonian heart, opened his folder and examined a few pages thoughtfully.

He knew, as I knew, and was reminding me as if I needed reminding: they don't die, the dead. They're not gone. Hence, not dead. They go on living and dying before our eyes, that is the afterlife, they remain with us, and with them they bring thoughts too viscerally distressing to tolerate. We cringe and avert our eyes, divert our attention.

Dead and not dead, as we are alive and not dead, and soon to be dead, and reminded of this when we cannot forget it; it is the primary purpose of our lives to expunge the thought of our own demise. Once we learn this it will not go away. This happens at some age or other – don't ask me, what do I know about the demographics of psycho-mortality? For me it happened rather late, really, with the late Suzy, who will not go away, who is more alive to me, and more present, than anyone I know, or have known. It has something of her habitual malice, this relentless persistence, this unwillingness to get into her damn grave, and stay there, transforming herself into fertile matter. Her liquacious, loquacious spirit transcends its boundaries, leaks out from her supposed resting place into mine, in which I too find no rest.

DS was inviting her in, as if there were room for all of us, as if only her presence could animate and unwrap the conundrum of her death.

Why make it easy for him, and me, and all of us? Why not resist this invasiveness, why not repel Suzy too? She doesn't need to be here, nor does she want to be. She'd be appalled.

'I'm not entirely clear,' I said, inadvertently dropping into a hint of a Scottish accent, a trace of the drear Enlightenment in my tone, 'not at all clear what would count as an answer to that question.'

He looked rightly puzzled.

'Ye might begin with "yes" or "no", and soldier on from there. But this is the right place for us to commence. Because what we have here is – isn't it? – a tragedy of love.'

'Is it?'

'And like all tragedies, it ends in death, and elicits our sympathy.'

I was being instructed on the nature of tragedy? By a policeman? He dangled the question in front of me, as if daring me into an embarrassing admission, or an even more humiliating exhibition of pedantry, some reference to Aristotle perhaps. Or might it have been, simply, an attempt at understanding, or – even worse – an expression of fellow feeling: there but for good fortune go I?

He was getting ahead of me. I hadn't yet disclosed whether I loved my wife. I did, and still do. I closed my eyes, and they waited, DS patiently, DC with the hostility of a rabid warthog.

If Suzy had been invited into the room, she bloody well wasn't coming. Good for her. Anyway, I knew well enough what her response and counsel would have been. *Fucking hell, James, tell that cunt to fuck off! What business is it of his?*

DS waited patiently. He had all day, all the days, and wasn't going to squander them on impatience, unlike his bristly colleague, who would willingly have knocked me into some kind of mis-shape. No, the longer this went on, the better DS'd like it. And, yes, it was his business, and his right to conduct it as he wished, even to the point of impertinently enquiring whether I loved – why the past tense? – my wife.

At which point, during this pleasant interregnum in our relations, while I pondered and he waited like Socrates for the right answer to the right question, he suddenly stood up.

'I'm so sorry,' he said. 'I haven't even offered you something to drink. Can I get you coffee, or tea perhaps?'

Nothing could better have indicated how little he understood me, how far apart were our worlds. As if I would contemplate a cup of police 'coffee', or even worse, their builder's tea. In a chipped and stained mug with lips as thick as his DC's, and almost as repellent.

'No, thank you. A glass of water would be welcome, though.'

He rose and left the room. It was obviously some sort of gambit: exit the good cop, remain the bad. He returned to the glowering silence a few minutes later, and placed the water in front of me. The glass was clean enough to see through, just, though it hadn't recently visited a dishwasher for delousing. One sip and I risked refurbishing my fragile DNA with that of a conga line of paedophiles and serial killers, whose dispositions would all too quickly commandeer my bloodstream, and pulse through my genes. On my journey home, I would find myself ogling the juicy children, as I shopped for knives.

DumbCroat watched me investigate and reject the glass, and sneered.

'Now,' said my watery benefactor, 'where were we?'

A rhetorical question requires no response.

'Ah, yes, we were talking about your feelings for your late wife …'

We weren't, but it would have been pedantic to say so.

He opened his file, on the top of which he had placed the copy of the statement I had read to them earlier. He read through it carefully, and stopped, with his finger on the page.

'You have said …' He peered down, as if myopically. 'That you gave the late Mrs Moulton a drink of tea in which you say you had dissolved "a quantity of Digoxin and Diazepam", and disguised the bitterness by the addition of honey. That she drank it, fell into a deep sleep, and died before the night was out.'

I nodded.

'Can you tell me what quantities of these drugs you administered? And what other drugs you might have added to the mix?'

'I wasn't thinking clearly, I was distraught, and had been drinking wine. I'm not sure I remember.'

'How much wine, sir?'

'I don't recall. It was a long night.'

'Do you take Digoxin yourself?'

'I take it as needed. So I often have a quantity available before I need to renew the prescription.'

'What dosage have you been prescribed?'

'I don't know. I take one tablet.'

'You don't know? Surely it says on the dispensing bottle?'

'I suppose so. I remember emptying the contents into a mortar, and then adding a lot of Diazepam tablets …'

'How many? And what strength are they?'

'I'm not sure of that either. I shook the bottle to make sure it had tablets in it, then opened it and put them all in, and mashed them into a powder. Then I put them into a cup and added some hot water until they dissolved, and added it to the tea. Then I stirred in the honey ...'

He looked more than puzzled.

'Surely, Dr Darke, surely you would make some attempt to calibrate the dosage, and to ascertain the possible effects. This information is easily available.'

'I suppose it is. But I didn't. I just assumed that enough would be enough ...'

'Enough for what?'

'To ease her distress.'

He looked even more puzzled.

'But if you wanted to offer pain relief, surely the doctor, and the nurses from the hospice, could have administered adequate and increasing dosages of whatever Dr Weinberg had prescribed. That is common practice.'

'She didn't want it. She said it made her go away, and she was determined to stay as long as she could.'

'I see. So you made her go away entirely then?'

'I suppose so.'

'You say that your intention in doing so was to relieve her distress?'

'It was. She was in terrible pain, and had been pleading to die.'

'So you say. Pleading with whom, may I ask?'

'I don't know. God perhaps?'

He looked up, and waited patiently for a moment.

'Was she a believer, then? I see she is buried in Oxfordshire, and you had a Christian burial service.'

'She was neither a believer, nor an unbeliever. She thought these are useless categories.'

'That's very modern of her, no doubt. What were her religious beliefs then?'

'We were members of that congregation – we joined it when we lived in Oxford – and were contributors to the restoration of the church.'

He dug out another page and perused it.

'How often would you say you attended services?'

'I'm not sure I can recall ...'

'Neither can the vicar.'

It was hard to see much point in this, and I must have looked irritated.

'I ask because it seems to me unlikely that the late Mrs Moulton would have made a last-minute appeal for God's mercy – though you can never tell – so perhaps she was asking for yours?'

'I hardly think myself an adequate stand-in for God.'

He looked up from his page and stared at me.

'Don't you now?'

Had someone blabbed to him? Sam, presumably. For if I recall that unhappy moment in the garden after Lucy had accused me of murdering her mother, I had claimed exactly this: that if the dying are to be delivered from their final agony, and God is char-acteristically unwilling, or uninterested, or otherwise engaged, then somebody has to act in his place.

Best not to answer, though DS waited patiently for a time. As did I. The room was increasingly stuffy, without a window to open, though there was some sort of dusty and cobwebbed vent in the ceiling. His colleague waited less patiently, made a gruff hoggy noise and was about to intervene when DS raised his hand to silence him.

'Tell me, doctor, what was your intention in giving this drink to your wife?' He looked at my statement again. 'You say that it was to relieve her agony ...What does that mean, exactly?'

'It means what it says.'

'You must forgive me,' he said, 'but it isn't as clear to me as it seems to be to you. Let me rephrase the question. At the time of making up this drink, and administering it, did you intend merely to put your wife to sleep or to kill her? Because if it was merely a strong sleeping draught, then I do not understand the presence of the Digoxin.'

Indeed.

'The Digoxin is prescribed for your heart arrhythmia, is it not? And the Diazepam for your anxiety? I can find no medical records for your wife being prescribed either of these drugs.'

'She took tranquillisers many years ago, when she had depression.'

'When was that exactly?'

'I'm not sure. In her late twenties, I believe.'

He made a note, and looked through the files again.

'When she died, how did you feel?'

'How did I feel? How do you suppose I felt? I was devastated, obliterated ...'

'Of course. Were you also surprised? Was this the result you expected? And if it was, surely you would have felt relief as well, that you had released her from her agony?'

I had addressed these questions in my statement, though he did not revert to it. Expected? I hadn't expected anything, other than the cessation of Suzy's distress. That was my intention: her death was, as it were, an accompanying by-product, not an intended consequence. That this answer was unclear, ambiguous, confused and unsatisfactory, was as obvious to me as it was to them.

'I see that the death certificate, signed by Dr Lawrence Weinberg, records the cause of death as heart failure.'

'That's what happened, isn't it?'

'Indeed. That is the cause of all deaths, or at least it accompanies them ... I have interviewed Dr Weinberg, who says he had no reason to suppose the death was in any way suspicious,' he said, suspiciously.

'Indeed,' I said.

'Can you tell me something about the relationship between Dr Weinberg and the late Mrs Moulton?'

'They met at a tennis club in London and formed a very

successful mixed doubles team. They were both Oxbridge tennis Blues ...'

'So I gather. They must have been a powerful pair. Did they have a social relationship?'

'We saw him and his wife several times for dinner.'

'Indeed. Mrs Weinberg says you cut off relations with them ...'

'That's not right. We just recognised, after a few meetings, that we were not socially compatible as couples.'

'Did Mrs Moulton see Dr Weinberg socially, outside of time on the court?'

'Yes.'

He went painstakingly through the details, of which he had a substantial number. Dates. Meetings at restaurants, receipts for rooms at hotels, the works.

'How did you feel about this affair?'

'It doesn't matter how I felt. I had no choice. I tolerated it. These things happen ...'

'I see. Was it a common occurrence? Are you suggesting that she had other lovers?'

'I don't know.'

He consulted the dratted file again, made a face, and continued his line of questioning. He circled back, to quiz me about my intentions, how and when I had decided to prepare the fatal draught, how I had mixed and administered it, what had happened afterwards, why I had afterwards locked myself into the house for all those months.

An hour or two, maybe more, went by. Question followed question, sometimes followed by answers; at other times I remained silent, as was my right. The details don't matter. Or no doubt they matter very much, but I can't be bothered with them.

'Well, Dr Darke,' he said, 'the position seems clear, doesn't it? Your wife was in her death throes, but she may have had a short time to live, according to her doctor. You decided to give her a drug-infused draught of indeterminate dosage, according to you, of Digoxin and Diazepam, after which she soon died. You had the stated motive of trying to relieve her agony, and a possible further motive in punishing her infidelity . . .'

I had anticipated this line of questioning, and did not rise to the bait.

He paused, and took several sheets of paper from his file.

'Can you tell me why you have not applied for probate on your late wife's estate?'

'Excuse me? I haven't what?'

'Your wife's estate hasn't been processed in any way. Can you explain this?'

I couldn't. I hadn't thought about it, assumed that Lucy would be getting on with whatever needed to be done. I don't need money. Though my parents' pittance went to some Australian charity for saving kangaroos or koalas, I had my inheritance from my grandparents to keep me warm, in its cosy, expanding account at Coutts.

DS continued rifling through the papers.

'Your wife inherited the full estate of Sir Henry Moulton, and later of her mother, Lady Moulton. That came to something just over two million pounds, some years ago. What happened to this money?'

'I have no idea.'

He looked surprised to hear that such a sum could evaporate into a cloud of unknowing, and even more unaccountably, indifference.

'I see. Was it in the bank? In property? In shares? Did your wife have a financial advisor?'

'If she did I have no idea who it might have been. You see, we didn't really need the money, we had ample for our needs.'

'Indeed. Your wife died intestate, did she not?'

'I think so.'

'You think so?'

'Yes. I do.'

'Which of course means that most of her estate, when you can be bothered to process it, goes to you, as her spouse.'

'Does it?'

'It does. Though she might, of course, have had a last-minute change of mind and drafted a will that was less generous to you ...'

I paused, appalled. This was enough, this was outrageous.

'Change of mind? Last-minute? She was dying, she was gone, she didn't have a mind to change. How dare you insinuate—'

He'd had enough too.

'It is clear to me, Dr Darke, on the basis of this evidence –' he pointed to his folder – 'and of this interview that you had ample opportunity, means and motive to cause and to profit from the premature death of your late wife. You admit that you administered a final dose of drugs, presumably sufficient either to kill her, or to hasten her death.'

I could find nothing to disagree with in this admirably succinct statement, so did not bother even to nod.

'I am, therefore, placing you under arrest, and referring the case to the Crown Prosecution Service. You will hear from them in good time. In the meantime, you will almost certainly be granted bail and asked to give us your passport, and an undertaking to make your whereabouts known at all times. Before you leave the station you will be fingerprinted and your DNA sample taken.'

The ensuing procedure was even more humiliating and discomfiting than my interview. While bail was being arranged I was placed in a holding cell for four hours, but allowed reading material from last week's tabloid papers, which looked as if someone had urinated on them. I closed my eyes, blanked out my cellmates, my surroundings, and myself. I believe I may have fallen asleep, a testimony to my considerable powers of denial.

I was then unlocked and escorted by a morose and distinctly

whiffy policewoman – *Come this way, please* – to a special room in which my 'samples' would be taken. First, the fingerprints, each fingertip rolled about on a screen. I breathed and tried not to panic, but the air resisted inhalation, was darkening and thickening, suffocating. My finger trembled, and the process had to be done again. I loathe having dirty hands; and someone else touching them, manipulating them into place, pushing them down, left me in need of psychiatric intervention.

I was about to explain my phobia, when to my relief we concluded our finger-pressing business, and I was allowed to wash off the residue of the screen debris, which took more time than the grumpy police lady was prepared to countenance.

'Let's get a move on, no need to scrub your fingers off.'

There was, though. As I soaped, rubbed, cleansed and dried – repeat until sane – she was opening a box of cotton-wool swabs for collecting 'a sample' from the inside of my cheek. I was instructed to open wide, and she took two dribbles of my saliva, presumably to test my DNA, if I have any left.

She put the samples into a tube, labelled it, took her rubber gloves off, threw them into a small white bin, closed the lid, and instructed me again to follow her. In a few moments, much shaken, I was back in my seat in the reception area, waiting to do the necessary paperwork. I spent the time examining my fingernails for oily residue, of which there was still a good deal. Though tempted, I did not pry one nail under the other, which would be both inefficient and as socially unacceptable as farting, though if I'd had a fart in reserve I might have offered it to my tormentors. But my sphincter was as tightly puckered as my mouth.

Bail had been granted, for I was, by all of our reckonings, no danger to members of the public. I was required to hand in my passport, and enjoined that under no circumstances could I discuss the particulars of the case with any witness or party in it.

That obviously included Lucy and Sam. Not likely! I left the station half an hour later, after further formalities were complete. On arrival home, I drank a bottle of claret that I had been saving for a special occasion – Calon Ségur 1959 – and smoked a remarkably good vintage Montecristo, as if I had something to celebrate.

In an hour I was fast asleep in my chair.

At eight o'clock the next morning the doorbell gave its single plaintive chirrup, which was quickly followed by a sustained, but not overtly aggressive, series of knocks, which gave no sign of relenting. I had been reading *The Times* in bed, my flat white on my bedside table, peacefully envisaging yet another morning with not much to do. I rose, and shrugged on my red silk mandarin's gown, a birthday present from Suzy all those years ago, so long ago that I once looked sexy in it, or so I was told. Nowadays, I think of it, if not myself, as regal. I popped my feet into my Turkish tessellated slippers – bit of a mix of cultures and styles, but I can be quite free-spirited when I put my mind to it. I ran my fingers through my hair, as I started down the stairs.

On the doorstep were – count 'em, one, two, three, with perhaps a fourth lurking – members of the police of various genders and ages, though their uniforms made them indistinguishable to my eye. The front one, a woman of severe aspect with a hint of a moustache, proffered her identification, while enquiring about mine.

'Dr Darke, is it?'

I agreed that it was.

She told me her name, and introduced her three colleagues, the final one of whom had recently appeared – like the last clown out of a tiny, pink and over-crowded vehicle in the circus – from the police car parked at the kerbside in front of the house.

'We have a warrant to search these premises.' She showed it to me, and I bent my neck to look at it, without bothering to read it.

'I see. Would you like me to fill out a parking voucher to put in the windscreen of your car? How long might you wish to stay? I should warn you that the local parking warden is a very strict Nigerian, and makes no exceptions. Last month he gave a ticket to an ambulance that had its light flashing and was picking up a victim of a heart attack, a woman I believe, of about your age. It was at Number 58 . . .' I pointed down the road. None of the eight police eyes followed my finger; they just focused stolidly on my visage, vaguely aware that I was having some fun with them. I would no doubt pay for that, but at my stage of life you have to find your amusements where you can.

'Do come in. I apologise for my dishabille, but it is a wee bit early for me.'

They crowded into the hallway, as if seeking another confined space to pop out of.

'You have arrived just in time for coffee,' I said brightly. 'Though I can do tea if you prefer?'

The woman officer was clearly Numero Uno, for the others congregated in a mass behind her.

'Thank you, doctor, but we've had coffee. Can I tell you how we would like to proceed?'

'That would be so kind.'

'First I have to inform you of your rights. You have a right to be present while the search is under way, and to be accompanied by a friend, family member, or legal representative. At the end of our search of the premises, we will give you a full inventory of what we have taken away, and I will sign it for your records. You may take pictures, or record any of the conversations.'

'Ah, that would be jolly, but alas I am no videographer . . . is that what they're called?'

If it were possible to amp up the wattage of her glower, she did so. Her cheeks contracted and headed east and west towards her nostrils, new lines appeared on her forehead. One of the two male officers, the youngest, who vaguely needed a shave perhaps because he hadn't yet formed the habit, was bringing up the tail of the conga line in the hallway, and smirked to himself.

'You have my permission,' I said graciously, fully aware that they did not need it, though I admired their adherence to the niceties of civilised discourse. 'Perhaps you'd like to come into the drawing room, and tell me about the procedure?' I opened the doorway on the right-hand side of the hall and ushered them through. I was careful sitting down in my armchair, as the dressing gown tends to ride up, and I had no desire to add indecent exposure to my charge sheet.

The police stood resolutely in the middle of the room.

'If you'd be so kind, sir, as to show us round the house, we can spread out, and try not to keep you too long.'

'And what will you be looking for?'

She had the grace to smile, but wasn't very good at it, so settled on a smirk instead. Incriminating evidence, obviously.

'We will just have a good look round. I need to take possession of your computer, and any electronic devices. We will look through the books – I gather you no longer have your valuable Dickens collection, but I promise we will be very careful – and any papers, letters, diaries or journals that you, or your late wife, may have kept. Also any prescription drugs – if you could be so kind as to find them and perhaps put them somewhere for inspection?'

The elder of the two male policemen stepped forward deferentially (not to me, but to his superior) to ask, 'Does this house have a basement or attic rooms?'

His superior glared at him. That would become clear soon enough.

'No, blessedly it doesn't. That's a bit odd for a Georgian house on this terrace. Most of them have cellars, if only for wine, but my theory is—'

'Shall we get started?' said the lady copper, as her inferiors fell back into line.

I went upstairs to shower and to dress, then for the next few hours I lay on my bed, Radio 3 in the background, finishing *The Times* and getting a stuttering start on the crossword, though the clues seemed more than usually perverse. I solved a few, stalled, gave it up, decided it might be more sensible to go for a walk in the High Street, pop into the bookshop, perhaps have another coffee.

I informed the first policeman I came across, who was seated at my desk going through my files of bills and receipts. I suppressed a scream of protest – after all, that's what he was there for – and told him I was going out, and would be back by 11.30.

'Thank you, sir, that's probably wise, and we'll try to get out of your hair as soon as possible. It can't be pleasant . . .'

'It's fine,' I said. 'You're just doing your job.'

He nodded, as if in confirmation of my acuity.

As soon as I had closed the door and walked far enough to be out of sight of the windows of the house, I stopped in the street and shook myself repeatedly, like a dog, drops of indignation, humiliation and rage threatening to soak the passers-by, who looked at me with some alarm. I had warded off this reaction by my display of *sang froid,* of which I was rather proud. They presumed to come into my house, rummage through my drawers and bookshelves, peep into the corners and crannies of my life, leaving their smudges and traces everywhere!

God knows what such searches might unearth elsewhere, but fortunately I have no secret stash of sexual implementa. Or pornography. I once viewed a pornographic film in Paris in my twenties, on a day when it was snowing in the Fifth, and I took shelter in a seedy cinema. It was disappointing: the French don't even offer popcorn. And as for the grainy black-and-white (literally) sex, one can only repeat the old *mot* about the First War: 'My dear, the noise! And the people!' I wouldn't exchange the time of day with the actors so rudely exposed on the screen, wouldn't drink a coffee with any of them, so why would I enjoy watching them nibble each other's bits? Within a few minutes I had closed my eyes and drifted off.

Thank God Suzy is dead. Dead as in: not in the house at this time. She would have been enraged at the imposition, fought and argued and insulted and cried, rung her solicitor, claimed a migraine, called her doctor, tried anything and everything to make them go away. And when they insisted on their legal right to search the house, she would have followed them around, tutting and admonishing and scolding at their handling of things, their brutish clumsiness amongst the porcelain, the pictures, the carpets, the crystal. She would have stood in front of her bedroom like Boadicea preparing for war before she let them examine her personals.

As I sat in the café with my coffee and a slightly stale almond croissant, I must have been muttering to myself. The lady with a sticky toddler at her side glanced at me, and moved to another table. What am I thinking? The police are only in the house because Suzy is not. They are there because she is dead. They are there because they believe I killed her.

On my hyper-caffeinated return I needed a tranquilliser – unless they'd been confiscated. I encountered DC Ladycop in the drawing room, a heap of my possessions on the console table on the far wall. There was a small pile of books, carefully arranged with the bottom edges aligned. Just what I had expected, indeed, I had placed them all together on the top shelf of the bookcase on the right-hand wall of my study. There were several books about medical matters, one on pharmacology, and a number on assisted dying, including a (very overpriced) copy of *The Peaceful Pill Handbook*, as well as *The Least Worst Death: Essays in Bioethics on the End of Life*, *Compassion in Dying: Stories of Dignity and Choice* and *That Good Night: Ethicists, Euthanasia and End-of-Life Care*, together with a number of American tomes on opioids and their effects.

Ladycop seemed very pleased with her haul. Picked up one, leafed through the pages, studied another, kept me waiting, put it down, pursed her lips in full satisfaction.

'Can you tell me about these, doctor? You seem to have a considerable interest in poisons and their effects, and on the question of assisted dying ...'

'Quite right,' I said, as if speaking to an eager but dim pupil. 'That's what the books are about. But they are not exactly what they seem, if I may put it that way ...'

She looked at me, sniffed, detecting the smell of rat.

I reached into the breast pocket of my jacket and produced two folded pages, which I had placed in an envelope.

'These are the receipts for the purchase of these books, printed out from my Amazon books account, about which I am happy to give you the details. You will observe –' I thrust the pages into her hands, and waited politely as she perused them – 'that all of them have been purchased in the last four months.'

Her eyes flashed as she made the obvious and easy calculation.

'They were purchased after the death of Mrs Moulton?'

'Indeed. They were.'

'They are studies about how to end a life by administering a fatal dose of drugs?'

'They are indeed.'

'I'm not sure I understand,' she said slowly.

'They are for me,' I said. 'When the time comes.'

The police had made a list of all the medicines in the bathroom and the drawer of my bedside table, but were of course obliged to let me keep them. They did, however, box and take away my computer, the few books, a file of bills and assorted business papers, and a cache of letters from Suzy dating back to our first years together. I'd hidden my journals under a floorboard, and they'd been too lazy to look.

I signed the necessary forms, and they left just before 1.00, promising to return the various items 'when the time comes'. I saw them out the door, as they silently trudged off with their booty.

A further coffee would have been a mistake, alcohol too. I mixed myself a lime and soda, and opened some smoked oysters and crispbread. Sitting at the kitchen table, I took out my phone – the purchase of which also post-dated Suzy's death, as I had explained and already proven to the police – and sent a text to Philip: *'Police just left. All as predicted. Thanks for the heads-up. James.'*

I then composed an email to Dragan, my Serbian computer wizard, suggesting he deliver the new computer that he had purchased on his own credit card, because I assumed the police would ask me if I owned any other computers. (They didn't.) He had already programmed it, and inserted all my files, which he had floated into a cloud, where they reside with the angels. The new machine is smaller than my desk version, and only costs £429, which I can now repay him. He had urged me to buy a Mac, a better, fancy computer, but I know what I am used to, and asked for more of it. He was disappointed, but soon gave in, as well he might considering how much he charges.

Chapter 11

Suzy was an actress by inclination if not much practice; addicted to claiming and declaiming histrionically, she took centre stage wherever she found herself, was happiest when eyes were upon her. She loved fancy-dress parties, and though I had no taste for them, I always joined in with bad grace. Our first was at St Anne's, in her final year. There was no need for me to debate my costume: if I had to go at all, it would be as Sherlock Holmes, though Suzy slyly suggested that perhaps Bertie Wooster would have been a better fit. Not going to happen, I said, donning my deerstalker and purchasing an elegant meerschaum pipe at the tobacconist's on The High.

We would make a pair of gumshoes, for she was going as Sam Spade, or more accurately as Humphrey Bogart playing Sam Spade in the film of *The Maltese Falcon*. At a second-hand shop in London she bought a dark pinstriped suit with wide lapels, a white cotton shirt and colourful deco tie, an appropriate dark overcoat, and pulled a trilby over her tied-up hair. She looked at herself in the wall mirror, turned this way and that, lit a Camel cigarette, drew in the smoke, puffed luxuriously.

'I always feel more powerful dressed as a man,' she said. 'I should do it more often.'

I was rather taken aback by this, and said I had no idea what she was talking about.

'I know,' she sighed, 'I know.'

As finals approached, she would give herself relief (not *light)* by reading thrillers. She urged Raymond Chandler on me so insistently that I reluctantly agreed to try *The Big Sleep.* Given her voluble examination anxiety and (not unrelated) libidinal energy, I certainly needed one.

It was dreadful, so bad and so incompetently told that it kept one *awake* with irritation. It was impossible to work out (in the words of that dirty limerick about the pansy and the dyke) *who had done what, and with what, and to whom.* Apparently Mr Chandler, quizzed on this very question, admitted he didn't know either. Somebody murdered somebody for some reason or other ...

For my forthcoming, fraught adventure tonight – I am almost as uncertain about my plot and motivation as that dumbbell Mr Chandler – I am dressing more like Sam Spade (I can never resist a pun, however grisly this one will be) than my beloved Sherlock, who is alas more likely to stand out in a crowd. Of course, there will be no crowd – the dreaded event will take place in the darkness.

I am staying at the local pub, which has a couple of almost clean en-suite bedrooms on the second floor, and a landlord of the requisite bushy stoutness, and chattiness too. That is enough by way of adjectives: such people, like the weather, should be endured, not described.

I entered the gloom at three in the morning, the rain scythed and bit at an angle, pelting my hands and what remained of my face under the brim of my trilby, with a sharp sting, as if the water were tinged with acid. I stationed myself under the yew tree fifteen minutes before they were likely to arrive, and lit a small Montecristo, which I would have to extinguish when I saw the approaching headlamps. Staking out, is it called, like what they did to Jesus?

The tobacco went straight to my head, and I soon had to lean against the tree to keep balance, which was a relief. It would have been intolerable had my senses been too keenly aware. The Montecristo heightened what the Diazepam had begun, and within ten minutes I felt as if I were someone else, somewhere else, as in a black-and-white film, noir as buggery.

I didn't want to be there, certainly didn't need to be there, needed *not* to be there. I had resisted the impulse – no, not the impulse, the throbbing compulsion – to make this visit, resisted it manfully for the week since I had heard the news, and only yesterday had I abjured the dictates of reason, and the clear direction of emotion, not to mention the urgent counsel of Philip (the only person in whom I had confided), and decided to come. I sheltered under my tree, hunched and miserable, until my cigar was a toxic stump and the first headlamps appeared down the lane. Over the next few minutes they were followed by others, as the cars – and a hearse – parked on the verge, and the various occupants made their slow way into the churchyard, holding torches and umbrellas. I was invisible, hidden behind my yew tree, but felt exposed, and likely soon to be discovered. What if they searched the area?

They set spotlights round the grave, by the light of which I could distinguish two police in uniform, two thick men carrying spades, a couple of people in white coats wearing masks over their faces, and a miserable-looking woman with a notepad, presumably the Public Health Official required at such procedures. Oh, and the vicar, standing slightly to the side, overseeing the operation on behalf of God.

If she had eyes Suzy would be studying their faces, their clothes, postures and gestures, delighted by the flickering light, which would give an extra challenge to her powers of observation. Her looks went everywhere. How eyes shine out of the darkness, like an animal's. How the colour of clothing changes as the light passes across it, or the person moves in and out of view. How facial features morph and coagulate in indiscriminate half-light, nostrils and cheekbones merging into monstrous mass, like a facial deformity worthy of a Victorian circus.

I could see some of this with her eyes, when she had them, but never did it for myself. Not that I couldn't be bothered, I just couldn't. She was at first sympathetic about this, as if it were some sort of disability, but later came to regard it merely as a form of laziness, this unwillingness to concentrate, to *see*.

'Look around. What do you see?' she would ask.

'What I need to see.'

'What's that?'

'Enough to navigate the hallways and keep safe in the streets.'

'What do you do the rest of the time?'

'Not a lot. Thinking.'

'What are you thinking about?'

By now – we had versions of this inquisition frequently in our early years together – I would be not so much bored as irritated, and would offer the one response guaranteed to make her shut up (often for the rest of the day) and walk away.

'*I think we are in rats' alley, where the dead men lost their bones.*'

Those lines, suitable for the seminar room and the colloquium, are also useful for prolonging marital discord. But here I was, verily in rats' alley.

On the side of the grave, facing the lane, they put up some canvas sheets on poles, lest the locals come a-rubbernecking, presumably an unlikely prospect at 3.30 in the morning. But the unusual volume of traffic, and the bright lights in the churchyard, soon attracted a trickle of locals, who posted themselves by the verge of the road to gawp. One could hear them murmuring in their soft Oxfordshire burr, as if they were some sort of small, furry animal, hobbits perhaps, sucking their pipes and thumbs.

While the spademen dug away at the moist grass, the other participants, experienced though they must have been, simply watched in silence, muted by the solemnity of the occasion. I rested against the far side of the tree trunk, my heart racing, and rummaged in my pocket for a tablet of Digoxin to supplement the Diazepam I had already imbibed. The irony, if it might be called that, was hardly lost on me.

For the next half-hour I stood as still as time, hardly aware of the sounds and motion, the *sotto voce* instructions. I peered out to see the spademen lower some ropes and engage some sort of lifting apparatus; it was impossible to tell in the unreliable half-light. I had insisted on the finest obtainable resting place for my dear one, a coffin of dark oak, impossibly heavy. The casket rose slowly, improbably, from the ground. Though it sounded spectral, the accompanying creaking sound must have issued from the strain on the lifting apparatus, or on the poor men themselves.

The vicar approached as if to offer benediction, but had something more welcome, two large teapots, a jug of milk and bowl of sugar, and some mugs on a tray. He consulted the various participants, filled the mugs, added milk and sugar when requested. His wife had baked some shortbread, which no one declined. Wet and miserable, I had to restrain myself from joining the party.

They all seemed in need of a break. A few shook themselves like drenched dogs, one walked off to smoke a cigarette, the others prolonged the emptying of their mugs, clutching them for the warmth. The hard work was done; all that remained was for the casket to be placed in the back of the hearse and driven to the mortuary for forensic examination. Of the body? I was unsure what the term now was, or is. Not *Suzy*, of course. Whatever was left. The remains of Suzanne Moulton? The corpse? It wasn't her. Her body had been embalmed, and might tarry awhile, or was there so little left, my imagination insisted, that there was merely a liquacious mass of decay, human compost? How invasively had the worms tried? Was she now an 'it'?

An *it*? I certainly was, my organs roiling and churning, wobbling like vile jellies. Hamlet apparently experienced something similar, though he was incapable of finding the right image:

O that this too too solid flesh would melt
Thaw and resolve itself into a dew!

Melt? Thaw? A dew? That's not a human body, that's a bloody snowman. I wasn't one of them yet, frozen and drenched though I was, nor was I a man either: just a thing in the darkness, a thing of darkness.

O dark dark dark, we all go into the dark. Stilled and bent with horror, gagging, bereft, I had a nigh uncontrollable impulse to reveal myself, to beg them to stop, to re-inter my poor lost wife, to *leave her alone! Leave her! Leave!* And then, too, to be taken into their arms, and comforted. I took off my hat, turned my face to the rain, listening in the pattering silence, lost in contemplation, of ourselves and of our origins, in ghostly demarcations, keening sounds.

I must have stood like that for some time, because when next I peeped, they were leaving. They had taken down the canvas sheets and poles – the curious locals had long departed – and begun wheeling the casket towards the waiting hearse. The police shook the vicar's hand and made for their car. The gravediggers put their spades over their shoulders and hunched off. It was all over.

When I could no longer see the tail lights, I made my way to the graveside, looked into the hole – it was now just about light enough to see, and the dawn cast an appropriate penumbral illumination, as if in an illustration to a Gothic novel. It seemed to go on into the bowels of the earth. At the top of the grave, the headstone read:

SUZY MOULTON
WRITER

Lucy and I had debated what should go on Suzy's gravestone, and it took some weeks to resolve the issue in my favour. I was after all paying for it. She and Sam thought it preferable that a gravestone have the deceased's full name, and dates of birth and death. 'And something right nice,' Sam opined, 'like "beloved wife, mother and grandmother".'

We settled, well, I insisted, on the simple eloquence of the final version, with her name as the top line, and 'writer' centred beneath it. I explained to the children that if this terse but eloquent epitaph was good enough for Philip Larkin's grave, it was good enough for Suzy's. This didn't cut any ceremonial ice with them, even after I began to explain to Sam who Philip Larkin was.

He was ready with the obvious.

'"They fuck you up . . ."' said Sam.

My experience under the blasted yew confirmed my general animus against trees, which are ill-designed and often overblown objects that block our light, clog our drains, and tear at our foundations, though I can grasp and even celebrate their occasional utility. Excellent for hiding behind. No log fires without trees. No paper, no books. I am told they are useful for making oxygen, so long as they reside in South America and drink the Amazonian waters. So when Suzy decided, when still a young woman, that she wished to be buried near a yew in an Oxfordshire churchyard, I did not demur. I didn't do a lot of demurring in our marriage, had soon learned that most of my ideas and opinions were best kept to myself. The same procedure and injunction, I once observed, might have served my wife, and our marriage, equally well, but Suzy was an expresser: no sooner had a thought, however contentious, entered her mind than it flowed directly onto her lips.

When we returned to our North Oxford flat after prematurely choosing her burial plot, Suzy took down our *Oxford Anthology of*

English Poetry and went silent for a few hours. I walked into town to the covered market to buy fresh bread, some prosciutto and sharp Italian cheese, and some tomatoes if they had any worth eating. When I got home, Suzy had earmarked a few pages that she wanted to share, which meant I was to sit still and listen. The yew, Suzy had discovered, was the most 'symbolically resonant' of trees. By this she apparently meant that a lot of poems have such trees in them, for they represent the darkness that will come to us all, particularly if you are buried right under one.

'If you wants yews, youse can have them,' I offered in my best Oxfordshire accent. This was apparently not funny.

I decamped from the pub as soon as I could shower and change my clothes, have a brief lie-down, and pay the curious publican, who wanted details about the goings-on in the night – he was far too indolent to actually get up, but said he'd seen lights and some commotion. He offered breakfast, which was included in the price, but I declined.

In twenty-five minutes I was back at the Old Parsonage in my junior suite, tempted to take more pills, sufficient to make me sleep long and hard.

Let the lamp affix its beam. How cold she is, and dumb.

How cold I am, too, how dumb, how numb.

In the restaurant I ordered a breakfast of two scoops of vanilla ice-cream and a flat white. Clara the waitress tilted her head inquisitively, but I was beyond explaining. When the bowl arrived my hands were shaking and I tucked my napkin into my shirt top, like an airline passenger in economy class hunched over his tray.

I'd been awake all night, soon went back to my bedroom, pulling the covers over me as if they could warm what was frozen. I spent the rest of the day drifting there, awake but not awake, asleep but not asleep. I have an extensive repertoire of nightmares, but today's were something new, without narrative, and I awoke scalded and boiled from the spectral images disinterred from the penetralium of mystery: ghostly, ghastly, fresh from the grave, rotten from the grave, a stinking, sodden, stench filled my nostrils. I looked about for the source, but of course there was nothing there. It was coming from me. I had no idea, none, no idea. Suzy is everywhere, every way. Solid, sullied, formed, unformed. Her. It.

I know what they are doing – how could I not? Know what they are doing. Now, right now. And now. Right now what they are doing is to *her*, or I would not feel so sharply the scalpel's call, each violation of the still flesh.

When they finish they will close her body and her box, put it back in the corpse-car, and thence to the cold dirt that is her home and destiny.

Cover her again, sheltered from the storm.

I have scant interest in the world. I've had enough, done enough, been enough. I'm insufficiently engaged any more even to be bored by it. I will not travel again – even my occasional visits to Abingdon have an epic feel, as if I were Wilfred Thesiger riding a camel, or perhaps an Arab boy. I have not abjured cultural activities, for I never -jured them in the first place.

Old places, new places. Old buildings, new buildings. Old people, new people. Mesopotamia and Manchester, Palladio and Lutyens, Aristophanes and Oscar, James Darke and Rudy. Words, for things. Pelicans, mangoes, cricket bats.

Churchill's brilliant, apparently unstudied (though if rehearsed even more extraordinary) last words were, 'I'm bored with it all.' I'd be so pleased to have that on my headstone, but Lucy and Sam would make a fuss. Wrong gestalt. Perhaps I should consult the stone-carver and have it ready in advance? It's a nice fancy, but unnecessary. It'll be the earthly fires for me, and I'll become a jug of ash before they can send me to the eternal flames. The grave is creepy, claustrophobic, terrifying: I'd rather die than be buried.

There's nothing left to discover. That's worth discovering. I'm out of patience with my old masters, with Wordsworth, Browning and Eliot, as if chipping away at long-abandoned mines, their valuable cargo stripped decades ago, nothing left but bare rock in the dry darkness. Wisdom-seekers, shit-slingers.

There are few available truths. You learn them early and enthusiastically and they erode as you do, until all you are left with is platitudes, and the dying of the light. Nothing to rage about there, just the encroaching blessing of the darkness, going to the inevitable.

I've done my required reading and writing, discovered what I needed to know. Unlike Suzy I had no desire to seek out, to expand my boundaries. If anything, I like contracting them, withdrawing and withholding, until like a sauce I am reduced to my essential flavours, more sour than sweet. All that is left is words. Hamlet says *words, words, words.* I concentrate myself into words now and they matter, they are matter, they are what I am. Reading was how I understood, writing is how I speak. I write me and read me, my sole impetus to go on. It passes the time, this self-interest. I grow gnomic in my final phase, doomed to spend my final days perpetually awake in the darkness, composing, soon decomposing.

Lucy says I am depressed, that I need 'to see someone', which tickles me, as seeing people is what I least wish to do. I am tolerably content in my own sedate company; it is only others who depress me, as – to be fair – I no doubt depress them. Why inflict myself on an otherwise cheerful counsellor?

A few days after that frightful vigil in the graveyard, with Suzy now back in her dark hole and me in mine, I requested a meeting with Philip, to discuss progress on my soon to be launched 'campaign'. He informed me that, unless the forensic analysis of Suzy's body reveals scant trace of the chemicals I introduced into it, I will certainly be charged. So I will. I wish to be, to have my days in court. The unexpected effect of my sojourn at the graveside was to strengthen this resolve.

Philip suggested a meeting in St James's Park, followed by a drink at the Athenaeum. Apparently he has been walking in that park since he was a toddler, and 'absolutely adores' the pelicans. He reeled off his names for them, but they were all wrong.

We sat companionably, two elderly gentlemen, lifting our pallid faces to the wispy midday sun, perching our depleted buttocks on the hard bench.

'I think this is one of the few things keeping me alive, James. Little else seems to matter any more ...'

His voice was faint. I leant over to catch what he was saying.

'... and, as it may be six or eight months before your trial, I have something I want to show you.'

He fished about in the pocket of his jacket. Looked puzzled. Checked his trouser pockets, nothing there. Properly clothed men have too many pockets. Anxiety clouded his features, the lines under his cheekbones contracted. He licked at his lips, which were always chapped and dry.

At last – right-hand breast pocket – he located the recalcitrant object and brought it out, in a closed hand, which he placed on his lap.

'But first,' he said, 'I need to make a wee admission.' He giggled at the phrase, as if he were a toddler needing the loo. Which perhaps he did; it happens to us old folk all the time.

'When I was discussing Keats with our little group, we talked somewhat – or I did – about the need to organise an easeful death. I think people were interested, and I got one or two rather ... how can I put it? ... delicate phone calls afterwards, seeking pragmatic advice.'

'Of course, I understand.'

'But you, though you were too delicate to ask, you may soon be in a different position to the others. Perhaps I am being presumptuous? If so, I apologise. But if you wish, I may be able to help you. I hope your trial, and campaign, may keep me alive. But if I don't make it, and before you go to the jail you seem so determined to enter, I have something to show you.'

He opened his hand, which had a small oval object in it, the size of a pullet's egg, ornate with faux-Fabergé enamelling, held together by a delicate clasp and fine gold chain.

'I carry this everywhere,' he said. 'It contains two pills, though one is certainly sufficient. If you want me to source one for you, just say the word.'

I was overcome by both his generosity and his resourcefulness. This cannot have been easy. He saw the thought heading for my lips, and intervened quickly.

'Don't ask,' he said firmly.

We stared peacefully across the water at the available pelicans. After a few moments of remarkably companionable silence, we rose to cross the park, ascended the great flight of steps in the stately manner of gentlemen of a certain age, and soon made our way into the bar of the Athenaeum. Philip insisted on buying a bottle of Krug, which we polished off so happily that we had to resist ordering another. An hour later, we bade easeful goodbyes, hailed our black cabs, and made our ways home, the close of a most satisfying day.

When I got home I settled in, poured myself an Armagnac, lit a cigar, and rang Lucy. We talked for perhaps twenty minutes. I even did some of it, perhaps most, chatting away about the sort of nothings with which she and her mother had filled the air. How I was getting on, what I'd eaten, how I slept, what was on TV (the news), how Rudy was, the dratted Sam, even.

'Gosh, Dad, you're in better form,' she said, relief all over her tone. 'Do you think maybe your depression is lifting?'

'I feel a lot better now,' I said. 'Thanks for asking. And lots of love.'

Most likely I will die in jail, of the one thing or the other. This will save Lucy the protracted agony of my protracted agony. Anyhow, the food might be sufficient to kill me, and apparently you cannot send it back. On the other hand, I won't be able to smoke or drink, both of which apparently shorten life, which is why I do them. Could jail actually be good for me? That'd be a right laugh, as Sam might say.

Chapter 12

I'm back. It feels better than home. I swooped into my junior suite, opened a bottle of 1955 Armagnac that I'd had the presence of mind to bring with me, and drank a few drams more quickly than usually sensible. It worked. For the first time in months, I slept through the night.

After a shower, I dressed more formally than required, and went into the dining room. The waitress knew me by now, and though she was cautious in her approach, granted me a smile.

'The usual, doctor?'

'Please.'

I'd trained her nicely: started out a difficult taskmaster, grumpy and fastidious, and became increasingly lenient as she became more compliant and efficient. She returned immediately with a copy of *The Times*, followed shortly by a double-shot flat white. The boiled eggs – three minutes exactly – and lightly toasted sourdough soldiers would follow soon enough,

I was just settling down, had folded the paper into the right shape for reading at table, and was finishing my coffee, when the chair opposite me was pulled back brusquely, as if by a poltergeist. I looked up to find the cause. It was worse than some itinerant spirit, it was Lucy.

A gentleman should never appear flustered, however much he is startled. Or appalled.

'Darling! What a treat. Can I order a coffee for you?'

'Coffee? Oh, all right. Just milk, no sugar.'

'Have you had breakfast? They have lovely . . .'

She made a dismissive gesture.

'Of course I've had breakfast. It's half-nine.'

The waitress hurried over, as anxious to please as a spaniel.

'An Americano, please. With milk.'

'Hot or cold, doctor?'

I looked across at Lucy.

'Cold,' she said.

When we'd finished, Lucy suggested that we have a talk in The Parks. I resisted for a few moments – 'a talk' is safer when one is surrounded by company – but eventually rose and put on my coat.

'We need to get some things straight,' she said, as we strolled amongst the bleary undergraduates and attenuated dons. 'I want to know what you are doing, and why, and what your plans are.'

'My plans? I've told you that already. To counter-attack – whatever you want to call it. I am not going to sit dumbly and be branded a murderer. I am not. I hastened your mother's death. I think I was dimly aware of this at the time, but in retrospect I accept that this was my intention. I caused her to die prematurely.'

'Get real, Dad. This is a court of law we're talking about. What the hell sort of defence is that?'

'A defence not of myself, but of my behaviour, and my actions. Of my heart. I was consumed by guilt after Mummy died, and hid myself away, but the more I have been called on to describe my intervention, the more clear I am. I acted wisely, and for the best. In Kantian terms, I behaved such that my action might become a universal law . . .'

Lucy waved her hand in front of her face.

'Above my pay grade . . .'

'It just means that anyone in the same situation ought to do the same thing. You remember that you said that if you'd had the nerve, you would have done so too.'

She nodded. 'I did. I accept that now. But I still have no idea what this so-called counter-attack of yours consists of.'

'Nor do I, quite. But I have to bring the whole messy business out into the open – to the court of public opinion if you like – and to plead my case. I suppose I will begin by writing something, then see if I can get it distributed, and made available.'

'You mean, like in the newspapers? You? You're going to become ... What? The leader of ... a movement?'

She put her hand over her mouth, to mask a grimace or perhaps to stifle a laugh.

'I am trying to think,' she said, 'of the qualities needed to lead a movement. Shall we go through them? There's—'

'Very funny! I know that, but there are all sorts of ways to lead, and all sorts of movements. What one really needs is a cause in which one passionately believes, and then the right catalyst, which in this case is most pressingly upon me. And then, the simple desire to speak the truth, and the vague hope that it might make a difference.'

'Waffle,' said Lucy firmly. 'Crap! It's all very well, but it's not you, is it? What, all of a sudden you're Nelson Mandela?'

'Now, now,' I said. 'No need for that. I have some powerful helpers. There's my human rights lawyer, and some literary people, and a doctor from the Chelsea and ...'

I could see Lucy giving up, and giving in: as she often said, 'If you can't beat 'em, join 'em.' A reprehensibly colloquial phrase, but not without sense.

'My only problem, Dad, to be frank, is *you*. You're not exactly charismatic leadership material ...'

'I don't need to be. It'll gain momentum as an issue – movements are like that.'

'The Darke Movement? Sounds a bit poo-ey, Rudy would like that. You should think of a better name.'

'I have. It's my own little joke ...'

'Do tell,' she said, smudging her tears with the back of her shirtsleeve.

'Darkeness Risible.'

She touched my arm, drew me to her.

'Very funny. And that's what it is, sure enough. Have you thought about . . . What this actually entails? What it *means* to go to jail?'

'Of course I have.'

'I'll tell you what it means – it means *me!*' She pointed to her chest, unnecessarily I thought. 'It means my heart will break, and Rudy's heart will break, and—'

I cut her off, unwilling to accept what was about to come out of her mouth, other than spittle and bits of drool.

'Sam's too? Come off it, you know full well that—'

'No. Not Sam.'

That was something of a relief, though if I could break his heart and leave the others' intact, it might have been a worthwhile project.

'I can break that by myself, thank you very much.'

We were owed a pause, and we got one. As Lucy stopped to catch her breath and to clear her throat, I considered the implications of what I had just heard. I sat down on the nearest bench, my presence sufficiently worrying to make the stringy cleric seated there glance my way speculatively, as if about to offer consolation, but Lucy bodged him over and sat down. He got up and left us to it.

'Darling Lucy, I'm not sure what you mean . . . I know you've been having a rough time, but Sam seems genuinely contrite. He knows he made a mistake. He has apologised for it fulsomely.'

'Mistake? You call that a bloody mistake? Well, you're going to end up in jail as a result, if you have your way.'

'That's right, love, perhaps that's right. But if I go to jail, it will be my own choice, not through Sam's error. I forgive him from the bottom of my heart. I even think I am grateful to him, for giving me my day in court.'

'Days in court, *years* in jail! Just to get some attention? When you get out Rudy will be a teenager, and I will be living on my own with the children. Is that what you want?'

I had no idea things between Lucy and Sam were in such disarray, and that she would contemplate moving out. While Sam has never been my cup of Assam, he is steady and reliable, a good father and I suppose a good man. As I inwardly reel off these attributes I feel depressed, and wonder once again what it is that Lucy ever saw in him?

'Integrity,' she once said by way of explanation, adding 'goodness', as if these were ingredients in cooking up a marital stew.

'Darling Lucy, have you thought about this, the details? Moving out, with a new baby ...'

She gave a weary shrug.

'You're about to talk about money, are you? And being practical?'

I'd been meaning to bring it up, and now was the right time. Since my confrontation with the interrogating coppers, I'd been doing some work on Suzy's estate, the acquisition of which was one of my alleged motives for murdering her. If it were, I would certainly have banked the loot by now, unless I am as deranged, inefficient, and sneaky as accused.

There was no will, so apparently I inherit the bulk of her estate. All that is now necessary, apparently, is that I discover what assets there are, and then do the paperwork and apply for probate. Mine, mine, mostly mine. Only I don't want it, never did. For reasons that were obscure to both of us, perhaps fastidiousness about talking about money, we did not know much about each other's finances, save that our savings generated sufficient income for a life, not of luxury, but of choice. We did what we wanted to do. Lucy will be able to do so as well.

Suzy's estate, when you added the cash in the bank, investments in the stock market and bonds, ISAs and the like, came to something over £2.3 million, most of which came from the sale of the family property in Dorset. If Lucy wanted to leave Sam, she would have adequate means to do so in comfort: to buy a little house, and perhaps generate enough income to live on modestly, though at today's interest rates she might have to spend some capital. But by the time she got through a significant amount of it, I'd have fallen or jumped off the perch, and she'd have plenty.

Sam was opposed to inherited wealth, which he regarded as the bulwark of class privilege. Money is not a genetic right, he maintained. I was never sure if Lucy actually agreed with this, but she went along. Anything for an easy socialist life. But she would surely have known, as an only child, that a shedload of cash would be sliding her way when the time came, and it beggars belief that she would consider donating it to some charity for the homeless of Oxfordshire.

'Darling Lucy, if you are thinking of leaving your husband – if it comes to that – then of course I am thinking about money. You should too. And I need to tell you something . . .'

She started to flap her hands as if attempting to levitate: *Stop!*

'Mummy died without a will. Most of her assets go to me, but you are entitled under law to—'

'Stop! No! I can't do this, talk about this. Not now, please.'

'Darling Lucy, I neither want my share of it, nor need it, and will transfer whatever money you need, or all of it, once probate is granted.'

She paused to rest her (left) wings, to consider. I could see her resisting the obvious and inevitable question. Opened her mouth slightly, as if to speak, closed it, opened it again like a goldfish. How much?

'It comes to a bit over £2.3 million. You're legally entitled to over a million of that. But I want you to have all of it.'

Her eyes went blank then rolled back.

'Pounds?'

'No. Rupees. She had an Ayah, you remember.'

She threw her head back, and looked up at the lowering sky.

'Thank you. For telling me. For being generous. I don't know what I think, so can I not say anything, not yet?'

'Of course,' I said.

She stood up again, and shook herself so violently that I expected drops of perspiration to fly about.

'This might change things. But it doesn't change the one important thing, does it?'

'What's that, love?'

'You. You being determined to go to jail, and to ruin all of our lives. Money isn't the answer to that, is it?'

'You mustn't worry so. I have internal resources as well as financial ones. I will cope. I will even find a way to make something positive out of the experience. I will be able to read. And to write. What else have I ever done?'

She came next to me to take my hand.

'Daddy, it's not a school library. It's a jail! If you're not out of your mind now you certainly will be. Locked up. Locked up day and night. You, a fucking claustrophobe who can't even go on a Tube? You'll be holding the bars, screaming your head off . . .'

'Not at all, not at all. I have looked into this. There are no bars, just a door that shuts, with a wee window that closes, and hey presto in you pop . . .'

She was crying again.

'In you stay, banging at the door, in your cute little prisoner outfit, so well-dressed, you who . . .'

'I shall think of it as a uniform,' I said. 'I approve of them, they erase differences.'

There was a long pause while Lucy dried her eyes and blew her nose, composed herself, stood up and paced the grass verge, kicked at some leaves, gazed miserably at a passing mother and child. I was taken aback that her pleasure in her new financial independence was so fleeting. It was because she loved me, I suppose.

'Tell me, would you – I have always wondered what "supercilious" means. You know, the derivation?'

'Do you mean as it refers to me?'

'Of course I mean you. But what I don't know is whether some mildly irritating people are "cilious", and unbearably superior people, like you, are supercilious?'

I was pleased by this line of enquiry, which, while it maligned me, nevertheless revealed a linguistic curiosity both appealing and unexpected.

'"Cilious" is not a word, and though "super-" is often used to indicate a greater degree (as in supermarket or supercharger) it need not be a prefix, as in superficial. It derives from the Latin word for eyebrow, as in the raising of. And may I add that I regard this description, if applied to my good self, is a misapprehension of both my tone and my nature? I am admittedly ironic, whimsical sometimes, sardonic to be sure, caustic and occasionally withering. But I am always serious, and a supercilious person is merely making jokes and gestures, whereas I—'

'Who gives a fuck?' said Lucy.

From that moment I found, as the time slowly passed, that the stench I associated with Yahoos began to fade somewhat, not because it was no longer present, but because I was gradually inured to it, as a worker in a tannery no longer experiences the smells that make a visitor swoon with disgust.

In my slow return, as Mary was wont to call it, to a life of domestic intimacy, the major incentive and delight was the company of my dear little Reuben, whose presence I found more and more necessary to the balance and happiness of my spirits. He was bright and inquisitive, and when freshly bathed smelled of lavender soaps and light powder. In his presence a small dab of scent under my nose was sufficient to block any residual Yahoo smell emanating from him, and I came slowly and grate-fully to regard him not as a noxious animal, but as a loving human child. Of an evening, when he and his mother were visiting, I would read to him before he went to sleep. He asked for Robinson Crusoe, *having heard much talk of it, but quickly found it as dull as I do.*

'Grandfather,' he said, 'these Adventures are paltry things compared to your own! Pray tell me more, Sir, of your own stories, and of the lands and people that you have known, and of the tribulations and trials that have been visited upon you.'

Though it was difficult to convey these mysteries to a child of eight, and likely to be unsettling to his as yet unformed nature, I nevertheless tried to give as placid an account as was possible, simpli-fied my language, and omitted much that was beyond his powers of comprehension. He lay still in his little bed as I sat at his side, as full of delight as I soon came to be myself.

'That is the best story, Grandfather,' he would say as I extin-guished the lamp. 'Pray may we have more tomorrow?'

Rudy chortled, and remonstrated.

'Not tomorrow,' he said. '*Now!*'

Only an extravagantly cilious man could have resisted this entreaty.

The next months would have gone by in increasing harmony, as I began once again to enjoy the company of my family, and the comforts of my home. But, alas, the ease of domestic life behind our own doors was rudely interrupted once those doors were opened. For, since my foolish and ineffectual attempt to make my tale public, the very persons to whom I had appealed had increasingly turned against me. I could not, under any circumstances, venture out during the hours of daylight, and my nocturnal visits to the stables to converse with my former stable-mates were fewer and fewer. Indeed, those poor horses were frightened on my behalf, and had begun to lose weight and sleep, as the infernal noise of the rabble shook the timbers of their quarters.

As the gathering vermin grew more and more confident, boisterous and vulgar, neither my life nor that of my wife and children cowering in the house nearby were at all safe. I enjoined Mary, who reluctantly agreed, with much relief passing upon her features, that she repair immediately to the country, to join our daughter and her children, until this wildness passed. She begged me to do similarly, but I was determined to face my new enemies, and if possible to explain to them, once again, what it was that I had learned, and how it might improve their lot to live in accord with the principles dictated by reason. I had been granted experiences that, though painful to undergo and to transmit, might be considered a blessing, for if they were properly conveyed, some improvement in the universal condition of the species might result.

My dear wife was confounded by my repeated folly, as she was wont to call it, but I insisted, and some days later she departed tearfully, begging me most earnestly not to behave foolishly, and privately giving our loyal servant and groom a shilling apiece to ensure their vigilance on my behalf. I felt relieved both for the sake of her safety, and for my own peace of mind. I had a task before me better undertaken on my own. I had used the diminishing income from the family estates to employ a gang of ruffians to stand outside the house to keep me safe. I had much to do, stories to relate, maxims and examples to convey. And much to write, for my travels would not be over until the final account of this, my final Voyage, had been written.

I knew that you can hardly reason with a Yahoo, or convert him from the ways that nature dictates. Yet I am myself an example of such a creature, who has improved as a result of right instruction from a noble being. Thus I may regard myself as a conduit through which this wisdom might be transmitted. It had an effect on me, and through me on my good family, who have transformed themselves for the better under the influence of my new understanding. And where I, and they, have gone, might others not follow?

Once I found myself alone in my house, and once it was clear to the rabble that I was not coming out, they got bored, as crowds so often do, and their numbers and their ferocity diminished. Within a few months I could once again venture out for a stroll, or ride in the carriage drawn by my two friends, whose health and spirits were immeasurably improved by such outings, with hardly a cry of 'HorseMan!' to disturb our peace.

'I think we need to stop here. Do you need the loo?'

He'd been still at first, but as the threats to Gulliver massed and multiplied, Rudy had begun to fidget, and to worry his hair in his fingers, as his mother often did.

'No. Go on.'

'You'll see,' I said in my most consoling tone, which is actually not very effective; I've encountered eiderdowns that are better comforters than I.

'It will come out well in the end. You know stories are some-times scary – like yours about the friendly Giant – but they always turn out for the best. That's why we like them, because they're exciting.'

He hated being treated like a child, particularly when he was acting like one.

'Go on! Read more!'

My foot is not very good for putting down, but I did it, got up from the chair, and put away the manuscript.

'I'm afraid that's enough for now. And you know it's always better for readers to want more. That makes us authors very happy.'

It didn't make my reader very happy, but there wasn't much he could do about it except pout and sulk.

There was some suspense building up, and the next episode – is that the right term? – has a different contour. And I have a problem, which is only coming to mind as things develop. It is possible – I almost think of it as likely, perhaps even desirable – that I will be going to jail in the near future. Might this be incorporated in the text? Gulliver might be sued or tried for sedition or blasphemy perhaps? Or does this intersect art and life too closely? Until I decide, I will withhold my next offering.

PART THREE

Darke Movement

Chapter 13

Long of neck as Margot Fonteyn, sharp of beak as Shylock, languorous and nasty as Kenneth Williams in a strop, swans are not entirely to be trusted, as Leda once learned. Aristotle observed that swans sing chiefly at the approach of death, though he never noticed, or noted, that this final song is the swan's most beautiful, its haunting exit from pond and air.

Consider a dying human and you will not observe, or hear, anything remotely similar. Suzy expired without so much as a whimper, and during her final weeks couldn't abide the harmonies of poetry or music, however ethereal. Yet my forthcoming evening with my poetry group is of course dedicated to her memory; it is her elegy and, not to put it too grandly, most likely to be my own swansong.

Having emailed my poem to the members, I gathered from their responses that they were unfamiliar with Wallace Stevens, and had never heard of 'The Emperor of Ice-Cream', a provinciality that I find both predictable and sad, having suffered from it myself. We were nourished on Rupert Brooke by our dowager aunties, damn their crimped, sentimental little souls. Well, let them have Mr Stevens as an antidote to all that auntydoting.

Call the roller of big cigars,
The muscular one, and bid him whip
In kitchen cups concupiscent curds.
Let the wenches dawdle in such dress
As they are used to wear, and let the boys
Bring flowers in last month's newspapers.
Let be be finale of seem.
The only emperor is the emperor of ice-cream.

Take from the dresser of deal,
Lacking the three glass knobs, that sheet
On which she embroidered fantails once
And spread it so as to cover her face.
If her horny feet protrude, they come
To show how cold she is, and dumb.
Let the lamp affix its beam.
The only emperor is the emperor of ice-cream.

They will protest, and ask what it means, but it is what it is, and it says what it says. If they want meaning, let them revert to soppy Mr Brooke, whose poems transform easily enough into homily and cliché.

I will tell them one thing, though: this Stevens poem is *true*. Harsh, clear-eyed, uncompromised, as befits an author who actually worked for a living: too much mooning about makes for mush. Mr Stevens was a posh insurance salesman, expert at sceptical figuration, exact and exacting.

No easy consolation for your grievers in his lines, just horny appetite and horny feet. We take our pleasures as and when: we come, then we go. It's necessary, all this death business: there's not enough room for all of us at the same time.

For the forthcoming evening, I will be the Emperor Redux, and Magimixer supreme. If I were sufficiently theatrical I would wear a gown of purple and gold brocade, and my Turkish embroidered slippers. Even-Stevens might have been amused, though there is no evidence that he had anything as simple as a sense of humour. When I play my LP of him reading this very poem, his tones are wry and dry.

He was fascinated by swans, the compelling contrast between beauty and danger, as if they were floating versions of the young Bette Davis, with feathers. One of his early poems is the immaculately titled 'An Invective Against Swans', which ends:

And the soul, O ganders, being lonely, flies
Beyond your chilly chariots, to the skies.

Suzy's soul has flown, mine will too, soon enough. All of our group's poems concern souls taking to the skies – that's why we meet and greet, take a gander, drink wine and eat our wafers in tolerable communion.

Soon enough, I shall sing my last, and be dead as a dodo. Another bird? A Chanticleer dinner. A pelican curry. A nightingale ode. Some ducks in a row. A swansong. *Death is a Thing with Feathers*?

Philip was the only member to reply at any length to my submission, and had the sense to do so without cc-ing the others.

Dear James,
  Well, what a treat your Emperor is. I am immensely in your debt, and have indeed spent the day first buying and then immersing myself in Stevens's Collected Poems. What a wonder he is, and such a relief after the earnestness of so much English poetry. Aren't Americans – is one allowed to say this? – fresh, sufficiently tempered by time not to be brash as Australians, but still original, and confident in their own newly acquired voices? I've read Eliot, of course, but he went off once he settled amongst us. But your Mr Stevens? Oh my, how impenetrably intelligent he is, how musical, how he teases and provokes.

Thank you, my dear. I feel so fortunate that you have entered our lives – my life, such as it is and will be.

See you soon. I cannot tell you how much I am looking forward to it.

Best, as ever,

Philip

First to arrive on the night was Miles, looking wan and drained of energy, no longer a priapic counter-example to the riddle of the Sphinx. He nodded and tapped me on the shoulder as he entered, took off his scarf and overcoat, and hung them in the closet in the hall, unbidden. He'd never been to our house, had he, so how did he know that was where the hooks were? Before I'd time to ponder this and to close the front door, Ethel and Patricia shuffled in clutching each other's arms like refugees, and behind them was Dorothea, beaming and making noise. They soon made themselves comfortable in the drawing room, admired and were warmed by the fire, settled in and down.

They were intrigued by and rather enjoyed my Golan Heights Muscat, and the nibbles of Bombay fat chicken crostini with red cabbage slaw were examined closely, and eaten quickly. They ran out in no time. The nibbles, I mean.

'Delicious! Never tasted anything like it,' said Miles, licking his fingers.

'Might I have the recipe?' asked Dorothea, failing to lick hers.

I put mine to my lips.

'Family recipe. Never revealed. Pain of death.'

They demurred. We respect each other's little secrets.

I refilled their glasses, and stood up, resting my arm on the mantel, unscrewing a tube containing a Montecristo. 'I hope you will indulge me if I light my cigar before I begin. If you dislike the smoke, think of it as an essential stage prop.'

After clipping my big cigar and rolling it gently with my fingers, I lit it and played them my recording of Stevens reading

'The Emperor of Ice-Cream'. Their silence was complex, as multi-layered as a millefeuille. And as unstable. They were by no means sure what to make of this austere, elegant American, but by the final lines they were not merely acceding to the music of the lyric, but moved by it. Not in a positive way, not entirely.

It was Dorothea, of course, who got the first words in.

'I'm intrigued by this, James, and I suppose grateful to you for bringing it to our attention. But it's a bit ... grim, isn't it?'

I puffed away philosophically on my big cigar. It was Patricia who answered.

'What, Dorothea, you think death isn't grim?'

'But, no, but I ...'

'Well, I for one am delighted that James should have offered this. It's so refreshing not be condoled and consoled all the bloody time. If you see as much death as I do ...' She paused for a moment, not quite finding the words. 'It's a relief to find a poet who isn't full of shit and sympathy.'

Before the conversation could gather any momentum, I gave a little cough.

'Who fancies an ice-cream?'

I went to the kitchen, accompanied by Dorothea, whose presence would be useful if uncongenial. I scooped my ice-cream into the sundae glasses, sprinkled the pomegranate seeds, inserted long-handled spoons, arranged the parasols deftly, and handed them to her. The look she gave me had, I reckoned, increased respect.

'How utterly adorable, James!' she said, pinching my shoulder in what was no doubt intended as a more than friendly gesture. I wanted to pinch her back, but might have dropped the glass.

She peered at the contents myopically, close enough to risk a parasol in the eye, or a dollop on the nose.

'What a lovely colour. Honey and Ginger? Butterscotch? Hokey-Pokey?'

I knew she'd get to the hokey-pokies soon enough.

'None of the above,' I said firmly.

'Another family secret?' I narrowly avoided yet another pinch.

'Let's carry them in, and all will be revealed.'

As we entered I wished I had dimmed the lights, placed a candle on each sundae and played the *March of the Toreadors* or something equally sugary and wet. I handed the glasses round.

'Ladies and gentlemen,' I declaimed, as if twirling a moustache. 'Concupiscent curds!'

'Goody!' said Miles, catching the spirit. Philip smiled sweetly, and bent to smell the offering. Looked a bit puzzled and sniffed again. Odd colour, odd smell. He took a small mouthful. Odd taste. None of the above disagreeable, just ... new. He tasted some more. Everyone was doing much the same, peering and sniffing, taking exploratory spoonfuls.

'Yes,' I said, 'this will be unfamiliar to you. It is to me too, since I invented it. If anyone can guess the ingredients, they win a fiver. My only hint is that I made it in my Magimix ...'

No one even tried to guess, being gracious enough not to spoil my fun.

'Please, emperor,' said Patricia. 'Do tell!'

They settled back, spooning gingerly.

'Well, we are a group who are, in our modest ways, interrogating ultimate things ... if that is not too grand a phrase. I fear it may be. What we are, really – or may I just say, what I am – is stumbling about, trying not to bump into more things. We suffer from loss, and are facing it. And we have, in our inchoate way, a yearning to understand what cannot be understood, to accept what is unacceptable, and to acquire some small modicum of wisdom that may guide us.

'This made me think, of course, of the wise men following the star – the Magi. And so what we are eating is their gift of frankincense and myrrh, whipped up in my Magimix for your delectation.'

My new friends (for a fleeting and certainly illusory moment I felt them as such) were, if I may say so myself, rapt. I had just said more words in a moment than I had in our two previous meetings combined. And having started I could hardly stop.

'Few of us practise a religion, though we are occasionally and ceremonially observant. The absence of faith is regrettable, for there was considerable solace embedded in the structures and strictures that our forebears practised and in which they believed. I almost envy them, for nothing – as Eliot remarked tartly – can *replace* religious faith. It's like virginity. Either you have it or you have to do without it. And scepticism and irony are such thin soup ...'

I paused to take up my sundae glass and to spoon a large helping into my mouth. No one could have called it delicious, nor did anyone actually gag. Anyway, it was a good gag.

'May I,' asked Patricia, fearing that I might soon be unstoppable, 'ask a question, or perhaps it is an observation masked as a question?'

'Of course.'

'As I said, I admire your Mr Stevens – this is a perfect little poem. But is it, I wonder, how *you* actually feel?'

I am not clear whether I had hoped for such a question, or dreaded its assumed familiarity. I decided, as Sam might have advised, to duck it.

'Say more, please. I'm not entirely clear what would count as a response to that, or – if I did – whether I would wish to make one.'

'I respect that. This poem takes the hard and cool view, it is materialistic. We are creatures relentlessly driven by appetite, and once dead are nothing more than matter freed from desire or attachment. Mr Stevens's vulgar revellers – it's so funny of you to make *us* into versions of them – give no thought to the corpse in the adjoining room, which is cold and dumb. Whereas they, by implication, are warm and dumb. They carry on, carrying on. Is that what you are doing?'

'Of course not. I haven't the energy,' I said, resisting an urge to explain, instead blowing an elegant smoke ring that inhabited the air round my head like a halo, then turning to add a log to the dying fire.

The conversation slowed at this point – as I had hoped it might – and though we carried on for another half-hour, the evening drew to a close, people donned their coats and scarves. Miles winked and pressed my shoulder, just before Dorothea pinched it again. It would take a few days for it to regain its peace of mind.

When I closed the door, I noticed that Philip had not risen from his comfy chair.

'Fancy a nightcap?' he asked.

I went to the drinks tray, poured two glasses of Armagnac, looked at them, and topped them up.

'Perfect,' he said, smelling the contents and then quaffing more than was usual or seemly. Shook his head as the liquid burned down his throat and into his stomach, smelled the glass again.

'That was a very amusing performance,' he said. 'Thank you, it was brave. I had no idea you were so inwardly dishevelled.'

I twirled my eyebrows – I can also make my ears wiggle, Rudy loves that – in my most Groucho-like manner.

'You mean I ought not to be?'

'Fair comment. I think in these situations it is best to depart from the emotional realities – they are what they are – and proceed to the practical ones. To this end, and not so much begging as assuming your permission, I have been sifting about for a defence lawyer of the highest quality, who is both available and willing to take on a case as unusual and as difficult as your own.'

He paused to finish his drink, and to lift and tilt the glass slightly for a refill.

'This has not been easy ...'

'I know, and I am most grateful to you.'

'I wonder if you do know. I am not referring to your actions with regard to hastening Suzy's death. There are many examples of such behaviour, though they very rarely reach the courts. But what is unusual here – and I have begged you to reconsider this – is that you wish to proclaim both your guilt and your innocence at the same time.'

I remained silent. This was a fair précis of my position.

'Consequently, though you wish to plead not guilty to the charge of murder, you intend to testify that you did, in fact, kill your wife in a premeditated fashion. You will give details of how you did this, and you will admit that she did not ask you to do so.'

I refilled my own glass.

'I have consulted a former colleague at my chambers, who has a remarkable record in the courts. He has represented some of the famous villains of our time, as well as some of the most obviously guilty malefactors of a superior sort. He is as good as it gets in that shabby outpost of the legal profession. I explained the details of your case – what happened, and your attitude to it. And you know what he said?'

I didn't, so I finished my Armagnac.

'"Wouldn't touch it with a bloody bargepole. I never mind if my clients look like congenital idiots, but I strongly object when I do! Any judge would think that my client was barmy and I was bonkers to go anywhere near him."'

Philip raised his glass, as if Caesar to a doomed gladiator.

'I'm not going to argue with you. What's the point? I have another chap, first-rate, young but experienced, who is willing at least to talk to you, on the grounds that while he hasn't been apprised of your arguments, he does, as it were, sympathise with the movement … His name is Cowper, Jonathan Cowper. He could see you – I hope this wasn't presumptuous – next Thursday at three. I can send you his details.'

'Do, please,' I said. 'That is so kind of you, and I look forward to seeing him and trying to explain myself and my situation.'

'Good luck,' said Philip, rising unsteadily. It was late, he'd drunk too much, and had only the dregs of the little strength with which he'd come.

'Let me ring for a car,' I said.

'Let me. I have an app that summons a black taxi. Can't abide those Ubers.'

It arrived in four minutes, and he was off into the dark, and soon enough I was too.

Jonathan Cowper: like an ale from the West Country. In the modern age, it sounds like an alias designed to frustrate googling. I tried, even added *lawyer*, but got so many of them that your actual Jonathan Cowper, of Fonthill Chambers, evaded me entirely. All I knew of him was what Philip told me: 'He seems unprepossessing, but he's very able. Give him a try and see how you get on.'

On first meeting what surprised me was how unsurprising the young lawyer looked, and sounded. He greeted me at the door, which opened into a small room lined with books and box files, and a dirty window overlooking the Clerkenwell Road. Neither the right room, nor the right road.

'Dr Darke? I'm Jonathan Cowper. It's good of you to come.'

We shook hands.

'Tell me, before we begin, how is Philip? I haven't seen him for a few months . . .'

'As well as can be expected.'

He seemed sorry to hear it.

He did not retreat behind his desk, but suggested we sat in a pair of worn leather armchairs separated by a side table covered in papers.

'Can I offer coffee? Tea?'

'No, thank you.'

'In that case,' he said, sitting back, 'tell me your story. I would prefer the full version, and I will not interrupt you. I think it best to begin this way.'

His accent, even to one whose ear is as finely calibrated as my own, was unlocateable as to class or region. He might have gone to a public school, and Oxbridge, as you expect of a barrister, but on the other hand he might be grammar school and a redbricker, risen like Jesus. He was well over six feet, slender in a way that might have been elegant but displayed as scrawny, with a prominent Adam's apple and shoulders that turned inwards, just a trifle. Nothing Uriah Heapish, but not the sort of charismatic figure you want at your side in court. His *café au lait*-coloured hair had an old-fashioned crisp parting on the left, held in place by some sort of goo. His suit might as well have had its Marks & Spencer label on the outside. Sam has one too; presumably they only make the one style, if style is the right word, and it isn't.

Composing myself after my failure socially to anatomise my new acquaintance – I, a student of Sherlock Holmes! – I gave him a full account, with a proper beginning (Suzy is diagnosed with cancer), a middle (it gets progressively more horrible) and an end (hers, aided and abetted by myself).

He sat still, did not take his eyes off my face, and they registered what I began to suspect was a remarkable responsiveness.

When I had finished, after fifteen or twenty minutes, he leant forward gently.

'Wonderful,' he said in a quiet voice. 'That was perfectly clear, and so helpful.' He rose and made his way across the room.

'Do you mind if I fetch a glass of water? Can I get you some?'

He returned from the small fridge I had noticed just outside his door, with two bottles of Evian water and two (clean) glasses.

'Now,' he said, 'may I talk for a bit too? And ask some questions?'

'Of course.'

'This is an unusual case, as you know. Indeed, it is the very unusualness that is so appealing, and so daunting. We lawyers always say – though it is not entirely true – that every case is different. But your case? It's differenter than different. In my experience it is unique. Usually lawyers can find chinks of light in the edifice of the law, some precedents and arguments that, if you deploy them with sufficient skill and clarity, might shift the mind of a judge or jury: *seen like this, rather than like that, you will understand that we have the law on our side.*

'And the fact is, we don't, not now, not in England. It is part of the appeal of your case that it may raise public consciousness and concern, and that we may eventually catch up with much of the rest of the world with regard to the moral and legal questions regarding assisted dying. I don't just mean Holland and Switzerland, for goodness' sake. Even the Americans are ahead of us on this one – or at least some of their states are.'

He was showing increasing signs of animation as he spoke, his voice rising in both volume and pitch, his hands moving to emphasise points. I feared that he might continue to speak in paragraphs, which lawyers are wont to do, and which is a certain way to lose your interlocutor's attention. When someone says more than three consecutive sentences, my eyes begin to close.

'Nevertheless, I've begun looking at precedents, and found one or two useful things. There was a case in the 1970s – I haven't yet found the details, but it'll all be in the relevant volumes – in which a man was accused of "aiding and abetting" the suicide of his wife and charged with murder. Similar case to yours, really. Wife dying a terrible death, begging to be released. Husband resisted, but finally gave in. Strangled her, I believe.'

Brave chap. Couldn't have done so myself, though I considered replacing the pillows from under Suzy's head to on top of it. Couldn't face that either.

'He was represented by an Irish QC named Comyn, I think it was, who said it was the saddest case he ever defended. And they got lucky, and found the right judge, who first agreed to a mitigated charge of manslaughter, but then gave the defendant an absolute discharge. He ruled that since this action by the defendant was never going to be repeated, and since he was no risk to others, it was not in the public interest to see him imprisoned. I was surprised by this. I will certainly do more work on it – and I shall certainly cite the case.'

'He let him go? I don't understand. Surely it is a precedent? Doesn't that mean that anyone who acts similarly will be treated similarly?'

Jonathan Cowper smiled, and put his hands out, as if beseechingly.

'If only, if only. Precedents, case law? They count, but not as much as members of the public think. They suppose that if you can find a precedent, then it determines what must happen in the future. But cases differ, and it is the differences that are crucial, not the similarities, and times change, attitudes change, and the courts evolve in their decision-making. Even what counts as a crime gets defined and redefined.'

All of this was marginally heartening, had my heart been ready to lift, rather than to attack me. But there were clearly misunderstood and uncalibrated legal and moral issues here, that ought to be researched and made public. That was what we were trying to do, though it was already beginning to feel like pissing into a typhoon.

'This is why I want to start a campaign, if that isn't too grand or unrealistic an expectation. Do you think doing so would prejudice the case?'

'Some judges might regard it as inappropriate . . .' he began.

'Really? Why would that be?'

'Never mind. For now you must do this on your own terms. It's you who have so much to lose – why make compromises along the way?'

'I have no intention of doing so.'

'I trust you are aware of the likely consequences? For every person who listens sympathetically, there will be another shouting you down. You will be vilified and demonised.'

'Indeed. Philip thinks that is the essential part of the process – without opponents there is nothing about which to argue. The moral war might be winnable in the long term, even if the legal one is not yet. I presume you think we are going to lose in court?'

'Of course I think we are going to lose, assuming the forensic results go against you. But I have no intention of giving up before we start. There are a number of promising issues to explore. But first, can we get one thing clear, because it is the greatest single stumbling block?'

'Of course.'

'You wish to plead not guilty to a charge of murder, and then admit in court that you did in fact take steps to kill your wife. Is this right? And you intend to reject the possible fallback of a plea of guilty to manslaughter, which the CPS may well offer in such a case?'

'That's right.'

'So be it. Are you aware that if you are convicted of murder the statutory sentence is life imprisonment?'

I was not. I should have been, I suppose.

'You're right to look alarmed. But of course "life" here does not mean life. In practice the tariff – that's legalese for the term of a sentence – is up to the judge. And this is at the heart of the problem. It will all depend on who hears your case. High Court judges, the ones you have to call My Lord, differ enormously in the severity of their sentencing.'

This might be where Philip came in.

'I always supposed – you know how things work? – that one might be able to influence who gets assigned to the case?'

'No. You can't. Rarely happens these days. And, to be frank, and making a genuine attempt to alarm you, I can think of judges whose very presence on the bench will condemn you – *if* you are found guilty – to a seriously long stretch.'

Only a damn fool could fail to take this seriously.

'Defendants – and indeed some lawyers I know – often make the mistake of concentrating their wooing on the jury, so anxious are they to get a not-guilty verdict. But what they neglect is that you have to seduce the judge as well, for if you are found guilty your fate is then in the hands of My Lord.'

All this was new to me, and alarming. Philip could certainly have apprised me of all of this, but – wisely, I suppose – held back, waiting for the right moment, and the right person.

'As I understand it, the key in this case is not what you *intended* – all the *mens rea* nonsense about premeditation and motive. No, the essential question is not what you meant to do but what you actually *did*. If you intended to kill your wife and then gave her three aspirins, believing them to be cyanide, you would be guilty of nothing other than stupidity, even if she died immediately thereafter. *Post hoc ergo propter hoc.*'

'Of course,' I said. 'I suppose the result of the forensic tests after the exhumation will settle that?'

'They might, and they might not. Too often such information is unobtainable, or ambiguous. That is why you will get forensic scientists arguing for each side in a case. I'm sorry to have to say this, but after so many months in a grave a body does not infallibly reveal its secrets.'

I stood behind the yew tree in the rain. For hours. As they dug up the casket with remains in it. Her remains, and mine. Whatever was in it, some refiguration of the slime and goo of being. Matter is neither created nor destroyed, but people are.

'When can we see the results? It's been some time now . . .'

He laughed. 'If only it were so easy. That information will only be divulged during discovery, when the CPS has to share with us all the information they are going to deploy, so that we may prepare ourselves accordingly.'

He stopped, and seemed to blush slightly.

'I hope you will forgive me – I seem to be racing ahead. When I say "we" I am assuming, inappropriately, that you will instruct me in the case. I'm so sorry. But speaking frankly, I very much hope you will. I admire you, Dr Darke. If I were to represent you, I would argue my heart out. Who was it, that philosopher who said the heart has its reasons?'

'Pascal.'

'Yes, that's it. Let's have our day in court. With a jury you can never tell. We need to move them, to open their minds and hearts to make them think new and better thoughts.'

He was just as Philip had implied.

'Well, Jonathan – if I may – I am impressed by what you have said, your arguments and your perspective. I would feel honoured if you would consent to represent me.'

'And I will feel honoured to do so. You will need to employ a solicitor – I can recommend one – as he must make the referral to me. It's one of the oddities of our legal system. And we need to have a discussion about costs. This kind of case can be very expensive, if it goes through the whole process ...'

'I assumed so.'

'My clerk will send you a schedule of my fees, but I would approximate ...'

'Don't. I trust you, I will pay whatever you charge. I have the motive and the means, after all.'

He had the grace to smile wryly but held up his hand, as if seeking permission to speak.

'You have been frank with me, and laid your cards on the table, but I fear I have not, and I wish to do so now, if I may?'

This was puzzling enough. What might he add to what he had outlined so admirably?

'I am – I don't exactly know how to express this – I am *personally* involved here, for the issues that your case raises have been in the forefront of my mind this last year. And of my heart, if I may include that as well. And I have been anxious to find a way to get involved, if we can call it that?

'My grandmother Esther, who is ninety-three years old, has lived for the last five years in a nursing facility – I would hesitate to call it a home – in Islington. She has advanced Alzheimer's, and spends her days in a chair, in a row of chairs carrying the husks and shells of other people. All unaware of each other's names or stories, unaware even of their own. When I visit she has no idea who I am. It is unbearable. I go not for her sake, but for my own.

'Granny is shrunken, lost in her own skin, all but vanished. I suppose that people in such an attenuated state of being still maintain their rights. You may not be able to access your personhood, but that is no reason for someone to deny or to terminate it. Other than yourself, if you are able . . .'

This was sympathetic, but – however worthy – a trifle long-winded for someone of my limited attention span. Why is it that the higher the moral register, the longer the paragraphs? I took a few sips of water, and nodded for him to go on, feeling mildly ashamed to seem uninterested. I wasn't.

'But Granny is dying now, of multiple cancers which swell and cause her agonies that she is unable either to tolerate or to understand. And now all efforts are being made not to help her to go, but to force her to stay in the land of the living. And there is no her. She needs to die, and is not allowed to. It disgusts me. You call that respect or reverence for life?

'I have wanted for some time to write something about this. I need to get it off my chest, if you'll forgive the cliché. I wanted to do something for the newspapers, *The Times* perhaps, with some pictures of elderly people marooned in their "homes" in rows of chairs, senile and shrunken, lost, dying and undead. And you know what? You know what!'

'What?'

'I googled and googled, searched and searched, but when you ask for images of the elderly and senile and demented in nursing homes, what you get is pictures of smiling carers and happy old folks dancing the cha-cha-cha. I searched forever to find a single image that shows what my grandma is experiencing, for an image that is *real*. Almost nothing. It's as if some prohibition were being imposed – it's a cover-up worthy of a Royal Commission, this abridgement of human rights. Because as I see it, the final human right is the right to die with dignity.'

I felt a glow of confidence that had nothing to do with my chances of acquittal in court. I had found what Pascal might have called a heart-speaker, if he'd had the imagination to coin the term.

'Of course I agree with you, Jonathan, as you would suppose. We have fetishised prolonging human life, in any way and for any length of time. I blame the God squad, not God himself, who, if he existed, would surely have released his poor creatures from their degradation. If he can slaughter the innocent and healthy, surely he could release the terminally ill? In a hundred years, when we allow the dying the right to depart gracefully, people will look back on us as barbarians and fools.'

Jonathan rose and took me by the hand, before remembering to shake it.

'Let's do it,' he said. 'I'm on the case!' He grinned, boyishly. 'I've always wanted to say that, but I was a bit shy ...'

'Next thing we know,' I said, 'we'll decide the game is afoot, and bring out the hounds and the Baker Street Irregulars.'

As I walked down the Clerkenwell Road seeking a taxi, I vomited in the gutter so suddenly and violently that I slumped on my knees, retching. Several passers-by offered assistance, but I waved them away, found my feet, and wiped my mouth. A few minutes later a black cab pulled over, reluctantly, to take me home.

I showered, went to bed naked, covered my head with the blanket and didn't get up for a very long time.

Chapter 14

There's just the three of us: Lucy and me, and Philip. I'd been uncertain whether he'd be able, or indeed willing, to take a role in the ... whatever you call it. He had a professional position after all. But as his health declined, he had relinquished his many duties and was keen to come.

'I have nothing to lose now,' he said, 'and it is a blessing to be able to join you in whatever way I can. I think I can just about see this out.' He had lost weight, walked now with the aid of an elegant walking stick with a carved ivory handle, and was having some difficulty breathing. He'd give it a go. Eventually, we would need some of the others: Patricia, Miles and whomever else we could usefully employ.

We were the unholy trinity, as Lucy called it. Or quartet, if you will, when Suzy graces us with an appearance, though she rarely does these days. At first she had inserted herself in my life regularly if unexpectedly, then less frequently, but recently only if invited, and sometimes not even then. She is fading again, dying again. *Where are you when I need you?* I enquire plaintively, without getting an answer. I can barely remember what she looked like. Which she? The diminished gasping skeletal final Suzy? The pretty, libidinously innocent girl in my bedroom at Merton? The young mother? The disappointed writer? The tennis player on court, swishing with her Jewish partner?

If whichever Suzy was unwilling or unable to attend, I would have to step into the breach, and be her. She would have approved of the ensuing affair, was happiest when most forcibly transgressive, and if the attention was still going to be on her, whoever she now was, then it would also have to be on me, who am less suited to a public role.

When I was informed of the charge of murder from the Public, um, Persecutor's Office, I was curiously elated. It was always unlikely that the Crown Prosecution Service would decide not to pursue the matter (which is to say, me) and if they did I preferred the charge of murder to the washed-out alternative of manslaughter. Not much fun in that, nothing to get your teeth into, and much harder to arouse public interest in. But a nice juicy murder? People love it. If there were still capital punishment, you'd get mighty crowds for a hanging, as they did in the eighteenth century.

Philip had the first words. His voice strengthened as the whisky took effect: 'The key is not how to present this argument, though of course you need to do that. But what is essential is that you mobilise the opposition ...'

Lucy looked puzzled.

'I'm not sure what you mean,' she said. 'Surely you mean some support?'

'Without an opposition there is no issue. It's all very well arguing that your father's case is of general interest – if, indeed, it is – and that it should be taken seriously. But unless you can get onto the front pages and on television, no one will know anything about the matter. And such coverage can only happen if James is roundly attacked, excoriated and vilified. Then he will become an object of interest, and once he is, and is able to respond, then the issue will slowly morph from his culpability onto the moral and legal problems that you are attempting to foreground. You can't fight for a cause unless people are aware of it.'

'Well,' I said, 'I am going to write and distribute my little pamphlet . . .'

'That is the catalyst,' said Philip. 'What matters is the reaction.'

Lucy twiddled her finger in her curls.

'What do you mean?' she said.

'Here is what I envisage,' he said. 'First, James prepares his public statement. I gather this is almost ready. It must contain the facts of the matter as James wishes to present them, but in such a way that they may easily be misquoted and misunderstood. You know, in the way movie reviews sometimes say that a film is an astonishing failure, and the marquee is lit up with the single word ASTONISHING!'

'Second, you try to get some immediate publicity, but this will not happen until – third, you get some responses condemning James in the most forthright, preferably hysterical terms.'

'How do you do that?' asked Lucy, nervously. Her father? Vilified and excoriated in public? And she to look on in horror, like Mary at the foot of the cross?

Cross? Suzy claimed that there was no such, they'd just nailed him to an available stake or a tree; the cross got added much later to sex up the story. A more compelling image, better composition to it. 'Crucial fiction,' Suzy liked to call it. And at that moment, catalysed by that memory, her faint presence entered my heart, and through it the room.

Suzy had her own understanding of the resurrection, and of the miracle of Easter. Jesus has risen: not like a balloon, or the FTSE 500. No, he was more like a soufflé, light and airy enough to ascend to heaven and be declared absolutely divine, darling. At Oxford we founded a sect, the Soufflarians, a secret sybaritic movement, the members of which would meet at our flat on Easter Sunday. Each would bring an egg and a passion fruit, the perfect symbols and ingredients, and I would make a soufflé in remembrance of that miraculous event, the Easter Uprising.

They were innocent happy times. We drank too much, played loud music, giggled and flirted. Suzy would dance and wriggle lasciviously in circles round me, teasing and laughing, shaking her hair and hips – eternally desirable, mine.

In her final year at St Anne's, Suzy wrote and performed a one-woman cabaret skit satirising the Anglican religion and its followers, with a particularly scathing portrayal of the Archbishop of Canterbury. After her bravura performance, with songs in the manner of Lotte Lenya, all Sobranie cigarettes and husk, various parents complained to the College Dean. Offensive? What more could a girl want? Her lines allowed her considerable interpretative leeway; there were few objections to the term *Archvillain*, which was pretty tame really, but *of Cunterbury* was not. Bearded by her irate Dean, Suzy claimed merely to be speaking in a posh accent, similar to that of most of her teachers, fellow students and their parents.

Prompted and amused by the memory, I asked Philip if we might be able to construct some clerical condemnation, the higher the better? After all, it is not man's role, but God's – when he can be bothered – to shepherd the dying into the eternal life.

'Maybe we could get the Archbishop of Canterbury to make a statement?'

Philip looked interested.

'Good enough chap really, not much harm in him. Bit worthy perhaps, but that's his line, isn't it? Let me have a thought . . . there's no sense initiating this until we have your . . . what'll we call it . . . foundation document, might that do it?'

'What's that when it's at home?' asked Lucy. 'You mean, like the Declaration of Independence?'

'Or the Rights of Man?' I was happy to add.

I had, of course, been thinking about this little essay since my lunch with Philip at the Athenaeum. I'd revised his suggested title, and sketched out a line of thought. Various lines of thought. My statement had to be long enough to be bound as a pamphlet, but short enough to hold attention, written in an approachable voice, unpedantic, not in the least schoolmasterly.

That is, not by me. I'd struggled, but made a start.

'May I read it to you? What I've managed so far?'

They settled down, and I took out my paltry two-page opening.

EASEFUL DEATH
DO YOU LOVE YOUR DOG MORE THAN YOUR WIFE?

My name is James Darke, and I have recently been charged with the murder of my wife, the novelist Suzy Moulton, who died last year. She was suffering from terminal lung cancer, was in agonising pain, ready for death, begging for relief. The usual painkillers did not help her.

One night I prepared a glass of sweet tea, into which I dissolved enough drugs to put her into a deep sleep. Some hours later, she died.

I was devastated by this loss, but relieved that she was at peace at last, and that I had helped her to go. After my actions, I was consumed by a combination of guilt and innocence. Had I killed my wife? Or had I released her?

I now believe that what I did was right, and loving, and just. What I feel today is not shame, but anger. Anger that a loving act of this kind is culturally, morally, spiritually and legally unacceptable, and that you can go to jail for having committed 'murder'. And that is ridiculous, and it is time to get up and say so.

Now let me tell you another story.

I have a friend, whom I will call J, a woman living in the north of England, who is a widow in her late fifties. Her children have left home, and her mother lives in a granny flat attached to her house. Though her mother is suffering from Alzheimer's, they manage to enjoy their time together. They are both devoted to their dog Pepper, a white poodle. Recently, though, their dog – who was fourteen years old – began to exhibit signs of distress, was listless and dragging herself about, and went off her food. J took her to the vet who said that Pepper had a tumour, and was dying. As the illness progressed, J visited the vet again, carrying her poorly dog in her arms, and that day it was given an injection, went to sleep, and soon died.

'She was suffering, and it was best to let her go peacefully,' J said. The next day, she and her mother, her children and grandchildren came, and they buried her beloved dog in the garden. J wept and wept, but knew she had acted for the best.

She has not been charged with murder. Indeed, everyone would agree that she did the right thing.

What is the difference, then, between these two stories? The circumstances are identical: the end of life approaches, suffering heightens, death is inevitable and imminent. It is time to make the final, loving decision . . .

I looked up.

'That's about it, so far. I'm not very good at this sort of thing . . .'

Philip was non-committal, and Lucy's protestations of admiration rang false.

It shouldn't have been so difficult. The subject involved my self-interest, enlisted my deepest beliefs, was of general interest. I can write my *Gulliver*, but this . . . what is it? Not *foundation document*, that's idiotic. *Manifesto?* All of a sudden I'm a Marxist? If so, I prefer Groucho: 'Whatever it is, I'm against it!'

I merely want to explain. To make clear. What I did, not *to* but *for* my Suzy, my lost and sometimes found dear one. But when I sat down to write my brain emptied and cramped, the unsullied white of the open page mocked me, threatened and cajoled: *Go on. Write!*

I can't. I know this project is both good and necessary, but it feels like someone else's idea, and that it has nothing to do with me.

It is impossible to say just what I mean.

Do You Love Your Dog More Than Your Wife? I'm trying to write about loving dogs? I detest the smelly slobbery hairy shit-slingers. And why would I want to write, publicly – for the *public*, for Christ's sake – about my dear lost Suzy? I should write only for myself, and for her. Between us. As I do.

I miss my Suzy. I'd give it all away to retrieve our days, our day together.

'Well,' I said, 'there's a long way to go before I finish. I have to discuss the state of the law with regard to assisted dying, cite international legislation regarding it, perhaps quote various writers and philosophers . . . And then, of course, find a publisher.'

'What's the hurry?' asked Lucy. 'And here's an idea – why don't we get Thomas involved?'

'Who?'

'You know, Bronya's boyfriend.'

'The scruff-bag? Why?'

She frowned.

'He's an international journalist. He was a stringer for Reuters, based in Amsterdam. He knows people, and how to do things . . .'

'Fine,' I said. 'Just what I need – an obscure Bulgarian so-called journalist. We can form a sort of Revolutionary Guard.'

Lucy didn't rise to the bait, scowled, twiddled.

'Why not ring him?' asked Philip. 'What do you have to lose?'

His face suggested that we had nothing to gain either. Between us we knew a lot of journalists, but he was taking Lucy seriously, which was more than I could manage.

Lucy already had her phone out.

'Thomas? Hi, it's Lucy.' She had it on loudspeaker, so we could hear his voice.

'Lucy! To what do I owe this honour?'

'A favour, Thomas. A big one, if you have time to help.'

'For you, anything.'

'Well, it's for Dad really. Have you heard the news? You know . . .'

'Bronya told me yesterday, she had it from Sam. Are you and he all right? I gather—?'

'Never mind about that. Let me explain what you might help us with.' She went on to fill him in about the statement I wished to write.

'How long will it be? Not very, I hope.'

'Just about long enough to publish as a short pamphlet – maybe eight pages?'

'Why would he wish to publish it?'

Lucy looked over at me. I shrugged my shoulders in an exaggerated manner. How dumb can you get? Leave it to the Bulgarians, right? The movement hadn't even started and it was already out of control.

Lucy offered me the phone, but I declined, feeling sheepish. I had originally underestimated Toe-mass, and treated him, as I remember, a bit dismissively.

'What can I do to help?' he asked.

'Come,' said Lucy firmly. 'We will be together again in the morning for coffee, say at ten. Could you join us at Dad's? We'd be ever so grateful.'

'Of course. Now I will bid you a fond farewell, and I'll see you in the morning.'

It was the first I'd heard of another meeting, but I didn't have anything better to do. Philip was in for as long as his strength allowed, and for Lucy it would make an excellent substitute for the domestic battle that she was clearly still fighting. When asked about this, she would deflect the question; if I persevered she would turn away and say she didn't wish to talk about it, which suited me just fine. I didn't either.

The next morning there was a knock at the door and a beaming Toe-mass entered, accompanied a step or two behind by a sheepish Bronya carrying a large paper bag that smelled of warm pastry.

'I come too. Maybe help a little?' she said, uneasy about whether she would be welcome at such a crucial and (to her) momentous gathering.

We greeted her warmly, and introduced her to Philip. What harm could she do? Toe-mass looked relieved.

I handed him a printout of my statement.

'This is the so-called foundation document, Toe-mass. I'm afraid it's not very good, not yet. It needs work. But everything flows from this. It will be printed and distributed, and we hope the newspapers and BBC will pick it up and get the ball rolling.'

He read it quickly, heedlessly one might say. I admit it is rough and incomplete, but given its importance it was due more ... well, respect.

He put it down on the table, carelessly.

'This is the modern world, James. You don't print "a statement", or "a foundation document". You set off bombs!'

None of us had the faintest idea what he was talking about.

'These days,' Toe-mass continued, 'you "publish" on social media – do tweets, join Facebook and Instagram, set up WhatsApp, grow the campaign that way. I can get us started in no time. I don't have as many followers as Jesus, but my numbers are rising and his are falling. I've been doing this for twenty years, and my contacts include major journalists, radio and TV newscasters, and the wire services. In forty-six countries.'

This palpable bit of showing off was presumably designed to establish himself as someone of consequence. It worked, and I was able to forgive his hubris. I'd mistaken him for a plumber at Christmas, and when informed otherwise had continued to regard him as if he were. Now a new conundrum emerged: if he is a journalist of some experience and reputation, why is he dating my cleaner?

'That is all very well,' said Philip, 'not that I know much about it. But what you need is not merely followers, but opponents. To launch such a movement it has to be controversial.'

Toe-mass laughed so hard his coffee waved in the cup.

'Philip! This is the Internet we're talking about. Within a week we will have more comments condemning James than there were for Judas. All we have to do is set off our bombs! The first tweets are essential. I can get it started, use all the available hashtags: *assisted dying, murder, religious debate, faith, Christianity*, you know?'

We most certainly did not. Philip slumped wearily in his chair, though it was unclear whether he was ignorant of such matters, or merely detested them. I made myself another flat white, triple shot, and scoffed a second croissant that would repeat on me all day, and got floury bits down my shirt. But Lucy seemed to be keeping up, just. She must know about such things from her work.

'So it'll go viral, will it?'

'Viral?' said Toe-mass. 'I hope so! I can get things going, and set up the accounts. It shouldn't take long before the first tweets go up. Then we should be trending within twenty-four hours. And then the C-word will kick in.'

Well, I could just about guess what he was referring to, but not why. I was wrong.

'Some celebrity or other will like you and retweet, one of those fuckwits with alternative inclinations, a big mouth, and millions of followers. Gwyneth Paltrow perhaps? She has a website called Gloop, encouraging her ladies to shove expensive stuff up their private bits, and then selling it to them.'

This was too much for me. I didn't understand it, felt sidelined in making my properly argued and distributed statement; instead Toe-mass was offering trendy bombs and stuffed vaginas.

He took out a piece of paper. 'Want to hear some of my ideas for the first tweets?'

We didn't have much choice. I drank my flat white bomb and started to quiver immediately. It felt appropriate.

'I've already set up your account. Your Twitter name is @JAMES DARKE, and your profile description will be "Accused of murdering my wife, and unrepentant". He opened his phone to show his own Twitter profile: Thomas Kovics, described as 'Journalist, TV presenter, and man about the world'.

'You understand the concept, I presume?' It was the first sign of stupidity he'd shown that morning. I didn't have a clue.

'Well, you are allowed a hundred and forty characters ...'

'That many? You mean, as in a Wagner Opera, Vikings with horny hats?'

'Yes, yes. Very funny. Characters, as in letters. Tweets have to be concise. The people who post and read them have a very short attention span, so you have to hit them hard immediately.'

'Is this where the bombs come in?'

'You bet.' He took out a page from his jacket pocket. 'We could start with this, that'll get them going!'

DO YOU LOVE YOUR DOG MORE THAN YOUR WIFE? WHEN YOUR DOG IS DYING YOU END ITS MISERY. WHEN YOUR LOVED ONE IS DYING, YOU MAKE THEM SUFFER TO THE LAST BREATH. THIS IS CALLED GOD'S WILL!

'Good,' said Philip. 'How long until this gets picked up in the media, would you say?'

'You'll be surprised,' said Toe-mass. 'But there is other work to do, and I haven't the ability or the time to do it. You will need to set up a website, James. I have already reserved the domain www. Jamesdarke.net. On it you can post your "foundation statement" – any length you want, there are no word limits – and you can tweet links to it. People interested in hearing more – and there will be a lot of them – can follow your arguments. I can recommend an IT guy who's good at website design.'

'I have one myself. Very clever chap, Serbian, I think, name of Dragan. I call him the Magic Dragan, because he can do anything.'

'PUFF!' said Lucy excitedly. 'How adorable! PUFF!'

'I beg your pardon? Are you being a bomb?'

'No, silly. Your joke. The Magic Dragon was called Puff. You must remember. *Puff the Magic Dragon*. It was my favourite song.' She began to hum. The tune had an unusual tenacity: once Puff got into your mind, there was no slaying him. Suzy would clasp her temples and howl, 'Puff the Magic Dragon is doing my head in!' When informed by an in-the-know friend that the song was actually about smoking dope, she changed into her kaftan, rolled and smoked a neat, tight joint, puffed and took a drag on it and listened to PUFF again in a heightened state of receptivity.

It was worse.

We dispersed an hour later, mildly elated but exhausted. Lucy had been up twice in the night, in spite of the absence of Amelie. I don't sleep much anyway, and Philip was just about bearing up. Toe-mass and Bronya, on the other hand, departed holding hands, having had fun.

'Isn't Thomas great?' Lucy enquired, as we closed the door on the departing trio.

'Yes, yes. I can see he will be useful ... But of course the key person is Philip, who will be an invaluable asset, if his strength holds out.'

'Dad?' Lucy turned, looked ... what? Pained? Puzzled?

'What?'

'Didn't you notice?'

'Notice what?'

She sighed and shrugged her shoulders, looked up imploringly as if for divine guidance, just as her mother had. Apparently I am *hopeless* sometimes.

'Philip. He isn't one of us ... It's dear of him to offer support and counsel, of course, very dear, but he's not ...'

I was rather offended by this.

'Whatever are you talking about? From the very beginning I have relied on him to—'

'He's not one of us. He's hardly part of your movement, whatever you call it ...'

'I don't.' I turned my back to walk into the kitchen. She followed me, unwilling or unable to shut up.

'Didn't you even notice? Of course you didn't. Whenever he referred to plans and strategies he never said "we" – it was always "you".'

'That,' I said, still moving forward and unwilling to turn round, 'is called reticence and good breeding. He would not presume—'

'Crap!' said Lucy fiercely. 'He has counselled against virtually every move you've made so far. He may lend his ear and advice, but he will not be out there, not with us. He knows this exactly for what it is.'

'What's that, then?'

'A stupendous folly. And your only real companion in this – how sad – is going to be me. A *folie à deux*!'

I turned. Took her hand, embraced her. As good and as fierce and as loyal as her mother, she is.

But if a folly, 'tis mine alone. Lucy must keep out of it. And I'm not sure my poor failing heart is up to it either. It's increasingly clear that this so-called movement has nothing to do with me.

Chapter 15

Toe-mass says I *must* have an image or photograph of myself to enhance and to particularise my forthcoming online presence. This will apparently make me more *real*. I prefer being the presence behind the curtain, chuntering away, like God. There's no reliable picture of him either.

We all argued about this for a time, and I lost, so we have compromised, and I commissioned this amusing linocut.

The caricature is fair comment, not exactly flattering but both serviceable and memorable. I will get the Magic Dragan to smallify and roundify it for my Twitter image that goes next to my profile.

It can also go on my new website, for which I have written a self-introduction to go on the front page:

Welcome. My name is Darke, James Darke. You may know me through the impending court case in which I will be prosecuted on the charge of murdering my wife, Suzy Moulton, whom I assisted to die when she was in the last stages of her terminal agony. The proper term for this is 'mercy killing'. It is certainly not 'murder,' with which I have been charged. I regard my final intervention, to hasten her death, as an act of love, and morally just. I would wish to be treated similarly.

On this website, you will see a statement entitled 'Do You Love Your Dog More Than Your Wife?' which is a defence of my behaviour. It is intended to serve as a catalyst, if that isn't too grand a concept, towards a change in our moral thinking, and our legislation: to allow the terminally ill to die with dignity, in what Keats called 'easeful death'. That this compassionate position is regarded as immoral, and in most countries illegal, continues to surprise and to appall me.

If you follow the menu and the various links, you will find a great deal of helpful information about the Easeful Death campaign.

I am no crusader, and ill-suited to spearhead such a movement. In any case, one cannot do much spearheading from a prison, which is where I am likely to be heading. My hope, when I don prison garb, will be that I have kindled a tiny spark, which may one day become a fire.

When I reread this, it sounds misguided and sanctimonious, as if written by a person more robust but stupider than I. It needs further work.

I'm pleased, though, to be adding the Twitter bluebird to my growing aviary. I am informed that his name is Larry, no idea why, short of the American obsession with cuteness: unless animals have names, they're just walking dinners. Their monikers have to be sweet, not meat: they cannot be called Porkchop or T-Bone. The soppy bluebird is presumably more attractive as Larry – no, not Dr

Larry – than he would be if his name were Shlomo. Are some birds Jewish? Could they tweet in Hebrew through elongated beaks? Can you circumcise them?

Toe-mass posted our first tweets the next morning. Within a few minutes, the replies came rolling in. At first, it was exciting, and seemed instantly to connect me to the world, and to people who might be interested in my plight and my opinions.

Most responses were supportive, sympathetic, and outraged not so much on my behalf, as on behalf of my behaviour. Of course there should be Easeful Death, and if the state or medical profession will not allow it, then this is the sort of situation that has to be dealt with discreetly, 'in-house', as one put it. In general these twits were boring, and I tired of them quickly. I was treated as if a member of a team. What a humiliation. Even groups (as in, poetry) are beyond me.

But increasing numbers of the twits hated me. I was accused of selfishness, Godlessness, self-absorption, and lacking a moral compass. This seemed to me fair comment, if over-enthusiastic in expression: I was threatened with every punishment from rotten eggs to crucifixion on Islington Green.

This kind of thing palls, and after the first few hours I barely looked at the twits again. Within forty-eight hours, the newspapers, as Toe-mass predicted, picked up the story. There was hardly any need to read them, for the headlines were sufficiently revealing, if largely witless. There was HEART OF DARKENESS, not to mention PRINCE of same. The headline in the *Mail* was admirable, though likely to confuse the very readership it intended to titillate:

CHARGED WITH THE MURDER OF HIS WIFE, SCHOOLMASTER PROCLAIMS HIS GUILT!

This was followed by a second wave of twit-attacks of increasing viciousness, presumably an indication of the spiteful disposition of readers of the *Mail*.

Lucy insisted that I refrain from reading either the newspapers or the twits. She has promised a regular update and synopsis, though I am not sure I will read that either, for the twits are particularly malicious and threatening.

*@**Watchyourback** We know who you are. We know where you live. We coming, we coming soon.*

*@**Ivillsnatchyerkidoff** Your daughter Lucy is suffering because of your criminal actions. She will soon be taken to a place of safety, and taken care of. Not in Abingdon. Ha ha.*

*@**DoublydisgustedX2** You will need police protection outside your home. And the taxpayer will pay for this?*

Lucy has been authorised – who gives a damn? – to answer these as she will, in my name.

*@**JAMESDARKE** Your comments matter to me. You are on a long queue, please stay online and I may answer eventually, if not later.*

I presume such threats emanate from sad, useless – and powerless – sociopaths, hiding behind keyboards and aliases. Pathetic, really. But when I said so reassuringly to Lucy, she was curiously retracted. Frightened, I suppose.

'What am I to do?' she muttered. 'Some campaign this is! Very high quality of debate!'

'Never you mind. It'll settle down,' I said, unconvincingly.

I didn't mind the threatening twits, not for a minute. What most disturbed me in this initial flurry of news coverage was not my detractors, loud and ugly as they were, but those who wished to sympathise and to support, but who found reason not to.

Another headline was eye-catching, and telling, but it was the content of the editorial that disturbed me.

THE QUALITY OF MERCY IS STAINED

The case of James Darke, the retired schoolmaster recently charged with the murder of his wife, the writer Suzanne Moulton, cannot fail to move us. Dr Darke will plead not guilty to the charge, maintaining that he assisted in the death of his wife, and that he did not murder her, but released her from her terminal agony.

Anyone who has had the experience of sitting at the bedside of the terminally ill understands how distressing it is. And though contemporary medicine has advanced in ameliorating pain, nothing can deny the torment of a difficult death. Death is not 'easeful', though both Keats and Dr Darke wish that it were.

Why do we allow this as a society? As Dr Darke has pointed out in his online manifesto 'Do You Love Your Dog More Than Your Wife?' we allow our pets an easier and more dignified exit from the land of the living than we offer our human loved ones. Why should this be?

The answer, of course, which Dr Darke does not adequately acknowledge, is that animals are different from humans. They have rights, but not many. Whereas a human being has extensive rights, both legal and moral, and must live within a framework of law.

Dr Darke is an inadequate and dangerous example. If you wish to pursue a case sympathetic to euthanasia, it is essential that the decisions about ending life are made under proper legislative and medical supervision, and at the behest of the terminally ill person. This is how such practices have evolved in Switzerland, in Holland, and in various American states. If a society is to sanction the deliberate ending of life, there must be cast-iron assurances that this is done in a manner sanctioned by the law, and carried out by medical practitioners.

Dr Darke, having taken the law into his own hands, and hence broken it, ought to plead guilty to the charge of murder. No other response on his part will contribute to the ongoing international debate about assisted dying.

Though I am no *Guardian* reader – I leave that to Sam and Lucy – this made me wince, as firmly delivered and well-argued remonstration often does.

But I got some support from friends. A charming, restrained email arrived from Dorothea, with only one *x*. I had a beautifully written missive from George, wishing me luck, in the firm belief that I would not need it: '*Those of us fortunate and strong enough to have endured prep school should have no problems in jail.*' He went on to enquire – in his mind a more important issue – about the progress of my 'little Gulliver *jeu d'esprit*'. Had I finished it? Might he once again offer an editorial eye? I responded graciously, and declined. I've got enough problems as it is.

Lucy reports that her tweets are trendy at a great rate. One of them received 673 'likes', whatever they are; yet another was immediately forwarded over a thousand times, but I don't know to whom. A hasty wetweet, as that dwatted wabbit B Bunny would put it.

Further comments, many of them hostile, apparently appear and vanish every few minutes. They don't matter, except as potential catalysts for mainstream coverage. If an issue isn't on the BBC, it is of no importance. Like Canada.

It's been a quiet news month, the maw is gaping, and I have been thrown into it. More stories followed, driven by the redtops. The broadsheets notice such matters once, and move on. But if you want sustained and venomous exposure, that's for the tabloids. Freed from the apparent necessity of reporting what is actually happening, and of sticking to the facts, what one encounters in such rags is the untrammelled popular imagination. I was soon christened Dr Death.

Lucy has sent me an update on all of this, but I hardly read it. She reports that I have a universal ecumenical appeal, having been roundly condemned by priests, rabbis, imams, pastors, monks and caliphs, and a host of other religious leaders. If anything can bring the various religions into harmonious agreement, it is me.

Next came a pleasing, ironic possibility. Miles, who has a chum who is literary editor of the FT, has suggested to him that I become their interviewee of the week, as if I were a writer. How unlikely. But the idea amused me sufficiently to prepare myself, just in case:

What books are on your bedside table?
I have stopped reading books. I have also stopped sleeping.

What is the last book that made you laugh?
The Book of Job.

What importance do you attach to literature?
I am something of a Benthamite in such matters: quantities of pleasure being equal, push-pin is as good as poetry. Of course, you could say the same with regard to serial killing.

What frightens you the most?
People. I am a claustrophobe. I cannot go on the Tube, and avoid crowds. If I am to be in company, I much prefer my own.

What is humanity's greatest achievement?
None of humanity's achievements is of the slightest importance. We are a nasty species, and the sooner our day ends, the better. I am thus an advocate for global warming: not only will we have better summers, but it will hasten the end of things, unless a nuclear winter comes first.

Who is your literary hero?
Jonathan Swift. He had the creative idea of solving the great famine by eating Irish children, of whom there were far too many due to the influence of the ubiquitous priests, who fathered a lot of them.

Who would be at your ideal dinner party?
I would rather go to prison than to a dinner party.

If you were allowed one luxury to take to your desert island, what would it be?
A suicide pill, to swallow when the available food runs out.

What projects do you have for the next few years?
I shall most likely be in prison. I am reliably informed that neither the food nor I will run out. I may need a suicide pill there as well.

To no one's surprise – even Miles thought it a long shot – the *FT* turned me down. Quite right too, and anyway I've had some fun composing my replies.

But *this* is not amusing, it is intolerable. The noisome people outside my door, shouting and gesticulating, many with microphones and cameras. There aren't many of them, but the few who come bear signs and placards as if at a political demonstration. One just says '**MURDERER!**'

I can hardly leave the house, an irony that is not lost on me. There is only the one exit, and that is into the midst of the cameras and journalists, who ring the bell regularly. Thank God it is so easily ignored. And, oh yes, on duty is a languid policeman, who has not the slightest desire to protect me from the hostility.

The demonstrations began following exposés in the *Daily Mail* and the *Sun*. Your average redtop reader is aching to find something new to hate and I fit the bill perfectly. A man may well murder his wife – the protesters knew that, indeed, more than a few may have tried after the pubs let out – but to have succeeded, and then to proclaim oneself proud of it, to have mocked God as an incompetent tosser, to have flaunted my 'three-million-pound mansion', my accent, my Oxbridge education and my utter contempt for public opinion, made me an ideal English villain.

On the afternoon of the first demonstration, I answered one of the knocks, having seen that a reporter from the BBC was on the doorstep. I opened the door and turned towards the microphone on my left.

'I would like, if I may, to thank you all for coming and to make a brief statement.'

I was shouted down, and soon retired behind my beloved black door.

That evening the news showed a clip of my undignified retreat, which soon drew a few more protestors, many of whom called themselves PRO-LIFE, as if I were by implication against it. Which I am: theirs, anyway. I would happily spray them with acid, if I knew where to buy some.

Lucy and Rudy came as quickly as possible after the ruckus began and had to push their way through the cameras and microphones thrust aggressively into their faces, which they covered with their coats. She was frightened and disgusted, and Rudy was white with anxiety, when they got through the front door and forced it closed. He went straight upstairs.

'Dad! This is what you wanted! An *opposition*! I'll bet you're pleased now!'

I allowed that I was not.

'I don't get it, I just don't get it. It's ruining our lives, it won't do any good, nobody gives a damn. And Mummy would be appalled. You think she'd admire you swanning about striking attitudes? Sacrificing everything! For nothing!'

Lucy is right.

Philip is right.

The twits are right.

The Darke Movement is a rotten idea. It stinks. Of rightness, or righteousness. I know what happens to crusaders: they pursue their exalted spiritual goals and then they die in the desert.

I am giving up a lot to gain very little. And *what* little, exactly? An alteration of hearts and minds? Of laws? Not likely: not now, not yet.

I've been trying inwardly to consult Suzy on these matters, for if this ruckus is not for her, exactly, it is certainly caused by her. But she is moving away. I have to hold my hand to my ear, I squint into the far distance, trying to catch her words or image as she recedes.

Lucy was waiting impatiently as I mused.

'The fact is, Lucy, I am doing this because I choose to. Or perhaps it is choosing me? I cannot be any clearer about it than that. I wish I could.'

'Enough, it's enough! You've caused this!'

I could see the thought cross her mind, though not her lips: *You, and Sam.*

'And you simply cannot go on living here.'

'Well, darling, you may well be right, though things will quieten down in time, if I don't give them a target. Crowds get bored. But it would be no good for me to come to Abingdon.'

'It's starting there. I've already had journalists ringing the doorbell, and we're getting these hideous threats!'

I hadn't foreseen this. That I would be the target of mass opprobrium seemed to me acceptable – the game was worth being singed by the candle – but I had not foreseen the malice directed at my family.

'Come,' I said gently, 'let's go into the kitchen. Do you want tea, or something stronger?'

By the time we had got halfway through the second bottle of wine – it was still only just past five, but needs must – we felt strengthened somewhat, and able to formulate a plan.

'It's either fight or flight,' said Lucy firmly. 'Let's get the hell out of here, and soon!'

'I've been thinking the same thing. It's intolerable. I'm already looking into it …'

'Into what?'

'A temporary relocation. Philip has had the most wonderful idea. A chap he knows wants a short-term tenant for his set in Albany ...'

Lucy looked puzzled, as well she might.

'Sorry. Albany is an eighteenth-century complex of purpose-built flats, the first in England actually, just off Piccadilly, and you call a flat there a "set", meaning a set of rooms.'

Lucy looked disapproving, and scornful.

'You've always wanted to move into the right set – it'll suit you just dandy. But why will it be any more secure than it is here? They'll find you out in five minutes.'

What she did not know was that Albany had been built, and has since been widely used, for country gentlemen to come to town to do business and to meet their mistresses in discreet and forgiving surroundings. Byron did so, and Aldous Huxley, Terence Stamp and numerous recent roués. Alan Clark used to joke that – like his mistress – Albany has an accommodating back passage that you can easily slip in and out of.

'Don't you worry,' I said almost happily. It was a grand prospect, living there for a time – apparently the set was going to be free for at least a year, though I was unlikely to need it for that long.

'The front entrance is off Piccadilly, which is where the media will congregate if they find out where I am. But there is a simple, unmarked back door that exits into Burlington Gardens. No one will know. The porters and staff of Albany are famously discreet. It will be ideal.'

'Well, bully for you, make it into a treat. You're good at that.'

Lucy hasn't my practised familiarity with alcohol – and shouldn't be drinking at all, according to her pill bottle – and was more than usually bellicose after a few glasses.

'And presumably you have something equally grand and perfect for me and the children?'

I wasn't sufficiently inebriated to miss the implication.

'You and the children?'

'You heard me. I am receiving death and rape threats, they know where we live, they even know the kids' names. And we have a throng on the doorstep – not as big as yours, of course, you're the big-deal news, but enough to make life intolerable!'

'My darling, of course you're right, I see that. I'm so sorry.'

I reached across the table to take her hand, but she wasn't offering it.

'If I had foreseen this I wouldn't have made such a fuss, just taken my punishment. Or got my ducks in a row. But did you say you and the children? Not Sam? You're still ... you're now ...'

'He can stay in the house! No journalist wants to talk to him – they don't know he caused it all.' She paused to think, creased her face, wiped her wrist against her runny nose and smirked. 'Unless I tell them. He's always wanted to be on the front pages!'

Sam? The front pages? Whatever for? Being a social-working twat? 'ABINGDON NINNY CAUSED MURDER INQUIRY!'

'I'm out. And the kids. Rudy knows something is up – he keeps asking for details. I just tell him that you saved Granny from suffering. He can see that is good, but you might want to talk to him about it?'

I don't.

'Anyway, I will tell him that we are just renting a place until things blow over. I've talked to his headmistress, who is not sympathetic to our case but she is to our situation, and I can home-school him for a term or two. It's not likely, is it –' she glared at me – 'to take longer than that?'

'No.'

She paused again. A lot was going on in her mind, and as always it registered thought-by-thought and feeling-by-feeling across her features, which scrunched and flickered and rearranged themselves. Old rubbery face, we called her when she was little.

'Hey! Here's an idea. Is that "set" in the Albany big enough for all of us? That'd be great, and Rudy would so love it.'

I must have looked discomfited, because she quickly added, 'And so would I. Of course.'

'Darling, alas, it's a marvellous idea. But the set only has one bedroom ... plus a servant's small room on the upper floors.'

'A what?'

'You heard me. But it doesn't matter, it won't work, and anyway I would be very, very bad company as things progress.'

I did not feel it necessary to inform her that children are not welcome in Albany. No sobbing or screaming are allowed there, except in ecstasy.

On reflection this was just fine. Once I had scarpered from the house, the media and protestors would go away, and then Lucy could use it, and I might visit them sometimes. This might take a month or two, so we would need to find them a serviced flat somewhere in town.

I don't know how to approach Lucy's forthcoming separation, for that is what it surely is, from Sam. Nor indeed how to approach him. Lucy will be delighted, she says, to let him stew, but I cannot allow him to just slip off into the distance. What sort of gestalt would that be?

Rudy was slouched in bed in the guest room, thumbing his little machine, his eyes glazed. He didn't look up when I came into the room, bearing a sundae glass of Cherry Garcia. I waited a moment, got no response, tapped the spoon against the glass. Ping! Head up. Spirits raised, like one of Pavlov's pooches. I put it carefully on the bedside table and handed him a napkin to tuck round his neck.

'Sit up straight. I'll put some pillows behind your back.' He budged up, settled himself into correct ice-cream-eating position, and took the glass greedily. I'd put some glazed cherries on top, and of course a parasol. Both of us love them.

As he ate, colour re-entered his cheeks, and his eyes looked, if not animated, at least less hooded. I pulled a chair to the side of the bed.

'Are you going to read to me, Gampy?'

'Would you like that, or would you prefer to talk a little? There seems a lot to talk about ...'

'Read!'

Thank God for that. 'A lot to talk about' means no sense talking about it.

I was concerned, though, about my final section of *Gulliver*. Things for both him and myself had gone as planned: the initial traumatic event, the madness and disgust, the withdrawal from family, the opprobrium and vilification, the attempt to justify, the gradual return to normality, the writing of the critical document.

But I had not foreseen how thoroughly my dear family would be implicated. In my Book V, family are of course involved and distressed, but it was sufficient that they leave home and move to the country. None of Gulliver's loved ones is physically threatened, or frightened for their life. It makes all the difference. What I had written did not foresee the crisis caused by modern communications: my tormentors were no rabble released from the pubs and coffee houses – this was a mob from everywhere, anonymous, malicious, delighted to threaten and to insult, without fear of consequence.

I will kill you. I will rape you. I will play with you.

I, I, I. You, you, you.

Lucy says Rudy hasn't read the headlines or articles, or heard the coverage on the radio and telly. Nor please God had he accessed the twit attacks and threats. But he knew what was going on. Only last week he was bullied in the school playground by a group of girls and boys, following him and chanting, 'Your grandpa's a murderer! Your grandpa's a murderer!' He was sent home in tears, and the headmistress suggested he might stay away for a while. From her tone, she meant for ever.

Events have outstripped expectations, moved unexpectedly. Opposition is building much faster than support. I should have foreseen this, perhaps. But who could? No one has been in a situation similar to mine. Except, perhaps, poor, brave Captain Gulliver. My reconfiguration and extension of his tale have been a source of great amusement, and no little comfort, to me over these months, Rudy too. Until now, armed, I like to think, with the prophylactic narrative arc of Gulliver/Gampy's tale, he has been remarkably resilient. Children are very good at dealing with adversity until it involves them directly. Mummy is tearful? Oh, well. Daddy depressed? OK. Gampy under siege? Oh, is he? But once this gets personal, and the press bang on his door and take his picture on the doorstep, and the bullies at school gang up against him, well, that's different.

I suppose this infantile fixation on self applies to me, too. Perhaps such self-absorption is generated by the very activity of writing? Or merely reflected? I can hear Lucy and even Suzy laugh as I say this. My Book V has been too focused on Captain Gulliver's predicament, and paid scant heed to what his family are experiencing, and likely to experience. But surely the self-absorption of which I am speaking is Gulliver's, not mine? My job is to help him to get over it. And in doing so to help, to comfort, and to strengthen Rudy.

The boundaries have shifted, and I need to write some more. It's all very well to relocate Captain Gulliver, after his period of assimilation into the family and the human community, into a late-life country idyll, his travels ended and sanity restored. But my trials, and my forthcoming trial, will not allow a quick flit into a happy ending, which is what my draft of Book V was intended to provide. No, what I need to do is find a way for Gulliver to apprise Rudy of the new threats to his well-being and to reassure him that all will be well in the end.

That's why we call this sort of stuff *fiction*.

Needs must. I will start reading, and if I sense that he is bored or unsatisfied, I can put my script down, and elucidate, or prevaricate, or just make up something else. Rethink, rewrite.

'You remember last time, about Daniel Defoe and *Robinson Crusoe*?'

'Yes. Read!'

Sometime during this period, I received a letter from Mr Defoe, announcing a visit to Redriff, and asking if he might call upon me, as he had heard wondrous stories of my Adventures, knew I was contemplating composing an account of them, and wished to make the acquaintance of so remarkable a traveller. I was sorely tempted to respond that, yes, I was indeed a traveller – unlike himself, I might imply – and that what would distinguish my forthcoming publica-tion was the simple fact that it was true. Instead, I merely pleaded pressure of work, and declined his kind offer.

I had by return a second letter from Mr Defoe, begging that I might reconsider, promising that he would impose himself but little on my time, as he wished simply to learn at the feet of a 'genuine and remarkable traveller'. He added, which was somewhat mysterious, that he had urgent need to communicate with me on a matter too delicate to put in a letter. Intrigued, I responded graciously, and invited him to visit and to take coffee a few days hence, when he made his journey to Redriff.

He arrived in a coach with four glistening but clearly unhappy horses, and descended from the carriage as if he expected to be greeted by a crowd of admirers. Dressed like a dandy, with a wig that reached halfway to the sky, he smelled strongly of scent and powder, and his nose was similar to that of his horses, only longer. When he greeted me, it was courteous but hardly deferential, as if he were honouring me with his visit, rather than the other way around.

It was soon clear that he was not really interested to hear my adventures – a few minutes established that he could not abide three sentences on my part without interrupting – and I made it a point to express no interest in his own fictions.

'May I be frank, Sir? As fascinated as I am by your many adventures, my reason for coming is more urgent and of greater moment.'

'Pray explain, Sir, you have my full attention.'

'Some years ago, at the start of this century, I was pilloried for my views, and sent to Newgate Prison. My supposed crime – the charge was seditious libel – was writing a pamphlet entitled 'The Shortest Way with Dissenters', satirising the clergy, and the full force of the law was directed against me.'

I had heard nothing of this, having been abroad on my travels at that time. I was amused, though, by the thought of the dandy Defoe being pelted in the stocks with fruits, vegetables and an occasional dead cat. But I wondered what this might have to do with me.

Mr Defoe leant forward solicitously.

'I am informed that there is most likely going to be a similar charge against yourself, even in advance of publication of your memoirs. It is regarded as sufficient provocation that you have spoken in public of your encounters with the accursed Yahoos, and that you insist that we Englishmen are as they: filthy, degraded, corrupt, and estranged from the love of God.'

I was little inclined to take such threats and rumours seriously, and said I was certain I had little to fear.

'Should it come to that, Sir, I am sure it will not be uncomfortable.'

'I felt similarly, Sir,' said Mr Defoe. 'It was foolish of me. I pray you will not make the same mistake!'

'What counsel would you offer, then?'

Rudy sat up, and begged me to stop.

'But Gampy, Captain Gulliver can't go to jail, can he? He hasn't done anything bad. He's just telling the truth!'

I struggled to reassure him, for he was now making the connection with my own plight, all too aware that Captain Gulliver's possible fate might be my own.

'Well, darling,' I said, attempting to lighten my tone, and failing. 'Let's look at it this way – it doesn't matter too much, does it? Captain Gulliver is going to spend the next few years writing his travels. So he could do that either at home, which would be best, or if necessary he could do it in jail. In the eighteenth century, if you were wealthy, you could pay for very comfortable accommodation in prison. And your family was allowed to visit, and to bring your favourite treats.'

Rudy knew enough to be aware that these privileges no longer pertained in modern jails.

'But Gampy, you're not . . .' His voice quavered and he turned his head away from me. 'You won't . . .'

I put my hand on his shoulder and gave it a rub. Huddled there, he seemed smaller, diminished by fear, his shoulder like that of a small animal. Which, I suppose, he is. A frightened small animal. And as I spoke I was too, a frightened larger one.

I hope that I have reassured Rudy. Time in jail need not be prolonged, nor uncomfortable, and the time can be used profitably. Family can indeed visit. Letters can be exchanged. If the worst comes to the worst, whatever Lucy's forebodings, it will be all right, quite all right.

*M*r Defoe counselled that I should flee as soon as possible, resume my voyages, and not return until the matter had been forgotten. This I was unwilling to consider.

'My voyages, Sir, are over. I have neither the appetite nor the endurance to resume my travels and would surely not survive any *further exposure to the rigours of life on board ship, and in strange lands.'*

'In that case, Sir, you shall have charges to answer.'

'Then I shall answer them, and I shall tell the truth as I have discovered it. And if many will shout in derision, some may listen, and perhaps amend their understanding accordingly.'

Mr Defoe smiled to himself as I said this, no doubt thinking me deluded, and likely soon to be behind the bars at Newgate Prison. This was, of course, not a pleasing prospect, nor was it a daunting one.

'I have faced perils compared to which a trip to prison is as nothing. There is much to be said for incarceration. A ship's cabin is far more confined than a prison cell, and the quality of provisions is similarly basic. Life in prison will allow me ample leisure to compose the memoirs which bear heavily upon me. By the time I am released, which will no doubt be in a year or two, I will have fashioned a tolerable draft of my story, or stories, I should say.'

Mr Defoe rose, and shook me by the hand.

'I can see, Sir, that you are a man of integrity. There are dangers in such high-mindedness, and I observe you are of sufficient moral strength to weather them. I trust your physical strength is as reliable. I wish you well, and will look forward to greeting you once you are released, and eventually to reading the remarkable volume which I hope you will produce whilst in confinement.'

'Wait, Gampy,' said Rudy urgently. 'It's bad to go to jail, isn't it?'

'No, darling, it is not. What is bad is not to tell the truth. Captain Gulliver has things to say to his fellow man, and a message that may, in good time and with good fortune, change the ways in which they think of themselves.'

'But ... but, Reuben will be so sad. And his mum and granny, they'll be sad too.'

'But they will also be proud. And don't forget, Reuben and the family are used to Captain Gulliver being away from them. He is a traveller, off on his voyages. This final adventure in jail will be the most exciting of all, because at the end of it he will have a book, and the world will know about his amazing stories.'

Rudy settled back and composed himself, looking unconvinced but slightly relieved.

Though life was now peaceful in and around my home, Mary had not returned from the country, for our house and its neighbourhood were now the location of memories so distressing and so tenacious that she regretted she would be unable to return, and enjoined me, instead, to come to the country, where we might perhaps purchase some land and live in quiet and harmony. This would, she believed, be beneficial to my health, my state of mind, and my progress with the composition of my Travels, which was advancing only slowly.

It was my painful duty to write to my dear Mary to apprise her of my decision, and to inform her that my final adventure was likely to delay my move to join her. Within a few weeks I had instructed our servants to prepare to close the house in Rotherhithe, in readiness for my imminent move. I did not, of course, tell them that I was likely to move to Newgate rather than to the country. They would find that out soon enough.

The initial tempest surrounding the prevailing accounts of my Adventures had now abated, and my demeanour was beginning to return, I do not say to normal but to its previous character. I was fully fit to stand trial, and to defend myself, fruitless though that might be. I no longer whinny, though my intonations have a foreign sound that makes my interlocutors wonder, sometimes, if I might be German, or perhaps Dutch. And I have altered and straightened my gait, through constant practice, so that I am no longer taken for a misshapen horse.

I am become, again, the Lemuel Gulliver that once I was, though tempered by experiences such that no man has previously undergone, and which I must hasten to compose, to edit, and to publish.

To fully recover myself, and to recapture, such as it is, replete with error and wickedness as it can be, my essential human nature, I had first to accomplish my major task, the task for which my journeys had equipped me. I was born, as it now seems, to have such Adventures, and to relate them.

I am Captain Gulliver, and I have tales to tell that will astound mankind.

Rudy was still and silent, as if his being had been placed on standby. It's probably better for authors to be in less close proximity to their readers, lest they worry, pander and mollify.

'Don't you fret,' I said. 'Stories always come out in the end. This one will too. But not yet.'

He didn't so much as shrug, and protested only mildly when I tucked him up for the night.

When I was little, we fed the ducks at the park, and Grandpa would say, 'Well, this is for the birds,' and laugh in a funny way. Grandma would turn her back. I was three, perhaps four. Of course it was for the birds, for the fat ducks and black moorhens, who gathered, squabbling for position. We brought a whole loaf of bread, and Granny would hand me little bits to throw. I did, quickly, lest the morsel be grabbed from my hands by a greedy duck.

For the birds. I'm thinking of that novel that had lots of endings. Can't remember the title. Or the author. Fowls? That's the chap, the book about the soldier's girlfriend. Suzy told me about it. Apparently there are three endings. It is unclear to me, not having read it, whether you have to choose between these alternatives, or whether all three pertain simultaneously.

Three endings? That feels very arbitrary. Once you start to write, once even I, who am no writer, start to write, the godly prerogative is yours. Mine. Anything can happen, it's in one's power creatively, anything.

I don't know what to do or to say, nor why it matters so very much. I know where I'm going, Rudy, Lucy and Sam, where we're all going, one after another, to nowhere special no time soon, which is what people do and what life is, till it ends, and we move off to make room for more people.

But this is different, isn't it? In some small way, different. Very few of us are charged with murdering someone or other, our wives for instance. Very few are going to jail. I might be, I am likely to, and that, well, that changes things. Not for me. I can tolerate it. I'm old enough not to give a damn, not really, worrying whether you are surrounded by these four walls, or those, imbibe this or that, shit in one pot or another. I am fond of my comforts, but I like to think, and find that I am thinking, that I can do without them.

But if I can face one ending or another with some degree of equanimity, I am by no means sure that Rudy can. He protested when *Gulliver's Travels* – the original, as Sam would have it – ended unsatisfactorily, open-ended one might say, which is to say it did not end at all. Like all children he has an implacable sense of an ending. If there is a problem, it has to be resolved happily, ever after. And then it says THE END. And then you get to read another book, and hear another story, and then you grow up and then you die. Like Suzy.

Rudy is waiting, and I do not know what to offer.

Three endings? Like Mr Fowls? That's possible – I can think of three, and four, and twenty. Any number you want. Captain Gulliver could turn into an Eskimo, or fart himself into orbit, or be reincarnated as a bumblebee, as in one of those magical works where any damn thing happens for no reason.

But let's start with the obvious:

1. Captain Gulliver is never prosecuted. Mr Defoe was either misinformed, or maliciously causing anxiety in one of his potential authorial competitors, slyly suggesting that he make himself scarce. So Captain Gulliver retires to the country and writes his Travels.
ADVANTAGE: reassuring, simple, clear.
DISADVANTAGE: diminishes the gravity of Gulliver's message and of his plight. Less fun to write.

2. Captain Gulliver is sentenced to jail, and feels rather relieved. Procures good accommodation therein, and lives comfortably and happily while writing his Travels. In two years he is released to rejoin his family in the country.
ADVANTAGE: Comforting; makes jail a pleasure not a punishment.
DISADVANTAGE: It's a lie. But of course lies are what hold things together. A life without lies? No marriage, no politics, no church. The land of the Houyhnhnms.

3. Captain Gulliver is sentenced to jail. Newgate Prison is every bit as bad as Mr Defoe had implied: dank, pestilential, the home of the dispossessed, the breeding ground of depravity, illness and desolation. Captain Gulliver dies during his second year.
ADVANTAGE: has the ring of truth. More fun to write. After all, it's only a fiction, compared to which our real-time reality will be almost pleasant.
DISADVANTAGE: Rudy will be distressed. But if he can assimilate knowledge of the yuck of sex at age five, then surely he can tolerate the muck of death at eight. When Suzy died, he gave a shudder, then a shrug, then he got over it. I don't expect more when my time comes, nor would I wish it.

So I have to choose. Unlike Mr Fowls, I am no chicken, and know that authors have to make choices. Only – I sympathise with him here – I don't know which of my endings to choose. Sophisticated as Rudy may be for his age, *au fond* he likes a clear and simple answer. He was unsatisfied and sulky when the original *Gulliver* didn't end properly.

I promised to make up the difference. What will happen?

How does it end?

How do I?

Chapter 16

My trial was scheduled for the third week of September, and according to Lucy's clippings, the newspapers picked it up again and made predictable noises, and the few remaining trolls frolicked and roared under their bridges. But the publicity was already waning: as one wag put it, there was a provocative Act 1 in the Darke Drama, and there would be a fitting climax in Act 5, but there was all too little in between to clarify, expand or elucidate the plot.

This was witty but untrue. What was in the middle were characters, *us*. Me in my righteous decline, Lucy in her marital muddle, Sam in his existential fug, Rudy engulfed by anxiety, buoyed by fictions. Oh: and the late Suzanne Moulton, as she is now. Not Suzy, on her long retreat into the clouds of unknowing, rarely glimpsed, hardly heard, become now an integer in a legal dispute. Not my Suzy, this one over whom we are arguing, making legal points, taking complex moral positions. That's not Suzy. The effect of drawing things so strenuously to this conclusion is that she has retreated from consciousness, is no more. I think this and weep, and hardly know what my tears may signify.

Things quietened down: there was a lot of bumf in the papers about Brexit (a most horrid coinage), which I failed entirely to understand, unlike most of the public, and all the politicians, who think they do. And America had recently acquired just the President it deserves, which soothed and amused me. The clippings from Lucy soon ceased. The only thing that could reinvigorate our increasingly futile campaign was my trial itself, which might get some coverage. Toe-mass kept tweeting and posting, rang his contacts and drafted press releases, but got fewer and fewer responses. I began to suspect that he wasn't as well connected as he had claimed.

As Philip had observed, ultimately my case was both too simple, and too much of a muddle. The public likes things clear, and I am anything but. If I was so proud of having dispatched my wife, why didn't I just plead guilty and suffer the consequences?

I accepted the decline from front page to no page with, if I may say so, considerable aplomb. I am uncomfortable in the public gaze, and on telly and radio I shrink and wither. It was a relief to live out the months before my trial in the airy confines of Albany, where the press never found me, perhaps because they were no longer looking. Lucy and the children soon moved into my house, and to my surprise settled in happily. Sam came down at weekends, and relations seemed to be easing, though Lucy assured me that nothing would be properly resolved until after my trial. The implication is that if I am sent away, Sam will be too.

But if Lucy was still angry with her husband, she was furious with me.

'It's all turned to shit, hasn't it? Your big campaign? Run by your daughter, two itinerant Bulgarians, and two hapless old men. Now you can go to fucking jail, not as a martyr but as an idiot.'

She was distressed, fair enough. But I am not, not just now anyway. I had a moment of unaccustomed clarity: *I am morally innocent, and legally guilty.* Simple really. It only gets complicated when you add that (1) I am only a moral agent and exemplar, if I admit my guilt under the law. That is what integrity demands, and integrity has ruined more relationships than adultery. (2) Lucy and Rudy will never forgive me if I plead guilty and hence go to jail, nor would Lucy ever forgive Sam.

I meant it when I said 'a *moment* of clarity' – it has passed already. Who could make sense of this? In the last months I'd sought ethical advice: enlisted Plato, sniffed up a bit of Kant, repaired to the blessed Hume. They scratched their heads furiously, and little flakes of wisdom fell off. Philosophy is the dandruff of hard thinking. I brushed it off.

I gave a shrug of doubt that Descartes would have been proud of, and tried to explain, but by now it wasn't clear any more. I stumbled, prevaricated, got lost in the words.

'Oh. Great . . .' she muttered. 'You were consumed by guilt and now you're consumed by innocence? You say one thing, then you say another. Make up your mind!'

'Hah. That's what you do with minds. You make them up.'

'What, like stories?'

'Exactly. Just so. You *tell* yourself.'

'I don't understand you.'

'Neither do I. I dislike people who understand themselves.'

Do I get to write the script of my own life? We make up our minds like our stories: we make ourselves up. I don't know who I am any more, I don't know what I did. I don't care. I am on the outside, looking out, on nothing.

There was a long pause such as you might find when a magistrate interrogates an idiot.

'Oh, my God. You are SO in trouble! You're trying to make a virtue out of not knowing what you mean.'

I was shocked and delighted by Lucy's accusation. How remarkable! What company I find myself in: that was what Forster once said about Conrad!

'Darling Lucy,' I said, 'have you ever read E. M. Forster?'

Lucy stood up, took hold of my jacket without pausing to admire the cashmere, and pulled me ever so slightly forward, not enough to topple, exactly, but I did stumble a little.

'Do stop, please, it's enough. No more silliness. I'm begging you. It's not too late. Accept a lesser charge. Plead guilty to manslaughter!'

'No.' This had become a possibility. The results of the forensic examination of Suzy's remains, we learned during discovery of the evidence, had been ambiguous. The administered dosage would have been less than fatal if administered to a healthy person. Though it may well have hastened Suzy's death, it was arguable that it did not cause it.

'In that case, go to court and plead innocent to murder, as you choose. You say it was a mercy killing. Let Jonathan make the case. You talk to him all the time, you're always directing him, but he's the damn lawyer! Take his advice. Let's get the ducks back into their row. Play the forensic card. You have a really good chance of getting off.'

'Lucy, darling, Lucy. I quite understand. What you say is sensible. But I am only going through this in order to make my point ...'

'It's made already. You've had your day, lots of days. You've been on the front pages, on telly, on stages and platforms. Everyone knows what you did, why you did it, and how you justify it. It's over now. There's nothing more to be said!'

There's always more to be said. And it was Lucy who said it, later that day. She'd gone upstairs, cried herself out, had a sleep.

I was surprised, stunned really, by her change of tone.

'You know, Dad, I'm sorry to be so harsh sometimes. I get frightened, and you ... you're so ...'

'I know. I am so ...'

She waved this away.

'What I really need to say, want to say, is that I'm so proud of you! This can't be easy, it's too raw and exposing, it's not you, and you soldier on ...'

'Well ...'

'It's very brave! But you know what I want to do when this is all over?'

'Do tell.'

'You know? All that money? From Mummy? I've been thinking and thinking, and I do want it.'

'I'm so glad,' I said. 'After all, it's really yours.'

'No,' said Lucy, firmly. 'It isn't!'

'Well, strictly speaking it is mine, there having been no will, but—'

'No! I don't mean it's yours. I mean it is Mum's. Her money.'

This was unhelpful, and Lucy raised a hand to stop me saying something obvious.

'I want it because I am going – I hope you will agree to this, don't know why you wouldn't – to set up a charity, maybe called the Suzy Moulton Trust, to promote the cause of assisted dying. Easeful Death, you call it.'

'I'm not sure I follow what—'

'I haven't worked it all out, of course. I want to provide information, and medical and legal advice, for people who are in the kind of position you were with Mummy.'

A wave of feeling washed over my nervous system, which tingled in response. Lucy! Just the right person for just the right response. It would allow her to channel, to divert, to redirect her energy and her life. Good, for her. For Suzy. And or me, thank God.

'Dad? You don't mind, do you? I'd hate it—'

'Of course I don't. I'm proud of you, to have thought of this, to want to—'

She came across to embrace me.

'Thank you,' she said, burrowing her head in my shoulder as she used to, when I would lift her into my arms, so long ago. 'Thank you so much.'

'No, it's me who needs to thank you, you know I never believed ...'

She clasped me firmly.

'Don't,' she said. 'I know.'

At last, the relief of being able to step aside. I never warmed to my self-proclaimed mission: to argue the case, passionately but also dispassionately, for assisted dying. I suppose that's why I had such trouble composing my little manifesto, as if my subconscious were stilling my voice and pen, saying, *This is not you, not you at all*. It's a worthy cause, but not mine own. My attachment is to Suzy, Suzy my girl, my wife, my departed, my ghost, and not to the idea of Suzy. I cannot, I will not, employ her as an example that leads to greater, bigger and better things. There are no such, not for me. My heart was never in it. It's with Suzy, with her heart, warm and mouldering in the grave. I yearn for our time together, fleeting though it may be, to lie beside and to hold her hand.

I declined most invitations, but was still occasionally interviewed, and appeared at a few symposia and festivals, where I was interrogated and sometimes mocked by my fellow panellists, when they weren't sympathising with me.

I was invited to speak on a panel at a meeting of the Oxford Humanist Cooperative, of which I have never heard. When I looked it up, it turned out to be an independent society, located in Oxford, but not associated with the university. This was encouraging: there's nothing so pretentious and cringe-making as an undergraduate society. When I looked up my fellow panellists on the Internet, there was a Catholic priest from one of the Oxfordshire churches, an academic from some polytechnic (now called university) in the north, and a stand-up comedian with a mordant line of death jokes, who styled himself The Terminator. The priest had not written anything I could find, the minor academic had published his little heart out, largely on the Internet and in obscure journals, and the comedian could be found on YouTube. He was modestly funny, though like many such he shouted too much. It was company in which one might shine.

I accepted their kind invitation. I rarely have an opportunity to visit Oxford without using it as a staging post on the way to Abingdon to see my family. The OHC offered train fare from London, followed by dinner. I said no thank you, being uncertain which I disliked more, travelling on trains or dinners with strangers. Both make me nauseous.

I did not, of course, tell Lucy about the occasion, at which I was intending to speak frankly if succinctly, and I had no desire for my poor daughter to hear it. She never knew the extremities of her mother's suffering, the malodourous shrinking awfulness of it. Yet, on the night, as we panellists entered the church hall, there she was standing at the back. With Sam!

'Daddy!'

'Lucy?'

'Why didn't you tell us about this? If we hadn't seen the notice in the *Oxford Times*, we'd never have known ...'

The *Oxford Times*! That would account for the crowd pouring in, come to see the villain/hero of the current euthanasia drama. There were only fifty chairs put out, in five rows of ten, and the organisers scurried about trying to find more. Their problem was soon compounded by an elderly man pushing a wheelchair, in which an ancient woman lolled, her head to one side, drooling like someone with Hawking's disease, almost dead but not dead enough. Her body was shrouded by a shawl, her hands crossed in her lap. A place was found for them at the front, just to the side so that she didn't block anyone's view, though for the moment all eyes were on her. Hers were closed.

'Darling Lucy, never mind, I'm sorry. I must go and take my seat up front. Shall we have a drink afterwards, before I drive back to the hotel?'

I didn't wait to hear her answer, and walked down the aisle, took the few steps onto the makeshift speaker's platform, and was directed to my seat. Apparently the mics had already been tested for sound. During a quick preliminary conversation amongst us, I said I'd like to have the last word, and the moderator acceded graciously, fully aware that no one in Oxford ever has, or could.

We began with the easy one: the RC priest who thought I must go to jail and thence to hell. The matter was simple in the eyes of God and should be equally clear to those of man: *Thou shalt not kill*. For a simple commandment this required some elucidation, and the reverend Father was in full flow when a voice from the audience shouted, 'What about soldiers then? Thank your God that they do the killing, or we should all have been saying *Sieg Heil* before we began!'

Ah, well, solving that question brings the priests in their long coats running over the fields; similar debate has kept generations of Jesuits well fed. But the caustic laughter in the audience rather discouraged him, and he decided enough was enough, pushed his mic away, and took a sip of his holy water.

The second chap was the beardy comic, presumably invited to lighten the tone. He amused himself by advocating a notion which had apparently originated from a child of Kingsley Amis, who believes that all telephone boxes should contain suicide pill dispensers, and a 999 hotline to the mortuary. The question of euthanasia was thus moot: *everyone* should be allowed – and many encouraged – to kill themselves whenever and whyever they wished. This might rid the world of a considerable burden of miserable persons, and contribute to solving overpopulation.

There were further benefits attached to such a practice: a construction boom in telephone equipment and boxes, building of myriad mortuaries, cemeteries and crematoria, and useful employment for thousands of new death services, both religious and secular. The Terminator was sufficiently convinced by his own arguments, he proclaimed, that he had set up a company which would soon be going public. The audience was invited to invest in its shares.

I suggested a trial run, in which Amis *fils* pops the first pill. That went down well.

But the fun stopped with our third speaker, Dr Whatsit, an elderly academic, scrofulous and pedantic. He rattled the microphone, which made a horrible screech, pulled it too close, and spoke into it loudly. The audience protested, and rather than moving the mic he began to whisper. They protested again, until our moderator adjusted the distance and whispered a few words of advice. He began.

'I have, as you will all know, written extensively on the subject of euthanasia, or "assisted dying", as it is now unfortunately and inaccurately described. I have adumbrated eight clear and discrete reasons why such a practice must never be sanctioned. Of these, five are insufficiently compelling, in and of themselves, to need discussion tonight, though taken together they certain strengthen my case. So I will confine myself to the three most cogent and convincing arguments.

'The first is that our medical practitioners are obliged to honour the Hippocratic Oath, which enjoins them to protect human life, and never knowingly to end it. Like all serious moral obligations, this must admit of no exceptions. Once you allow killing the nearly dead, you soon start to dispatch the very nearly dead, and then the distinctly poorly, and then those whose sneezing and hacking are so irritating to others. No, a principle, to be a principle, must admit of no exception. If we allow even one, perfectly conceivable deviation from this obligation, we are on an ethical slippery slope. The next thing we know the boundaries shift, and we are sending to Switzerland – and soon enough it will happen here – all of those terminally ill or disabled persons who say they wish to die. And soon enough, inevitably I would say, members of various disabled groups, the senile, the mentally deficient, the insane, the crippled, might be dispatched as well. No doubt the previous speaker would regard this as a boon, but I do not.'

He looked up at his audience, some of whom were listening, but the slippery slope of their attention was waning. The woman in the wheelchair was either asleep or dead. I'd been watching her; she had that alabaster sheen that Suzy had in her last weeks, flesh preparing for its own dissolution. I had wondered if Suzy might put in one of her appearances, in my heart or to my eyes, but there were no signs of her, only memories. They were enough, they were too much. I looked towards the back row, where Lucy was sitting on the aisle, head cocked to the side.

'Second, of course, is the question of palliative care. Once you allow the premature death of those who – under whatever legislation and control – choose how, when and where to die, the next thing is that there will be pressure on the dying to make such a choice. To get it over with tidily. It has been empirically demonstrated that states which allow assisted dying suffer a decline in the quality and availability of palliative care in hospices and hospitals.

'And thirdly, Dr Darke has published a widely distributed "manifesto", arguing that we treat dying dogs more kindly than dying relatives. That is true because, as would appear obvious enough, dogs (I include other pets in the category) are different from *persons*. Not because they have immortal souls, which specious argument I leave to our ecclesiastic friend, but because they have rights, not the least important of which is that they must not be dispatched prematurely.

'A dog owner cannot profit from the death of their *pet*. An unscrupulous relative certainly can, for a dying *person* may be influenced, indeed pressured, by a living relative who has something to gain from their death . . . And if they resist, they might just be helped on their way.'

He turned and looked at me.

'I presume, Dr Darke, that this was not the case in the death of your late wife Susan?'

There was a collective gasp from our audience, and several members cried, 'Shame!' at the sheer audacity of this. I didn't object, or respond in any way.

Failing to get a reply, he pushed his chair back and the mic forward.

'I believe that is a fair outline of my argument, though I would urge members of the audience to look into the matter more thoroughly. I can recommend—'

He was, at this point and at last, interrupted by our moderator, who had been casting sympathetic glances my way, which I also ignored.

'Thank you for your cogent, indeed provocative, exposition. May we now turn to our final panellist, Dr James Darke, who needs no introduction?'

There was a round of applause which might have signalled incipient support for me, but was more likely just relief at moving on to the final speaker.

I looked round the room. Lucy and Sam were perched on their seats. She was wiping her eyes, he holding her hand. The woman in the wheelchair had opened her eyes; weirdly, they seemed to be on the side of her head, which rested almost on her shoulder. They were aglow with blue, focused intensely on me. It might have been unsettling, but to my surprise I felt animated and enabled.

'Thank you, moderator. I accept the previous speaker's arguments in the spirit in which they are offered, which is that of a student of Agatha Christie. But unlike her fictive world, ours is distinctly underrepresented by unscrupulous relatives in desperate need of a premature inheritance. I daresay there are some such, on the basis of whom we have chosen to stifle the greed of the few with the prolonged suffering of the many. For every murderous, unscrupulous nephew there are tens of millions of people dying in agony.

'And yet, you know, I am more than happy, but anxious, to acknowledge the weakness of my arguments, and indeed my case.

'Yes, people are different from pets, have more rights and exist in a more complex moral and legislative nexus. Fair enough.

'I have taken things into my own hands, and even doctors have no right to end life. Agreed.

'It is indeed possible that once we let the cat out of – or into – the euthanasia bag, various problems and extensions of the practice may ensue. That is plausible.

'These are interesting ideas, and provocative questions, but I am not interested in them. Not at all. What happened to me, as I sat at the bedside of my poor dying wife, was not a matter for discussion or debate. It was particular, and particularly harrowing, and not in any way general. Indeed, language had nothing to do with it. It was indescribable – no words do justice to the visceral reality. To being unable to comfort or to aid my wife, who lay dying, gurgling and choking as her lungs failed, at my side, dying. But not yet dead. No one could suppose such a life preferable to the beneficence of a final release.'

I continued for a few minutes, longer than I had planned, describing for those who had little experience of such, the actual physical realities of Suzy's last days and nights: her tenacious will to live, her terrible struggle and fear, her will to die, and inability, quite, to do it. I didn't dare look at Lucy in the back of the room, directed my gaze at an upward incline, as if seeking the God who was so obviously not there. I could sense the reactions in the room, the corporate wince. I shifted my gaze downwards by thirty degrees and scanned the room slowly, counted to ten, and concluded with the only question that mattered:

'You know what is right and what is wrong, do you? So what would you have done?'

There was a long hush, and a round of applause, which lengthened, and a few members of the audience stood up and continued. I took hold of my mic.

'Thank you for listening so sympathetically, and thank you too to my fellow panellists, who have made this a stimulating and provocative evening.' The moderator said similarly, and we were through. The priest and academic left the dais without saying goodbye, but the amiable comic came up to shake my hand.

'See you at the phone box ...' he began, when we were interrupted by the elderly gentleman and the shrunken woman with the beautiful eyes. They stopped, and he leant forward and put his ear to his wife's lips, listened carefully.

'My wife has asked me to thank you so very much.'

The woman made a sound, and he leant forward again to listen. He rose and took my hand. He looked exhausted.

'Bless you, she says. I do too. And good luck!'

I took my hand from his, reached down to take hers. It was as I had expected, and feared, reduced to bone, soon to be dust. Suzy's.

'Of course, of course. Thank you for coming.'

It took me a few minutes to pull myself together, honking and wet, in a stall in the lavatory. I was touched by the plight of the poor woman, of course. But I resented the intrusion, and felt in danger of becoming a spokesman for all such. I am not, I am merely acting on behalf of Suzy, and of myself. Particularly particular, not general. I waited for enough minutes, I hoped, knowing it was in vain, for Lucy and Sam to have departed. But when I went back into the hall, there they were, as a few cooperative humanists began to put the chairs away.

Lucy looked at me intently, and had the good sense to be quiet. Even Sam did, more or less.

'You look like you could do with a drink,' he said. 'We all could! There's a pub down the road ...'

It was impossible to say no. But the drink, and a further drink, didn't loosen our lips. Too much to say, and as often with ultimate things, no way to say it. We drank, though, in companionable silence. Lucy and Sam sat close, shoulders touching. I found, somewhat to my surprise, that I was pleased.

'One thing, Dad,' she said. 'Thank you.' She glanced at Sam. 'I think we know what to do now ...'

'What's that?'

'Not now, we're all wrung out. But I'll talk to you about it. We both will. You've given us a way forward.'

However bemusing this was, I was pleased to hear it. I'd never done that before.

I had parked nearby, and they walked me to my car. I hugged them, both, and they watched the tail lights of the car as I drove away.

Sam and I hardly talk. So it was a very considerable surprise, and caused a frisson of apprehension, on picking up my phone some ten days later, to hear his voice.

'Sam? Hello ...'

'I'm in London for the next three days, just on my own, you know, attending a conference ...'

'Oh, yes, a conference?' Presumably to do with his running groups, which must be more taxing, even, than my poetry one.

'And I wondered if I might pop by one morning for a coffee. And a chat? Are you busy tomorrow?'

I was flooded by feelings and questions. Of course, I will not be 'busy' tomorrow. I am never 'busy'.

'Sam, is everything all right? Has something happened to Lucy? Or the children?'

No, no, none of the above, everything was grand.

'Do come tomorrow morning. Perhaps at ten?'

'Works for me. I don't have to deliver my paper until noon.'

'Deliver the paper? I'm not sure what you mean.'

He laughed a little uneasily.

'I know, I know, it sounds a bit pretentious. I prefer to say "read my paper".'

'I'm still not sure I understand ...' I began. 'Is this for your exercise class?'

He cut in brusquely.

'No time for this now, James. I'll see you in the morning. Thanks.'

And rang off before I could compose my next response. Why would Sam be coming to talk to me? On his own. I never thought he was that courageous.

A few minutes before he was due the next morning, I peered out of my peephole to see Sam pacing about on the pavement in front of the house, consulting his watch. He's a literal fellow. Ten means ten.

I opened the door.

'For goodness' sake, Sam, do come in.'

I made coffee as he made small talk, filling me in on the conference he's attending, which has something to do with grief and counselling. I didn't listen. A barista has enough to occupy his mind, and hands, and I was determined to make the *non-plus-ultra* flat white that would teach him a lesson. When I'd finished, and made a spiffing fern design on the top, I handed him the result. He didn't look, slurped a bit and got fern on his upper lip, which he wiped with his fingers.

'Mmmm, thank you,' he said.

'Shall we go into the sitting room?'

We sat down, and there was a pause, which I made no effort to end.

'Well,' he said, 'may I fill you in on what's been going on?'

'I'd be most grateful,' I said. 'Lucy has been a bit evasive. Said you'd explain ...'

'Yes. I want to. But I'd like to begin with an apology ...'

'I don't understand. You have nothing to apologise for, or I suppose more accurately, you already have, and I entirely accept that your revelation was unwitting, and that you regret it.'

'No,' he said. 'I regret the storm I have caused, but I don't believe it was "unwitting", as you call it. I think I did it on purpose. But unconsciously.'

I was confused by this: the terms 'on purpose' and 'unconsciously' don't go together in my lexicon. Not that I understand, quite, what people mean when they talk about 'the unconscious', a murky region peopled by the therapeutically inclined. I find it sufficiently perplexing to understand what people do consciously. Add another dimension and I'm totally at sea. Not my gestalt.

'But Sam, you explained this. You assumed that you were speaking to your group in confidence. The phrase, if I recall, was, "What is said in the room stays in the room." I accept that.'

'Yes, well ...' He took another sip of coffee, put the cup on the side table. Picked it up again, drank again.

'That's exactly what I said. And it's crap. People in therapy get obsessed with their sessions, and talk about them incessantly to their partners, their friends, to anyone who will listen ... Any therapist knows that. So when we tell a group or individual what the rules are, we know they will ignore them.'

I could immediately see the truth in this. When Suzy was suffering from 'writer's block', failing to work on a novel in Oxford, she engaged a therapist, who not only exacerbated her problem, but caused new ones. She talked about it constantly. Soon enough she was blaming me for her creative paralysis, claiming that my criticism of her drafts lowered her confidence. I was sorry to hear this, but of course had no such intention – quite the opposite.

After her sessions she shared the details with me, until I begged her to desist, not because it was private, but because it was boring, and irritating. After which she made transcriptions of each session in a diary which she kept in the top drawer of her desk, and which I read, as she knew I would. They, too, were rather dreary, but contained occasional titbits about me that I was too curious not to ignore. I hardly recognised the person she was describing.

'Let me start at the beginning,' Sam said, 'in the garden at our house, when you told us what you'd done, and Lucy was crying so much.'

No need to remind me. I'd immured myself in my house, broken contact with the world, all of it, everyone, and stayed there for some eight months before braving the outdoors and making my way to Abingdon to see Lucy. I rang her anxiously from my Oxford hotel, and was soon knocking on her door like a supplicant, and meeting with the disdain that I both expected and deserved. Sam had come home, just for the occasion, 'to lend support'.

In the garden, I tried to explain, and failed. Yes, I had caused Suzy's death, and I was, however ambivalently, proud to have relieved her suffering. It was – I was – *merciful*. I felt wretched, eviscerated, but combative. Whatever simplistic '*thou shalt not*' categories pertained in their view of things, I would accept agency, but not blame. Both guilty and innocent in mine own eyes, I begged her forgiveness without, quite, requiring it. I did what was necessary, and Lucy was soon tearfully to admit that she would have done the same, had she the courage.

As I mused, Sam sat quietly and finished his coffee, having the sense to allow me the next word.

'Yes. I'm hardly likely to forget that.'

He gave a brief nod, or perhaps it was some sort of bow.

'Lucy was in a state, yes, and so was I. She says she suspected what had happened, but she hadn't said a word to me, and I certainly never would have thought of such a thing. I was – how can I say it? – very shocked.'

He paused to catch my eye, but I wasn't offering it.

'Was that naive of me? I've had very little actual experience of death – I just talk about it. Some of my clients have had the impulse to end the suffering of a loved one, but none ever seriously contemplated doing it. They recognised that it was murder . . .'

'And you agreed?'

'I did. And I said so in my group.'

'Let me see if I have this straight. You knew your group members would talk about Suzy's death and my role in it?'

'Yes, though that was not my intention.'

'Not *consciously*, as you put it.'

'No . . . Yes.'

'One final question then. Were you aware that a member of your group was married to a police officer?'

There was a pause and some copious facial adjustment. I'm not sure if I've ever seen anyone wringing their hands, but his were wrung out.

'Yes. I was. At the time I spoke it was hardly in my mind . . . But I accept responsibility, James. I am so, so sorry. This is all down to me.'

As they put it in those wonderful old gangster movies, he'd dobbed me in, though black-and-white film snitches did so consciously, choosing their own fates and often meeting them. Sam was meeting his, I suppose, though I was unclear what had prompted this gratuitous extra confession. Guilt perhaps, Lucy more likely. Or both: they go well together.

There was only one further question, and then I would have to reflect a bit, to process this new material, like cheeses.

'Thank you, Sam. It's hard enough to find a person who takes responsibility for what he does consciously, but . . .'

'I'm so sorry. It's all my fault.'

'No, it isn't, Sam. It's mine. And I accept responsibility for what

I chose to do, and I am actually not ... *glad* that you exposed the situation, but *grateful*. I will have my day in court. That feels right to me.'

'That's where Lucy comes in, and me too, I hope. I want to help,' he said.

'Help?'

'With the campaign, you know, like she told you – getting publicity about assisted dying, making the issue public. Causing a change of hearts, and minds. And eventually laws. What you called the Darke Movement we'll make into the Suzy Moulton Trust. We want to be in charge of the website, and fill it with important material, do the social networking, organise conferences and rallies, enlist the support of various experts ...'

Too fast, everything was happening too quickly.

'Wait! Let me get this straight. First you were horrified by what I did, and called me a murderer. And now you're a supporter?'

'I am. Since then, I've thought and read a lot, and talked with Lucy ...'

He shrugged and laughed uneasily.

'That is, when she would talk to me. She's held me responsible for what has happened. And I am!'

'Let's leave that, Sam. Or share it at the very least.'

'But the final straw was your talk in Oxford. It was so moving, and convincing that I ...'

'Yes. Yes, I see.'

'So, may we have your blessing?'

'No. My gratitude. Thank you.'

That was it. After a bit of conventional toing and froing he went off like a dutiful newspaper boy to deliver his papers, and I sank into my armchair after making another flat white.

Leave it with them, leave it with Suzy Moulton. Trust. I'm no leader. Next thing I know I'll be followed by a train of terminal old ladies in wheelchairs chanting my name: *Darke! Darke! Darke!*

No thanks, not me, not for me, I have no desire to be that good. Nor the capacity.

Sam and Lucy can generalise – go on, be the generals, plan their campaign, do whatever needs to be done.

I don't care. I'll be deep in the trenches with the mud, the corpses and the rats.

With Suzy.

Chapter 17

I was tried for Heresy and convicted. The papers made a sensation of it, and for a few days my strange story was on everyone's
lips. And then it was superseded by other news, and forgotten. I
was given a sentence of two years, which – though I tried not to
show it in court – pleased me greatly. It would suffice to finish my
memoirs, and thence to retire to the country to see them through
publication.

As I had anticipated and arranged, my lodgings at Newgate were
comfortable, the provisions better than I was used to, and I had sufficient paper, pens and ink for my ambitious purposes. There were
hardships, of course, most particularly the noisome presence of my
fellow men, but I bore them bravely. When a vile Yahoo has shat
upon your head, what worse can befall you?

I set myself the daily task of relating these Adventures, then of
refining and editing them so that readers of all sorts might profit from
them. I sought a style at once simple and direct, which would yet not
diminish the complexity of what I wished to convey.

My efforts to sustain my writing have been impeded by diminished powers, for I am grown old now, and my strength is reduced.
Though I take exercise in the prison yard, and my diet is much
improved from the staple of oats, milk and honey, still I cannot but
recognise that my days are drawing to a close.

It was a great surprise when I was informed of my imminent release, for unlike most prisoners I was content in gaol, and so concentrated were my efforts of composition that it astonished me that two years could pass so quickly.

On the morning of my release, Mary, Lucile and dear Reuben were at the prison gates, their faces wreathed in smiles and their arms filled with bouquets. I was embraced by those who loved me, and whom I once again love with all my heart, and I wept with joy as I entered their carriage, and hardly stopped weeping until we arrived at my new home.

It took no time to settle in, and to begin the final task of editing my memoirs for publication. In these efforts I could not concentrate without the encouragement and aid of dear Reuben, who is constantly by my side, and whose wise love expresses itself sometimes in encouraging my labours, and at other times urging me to suspend them in order to eat and to drink, and to rest. He is now almost eleven years old, and has grown into a beautiful and strapping child, indeed already a man in the breadth of his understanding and the depth of his affections.

He and I often ride in the afternoons, perhaps more gently than he would wish, for his horse Enigma is young and anxious to display his powers, but both he and his young master hold themselves back to accompany me in my more stately passage across the fields. After our return, since I now tire easily, I fall asleep for a few hours, else I can hardly hold the pen to complete my compositions.

I first read my stories to Reuben, in order to refine their presentation and to profit from his many comments. He is my best audience. Now he is older, and I weaker, at times he reads the text to me. I sit back, and close my eyes, listening to his mellifluous voice reciting my own words, which are now also his. My eyes fill with tears, close, and sometimes I fall asleep, to dreams no man can have dreamed before.

I owe this new life, of course, to the passage of time and the regaining of my residual, I would not say sanity, but sense. The influence of my dear family has been essential to this slow return to the land of the humans.

Though I cannot share dear Mary's dismissal of my formerly dear Master and his noble race as cold and loveless, yet have I come to see something thin, pale and lacking in their attitude to each other, and to their world. Had they a better understanding and greater discrimination of the emotions, they would never have sent me away, and I would have spent my final years happy in their company and service.

And thus, by that great irony, I was returned to my fellows, and eventually recovered both my demeanour and my understanding. I have not, though often mistaken for it, been a madman, merely one who has been exposed to trials and experiences of a kind so diverse, so powerful and so reformative that I have had too much for one man to learn from and to assimilate without the passage of a great deal of time, and a great deal of thought. I have been reduced to the size of a flea, enlarged to that of a giant, wandered amongst the eternally dead and the immortal Struldbrugs. And finally I was tormented by the vile Yahoos, recognised a fatal kinship with their race, then had the privilege to reside in a community governed by reason and fondness.

And then, against every inclination of my being and my reformulated nature, I was transported back to Redriff, to live, once again, amongst my fellows. The images of the Yahoos have receded, and fade with every day, though their essential truths reside in me permanently, and recur with shocking power when I least expect them: images of the degraded body, of the noxious odours and foul-smelling excrement, which had made me ashamed to be human, and unwilling to tolerate the presence of other such. They shat upon my head: a truth and a metaphor that imprints itself indelibly, for my head has neither recovered nor forgotten, nor have my fingers, that wiped it away, ever lost the smell of the vile excrement. When the mind is inhabited by such images it only slowly regains its equanimity, and *never permanently. For if Yahoos are not what we are, yet they are like us, and we them. It is a truth worth forgetting, yet impossible to banish.*

For our species, imperfect as it may be, is not entirely that of the Yahoos, who are merely a degraded version of it, and not to be mistaken for that much preferable species, mankind. For men, however venial and disappointing, are touched by grace, and made in the image of a divine spirit, and – for my dear and fragrant Mary constantly reiterates and exemplifies this – have a spirit informed by love.

And so I rest, with my dear family, weary but in complete happiness, restored in every manner.

THE END

Listening to this conclusion, Rudy rubbed his eyes – I think he slept through a good bit, but woke at the last – and turned his head on the pillow.

'It's really good, Gampy,' he said. 'I feel much better now.'

I bent to kiss his forehead. He was soon asleep.

I sat by his side in a reverie, replete for the moment. I'd done my duty. I looked over at his sleeping face, stroked his head, gazed with – what? – a sort of wonder, at the tiny blonde hairs on his lip. When he was little, only just a few years ago, indomitably toddling, imperious, Suzy would study his face, and tickle those tiny hairs, which eventually migrated onto the face of a child in one of her stories.

I admired and envied Rudy, reassured and so easily satisfied. I'm not. I wrote this for him. If I have simplified, indeed distorted, what must happen to Gulliver and has happened – and may happen – to me, I have done so for Rudy's sake.

I am embarrassed by the easy facility of my story, the sentimentality, the imposed, happy ending. Have I converted

Swift, lovely misanthropic, gnarly, fastidious-enraged-inventive-indignant Dean Swift, into Mr Dickens, slobbering away? Next thing I know I will write a sequel about Tiny Tim, in which he grows up strong and tall and healthy. God bless him, one and all. What an irony, what a humiliation! Had Lucy been eavesdropping outside the bedroom door, she would have wept with astonishment that I was capable of composing such a heart-warming and consoling story. As do I.

This is what integrity is for, isn't it? To be sacrificed again and again, abandoned in the services of love.

I sit, still, waiting, breathing, looking. 'Wise passivity,' that stupefying prelate Wordsworth called it: breathe and wait and look, and the feelings will come, unbidden. And with them, or with the recollection of them, the appropriate words. I've unfurled my folding chair under the poisonous Tax-us tree, sat down and stretched myself out, closed my eyes to the afternoon sun, listened to the rooks in the trees, strained to hear the insects on the ground beneath my feet, the grass growing. My eyes closed, my head thrown back in readiness.

Nothing happened. The opposite of feeling invaded me, anti-feeling, the numbness that seems my destiny. I could not speak, and my eyes failed, I was neither living nor dead, and I knew nothing. Nothing is what we know; when we know nothing we know everything.

Perhaps it's the wrong way around: the words come first, then the feelings? Find the right words and everything follows; you follow, I follow.

I'm here now, love, I'm here. We're here, both of us, lost here. I miss you too much to say. How can I when the you that is you is no longer you? All we have now is words, mine, yours are faint echoes that touch the ear like a breeze, but do not enter.

Am I talking then to myself?

I'm carrying on, I know that. You used to tease me, sometimes strict, tell me not to carry on so.

You've slipped away. The richness of your voice, laughing or singing. All we are left with is words. Words are all we have. Pellybelly, Captain Gulliver, Suzy.

But I will not let you retreat into the gloop, morph into bacterium and sludge, the you that is not you. You will have your day, I will have mine. We will. Miss Moulton will be received at Court; she was of royal blood, she was a princess.

I am making this up, making you up. A maker's rage to order words, the fragrant portals, to make something of nothing?

Not at all, nothing as fancy as that. Just faltering words of goodbye, again, never, at last. There is no last. Is there?

The vicar is talking to some doughty parishioners, who laugh ingratiatingly at words that are not jokes. Over their shoulders he sees me at the graveside in my folding chair, talking to myself. He knows who I am, and resolves that even I am a worthy recipient of God's grace, which he steels himself to offer. He walks my way, dignified and withheld, smiling gently in unwelcome benediction.

'Dr Darke.'

'Vicar.'

I last saw him when hiding behind the yew in the rain. He didn't know I was there, else he would have offered me some of the tea and biscuits he distributed amongst the grave robbers who had come to heave the earth in many a mouldering heap. As if to atone for this unwitting remission, he offers to fetch me some tea now, unless of course I would like to join him and his wife in the vicarage? He knows I will decline, else he would not offer.

'Thank you, no.'

'I haven't seen you since the funeral, I believe?'

'No. But sometimes I come to her grave with my daughter and her family.'

'Ah, yes.'

'But today I wanted to come on my own.'

I found myself wanting to say more, and had to throttle the compulsion. What use to explain, and for that explanation to be received with understanding or even worse, forgiveness? I have no need of bloody vicars demonstrating the elasticity of their charity.

'Do forgive me, vicar, if I simply sit here on my own. It may be some time before I can come again . . .'

'So I gather,' he said, and turning without a word of farewell, strode into his church, and would have shut the door firmly if it wasn't so heavy, as if I were not welcome in the house of God, amongst the brethren of Cunterbury.

Time passes, that's what it does, what it's for. I drink my coffee from the Thermos, unwrap my two shortbreads and eat them, allowing the crumbs to float and drift, as is their wont. The ants congregate for their unexpected feast. The sun is beginning to withdraw, shadows cross my path, and I peer westwards in hope of a sunset to fix upon, perhaps to console or perhaps to exacerbate my grief. I wish nature would get its metaphors straight sometimes.

You loved that aria, would have swapped your dusky imprecise haunting contralto for a weedy soprano if only you could have sung 'Là Ci Darem la Mano' with Don Giovanni, as wet with desire as a hyacinth girl.

The dusky falling, the shade. You made the sky acutest at its vanishing, measured to the hour its solitude. You were the single artificer of the world in which you sang.

Before I pack up and leave, I want the benediction of that beautiful music of Mozart's, the haunting paradox of that seduction, the memory of your voice singing, along and alone. That aria is a recurrent constituent of my inner life, frequently playing in my ear and my heart.

But today all I receive is *'Let's Hang on to What We've Got!'* It's a tribute of a sort, I could suppose. Got? Had?

Never you mind. Be with me, bear with me, I'll be back, in a while. Soon enough. Be with me in the passion of our risen Christ, who was our delight.

Time to pack up and go home, and face some other music. I'll hang on.

Goodbye, love.

Goodbye love.

Chapter 18

Though I could sense them thinking it, the phrase 'the condemned man ate a hearty meal' will certainly not pass *my* lips. It is a disgusting sentiment – The Last Supper! – to apply to our dinner together, delivered to my set at Albany, from the wonderful Hakkasan Restaurant. *Hearty?* Perish the adjective, justly applied to Lancashire hotpots. Before us was a most wonderful feast, perhaps one of the last that the likely-condemned man might gather into himself.

My trial begins tomorrow, so we are met for dinner at Albany because my house is again under observation by the media. But not many of them. Now that we've reached Act V, I'd rather hoped that we might be more ... *noticed*, I suppose is the word. According to Lucy there are only a few scraggy end-bits of reporters outside the house. Between the forthcoming referendum, and the disgusting ascendency of the Drumph, no one is much interested in me and my trial(s). Even me, really.

I laid the table with care, using our best Bow china and Georgian silver, a white damask tablecloth, candles aglow, the lights dimmed, Mozart in the air. The fresh air of civilisation: fragrant and easeful. When he entered just before 8.00, Philip looked about panoramically, smiled, and nodded his head before settling in my comfy chair. He'd made it thus far, depleted and diminished, and he was beginning to look forward to the end. His little pillbox would be in his waistcoat pocket.

He was soon followed by Lucy, and she by Sam. Rudy and Amelie were at the house, where Toe-mass and Bronya would be spoiling them. Bronya would be entrusted with them during the trial, much as she wished to attend. Rudy is furious – it's so unfair – that he isn't allowed to come.

Toe-mass has promised to transcribe the proceedings. As a cub reporter in Sofia he'd learned shorthand, and can still do it. 'It's like hitting a backhand. The body never forgets.' So Bronya would have a daily record, and Lucy and Sam could post the relevant material on the website, once the trial was over.

It's not likely to take long. Most law cases are mirror images of each other, opposite ways of seeing what is often agreed to be the same thing. Given that my side are unlikely to contest any of the facts, we and the prosecution will be in considerable harmony, and can get on with things, and judge and jury will take their views.

Jonathan begged off dining with us, says he needs the evening to polish his preparations, which seems overzealous of him, but Philip assures me it is essential to avoid complacency.

'You have to keep your head down,' he says, as if coaching a tennis player.

Ours were soon down too, eating an exquisite meal accompanied by two (genuinely smooth) bottles of Schoelhammer Riesling. It's lovely, sexy food; being tried makes for a good appetite. We start with 'Supreme dim sum platter' – Suzy called dim sum 'cunty' – and sesame prawn with foie gras, followed by stir-fry Alaskan king crab in XO sauce, Mongolian-style lamb chop, Chinese vegetables, steamed jasmine rice.

Sam bent over his plate, slurping his way through the delicacies as if they were chop suey from his local takeaway. He can hardly tell the difference – both are right nice – though he no doubt wishes we'd added an order of spare ribs, to enhance what he'd called a 'Chinky nosh-up', before the phrase fell into ideological desuetude. Lucy had no appetite at all, picked at a few bits, preferred to drink. Philip ate even less than she, drank less too. He's living on borrowed time's borrowed time, bless him.

So am I.

DAY 1

I'll be back, wasn't that a phrase? Jesus, perhaps? Well, I am too. Back. At the scene of my humiliation and collapse, that old Old Bailey, back again, this time on the other side of the whatever you are on the other side of. The law? Maybe that's it. It is no less intimidating, but I'm not so anxious now, though this time I really do have something to lose.

In America, if the films get it right, lawyers choose their jurors, and may reject those who don't suit the case they wish to make. They get the gestalt right. Would that we could have done so: *Do you practise a religion? Do you believe in God? If so, thanks for coming, you can bugger off now. Are you an atheist, a free-thinker or a sceptic?* Welcome aboard.

God alone knows who we've got stuck with. Jonathan thinks the jury demographic is not too bad: seven women and five men, median age fifty-eight, median weight fat, median tint beige, a few of them at least minimally educated, if you can tell by looking, which I can. I hope many of them have pets, but that I cannot ascertain. I might if I sidled closer and sniffed them, but they'd think me odd.

But I don't need to sniff to look, and when I do concentrate my attention, something ... well, astonishing ... something, well, horrifying happens. At first I could hardly take it in, shook my head, looked again.

Yes, I was right, how could that be? That Teutonic tuba player called it 'eternal recurrence'. I've never understood the term, merely assumed it was by way of self-description. He does go on and on tooting the same old *oom-pa-pa*.

And here I am at the Old Bailey, as if inevitably, again, again. Of course, hardened recidivists have more visits on their CVs, and I'll only ever have the two. But my two are sufficiently recurrent to qualify as *sub specie aeternitatis*. I don't mean the obvious: the building is the same. Why wouldn't it be? The corridors, the huddled lawyers, retracted clients, implacably vague judges are mere incarnations of the same old archetypes. Of course. Things come and they go.

But the jurors: these are neither types, nor tropes, nor figments. They are the same! The same persons, if one might honour them with that appellation, the same peers, ditto, as they were a year ago, when I collapsed within their midst to their amusement and derision. The same. Have they simply been lurking, slouched over their tabloids, fiddling with their phones, slurping their tannins, ready for assignment to a trial, and after an infernal eternal passage of time been assigned to mine?

I recognise the faces, the postures – the people, if I might so describe these recurrent wraiths – the shrunken hunched shoulders, the hoodies and tracksuits, the Arsenal shirts. The clothes are the same (presumably in the eternal life you don't have to change), the bulges, hunches, pimples, frazzles and pouts, the expressions that mix ennui with contempt. Each of the twelve stares at me as if with long-concentrated animosity: *Ah, there you are again. You. You are SO fucked!*

I shook my head, unable to dispel this Zarathustrian illusion. *A jury. Peers?* Not landed gentry from great estates, but the ill-educated denizens of council estates. These are my equals under the law. *The law is an ass*, said Mr Dickens, though I doubt he knew why. He merely thought the legal process ponderous and balky, braying, silly. But what is actually wrong with the law is that, of necessity, it erases differences. Scorns the minute particulars in favour of idiot generalities. If you murdered a person, you got hanged. If you stole, you went to jail. No *who*, no *how*, much less *why*. Punishments must fit the crime not the criminal, which is in itself a fine reason for staying on the right side of the law.

I'm on the wrong side.

Several of the huddled dozen might have come from the pages of *Oliver Twist*, so pasty and malnourished are they, so lacking in the spark that might define them as sentient beings. Two of the younger men wear the same old jeans and unlaundered shirts which they do not bother to tuck in, and slouch in seats 5 and 11, looking desperate for a fag, or a wee, some form of escape.

They look like convicts, but they can convict me: my fate is in their hands. They all think they're important, generatively, ultimately. They are all that matters. They get up in the morning and they Me. They Me all day, sleep their Me sleep and dream their Me dreams, then they wake and Me again until they die. And before that, they can send me to jail.

The humiliation of this, the outrage, is so palpable that I want to stand and shout, *STOP! THIS IS A FARCE! Find me some peers!* There's plenty of them about: well-educated, articulate, thoughtful, disinterested. If I put my arguments and state my case, my equals would, by virtue of our peerness, at least understand it, and me. And if they found me guilty, so be it. After all, I am.

But this basket of lumpies? I am peerless. Mrs Tinto, straight from the factory floor where she is paid less than minimum wage to make sari-garments for her ghetto-sisters? Mr florid Golf Club, an insurance salesman keen on his rules and his birdies? Mrs Grey, a housewife of indeterminate origin and age, dressed as if she were a randomly outfitted mannequin for the lady's section of an Oxfam shop? I remember them vividly. Don't I?

Suzy would be peering and screwing up her features, describing and transcribing, but I can barely stand the sight of them; the effort of writing this makes me weak with nausea, and shame. Worse than shame. It is shameful to be exposed, found out and judged, naked in the chambers of My Lord. To have one's secrets exposed and paraded: he picks his nose, or likes to be spanked, steals from the communion money. Yet being shamed is a process of reckoning, making the personal, public. It is, considered rightly and disinterestedly, good for one. Being humiliated is not. To be rendered null, loathed and self-loathing, valueless as slime.

I have ceased to look at my tormentors, but I feel their eyes on me constantly. Something in my mind is poisoning everything else, or perhaps it is the other way around?

It will be Jonathan's job to convince these soporific nitwits that what I have done, in allowing my wife an easeful death, is both morally justifiable and, properly understood, a form of mercy and not of murder. I once employed this very argument with my daughter and son-in-law – who I supposed might just squeeze into the 'peers' category – and they found it impossible to comprehend exactly what I meant. So this bench of bumblers? They will catch the nuances? Appreciate the moral ambiguities? Find a way to make the law bend its knee in sympathy to the suffering and the bereaved? Bend theirs?

When I expressed these doubts and observations about the jury to Philip, he looked more than disapproving, he was shocked.

'You should know better,' he said. 'But of course you don't. You've never been on a jury, nor been in court. But one thing we learn, and that you must learn right now, is that jurors, like the rest of mankind, are various in their abilities, however unprepossessing their appearances may be. Every jury will have on it persons of very considerable acuity, education and moral discrimination. If you go into court with contempt for them, they will mirror it right back to you ...'

'I'm sorry,' I said. 'Of course, you're quite right. But it is impossible, when your fate is in the hands of random selected others, not to doubt whether they are capable of making the right judgment.'

'It's far better,' he replied, 'if you have confidence in them. Then they may.'

Philip had groaned when we learned which judge would be presiding. Charles Highgrove is a conservative, punctilious pill of establishment. As a boy he'd apparently been called 'Chucky' by his elder sisters, and had the terrible misfortune to have this overheard by one of his schoolmates. The name spread round his house, and soon morphed, as nicknames do, and ended as Chuckles, which was mordantly inappropriate, as he had never been known to smile. He was not a morose youngster, merely serious, inward-looking, and totally lacking in humour. Dragged in front of *Monty Python's Flying Circus*, he would sit through the programmes, trying desperately to understand: why is a dead parrot funny?

His judgments in the High Court were acerbic, minimally but stringently argued. He particularly enjoyed tormenting wrongdoers who ought to have known better. Like me. I had made a jamboree of my case in public, such that it would be difficult to find jurors who hadn't already formed an opinion. This was worse than unseemly – it was improper – and from the beginning he let me know it, referring to me with languid contempt, as Dr Darke, lightly pronouncing the final *e*, so that it sounded like Darker. Darker than dark.

The prosecutor did similarly, Dr Darker, though with less contempt. His opening address to the jury began almost as if he were representing, rather than prosecuting, me.

'Ladies and Gentlemen of the Jury. This case has received much attention in the media, and Dr Darke has broadcast his own arguments and rationalisations widely on social media. I assume some of you are familiar with this, and beg you to wipe your minds clean of what you have read or heard, and any opinions you may have formed, and to start afresh, today, in this courtroom, with genuinely open minds.

'If you are to believe much of what you read in the newspapers, Dr James Darke is a wicked man, who has transgressed and mocked the laws of both man and God. He has been reviled, spat at, hounded by the press and the media, and regarded as evil.

'Do not believe this.

'He seems to be a man who loved his wife, could hardly bear to witness her suffering, and acted to relieve her of her pain. No one can fail to understand this. He is, to this extent, deserving of our sympathy.

'There is some danger in recognising this, for you are not here, ladies and gentlemen of the jury, to decide whether the defendant is sympathetic or unsympathetic. No doubt you will understand his predicament, and sympathise with it. We have all had similar problems to deal with.

'But your job is to find him guilty or not guilty. Under the law. And of his guilt, I shall demonstrate, there can be no doubt. No reasonable doubt, for that is the rule of law.

'My honourable colleague Mr Cowper will argue that there are extenuating circumstances, and cite both precedent and further legal and moral arguments. At the end of his presentation you will find yourself scratching your heads, and wondering if Dr Darke deserves lengthy imprisonment. Surely there is some way out of this?

'I am sorry to say there is not. The law in such matters is clear, and it must be upheld. That is going to be your job, and I do not presume that it will be an easy one emotionally. But it is your duty to see that justice gets done.

'To convict someone of murder you must find conclusive evidence of premeditation, and demonstrate how the murder was committed. We shall show that on the night of his wife's death Dr Darke prepared a fatal concoction of drugs, which the late Mrs Moulton drank, and that she died, as a direct result, some hours later.

'It's tragic, but simple – Dr Darke is guilty. He had the means and the opportunity, and as we shall show, the motive. It will be your duty to say so.'

He went on and on, filling in the blanks, and as he spoke his tone darkened. Enough sympathy. More accountability, more justice. Facts are facts, whatever his right honourable colleague Mr Cowper might argue. As he concluded, his reference to my doctorness seemed, to my ear, to be contemptuous, as if attempting to convey the impression that I was some sort of deranged medic, fatal pills and syringe in hand, like Dr Shipman.

Jonathan fidgeted and picked at his thumbnail, below sight level lest the jurors take notice. When he stood to make his opening address, he tackled this very point: his client was *not* a medical doctor, but a PhD – a doctor of *philosophy* – in English literature. Not a physician, but a *scholar*. The jury seemed uninterested in the distinction.

He would not contest the facts, Jonathan said, he simply wished to throw fresh light on them for, properly seen, mine was a case, as his right honourable colleague had stressed, deserving not merely of sympathy, but of legal exoneration.

Undeterred by the initial coolness of the jury, Jonathan later told me he believed our case was sufficient. There was only one thing he was worried about, and that was me. He didn't need me to take the stand; he disliked the very thought of it. Apparently I am the major weakness in my own case: on the witness stand, each time I open my mouth will be a potential disaster. My disquisitions on Pascal, and explanations of the law of non-contradiction, would undermine sympathy, and sabotage our case.

Philip agreed: 'You know what you want, but you have no idea what you need. You'll be a disaster on the stand. It's not a pulpit, or a stage. The jury are not an audience.'

Lucy was more than adamant. I'm not sure there is an adequate word for her degree of vehemence: 'Are you crazy? No way. If you testify I swear I will walk out of the court and never come back!'

I pointed out that there would be no need for her to come back, as my trial would soon end, and likely enough I will be incarcerated.

That night, even Rudy took up the entreaties, with tears in his eyes. I don't think he actually understood much of it, though I had primed him with my Gulliver story, but he certainly understood that his life might be diminished without my input of ice-cream, Blades memorabilia and bedtime stories.

'Please, Gampy. Don't do it!'

What'd he know about it anyway?

'Do *what*, darling?'

'Get up and talk too much.'

OK, he understood.

I did what I always do in a minority, and insisted on having my own way. My trial, my choice, my life, my show. I was the piper, and my representative could dance to my tune.

Concluding his admirably succinct address to the jury, Jonathan described me as a victim of the depth of my own love. Suzy was close to death, but I, who had everything to lose, nevertheless had risked my future in easing her final passage. He made much of the compassionate verdict in the case defended by the Irish barrister James Comyn, though he neglected to mention that the husband, after dispatching his poor suffering spouse, had immediately given himself up to the police.

After a break for lunch, the prosecution began to present their case, calling first my old antagonist DS, who was full of information, and bursting to divulge it. He began with an account of our first meeting at the doorstep of my house, my rudeness and recalcitrance. But, he smirked, Dr Darke 'finally condescended to join us for a wee chat, and to read a copy of the statement he wished to make. I will now read it to you, if I may?'

'You may,' said the prosecutor.

When DS had finished reading my self-exculpatory explication, he paused, and waited for the next question.

'So, according to Dr Darke, his only motive was to release his wife from her pain?'

'So he said.'

'Had you reason to doubt this?'

'I had.'

'What further motives might Dr Darke have had?'

The next few hours were taken up with the minutiae of these imputed motives. Suzy's relationship with Dr Lawrence Weinberg, and their (fully documented) affair. His inadequate death certificate was cited, and sniffed over. If you're looking for a motive, opined DS grimly, you have one here.

And another one here. There followed a forensic account of Suzy's financial affairs, her unsettled estate, for which probate had only recently been granted, and the fact – DS raised his eyebrows as high as Ben Nevis – that given that she had died intestate, Dr Darke was the major beneficiary of the will.

'A sum of £2,320,168 . . .' said the DS, looking the jury squarely in their bleary impoverished eyes.

'Though Dr Darke certainly had more money than that in his various accounts, trusts and investments.'

Details followed. This apparently made it worse. I had plenty. I wanted more. It was disgusting. DS's lips curled accordingly, and my peers listened attentively, as the rash of suspicion rouged their cheeks. So much for the innocent, suffering Dr Darke, the compassionate, the merciful. All it comes down to is sex, jealousy and greed!

In the morning, I gather, the newspapers had me on the front pages, but I neither read them nor allowed any of our little circle to tell me about them. Bronya could cut them out and put them in her scrapbook. Things were getting worse. Jonathan would have to rebut these impugned motives, and was still determined to do it without my help.

'Look, James, I can understand you want to explain, but the more explaining you do, the worse it will look. The jury are already turning against you – all it now needs is your presence to confirm their judgments. The better and more articulate your explanations, the worse they will think of you. *A Doctor! A PhD! Bit of a smooth talker, that one. Thinks he's better than the rest of us!'*

I am not without some smattering of knowledge, of both self and others. Yes, I can seem cilious, or even supercilious, to those inadequately versed in registers and tones. And juries can jump to conclusions, stomp them half to death, and then proudly display the corpse. I am not a good fit with these peers.

Nevertheless it is quite wrong to ask Jonathan to make my excuses, explain my motives, try to banish the harsh insinuations of greed and jealousy. He is only a barrister. His heart may be in the right place, but his capacity to find the right words and tones will be diminished by the very fact of his profession: lawyers think like lawyers, they talk like lawyers, and however agreeable they may be over a drink, once they are in court they are transformed, in their wigs and gowns, into droning, insistent, preening pedants. Juries, in their peer-wisdom, hold them in disdain; you can see it on their faces, when they are awake.

If my case is going to be made fairly, and articulately and movingly, it will have to be done by me. I am resolved to turn up my charm to its full 40 watts. I can't wait to take the stand. Here I am, Dr James Darke in the dock, defending my behaviour in assisting my late wife to die. Why should I be sent to jail without having explained myself? It's up to me to convince the dunderheads, both the twelve in a row, and the one on that other, higher and grander bench.

That evening there was no time for feasting – though some drink was taken – as Jonathan took me once again through my paces. If I was foolishly determined to take the stand, I should at least prepare properly for the examination. Surely any teacher knew that?

He and Philip put me through mock cross-examinations, again

and again. We are agreed that though I tell a jolly good story, I never tell it the same way twice.

'Why should I?' I demand. 'Stories have an infinite capacity to alter, to deviate, to improve, to add this or drop that, to hold or to deter attention. Any good novelist or competent raconteur knows that narrative arcs improve with retelling . . .'

Philip laughed when first I said this, though by now he had little laughter in him, but my sally drove Jonathan, a less urbane fellow, that little bit bonkers.

'When you are being cross-examined, any competent prosecutor will make you go over your story, point by point, again and again . . .'

'How very dull of them. Don't they listen the first time?'

'They do. Carefully. And then they seek elucidation, amplification, the answer to a slightly different question, change the angle of approach . . . And what they are really doing is trying to get you, not to make a fatal admission, but to contradict yourself. To make the error of seeming untruthful, prevaricating. A liar. And once the jury see that happening, and happening again, then you're finished.'

Perhaps there might be some fun in this, like a sort of bad party game: who can tell exactly the same story twice in a row? Jonathan had warned me to do so assiduously. Concentrate, stick to the script.

On his chambers' wall he had framed the old Second World War poster:

CARELESS TALK COSTS LIVES!

So does no talk, doesn't it?

DAY 2

The action onstage, if I might call it that, was proceeding inexorably. If this is a play, it's a jolly dull one. Not enough plot, rotten cast of characters, except for me, and I haven't said a word yet. Our respective forensic specialists are in court: one for their side (guilty!) and one for ours (not guilty!). If you pay them sufficiently they will say most anything to advance their bank balances.

We began with a detailed account of the exhumation of the body, and the forensic analysis of the remains. I am no good at figures, all those millilitres and micrograms and dosages, but it appears that my cup of Manuka honey, tea and drugs had contained less noxious content than I might have intended, apparently because the many Diazepam tablets I had administered were only 2ml each.

According to the prosecution's Dr Tweedledum, a dog might have survived, even enjoyed, the dosage I'd mixed, but when administered to a dying woman in an extremely depleted state, the drugs might not, strictly, have *caused* death, but they certainly would have *hastened* it. Mrs Moulton had died shortly after imbibing my glass of tea. Cause and effect were clear enough.

Contrariwise! insisted Professor Tweedledee, if the dosage administered by the thoroughly befuddled and incompetent Dr Darke would only send a pet to dreamland, they were hardly adequate to send his wife to the promised land. No, Dr Darke had not killed his wife.

Did so! said Tweedledum.

Did not! countered Tweedledee.

Everything that is being divulged with such excruciating slowness is already known to me. On trial for murder, I am bored. Everyone else is bored too. His Honour is nodding off like a dowager aunt on Boxing Day, the jurors are propping their eyelids with matchsticks, from the public gallery come shuffles, wheezes, coughs, whispers and snores.

But at least, in the midst of the gathering gloom, there is something to look forward to. Tomorrow morning that oleaginous fornicator Dr Larry will take the stand. From my memory of DS's folder, there was reams of information about various trysts, hotel rooms, car rentals, meals in fancy restaurants, gifts of one sort or another: all of the transactions that make infidelity so expensive, and so traceable.

But our daughter will be there, listening. If Dr Larry deserves his comprehensively detailed exposure, Lucy will once again be the innocent victim of her parents' behaviour. I wonder if I could talk her out of coming? Not likely, but that evening I picked up the phone.

'Lucy here.' It was late, but she sounded wide awake, had hardly slept for weeks, she said, between the dual trials of her still-fretful baby and recalcitrant father.

'Darling Lucy, it's Dad.'

'Yes.' She was still angry at my insistence on taking the stand.

'I've been thinking. About tomorrow, you know ... Perhaps you might give it a miss? It's likely to go on and on, bit upsetting, bit grisly, and you could use a day off. What do you think?'

'No, I'm coming. I'll be fine.'

'I see. Well, of course it's up to you, but ...'

'What you're really worried about is Dr Larry, isn't it?'

'Why should that be? He's going to be quizzed about the incompetent death certificate, I presume ... Not much interest there.'

'Oh,' she said, drawing out the word into several syllables, or breaths perhaps. 'Ooooooh, I suspect he'll have more than that to discuss.'

'What do you mean?'

'I mean that he and Mummy had an affair. Surely you knew that? Even you can't be that blind ...'

'Yes. I suppose I did. But how do you know? I thought it was a secret.'

She laughed.

'She and I often talked about things – not in detail – but she told me it had gone on for some time, but was long over.'

I was astonished, and relieved. Now I can revel in Dr Larry's comprehensive humiliation without worrying about its effect on my by-no-means innocent daughter.

I can't wait.

DAY 3

He was wearing the same old tie. Ermenegildo Zegna, muddy swirling reds – a gigolo in Milan might have pulled it off, but on Dr Larry it looked foppish, appropriate only for proclaiming his idea of himself. He wore it in his Wigmore Street office on our meeting when Suzy's diagnosis was first confirmed, and I made my appraisal and disdain of his neckwear a clear instantiation of my attitude to him.

Was it some sort of message? A reminder, perhaps, that we are united in our suffering, had loved the same woman? Suzy laughed about how insecure he was, how much he needed my approval in matters of attire. 'He dresses for you,' she would laugh when he visited at her bedside, each time in a different suit and tie, though the unobjectionable white cotton shirts were a constant.

When he took the witness stand he glanced in my direction, but I lowered my head. To my dismay he looked confident, sat tall in the uncomfortable seat with his shoulders back, pulled his trousers into position, folded his hands carefully in his lap. An eminent specialist, offering his services.

Suzy had certainly had enough of them. That much became clear in the ensuing hours, as the prosecutor guided him, in a day-by-day bonk-by-bonk schedule of their relations. Their credit cards (his Visa Debit card, her Amex Platinum) revealed the details: dates, hotels, meals, bottles of champagne. When he was paying, they used the Novotel near Queen's Club, the restaurant would be one of the local bistros, the champagne low end. When she paid, it was a deluxe double room at Brown's Hotel, early supper from room service, Taittinger Rosé. Presumably she had more money; she certainly had better taste, and was more spoiled.

He should have been embarrassed.

I should have been indignant.

Neither of us was. He carried on answering question after question; I drifted into a reverie and ceased to listen.

He could well afford his equanimity; he wasn't on trial himself, was simply the canvas on which the motive of my jealousy might be painted. From his own point of view, he'd done nothing wrong. Affairs happen. He and Suzy had conducted theirs discreetly. Both his wife – Mona, was it? – and I knew of the relationship, and made no serious effort to end it.

And there, faintly, is her voice, is it?

Leave it alone, James, just leave it. Why care now, why feel vengeful? You weren't angry at the time, took it on the chin, it's gone, it's over, all gone, all over. Give him a break, won't you? It doesn't matter a hoot.

The tone is wrong: either I've become a very inadequate medium, or I'm making this up entirely. A ventriloquist then, and she my dummy, dumb yet still faintly audible. We are reduced to this. She not even a whisper, her voice hardly a memory; I have to make her up. She's a story.

To take an enlightened view of adultery, you need to be of a certain disposition, upbringing, training and education. To have been taught how to behave. And when I scanned the faces of the jury, as they listened to these details of privileged infidelity, I could sense the hasty rush to judgment, my peers straining to work out who was worse, the philanderer or the weedy cuckold? Both. Both worse!

There was more to come, more dates and assignations, and a final, probing and hostile attack on the issuance of an inadequate death certificate. Had the doctor had any doubts about the cause or circumstances of the death?

No, he had not.

The curious problem was that we had ceded to them the problem of proof. No burden there. I had admitted administering the final dose – hence the reason, thank God, that neither Sam nor

Lucy was required to testify – so the question was not my intention in doing so, but whether it proved fatal. That depended on who you asked. Serious grounds for reasonable doubt, one might suppose, supposing that the jury were reasonable and could doubt.

As a fortunate result of all this, my intentions and motives were irrelevant: I may have been in a jealous rage, or perhaps hastened her death in order to inherit her money before she left it to someone else: it doesn't matter, or matter very much. What matters is what I did.

I will take the stand not to self-exonerate, but to try to explain that even if the dose was fatal, it would not, in my eyes, constitute murder. That is a category mistake, but alas one sanctioned by the law. Jonathan says he will ask me the questions I require, but has some doubts that the court will allow such a line of questioning (by which I mean answering) to be sustained for long. Because I have a lot I want to say.

It seemed easy enough, before the forensic disclosures. Since the day of Suzy's death, I have accepted that by my action I released her from suffering. This was both impermissible and it seemed to me, loving. I was both guilty and innocent. This became the basis of my press campaign, my justification for my own intervention, and my belief that minds and laws had to change to allow an easeful death to be administered to the dying.

I am only of interest if I killed Suzy. That was the basis of a moral campaign. But if I am merely an incompetent bungler, unable even to provide a fatal concoction, what then? What a muddle. *My example only has moral weight if I am guilty.* Of killing. But of murder? No, that's where I draw the line. I rather doubt that the jury will see this.

DAY 4

I love swearing, and adore oaths. As a schoolboy I had an anti-quarian phase in which I not merely collected but actively employed a variety of antique expostulations: *Zounds! 'Ods Bodkins!* and an associated set of curses and insults: *A pox upon thee! Varlot! Whoremonger!* which were sufficiently irritating to my schoolmates that they often replied with the colloquial: *Wanker!*

This quietened but did not silence me entirely, such that in my first year at Oxford I actually used one or two of my choicest specimens – I think we'd been doing Chaucer – in front of my tutorial partner, the attractive Suzy Moulton. As we left our tutor's rooms, she turned and said, 'Zounds? You've got to be kidding! It's an anachronism, James, it makes you sound a prat. Words come and go – it went. These days if you want to insult someone, just call them a cunt and get on with it.' This would have been shocking if it had any preening or self-display, but it was offered matter-of-factly, as if advice on how to spin a lettuce. It was one of her favourite terms, and it applied not merely to disagreeable persons but to things in general: *Life's a cunt.*

'Is that bad or good?' I asked.

'Yes,' she said. 'For sure.'

I didn't adopt the word, was much too shy, and for a time gave up swearing altogether, antique or modern. But an unsworn life is not a happy one, needs must when needs must, and I eventually succumbed to the spirit of the times and said 'fuck' occasionally, though I never warmed to it. Like most modern locutions, it lacks elegance and texture.

I shall have to swear an oath before I testify. I am in principle delighted to do so, as I intend to tell the truth, the whole truth, and nothing but the truth. That's why I'm going to be there. But I was under the impression that the standard form of words concludes (as used by the previous witnesses) with reference and deference to the Almighty: *So help me God.* He's never helped me before, he has regularly tormented me, I'm one of his latter-day odd-Job substitutes – so why would he show up at the Old Bailey to offer assistance?

The judiciary may insist that God comes in somewhere, but this I will not permit. Not that he is *out* of it, he's on trial every bit as much as I am. If he is indeed in court – and I am informed that, like bacteria, he is everywhere – I am anxious to swear *at*, but not *by* him. It is God who needs to be convicted: condemned as lazy, capricious, callous and perverse.

My dear lawyer is worried not on the good Lord's behalf, but on my own. He knows I love a rant. 'Leave God out of it!' Jonathan demanded, to which I have agreed. The Almighty (hah!) is sufficiently out of it that he couldn't make his way to the Old Bailey if you picked him up in an Uber. Who gives a damn about God anyway? For a being with such limited powers and understanding, he does the best he can. And, as Jonathan points out, some members of the jury might love him to bits. Why piss them off?

I was informed that we atheists and free-thinkers get our very own secular oath, or affirmation as it is called, and no one will throw thunderbolts at us if we break it.

'I do solemnly, sincerely and truly declare and affirm that the evidence I shall give shall be the truth, the whole truth, and nothing but the truth.'

Weak soup. I said the words crisply, my hand raised, the jury watching attentively. I can hardly be as wicked, standing there so upright and dignified, as has been made out by the media, and prosecution. An elderly retired schoolmaster, well but not foppishly presented, open-faced and presumably open-hearted, wishing to have his say.

Jonathan did his best, offered the questions that I had requested. I tried to elucidate the moral complexities of my position, but was cut off in mid-flow when the prosecution objected, or the judge wouldn't allow me to continue. Mostly it was like that radio show. You get just a minute. No Deviation. Repetition. Hesitation. Irrelevancy. Or justice.

I was delighted to look benignly at my antagonist, the

prosecutor, as he rose and oiled his way across the floor to confront me, a look of disdain on his features, as if I were Dr Crippen risen from the grave. What right has *he* to look askance at *me*, when he is dressed in a greasy wig and a hideous black gown like a pervert in fancy dress? I have to be wary, careful and exact. To get my ducks in a row. I look up and see Sam sitting greenly in the public gallery, next to Lucy, who looks white.

The prosecutor did as predicted, took me through the facts, questioned the details, went round and round. This was supposed to be the moment in which I told my story, made my case, gave my moral justifications. But each question was tightly framed, and asked something specific, and when I attempted to deviate I was slapped down.

The prosecutor's final question surprised me, though it was the moment for which I had been waiting.

'Tell me, Dr Darke, do you regret having caused your wife's death?'

I could see Jonathan rising to object, but I nodded to him, and he sat down. This was the moral crux of the matter.

'No, I certainly do not. I—'

'Thank you, doctor. I have no more questions.' He made his way, with a triumphant air, back to his bench.

'But I wish to explain!'

'There's no need for that, Dr Darke, you have answered the question. And you've done plenty of "explaining" already.'

At this point, for almost the first time, Judge Chuckles intervened on my behalf, allowing me to continue.

'Thank you, My Lord.'

I commenced an account of Suzy's sufferings, her stated desire to die, and what I had done (however inefficiently) to hasten her demise. But as I continued, rehearsing the arguments I'd made in my little manifesto, I was interrupted by the prosecutor's objections, alleging irrelevance. I lost my thread, looked to the jury to see if my tale was touching their hearts. It wasn't.

The judge was getting restless, and encouraged me to carry on, but be brief, reminding me that this was a court of law, not a stage or a pulpit.

I met Jonathan's eye, and he gave a slight nod. Time to go.

'That's all I have to say, My Lord. I am sorry to have said it so inarticulately ...'

'You may stand down.'

On my way back to my seat, the jury's hostility was palpable. Lips pursed, frowns of disgust spread amongst them as if they were all sniffing the same fart. That would be me. No remorse. None. He stinks!

Good, I think. I think, good. Isn't it? Guilty therefore? That's good too, isn't it?

I have no idea, no ideas any more, want simply to be taken away and put in a room for a long time.

I sat down, thinking that Rudy is the right example after all: boys like simple answers, and endings. I should have provided one, that's what people understand and need. Whereas all I offered is yet another example of the fact that life is a blasted heath of ill-understood obligations and motives, inadequate actions and reactions, improbable explanations and diagnoses. How do I say this, without exemplifying it?

I made the effort, and the mistake, of trying to understand. Looked this way and that, scrunched my features, posited, formulated, cared. Some ideas stuck, for a time. But they faded as fads do. I had the desire but not the capacity to make sense of things. And now? I have made sense of them: what I regretted as a muddle *is* a muddle. That's all there is.

MUDDLE: chaos, confusion, disarrangement, disarray, dishevel-ment, dis-order, mis-order, disorganisation, free-for-all, havoc, jumble, messiness, shambles, snake pit, tumble, welter: life, things as they are . . .

I am nearly seventy years old, what can I have been doing that I am still in a muddle? But everyone else is, too; our muddles are concurrent forms of wisdom. Scant consolation there.

Chapter 19

There's too much time to kill, waiting for a verdict, without the ongoing trial, however dreary, to focus on if not to hold one's attention. As the hours passed, and we waited for the disagreeable and obviously disagreeing jury to return its verdict, I fidgeted and nodded off. Tried to read a magazine – not the newspapers, they are forbidden – but could not concentrate.

I have neglected my reading of late. Too much on my mind, of course. But when the trial is over, there will be plenty of time to extend my literary boundaries. I've made a list of books that (a) I have not read, and (b) might prove useful to me, in one way or the other. I did some googling last night, and came up with the following, located and charged my Kindle – unused and totally unloved since Suzy's death – and, after an hour's frustrating trial and error, managed to download them all:

PROSE AND CONS:

- Cervantes, *Don Quixote*. Rudy would be pleased that it has an amusing horse in it.
- Raleigh, *The History of the World*. Volume 1 will be all I need – how much history can a world generate, after all?
- Malory, *Le Morte D'Arthur*. In spite of the fact that I hate the

Middle Ages, which are only useful to prove that there is such a thing as moral progress.
- Rustichello da Pisa, *The Travels of Marco Polo*. Plenty of spicy tales.
- Sade, *Justine*. A bit grisly, though tales of the foolishness of innocence are always amusing. Bit like *A Portrait of a Lady* perhaps?
- Thoreau, *Civil Disobedience*. Yet another philosophical American windbag, but an appropriate theme.

If I manage to get through these there's plenty more where they came from. Or went to. I suppose it's a form of genre literature? *Books written in jail*. A professor could teach a course on such books: it would be a better way to teach and to encourage 'creative writing'. Not that one should.

I wish I could say I was sitting comfortably, looking about attentively, both in and of the moment, but I was not. My trousers and pants had tucked between my buttocks tight and sweaty, my back ached from the days on un-upholstered and ugly seats, I was hardly aware of my surroundings, lost in a fug, or is it a fugue, of wispy awareness that took in nothing and everything, which is the same thing.

The air would have been stifling, were I in a state to stifle. I was unaware of it, not that one usually is, one just uses it, it is the very basis of awareness. Useful stuff, air, you can take it entirely for granted until – like dear Suzy's final days – the time when you can't, when it becomes a reluctant companion, and you an imperfect reservoir. Yet for that critical courtroom moment I was as still as if in a coma, taking no breath, no revivifying humid draughts in my lungs, nothing in, nothing out. Nothing, again. Torporous, inert, I must have appeared as if in suspended animation, eyes closed, breathless, yet my poor beleaguered heart bumbled and whirred and whirled in my chest, seeking release. Deep breathing is recommended. Any breathing would be a balm. I dosed myself with Diazepam, which stills everything but my heart and my mind. I should have known better. 'Avoid stress,' a dimwit doctor had advised, envisaging all sorts of internal disorder if I did not. He looked at his computer screen: I have a 52 per cent chance of a stroke or heart attack at the best of times.

The jury was re-entering the courtroom, the judge had slipped on his gown and refitted his wig like an elderly diva and sat at the bench. Lucy and Sam, George and Toe-mass were in the gallery, smiling at me reassuringly and apprehensively, crossing their mass digits. Philip had been there earlier, wished me well during the long interval of the jury's deliberations, and had to go off 'to rest', he said. I was glad he was gone, wished they all were. I did not want to be alone, I was alone, in the midst of people and portentous events to come in a single sentence, perhaps followed by a long one ...

Alone, a thing in a world of things. I looked about, at the chipped mahogany reach of the judge's bench, the fluorescent lighting flickering above, the windowless expanse, my black, waxed shoelaces immaculately tied, a small creature creeping on the floor, the faces of the jurors as they filed back. Bench. Lights. Walls. Shoelaces. Insect. Jurors. Words, words, words. The things were being denuded of their characteristics, as if adjectives no longer pertained, the world stripped to pure thinginess, the skeletons hovering below the wordskin. Material. Stuff. And when that is morphed into oneness, what revelation is at hand?

They would find me 'guilty' or 'not guilty', and certain consequences would ensue. Either I would be released to the arms of my loved ones and the waiting car service, the drinks, the hoo-ing and ha-ing of celebration, or escorted down the corridors to the requisite holding rooms, and thence to jail. Not guilty, or guilty. I knew which: both, as I had tried to maintain, staunchly proud, ambivalent, ambiguous, upright.

I have been reviled and rejoiced in, noticed and dismissed, relentlessly observed, prodded, examined, dissected, have made my point and my points, caused something of a reaction, though whether it would come to anything was, well, unlikely – it takes more than James Darke to affect a shift in moral consciousness. That might have been altered slightly, might it? I had done what I had to do, did my not-good-enough best. Served Suzy, now known as the late Suzanne Moulton, my evanescent wispy memory of her and of my love for her, served as best I could, in favour of the dying, the living and the dead.

Looking at the jury, at the gallery, at the judge, I didn't have even to squint my eyes to see their incipient decay and too-soon-dying figurations, the skeleton beneath the flesh readying itself, after all those years, to re-emerge in the oven of the crematorium as the fat crackles and then liquefies in the flames. Or like Suzy's bones, now reinterred beneath the sod. Lucky sod. Lucky Suzy.

We start the same, we end the same, we are the same. Things come and they go, indistinguishable not as sub-atomic particles or gross matter are indistinguishable, but simply this: the same. Things as they are, are lost in the ether, then played upon a blue guitar. Imagined. What we are surrounded by are not things but words. Pellybelly, mangoes, cricket bats, judge's robes, bugs, comb-overs, blades, emperors, ice-cream. Thinking this makes me smile. Smiles, too. None of the jurors are smiling, they look down, and out: exhausted and fed up, anxious to be released to the delightful tedium of the everyday. Released from their duties.

Released? I am. I have done what I needed to do. It doesn't matter at all. Nor does whether I am found guilty, or not guilty.

They're the same too. Words. Home has been a jail, jail may be a home. Did that damn fool Oscar Wilde once feel the same, that day in the dock? He found out: there is a difference between Tite Street and Reading Gaol, between fame and comfort and penury and humiliation. He lasted only three years after he was released, his health destroyed. He killed his wife too, broke her and her heart; she died before him. Surely there is something to be learned from this? A warning?

Yet poor innocent Oscar was emblematic, deluded and heroic in his intransigent love, making an example of himself. He'd dressed splendidly for the court occasion, courtly, made his trial into theatre, scripted and staged himself meticulously, declaimed, attacked, and told the truth. He was proud, an example to his audience, made himself into a spectacle. I wish I could have done as well. He did not feel guilty. He was not guilty.

Our prisons attract the wrong sort of people. The greedy, the devious and envious, the brutal. We need to reopen Newgate Prison – call it New-New Gate – and set it aside for the free-thinkers and spirits, those in whom the impulse of challenge and opposition is unrestrained, who dare to think and yearn to speak. Who are guilty by virtue of virtue. Who transgress and subvert, who say the thing that is not, not allowed, and who are sent to prison for believing and for saying the wrong things because they are the right things. Like my Captain Gulliver.

Take these new convicts, these people of conviction, give them basic facilities, security and quiet, and allow them their tools. Think of it as a writer's retreat.

In his unaccommodating, stark and severe prison, Oscar served his time, and used it assiduously, when he wasn't contracting the inner-ear infection that was to kill him. Wrote *De Profundis*, a blowsy missive to the scabrous Bosie, and later *The Ballad of Reading*

Gaol, which isn't as much fun as it sounds. They gave him some pencils and paper, which was unusual.

Each man? Kills? The thing? He loves? Each makes no sense at all, and the stress is not on *kills*, or indeed on *loves*, but on *thing*. That's what we are, things, all of us, bits of matter sometimes alive, and other and longer times differently alive, which is dead. We are created and cannot be destroyed. Matter as flesh or as bacterium. Things. That's what's the matter, what does it matter? The heart of the matter, m'lud, is simple; did the defendant wilfully administer a drugged drink that caused the demise of his beloved wife?

The answer is yes, though it is also no, or maybe. Pharmacologically, morally, legally. Who gives a damn? I am uncleanably darkened, and virginally unsullied. Innocent and guilty; they are entwined, I can't have one without the other. And as for jail? I've been there already.

This isn't about me. They want me to be a campaigner, a victim or a villain. I am in court where 'James Darke' is on trial, and I'm not him. Who is? How did my name and identity get appropriated, and slither away into these remote parts? It has something to do with me, surely, but I refuse to be that person. Not me. The me that I still am, adhere to and inhabit, is coming to some end in which I need not participate. I'm not on trial, though I am severely tried.

Out of my body. Floating in the dusty air, looking down on 'James Darke', these wiggy lawyers, this peerless jury? I am above them, observing as a fly, or God.

I detest neither this, nor them. The sooner it's over the better, and 'he' can get on with the rest of his life, and I with mine, whatever, when and wherever. Yawning my way to the grave.

This is pellucid to me. When I tried to explain to Lucy, she furrowed and remonstrated, raised eyebrow and voice. Apparently

'I' am in need of explanation and diagnosis, encouragement and counsel.

I'm not. Not I.

Awash in this linguistic and conceptual delirium, I was startled by the Clerk of the Court instructing us.

'Please rise!'

I did. Why not? Took some deep breaths, as if I had forgotten how to replenish my lungs, stood up straight. I felt distinctly biddable, without needs or will.

The judge addressed himself to the foreman of the jury, a porky chap with a comb-over and florid face, dressed in a navy blazer with brass buttons, soggy white shirt with the collar rolling, and striped tie. One of my peers. Jurors, my readers, masters of my destiny. Mangoes, pelicans, cricket bats. Suzy, James. Lucy.

The foreman stood gravely, teetering slightly with exhaustion. The jury had been out for almost two days.

'Ladies and gentlemen of the jury, have you reached your verdict?'

'We have, My Lord.'

* * *

*P*ublishers print THE END *at the conclusion of a book to confirm to the reader that nothing else will follow; yet stories can migrate from paper into hearts and minds, seeking new and unforeseen life beyond their original covers.*

When I said goodbye to my weeping family at the prison gates, held dear Lucile, embraced my Reuben, I was overcome by an unexpected feeling of relief. All things end, all things had come to this, my ship now arrived at its final destination, my Travels are over. And as desolate as they were to see me taken from them, I was curiously relieved to have them taken from me, to be freed of the obligations of family ties, from the burden of love.

As I accompanied the gaoler through those heavy gates, my spirits lifted, and though I did not turn to look back, I lifted my arm in farewell, and benediction, as if I might ne'er see them again. This thought was instantiated by the waving of my hand, with an elegant twirl of the fingers, as if a Bishop drunk on port, celebrating the birth of our Lord Jesus Christ.

Acknowledgements

When I published *Darke*, in 2017, I noted that its protagonist's insistent voice had come unbidden into my head, and that writing the novel was, in some unfanciful way, an attempt to exorcize him from my consciousness. The next year I published *A Long Island Story*, which was written in an entirely different voice and register. Some readers quite liked that, but many hoped for more Darkeness. I had no such plans, but it seems that my character did. He returned, demanding as ever, and it was once again easier to write him down than to expel him from my mind and life. So my chief acknowledgement is, I suppose, to thank him for this reappearance. He's good company, really.

My second and unambiguous thanks are to my wife Belinda, which is rather ironic as she and James Darke have never got on. But in my life nothing much happens without Belinda's loving support, and she has guided me through this book with a steady hand, eye and ear.

Multiple friends and loved ones have read early drafts of *Darke Matter*. I am particularly grateful to Bob Demaria, Bertie Gekoski, Matthew Greenberg, Ruthie 'The Eagle' Greenberg, Declan Kiely, Cliff and Gill Leach, Sandy Neubauer, Rosalind Porter, Lorna J Reeves (retired Manager for Forensic Services for the Metropolitan Police), Fiammetta Rocco, John Simpson, Peter Straus, and DM Thomas.

Homages to all the good folks at Constable for producing this handsome volume: especially to Claire Chesser, who guided me so patiently through the preparation of the text, and to Publisher Andreas Campomar, to whom this book is dedicated in gratitude for our long and happy association, and friendship.